FOR A REAL HERO,
BILLY DIMICHELE

With thanks to John Steinbeck, whose novels, particularly
East of Eden, still resonate with readers today.

Library of Congress Control Number 2017939754

978-1-338-74106-3 (POB)
978-1-338-23037-6 (Library)

10 9 8 7 6 5 4 3 2 1   21 22 23 24 25

Printed in China   62
This edition first printing, August 2021

Edited by Anamika Bhatnagar
Book design by Dav Pilkey and Phil Falco
Color by Jose Garibaldi
Creative Director: Phil Falco
Publisher: David Saylor

Tree-House Comix Proudly Presents

DOG MAN AND CAT KID

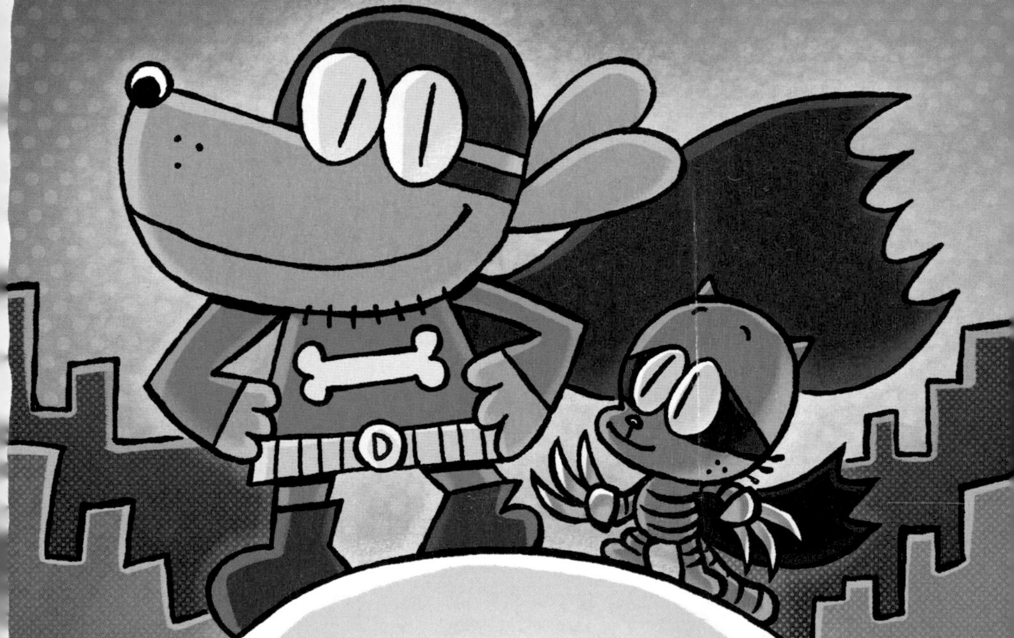

WRITTEN AND ILLUSTRATED BY **DAV PILKEY**

AS GEORGE BEARD AND HAROLD HUTCHINS

WITH COLOR BY JOSE GARIBALDI

graphix

AN IMPRINT OF

SCHOLASTIC

CHAPTERS

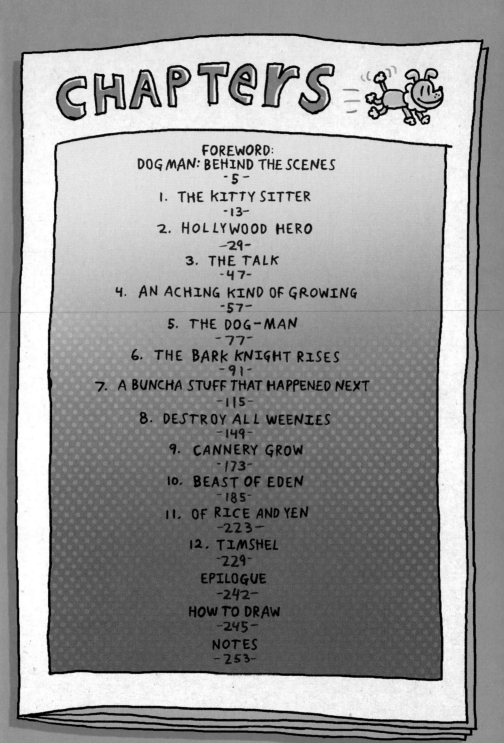

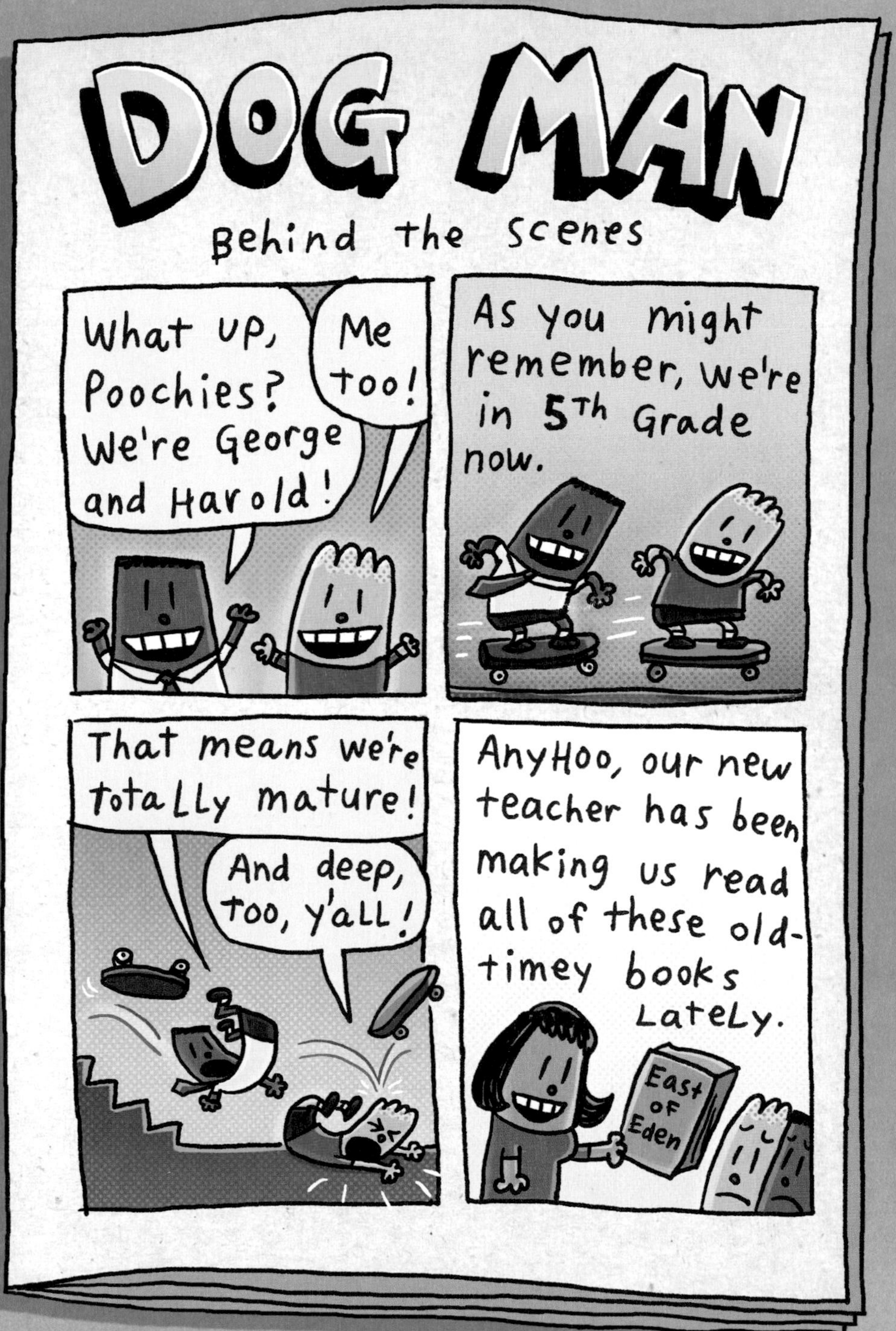

DOG MAN
Behind the Scenes
What up, Poochies? We're George and Harold!
Me too!
As you might remember, we're in 5th Grade now.
That means we're totally mature!
And deep, too, y'all!
AnyHoo, our new teacher has been making us read all of these old-timey books lately.
East of Eden

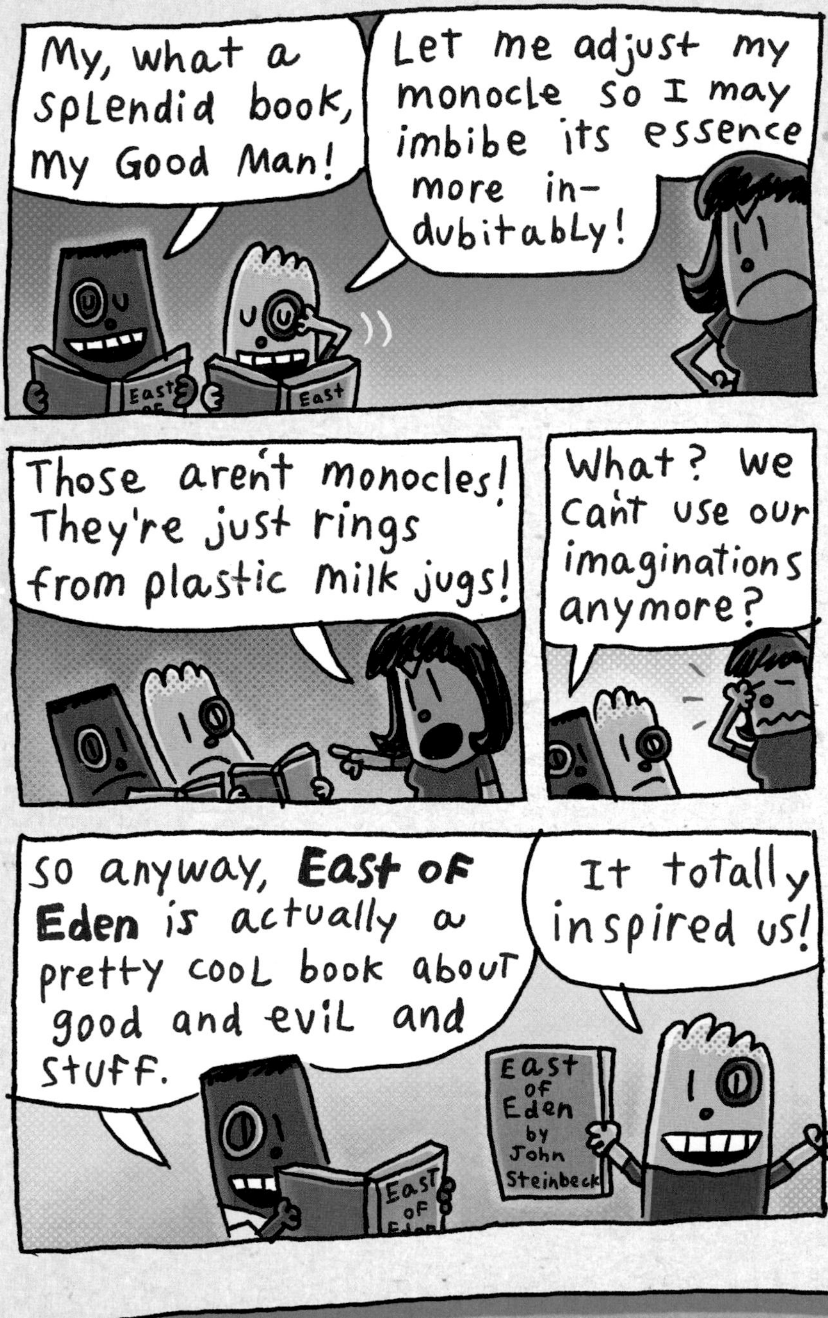
My, what a splendid book, My Good Man!
Let me adjust my monocle so I may imbibe its essence more in-dubitably!
East
East
Those aren't monocles! They're just rings from plastic milk jugs!
What? We can't use our imaginations anymore?
so anyway, **East of Eden** is actually a pretty cool book about good and evil and stuff.
It totally inspired us!
East of Eden by John Steinbeck
East of

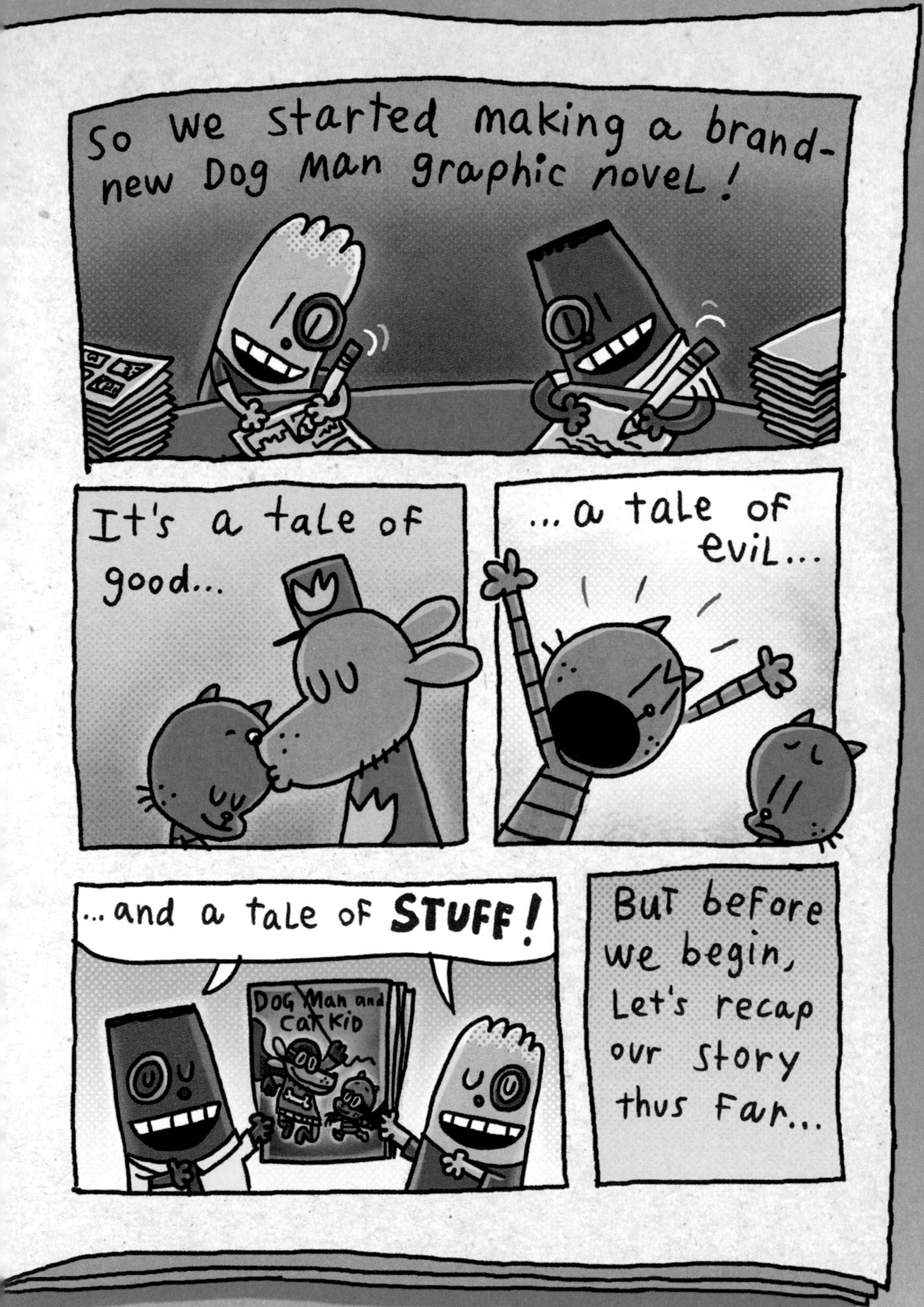
So we started making a brand-new Dog Man graphic novel!
It's a tale of good...
...a tale of evil...
...and a tale of STUFF!
DOG MAN and CAT KID
But before we begin, Let's recap our story thus far...

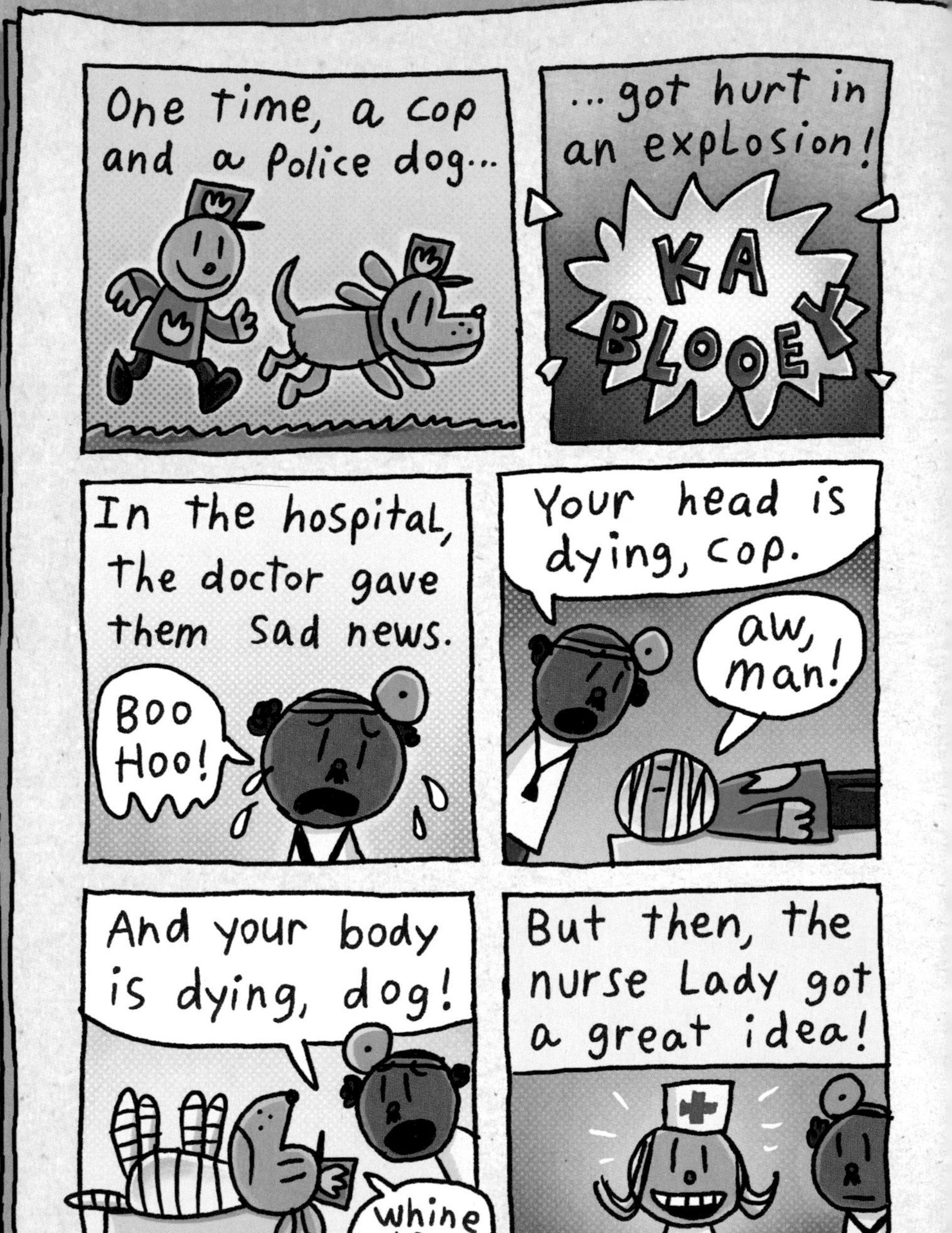
One time, a cop and a police dog...
...got hurt in an explosion!
KA BLOOEY
In the hospital, the doctor gave them sad news.
BOO HOO!
Your head is dying, cop.
aw, man!
And your body is dying, dog!
whine whine
But then, the nurse lady got a great idea!

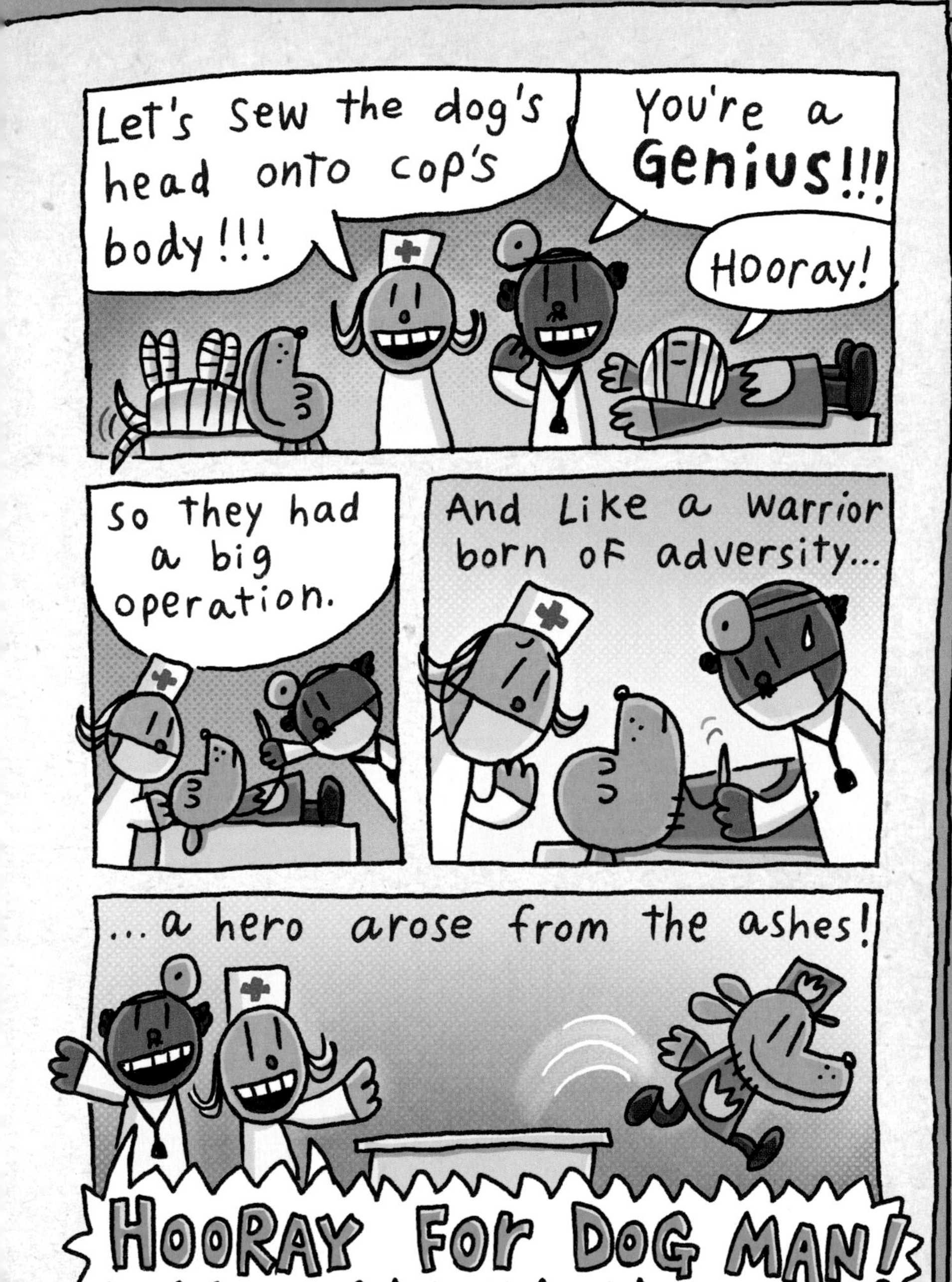
Let's sew the dog's head onto cop's body!!!
You're a Genius!!!
Hooray!
So they had a big operation.
And Like a warrior born of adversity...
...a hero arose from the ashes!
HOORAY FOR DOG MAN!

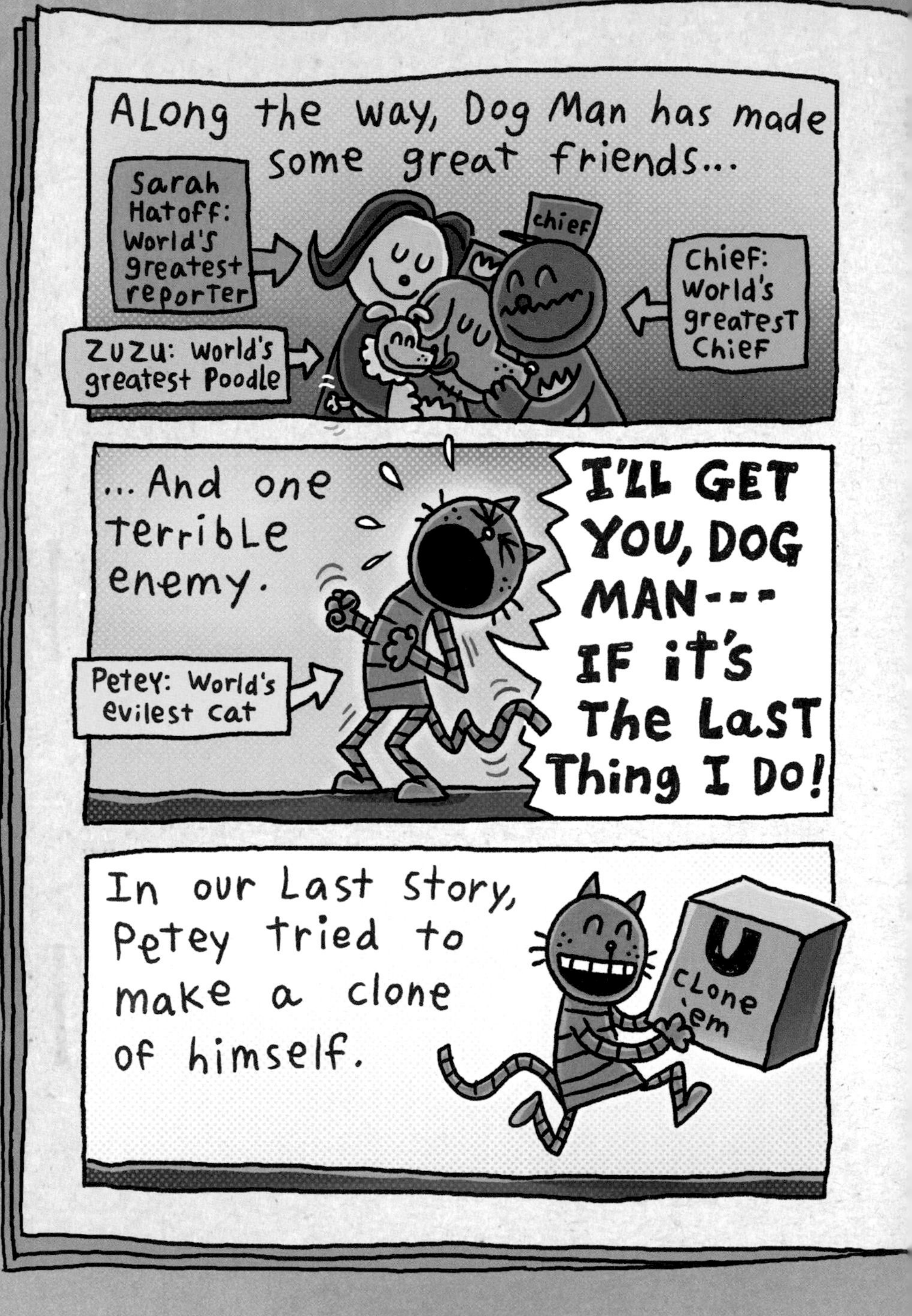

ALong the way, Dog Man has made some great friends...
Sarah Hatoff: World's greatest reporter
chief
Chief: World's greatesT Chief
ZUZU: World's greatest Poodle
...And one terrible enemy.
I'LL GET YOU, DOG MAN--- IF it's The LasT Thing I Do!
Petey: World's evilest cat
In our Last Story, Petey tried to make a clone of himself.
U
cLone 'em

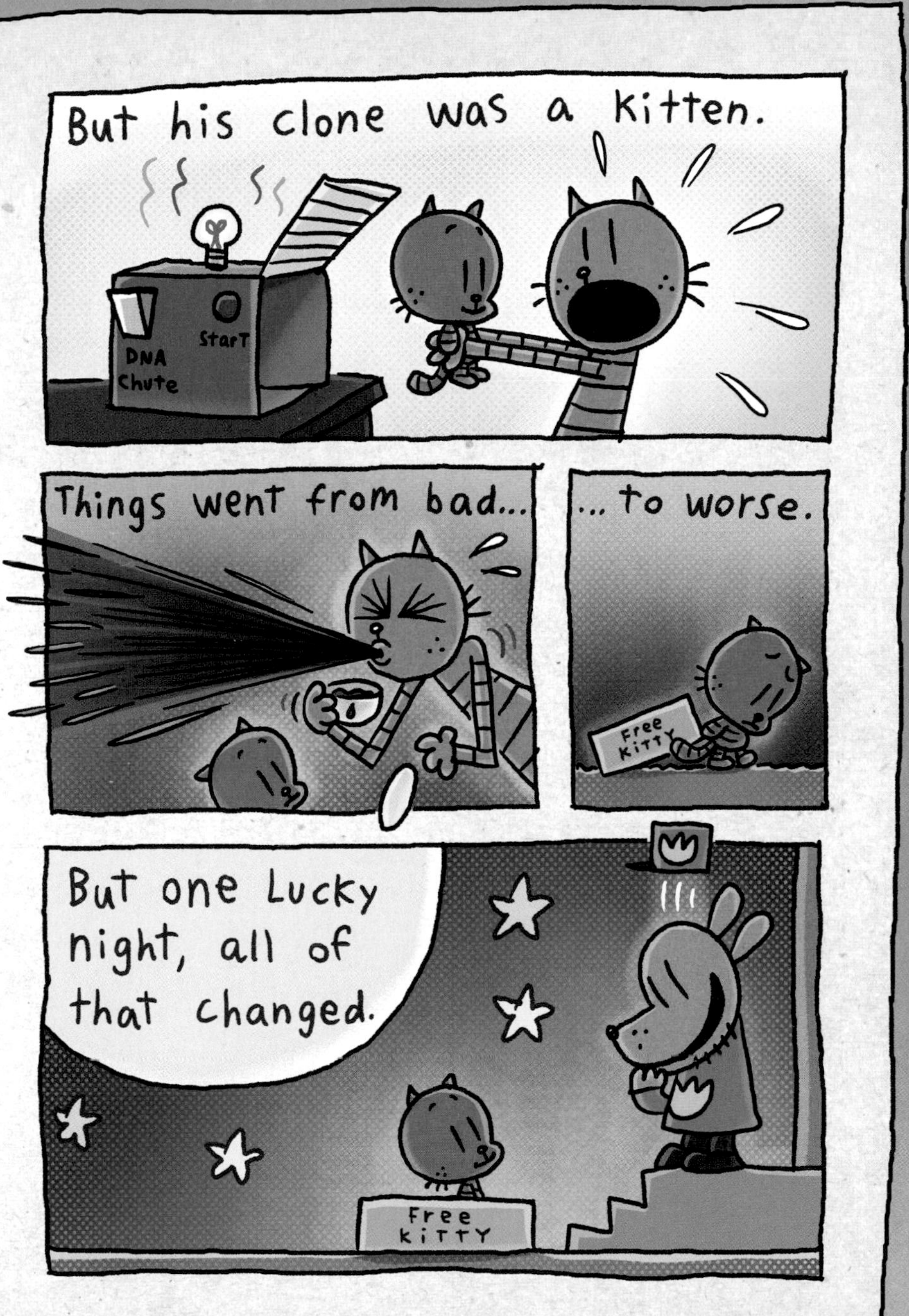
But his clone was a kitten.
DNA Chute
StarT
Things went from bad...
... to worse.
Free KiTTY
But one Lucky night, all of that changed.
Free KiTTY

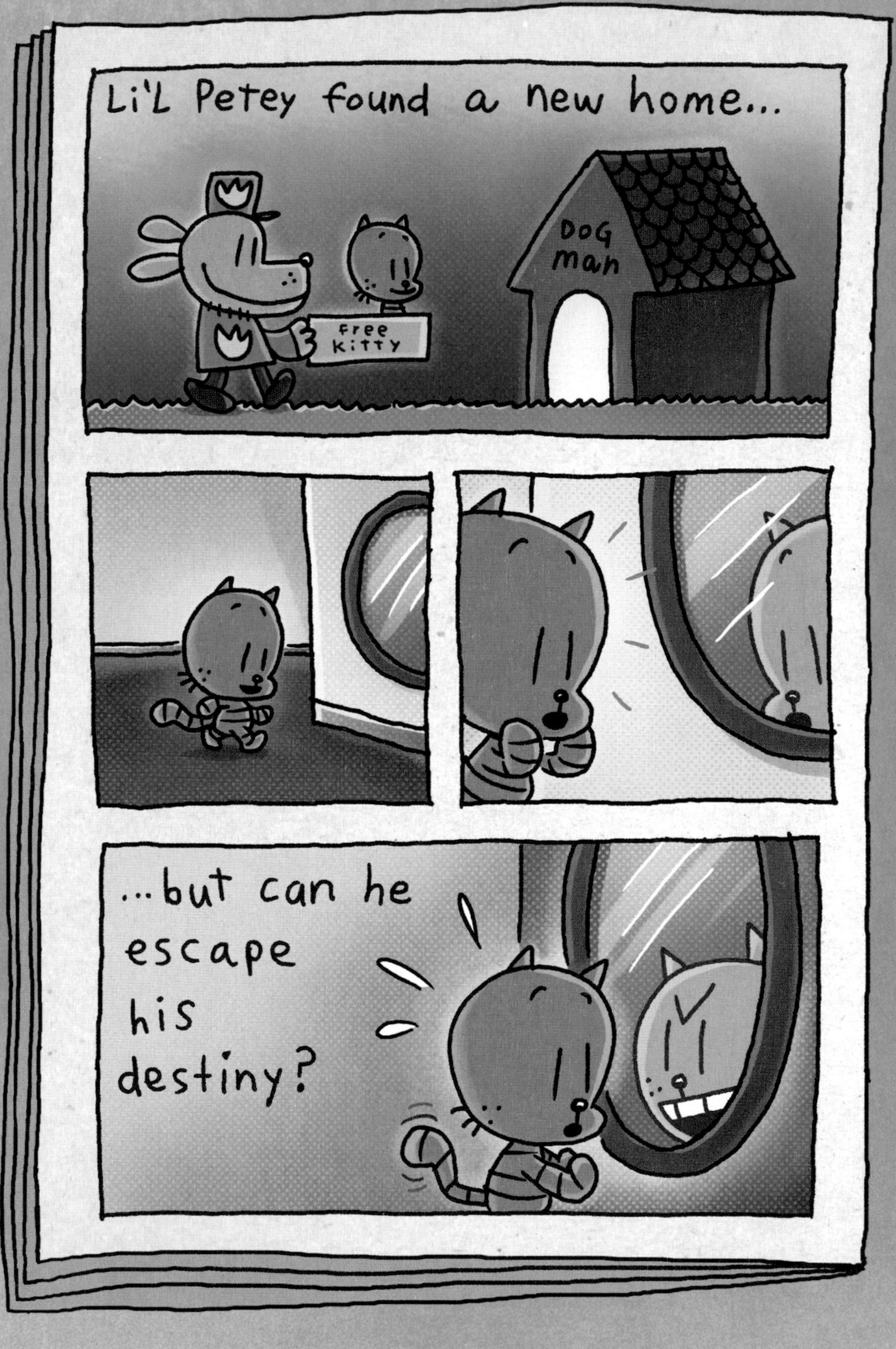
Li'L Petey found a new home...
DOG man
Free kitty
...but can he escape his destiny?

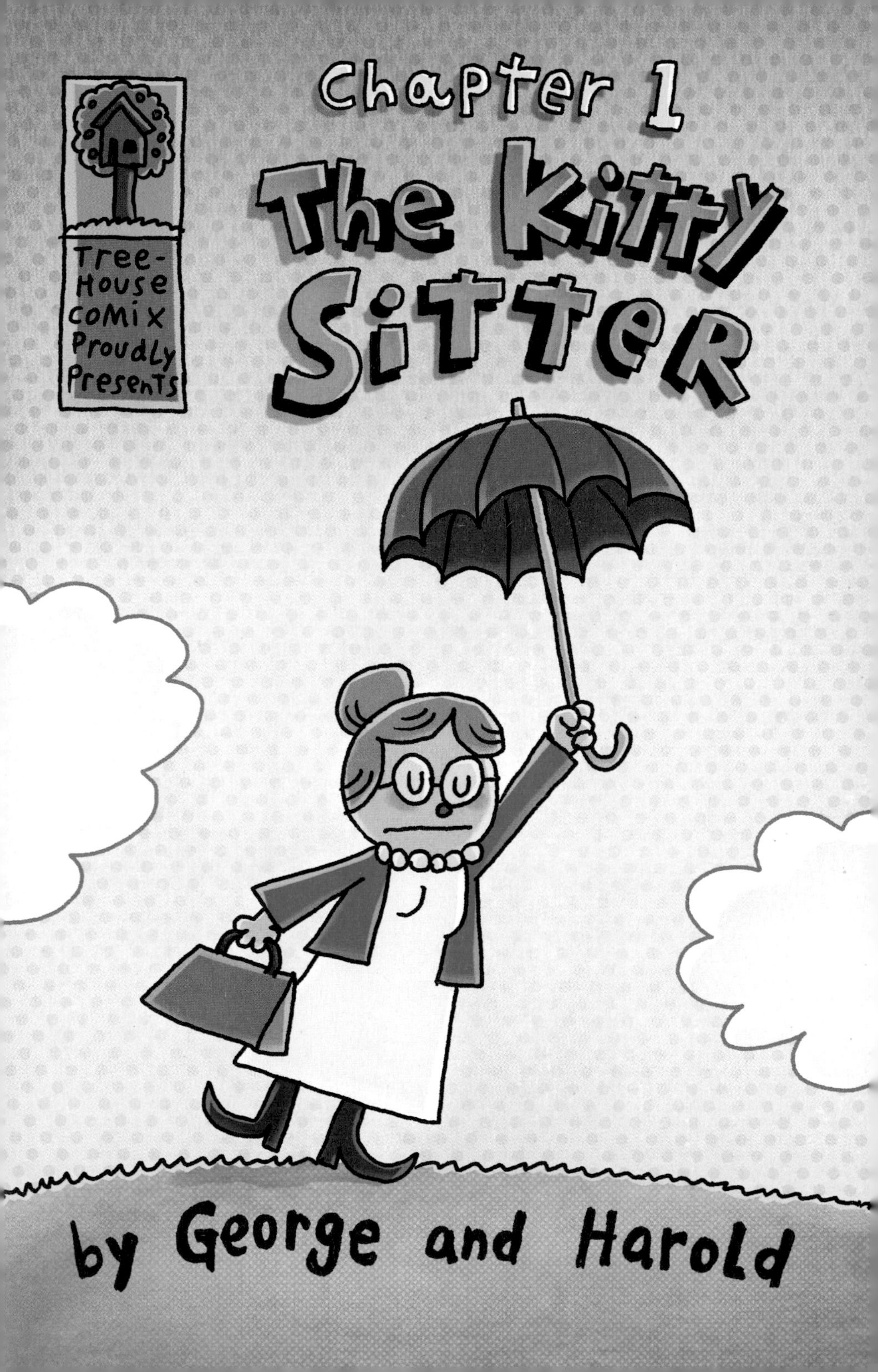
Tree-House Comix Proudly Presents
Chapter 1
The Kitty Sitter
by George and Harold

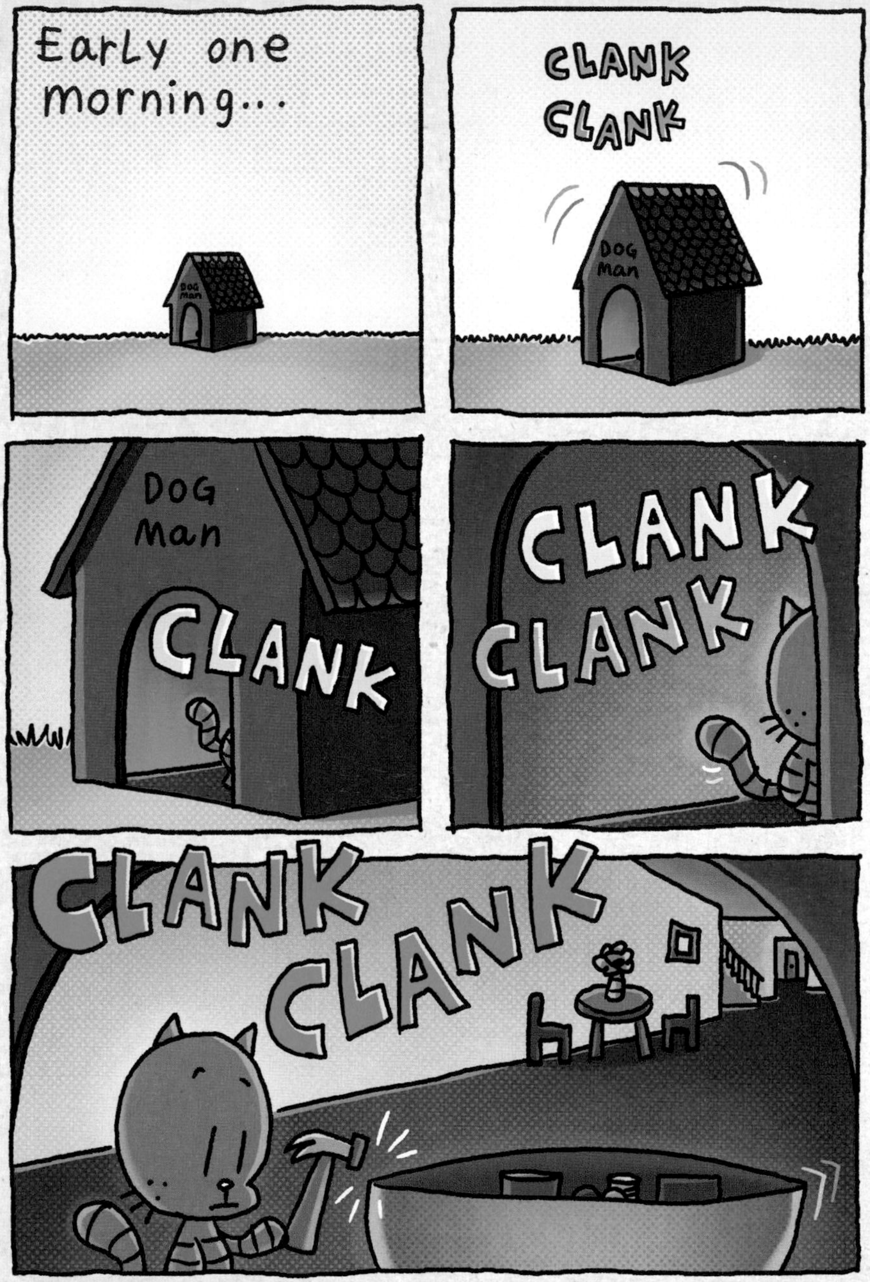
Early one morning...
CLANK
CLANK
DOG man
DOG man
DOG man
CLANK
CLANK
CLANK
CLANK
CLANK

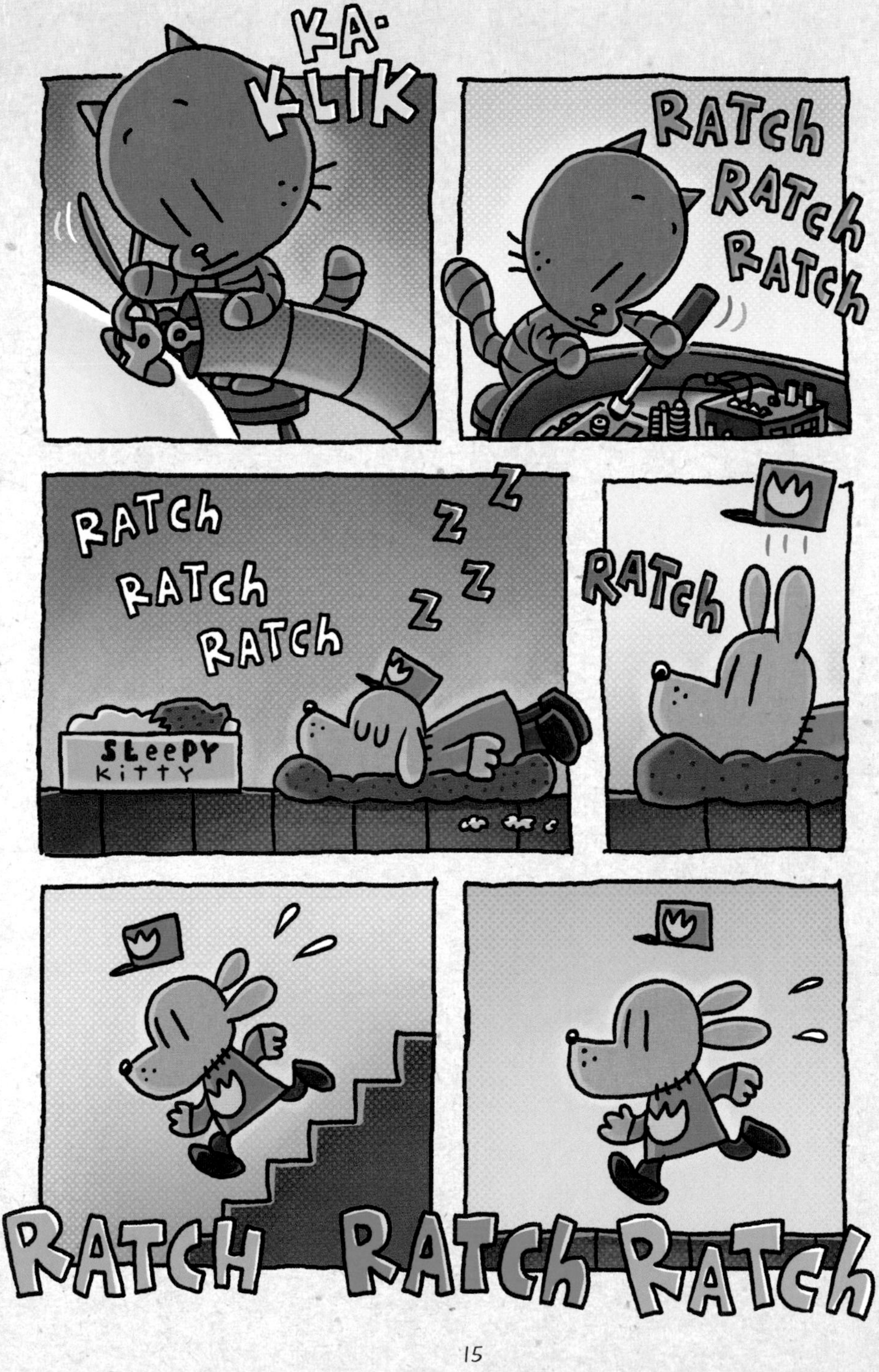
KA-KLIK
RATCH RATCH RATCH
RATCH RATCH RATCH
Z Z Z Z
SLEEPY KITTY
RATCH
RATCH RATCH RATCH

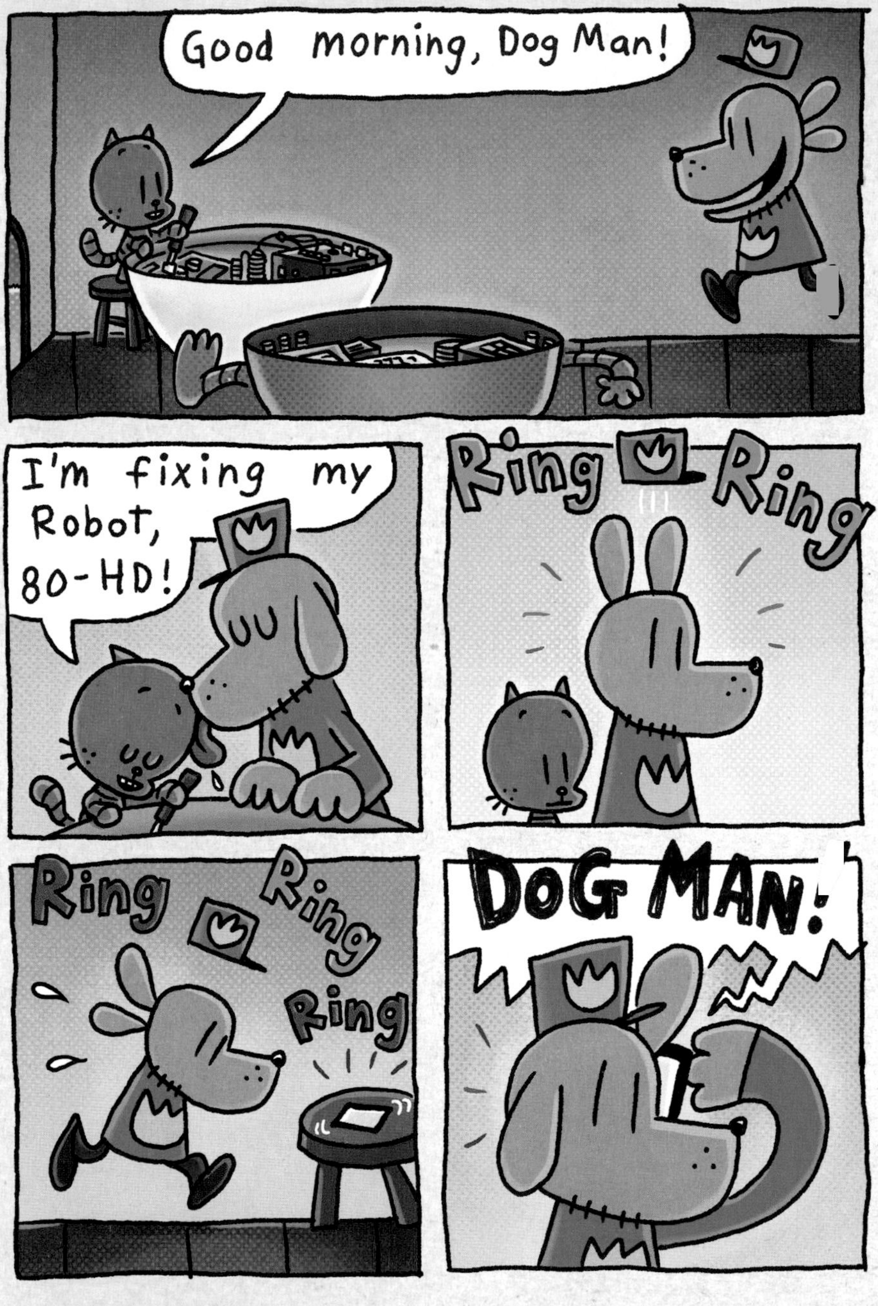
Good morning, Dog Man!
I'm fixing my Robot, 80-HD!
Ring Ring
Ring Ring Ring
DOG MAN!

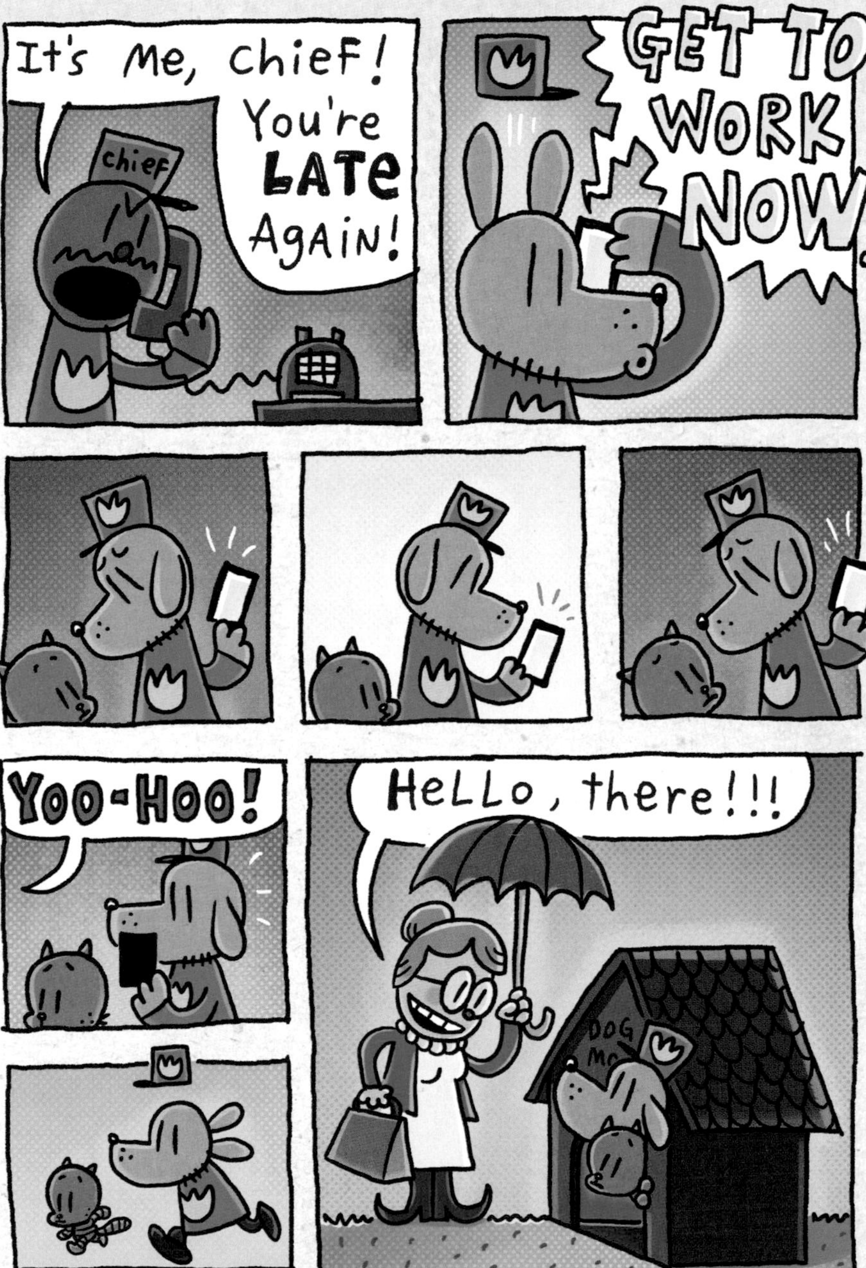
It's Me, chief! You're LATE Again!
chief
GET TO WORK NOW!
YOO-HOO!
HeLLo, there!!!
DOG MA

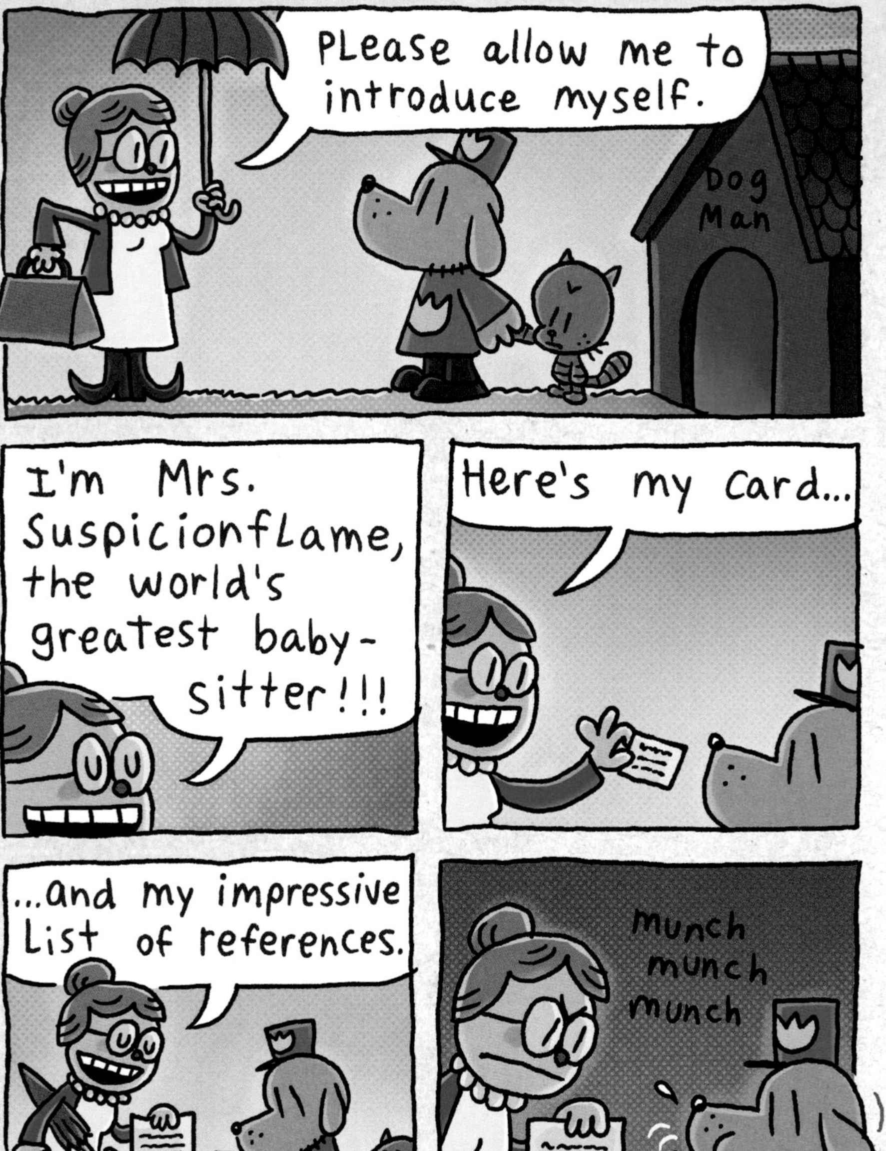
Please allow me to introduce myself.
Dog Man
I'm Mrs. Suspicionflame, the world's greatest baby-sitter!!!
Here's my card...
...and my impressive list of references.
munch munch munch

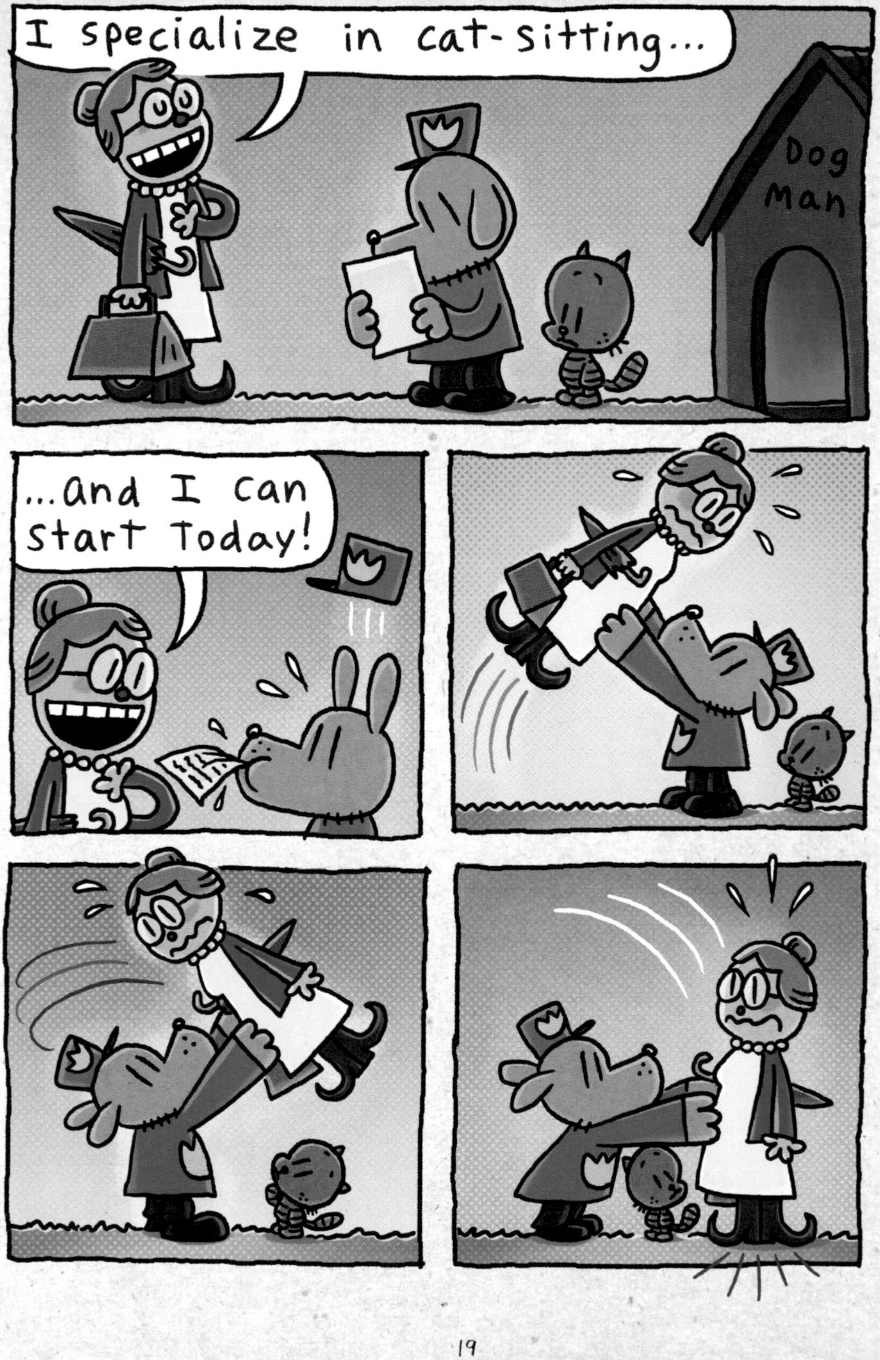
I specialize in cat-sitting...
Dog Man
...and I can start Today!

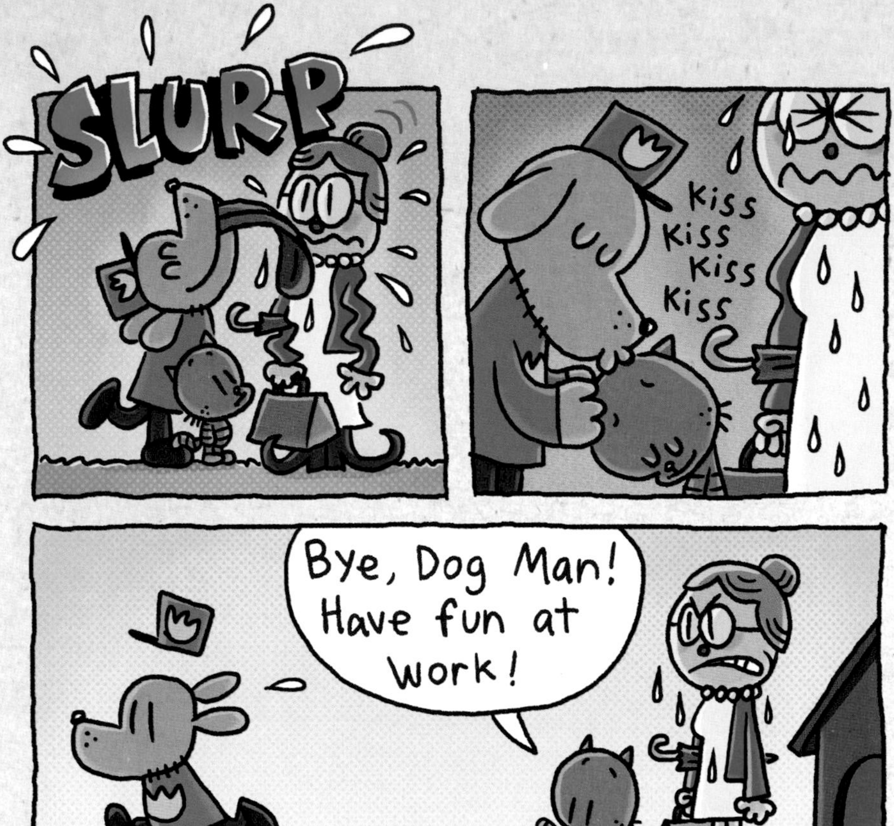
SLURP
KISS
KISS
KISS
KISS
Bye, Dog Man! Have fun at work!
Well, uh--- hello there, young man.
Hi, Papa.

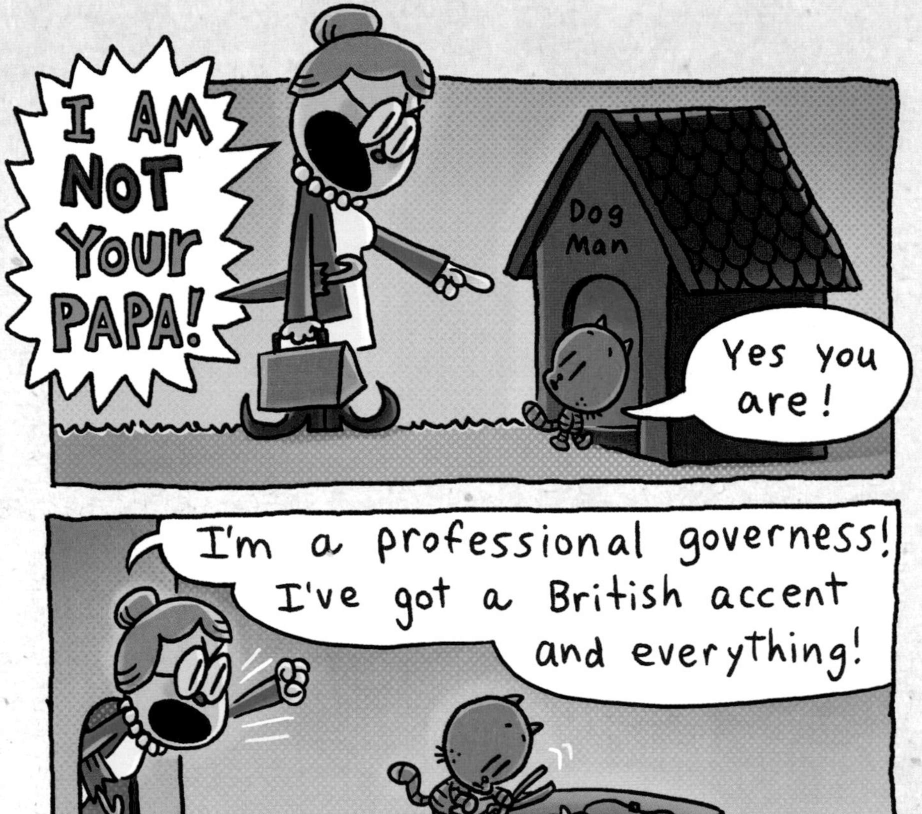
I AM NOT YOUR PAPA!
Dog Man
Yes you are!
I'm a professional governess! I've got a British accent and everything!
I sing songs about how much fun it is to clean up your room and stuff!
OK, Prove it!
Sing me a song.

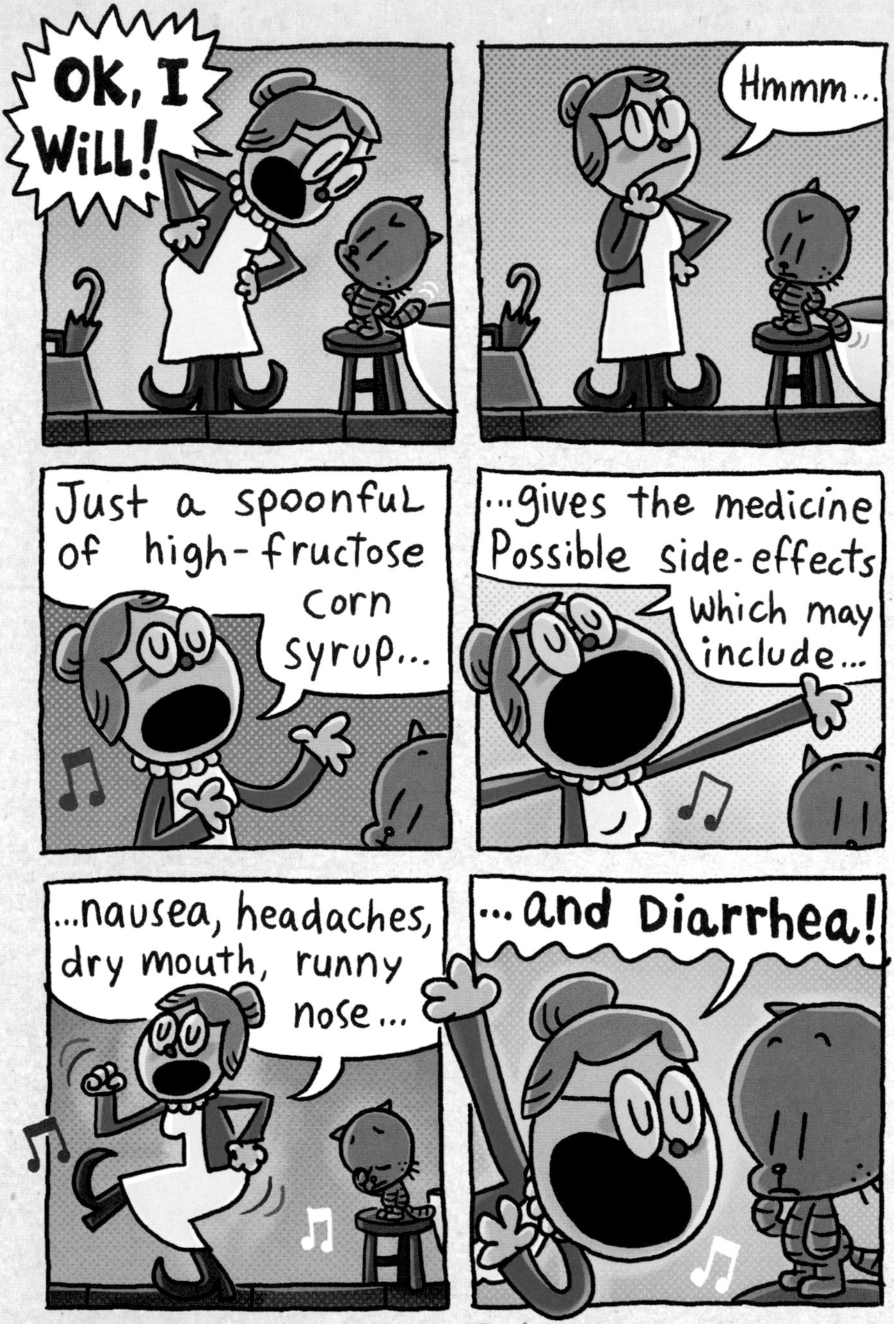
OK, I WILL!
Hmmm...
Just a spoonful of high-fructose corn syrup...
...gives the medicine Possible side-effects which may include...
...nausea, headaches, dry mouth, runny nose...
...and Diarrhea!

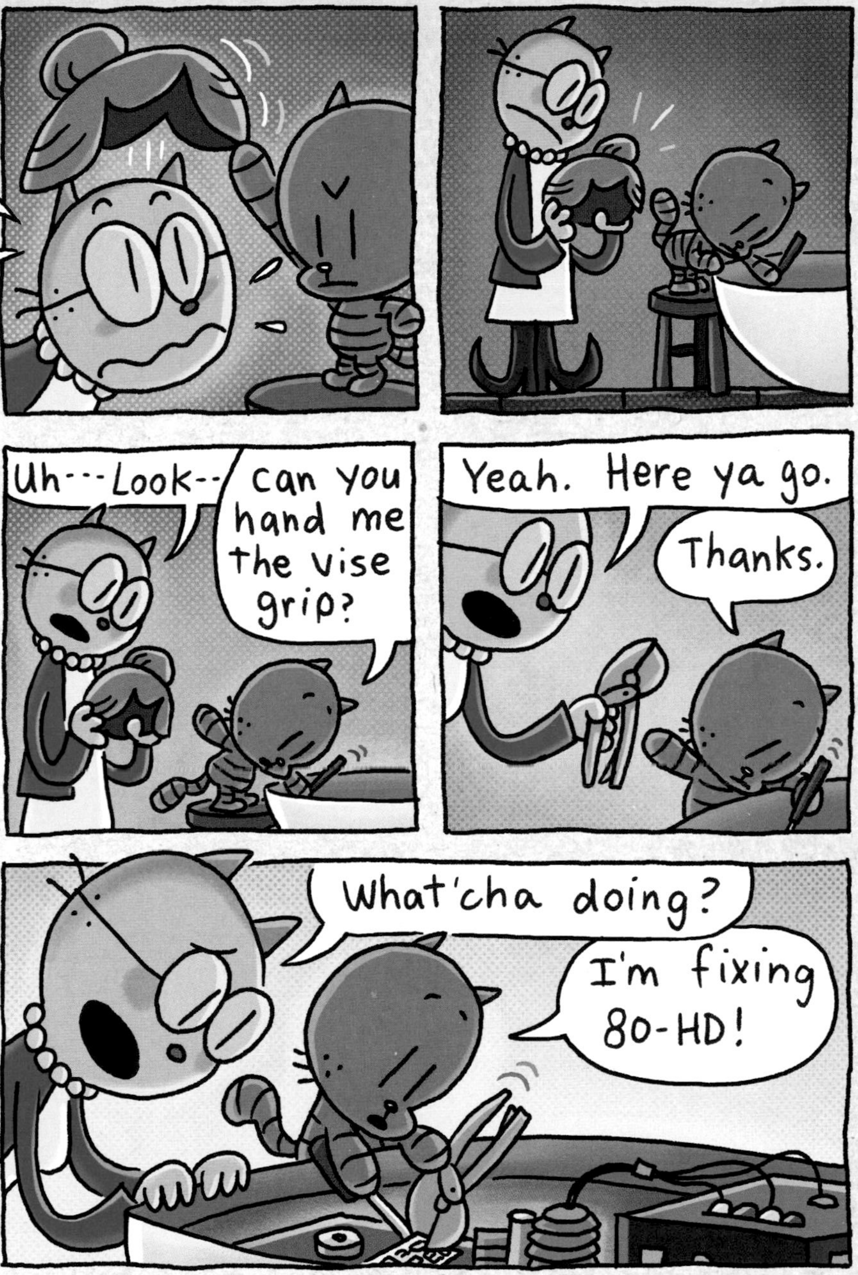
Uh···Look··
can you hand me the vise grip?
Yeah. Here ya go.
Thanks.
What'cha doing?
I'm fixing 80-HD!

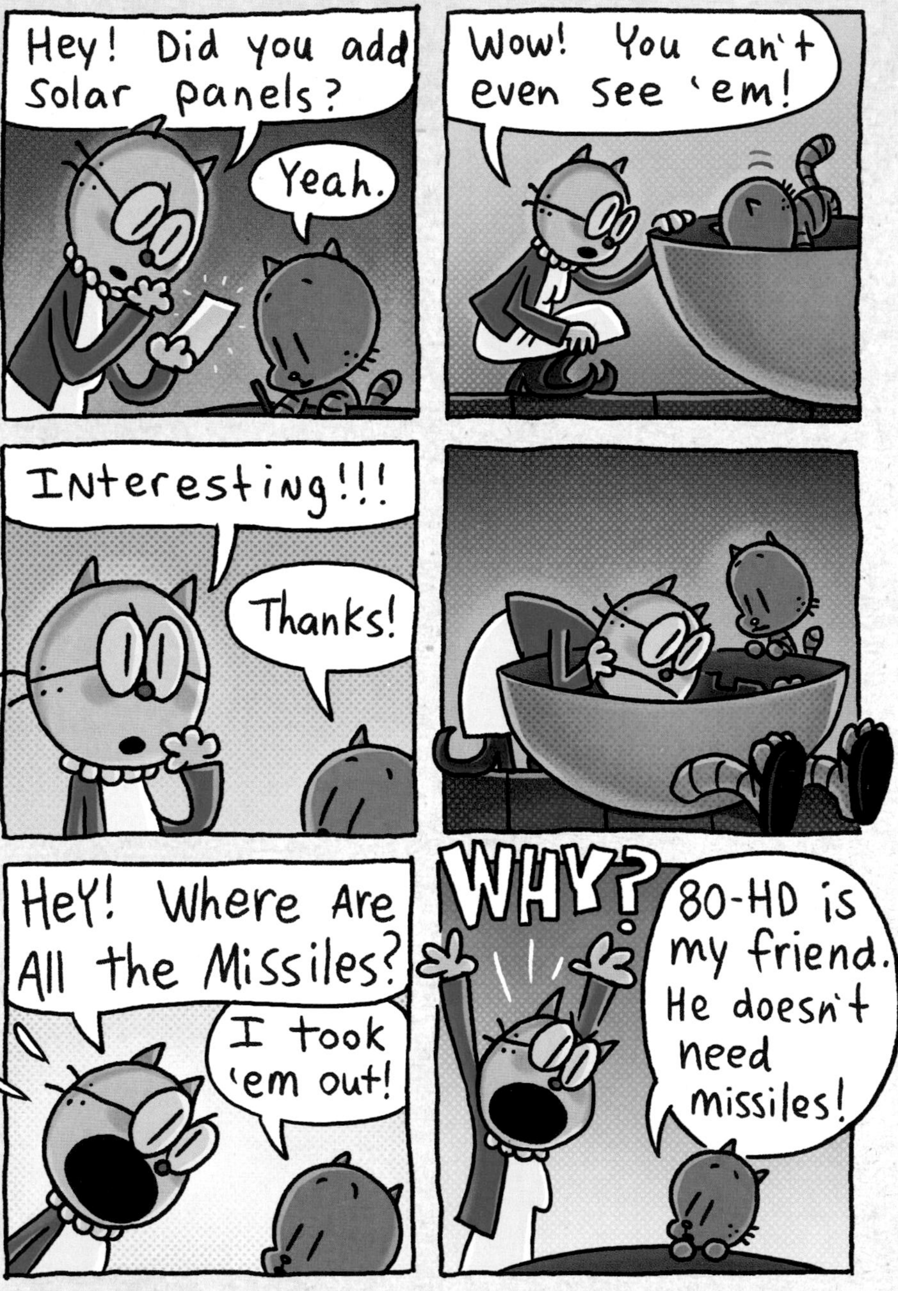
Hey! Did you add Solar panels?
Yeah.
Wow! You can't even see 'em!
Interesting!!!
Thanks!
Hey! Where Are All the Missiles?
I took 'em out!
WHY?
80-HD is my friend. He doesn't need missiles!

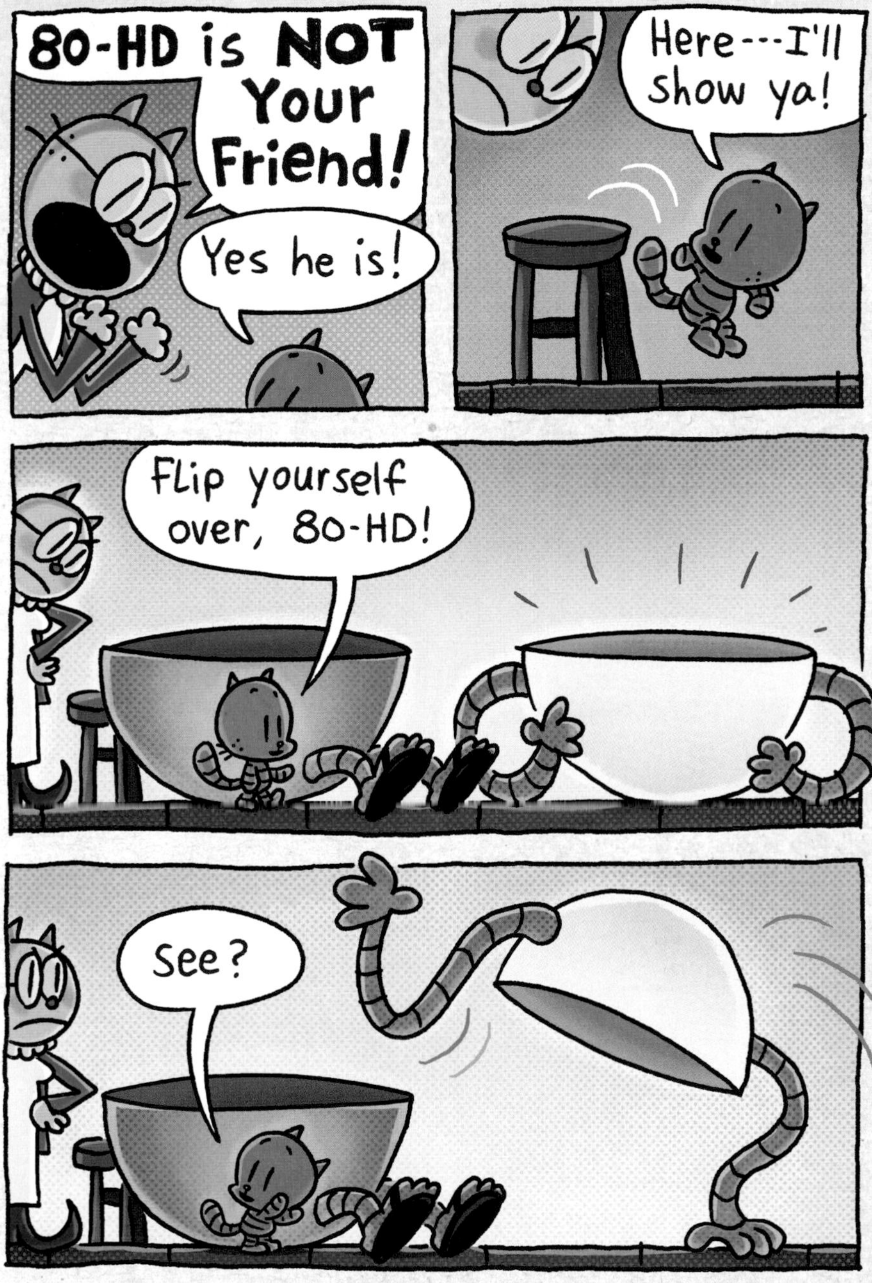
80-HD is NOT Your Friend!
Yes he is!
Here---I'll show ya!
Flip yourself over, 80-HD!
See?

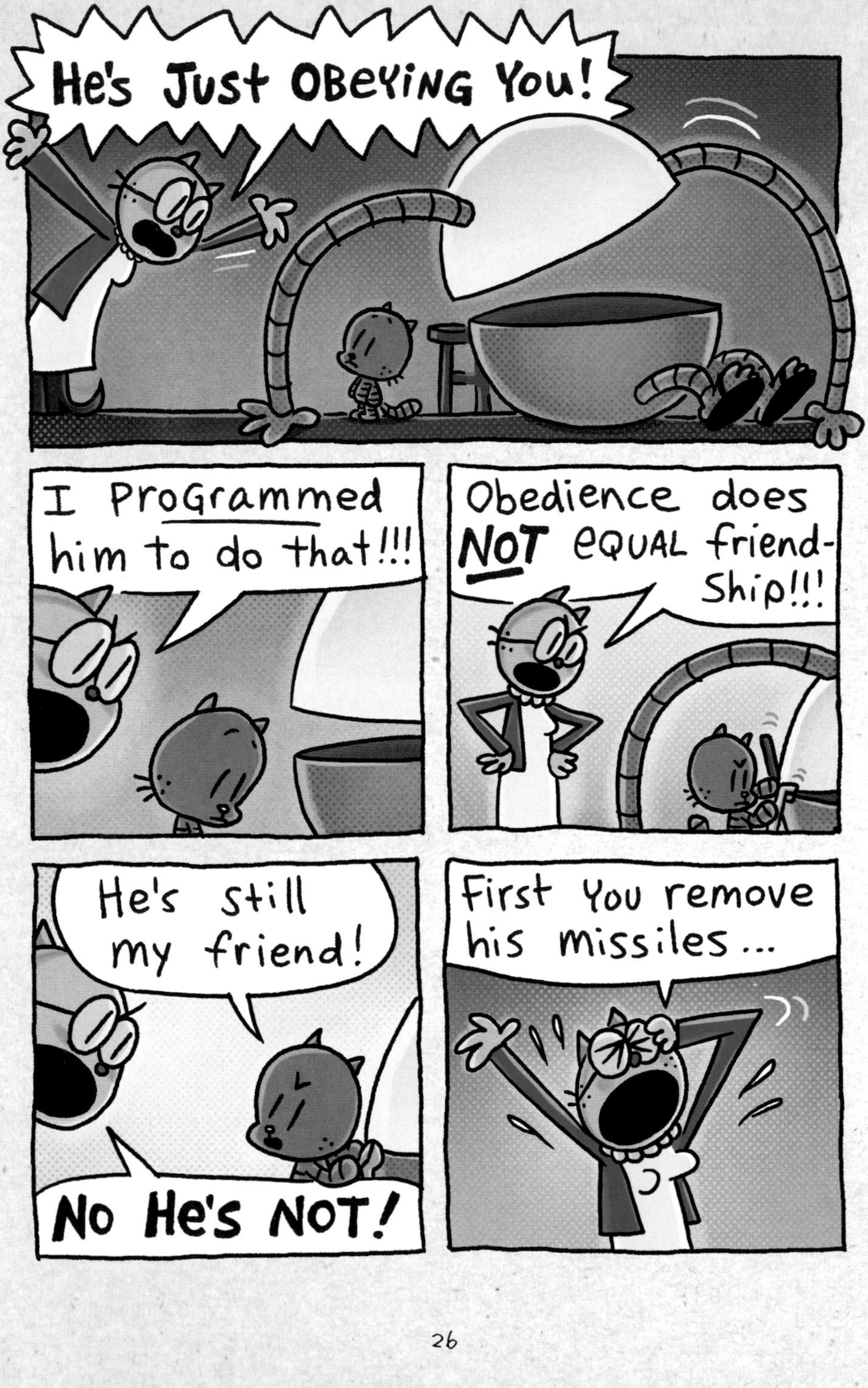
He's Just OBEYING You!
I PROGRAMMED him to do that!!!
Obedience does NOT EQUAL friend-Ship!!!
He's still my friend!
No He's NOT!
First You remove his missiles...

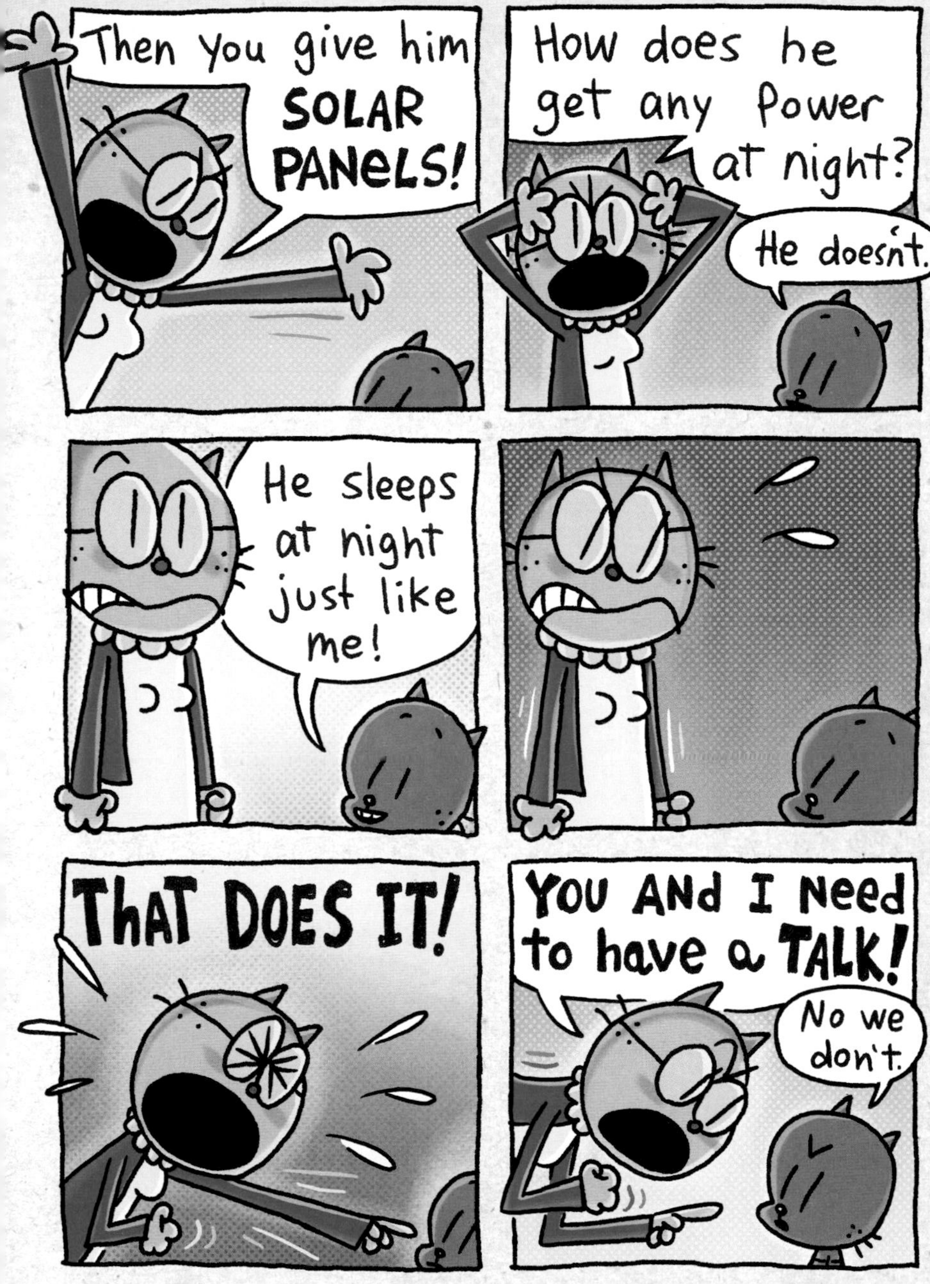
Then you give him SOLAR PANELS!
How does he get any Power at night?
He doesn't.
He sleeps at night just like me!
THAT DOES IT!
YOU AND I Need to have a TALK!
No we don't.

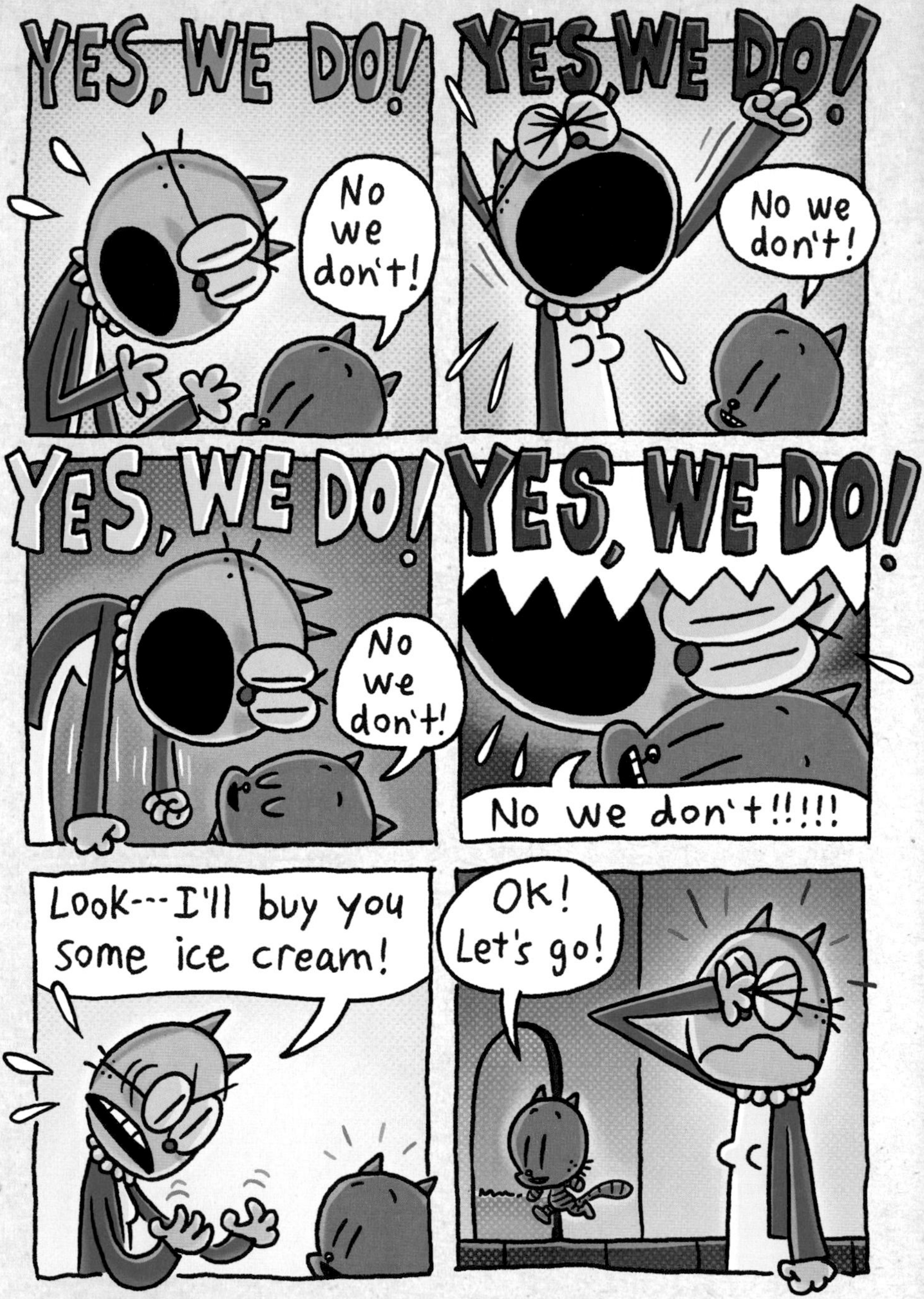
YES, WE DO!
No we don't!
YES, WE DO!
No we don't!
YES, WE DO!
No we don't!
YES, WE DO!
No we don't!!!!!
Look---I'll buy you some ice cream!
Ok! Let's go!

Chapter 2

Hollywood Hero

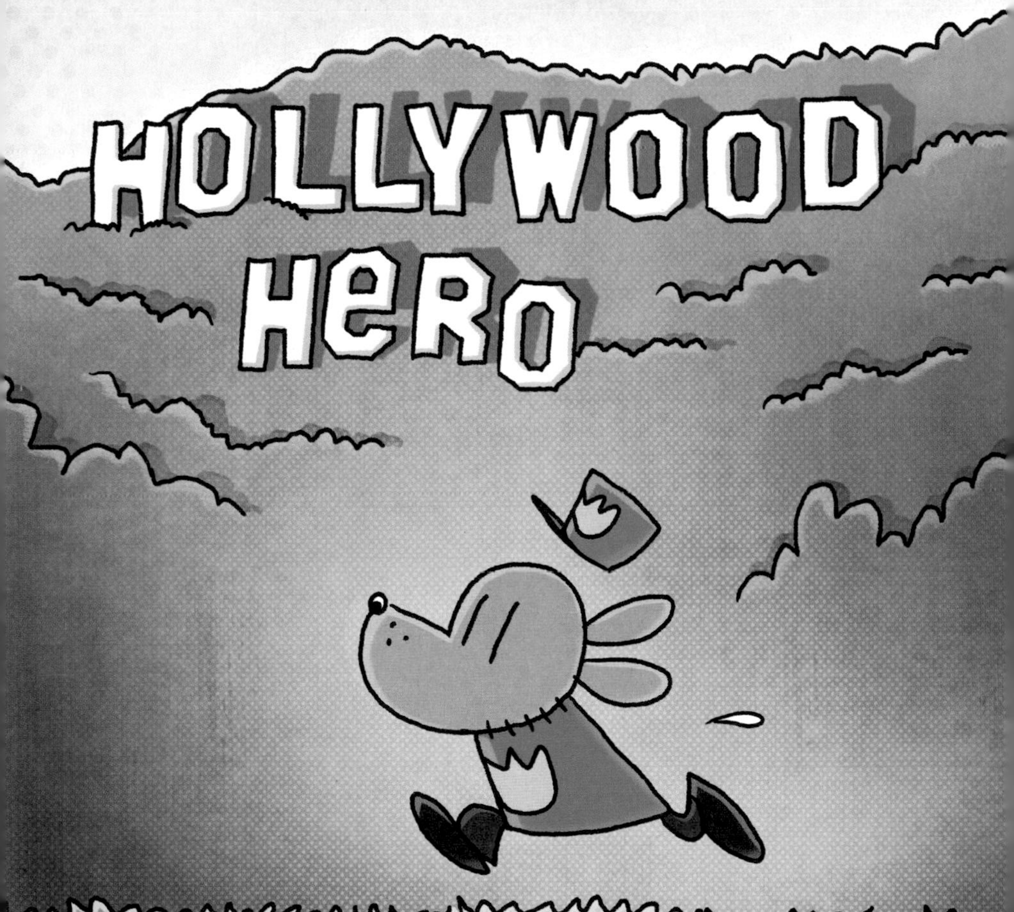

by George and Harold

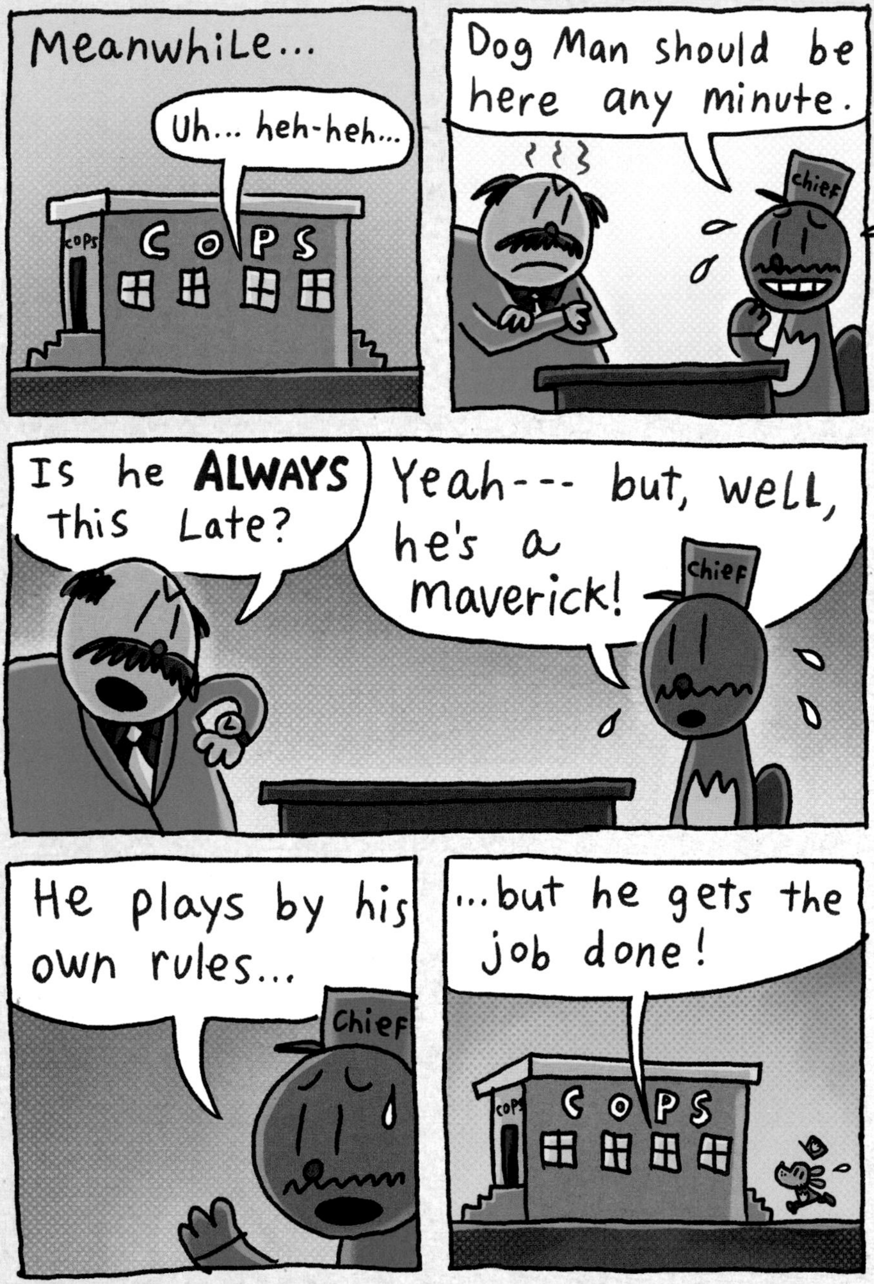
Meanwhile...
Uh... heh-heh...
COPS
COPS
Dog Man should be here any minute.
Chief
Is he ALWAYS this Late?
Yeah--- but, well, he's a maverick!
Chief
He plays by his own rules...
Chief
...but he gets the job done!
COPS
COPS

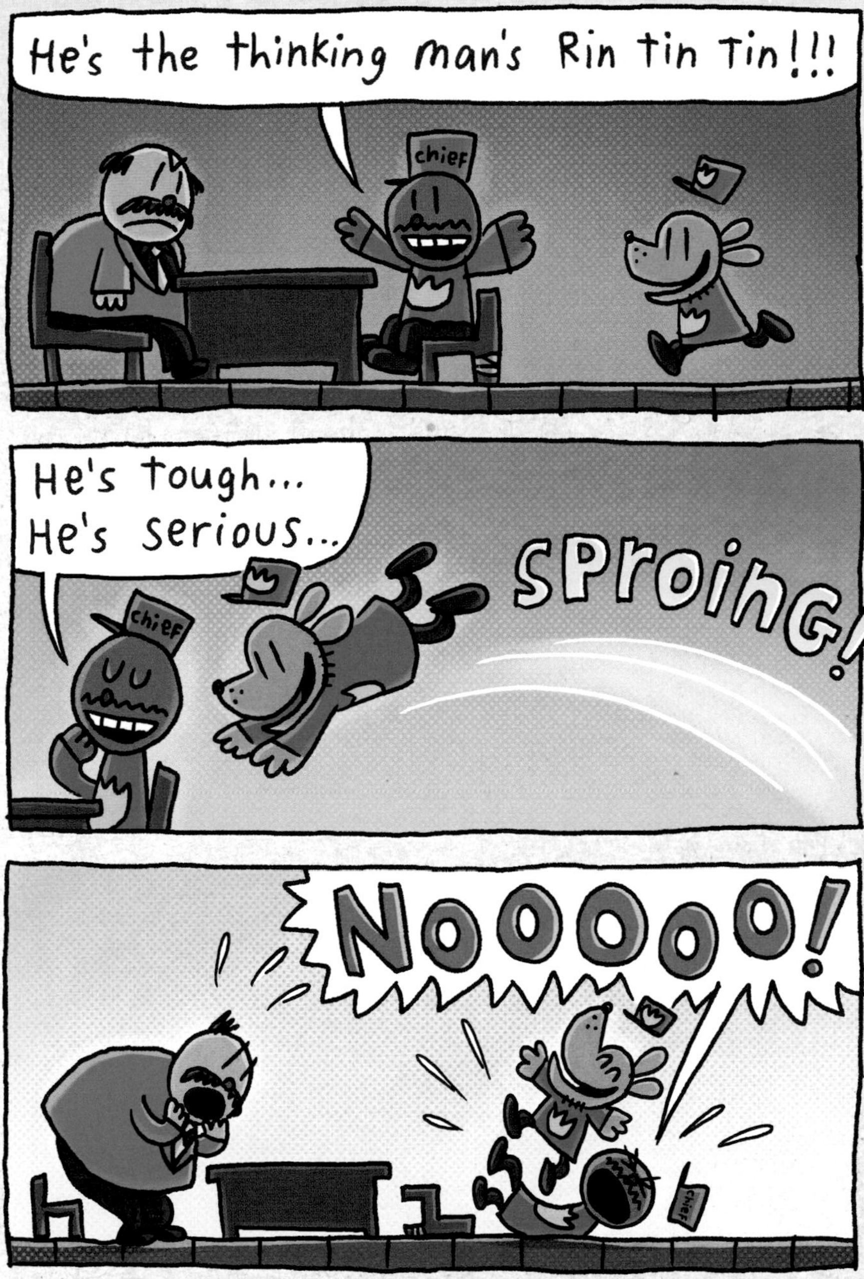
He's the thinking man's Rin tin Tin!!!
chief
He's tough...
He's serious...
chief
SPROING!
NOOOOO!
chief

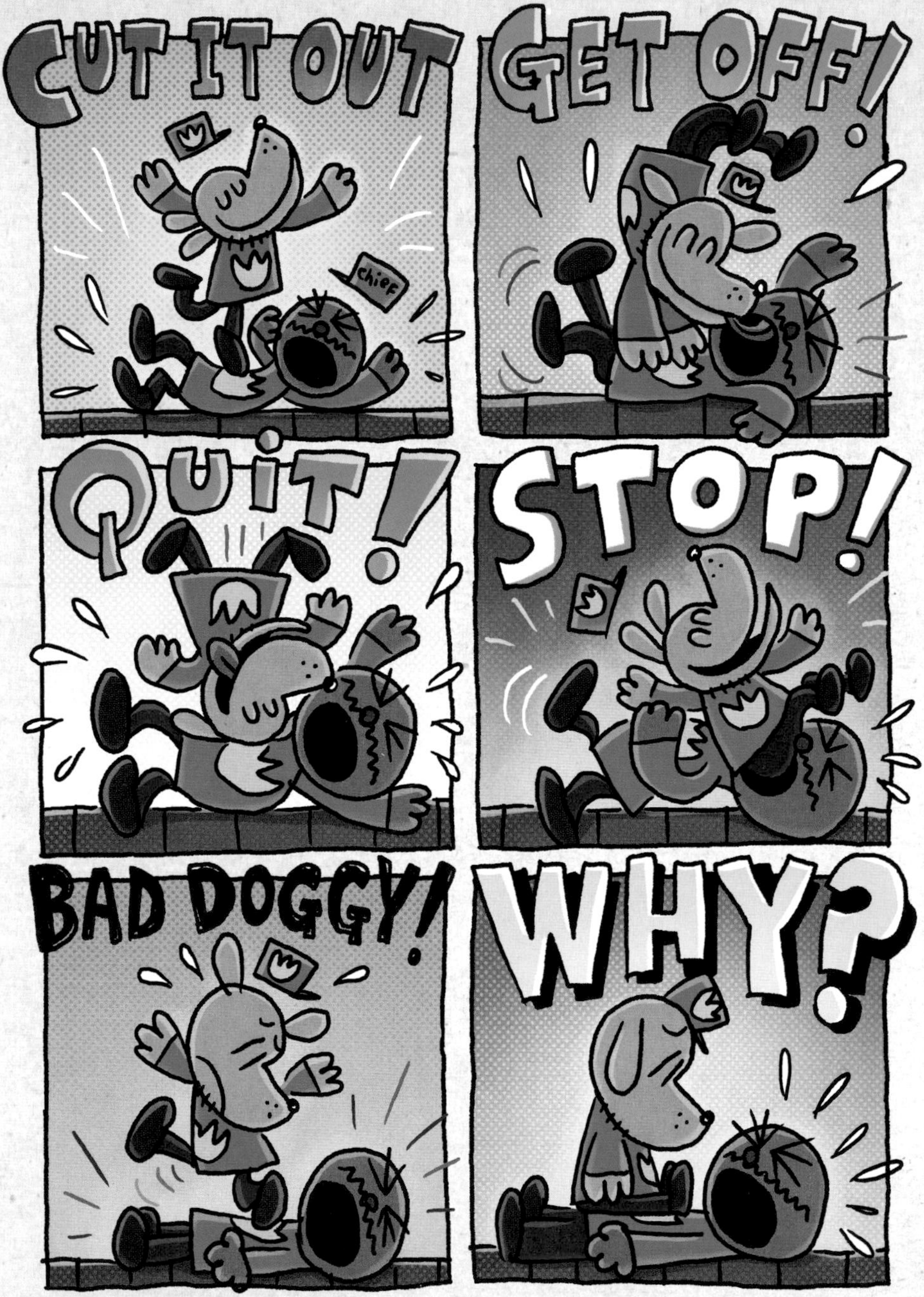
CUT IT OUT
chief
GET OFF!
QUIT!
STOP!
BAD DOGGY!
WHY?

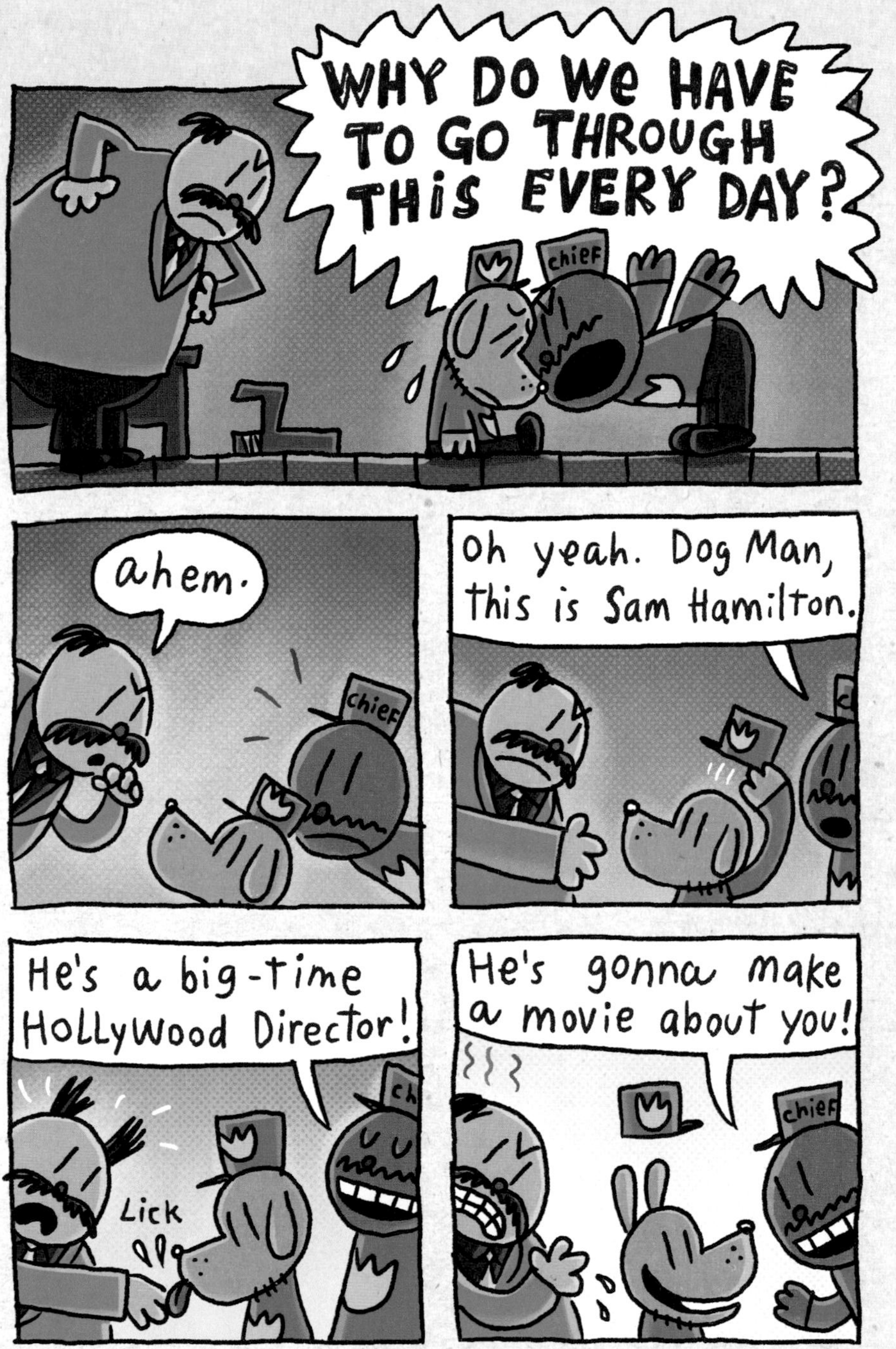
WHY DO WE HAVE TO GO THROUGH THIS EVERY DAY?
chief
ahem.
chief
Oh yeah. Dog Man, this is Sam Hamilton.
He's a big-time HoLLywood Director!
Lick
He's gonna make a movie about you!
chief

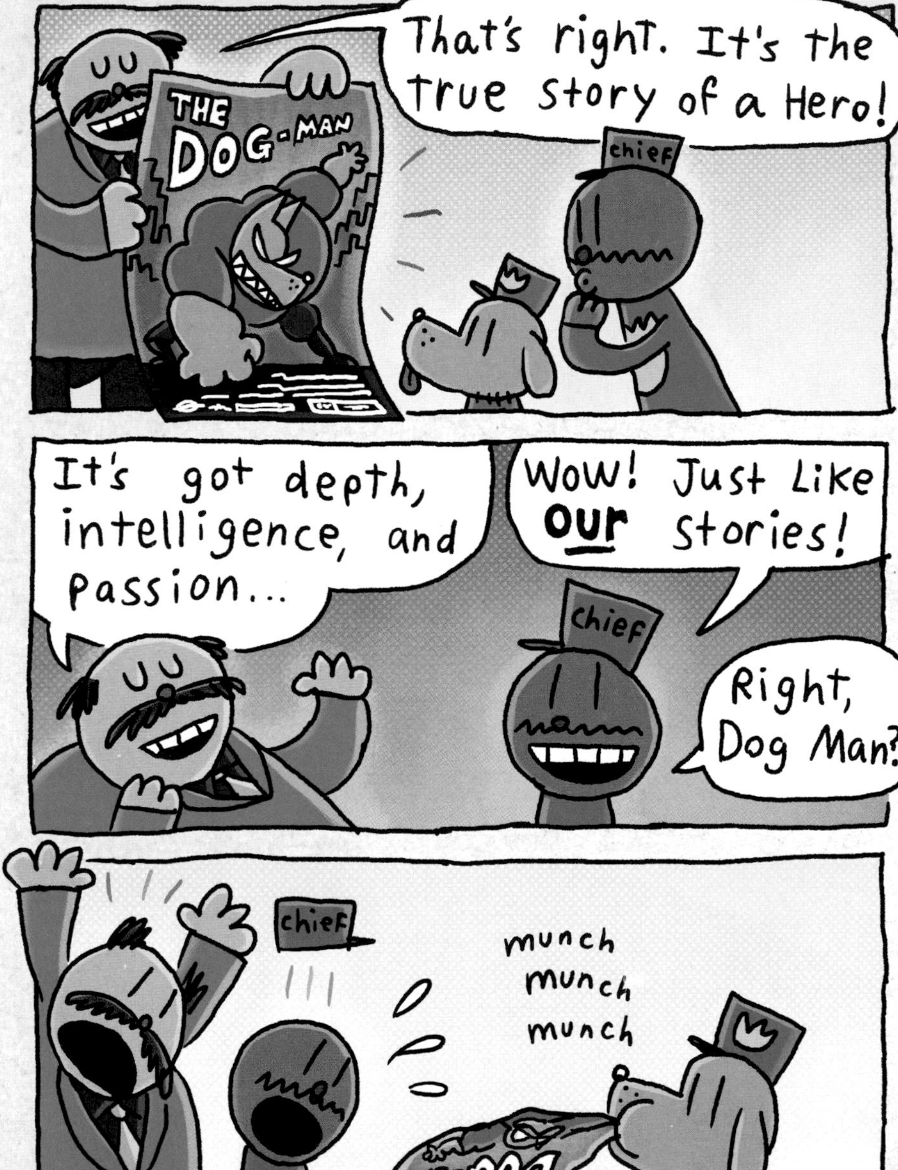
That's right. It's the true story of a Hero!
THE DOG-MAN
chief
It's got depth, intelligence, and passion...
WOW! Just Like **OUR** stories!
chief
Right, Dog Man?
chief
munch
munch
munch
THE DOG-MAN

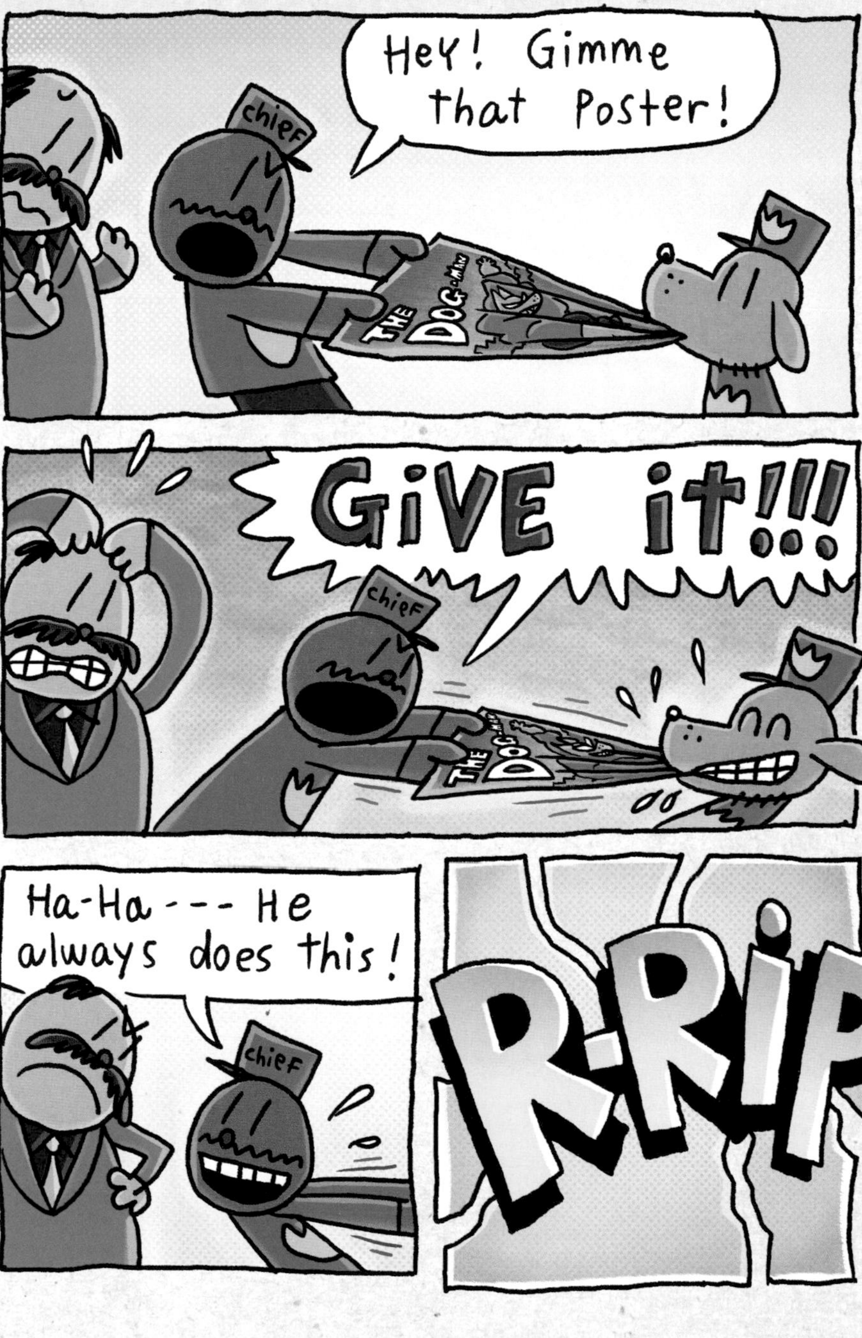
Hey! Gimme that Poster!
chief
THE DOG-MAN
GiVE it!!!
chief
THE DOG-MAN
Ha-Ha --- He always does this!
chief
R-RIP

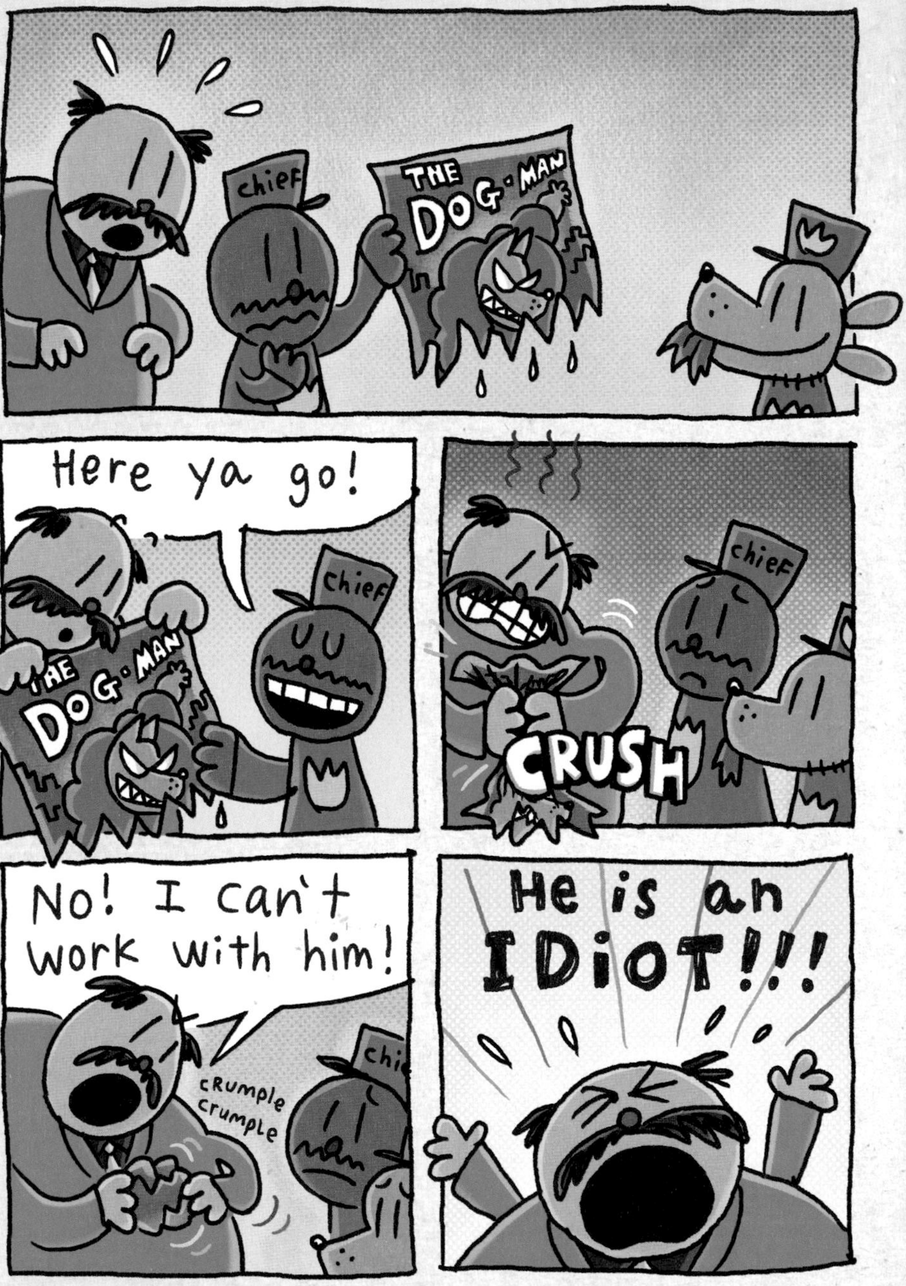
THE DOG-MAN
chief
Here ya go!
chief
THE DOG-MAN
chief
CRUSH
No! I can't work with him!
crumple crumple
He is an IDIOT!!!

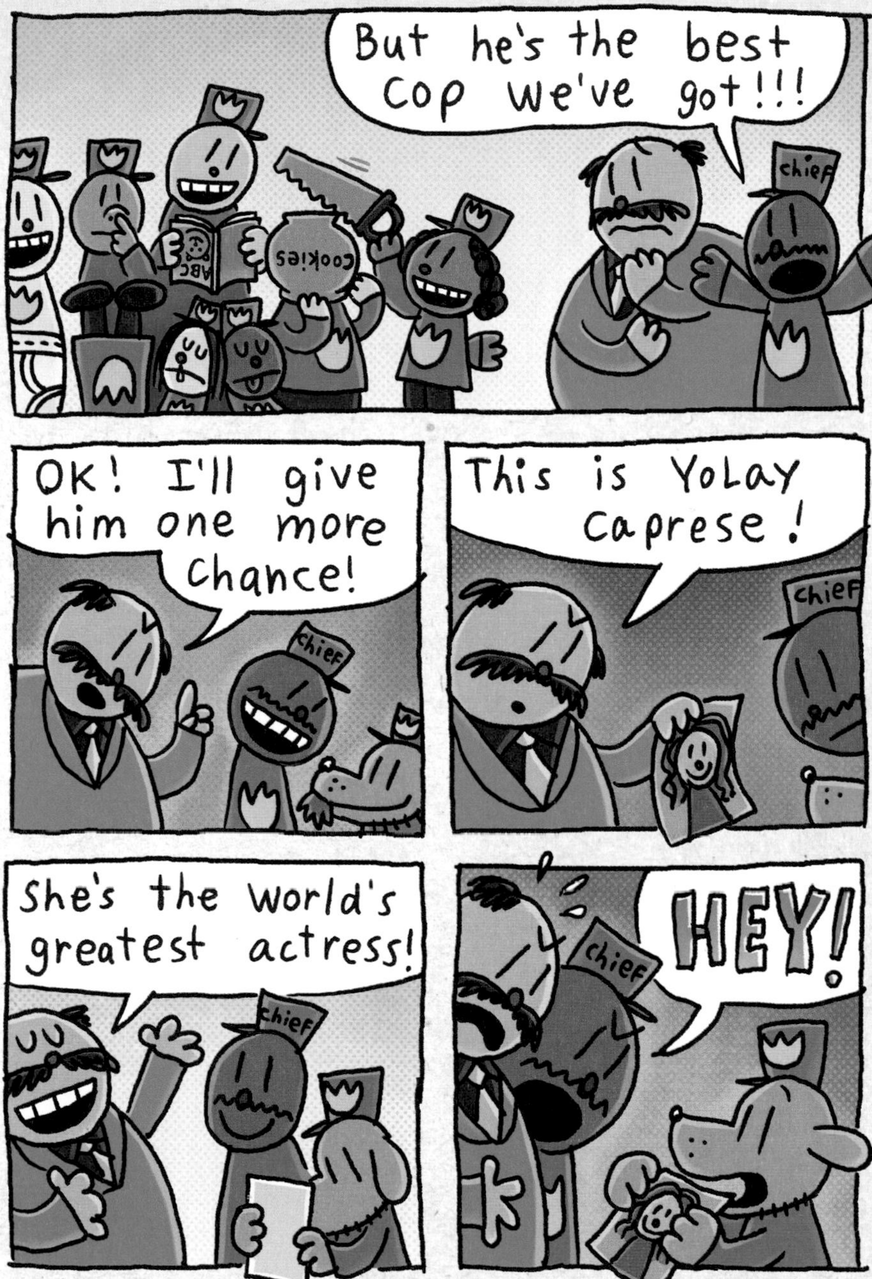
But he's the best cop we've got!!!
Cookies
ABC
chief
OK! I'll give him one more chance!
chief
This is Yolay Caprese!
chief
She's the world's greatest actress!
chief
chief
HEY!

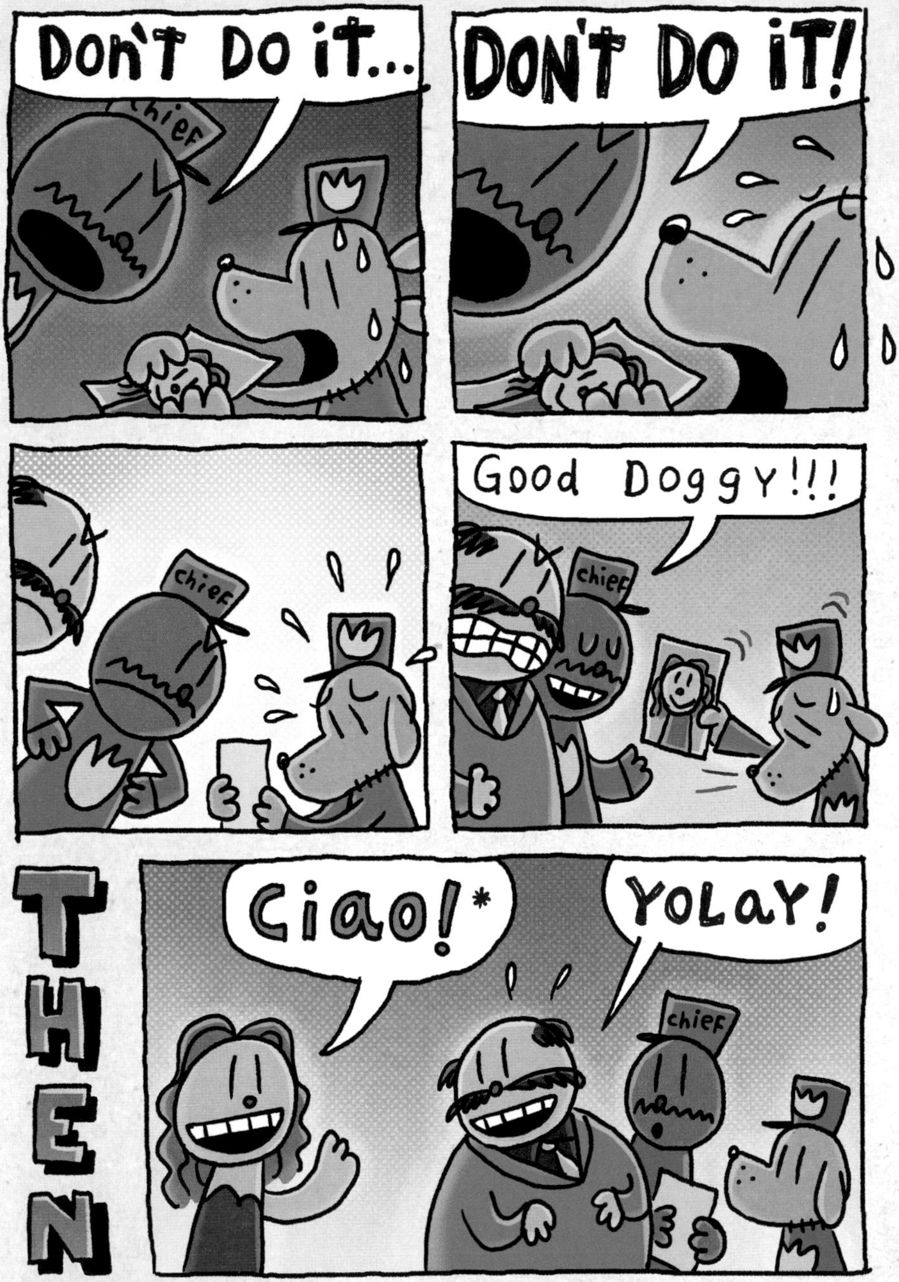
Don't Do it...
DON'T DO IT!
chief
Good Doggy!!!
chief
THEN
Ciao!*
YOLAY!
chief

* Italian for "hello." (Pronounced "chow.")

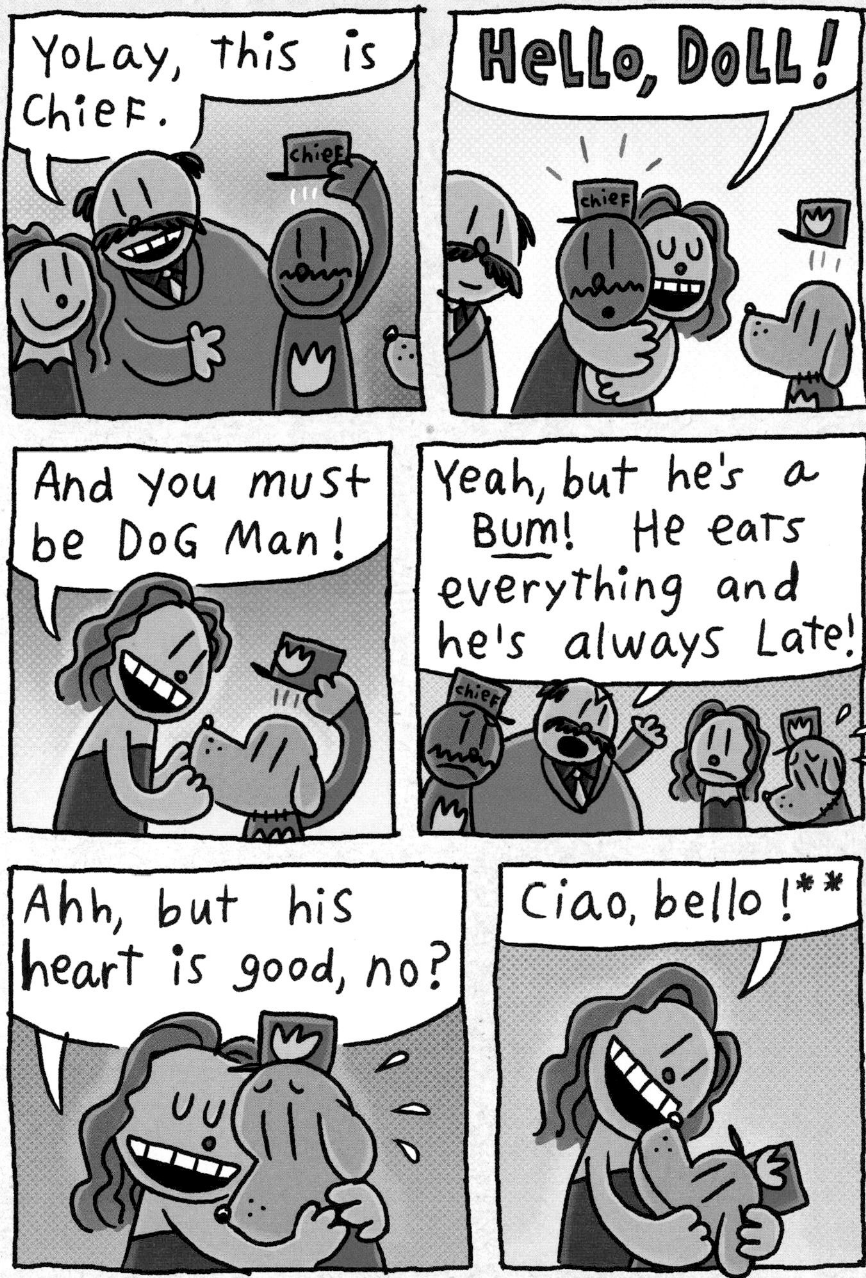
YoLay, this is Chief.
chief
HeLLo, DoLL!
chief
And you must be DoG Man!
Yeah, but he's a BUM! He eats everything and he's always Late!
chief
Ahh, but his heart is good, no?
Ciao, bello!**

** TransLation: Hello, handsome!

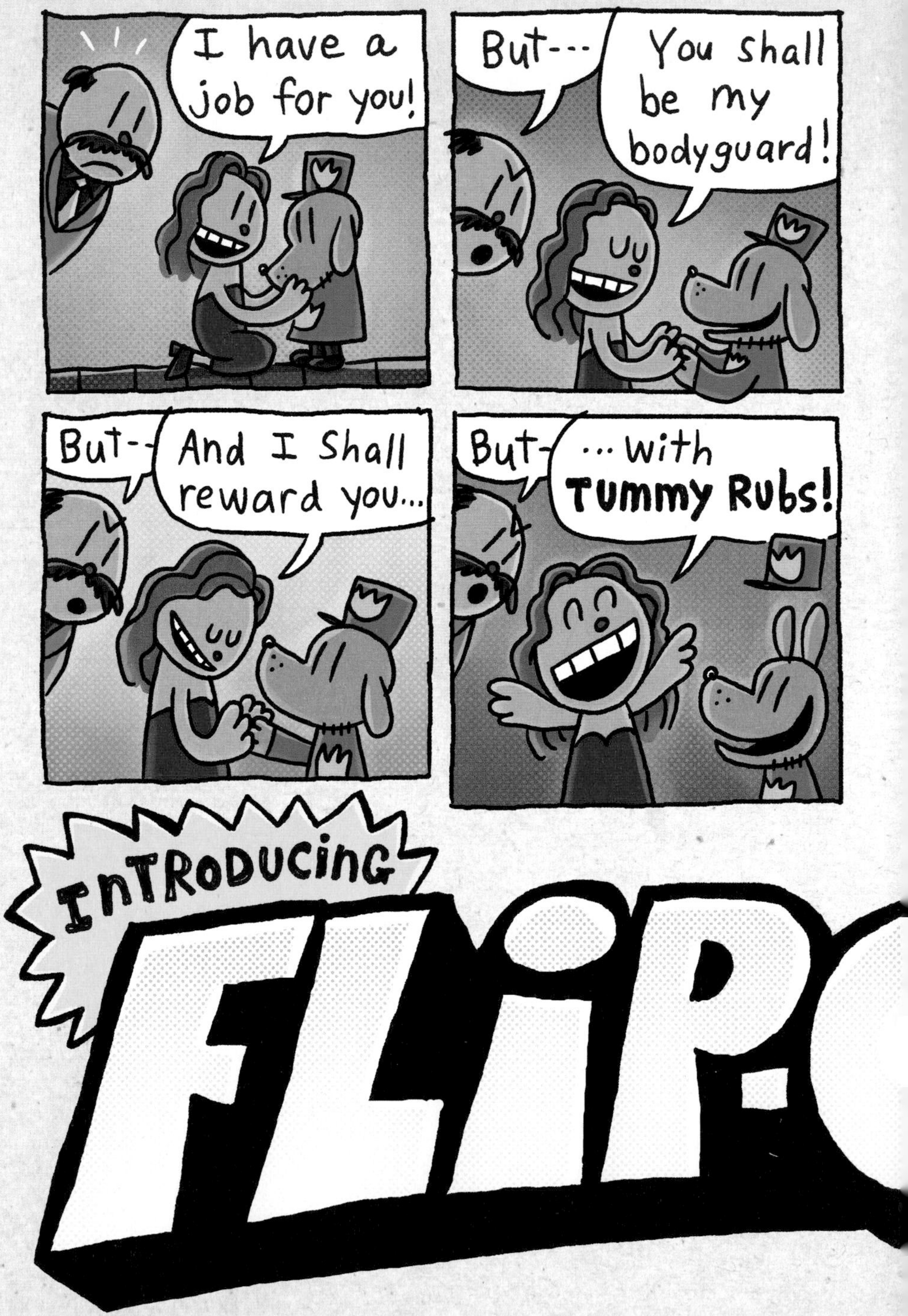

I have a job for you!
But---
You shall be my bodyguard!
But--
And I Shall reward you...
But-
...with Tummy Rubs!
INTRODUCING
FLIP

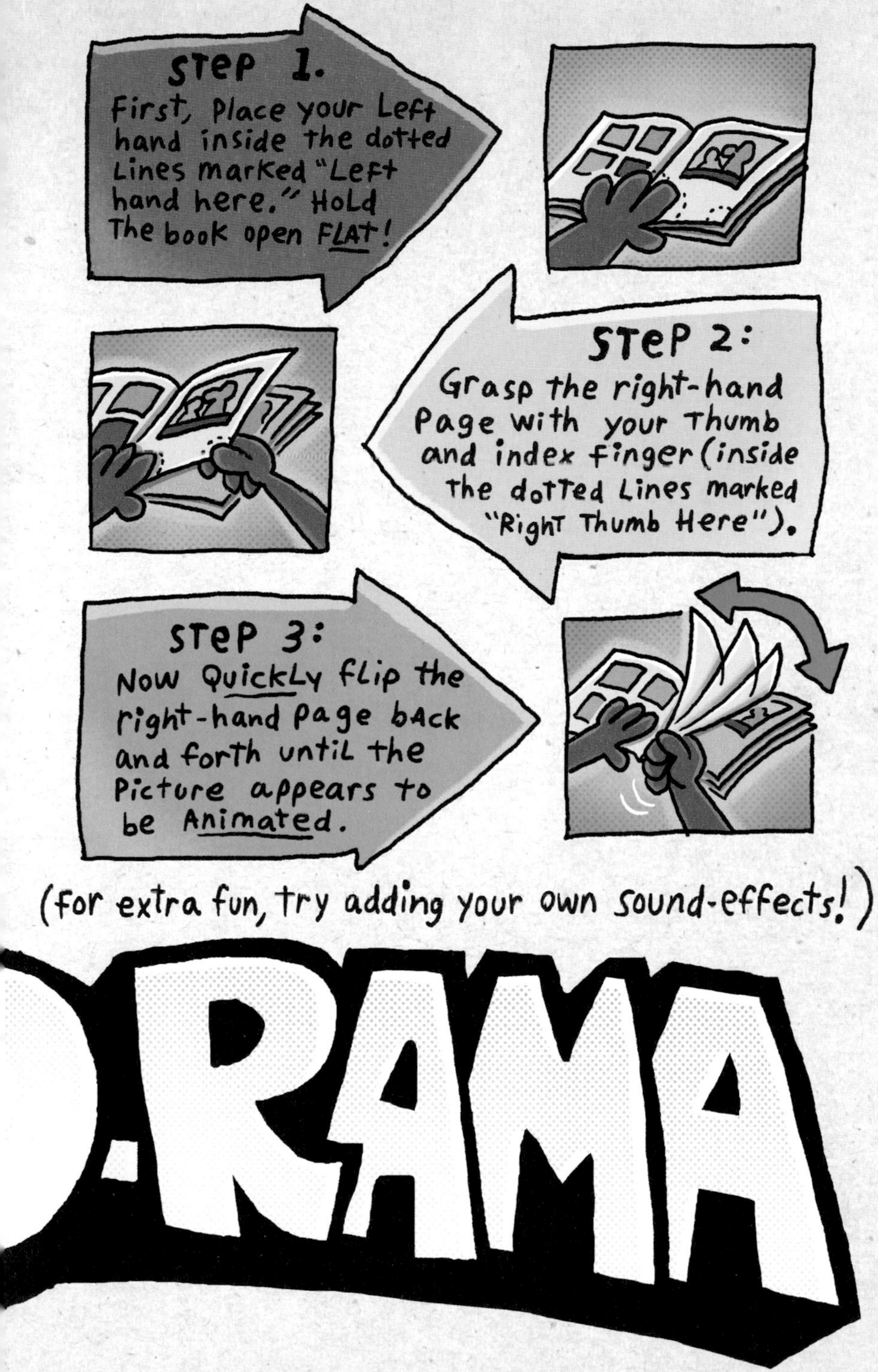
STEP 1.
First, place your left hand inside the dotted lines marked "Left hand here." Hold the book open FLAT!
STEP 2:
Grasp the right-hand page with your thumb and index finger (inside the dotted lines marked "Right Thumb Here").
STEP 3:
Now QUICKLY flip the right-hand page back and forth until the picture appears to be Animated.
(For extra fun, try adding your own sound-effects!)
-O-RAMA

Remember,

while you are Flipping,
be sure you can see
The image on page 43
AND the image on page 45.

If you Flip Quickly,
the two pictures will
start to Look Like
one **Animated** cartoon!

Don't forget to
add your own
sound-effects!

Left
hand here.

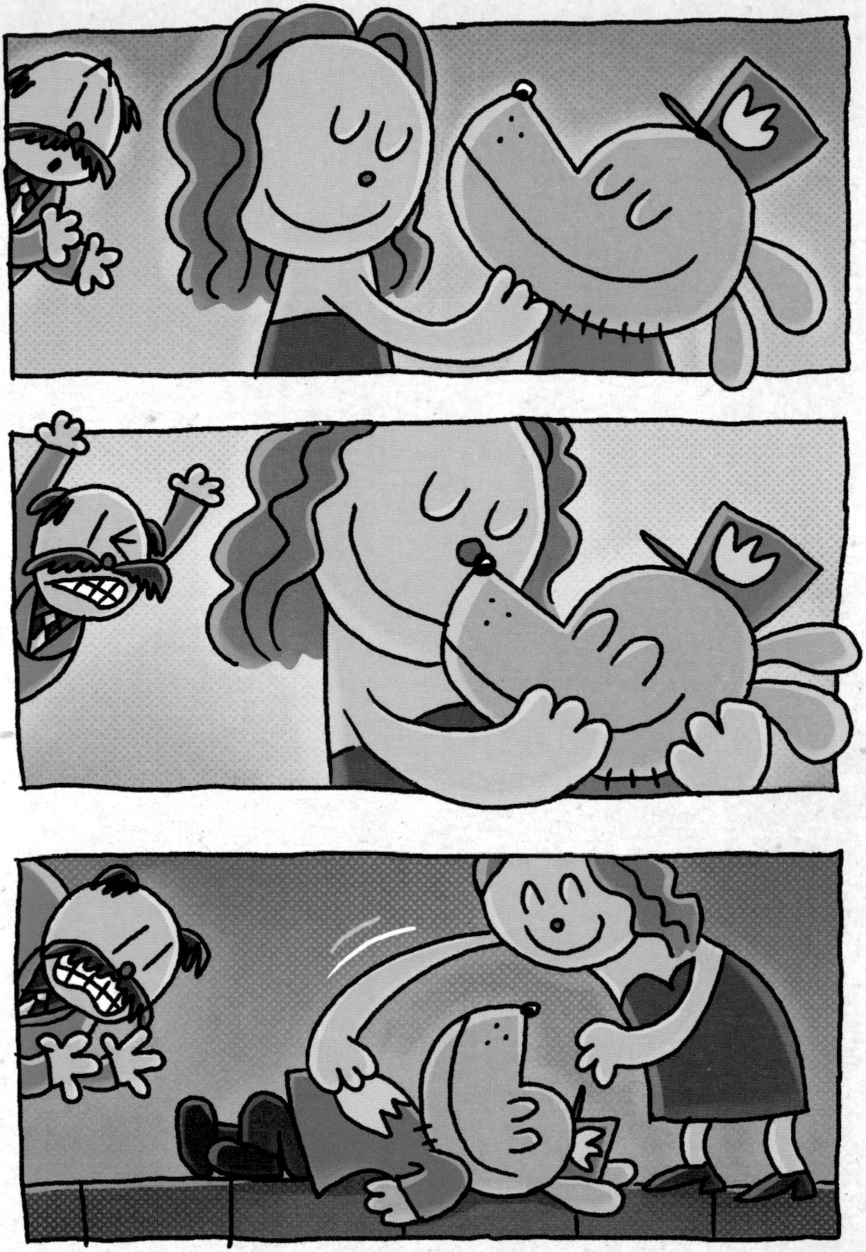

Right Thumb here.

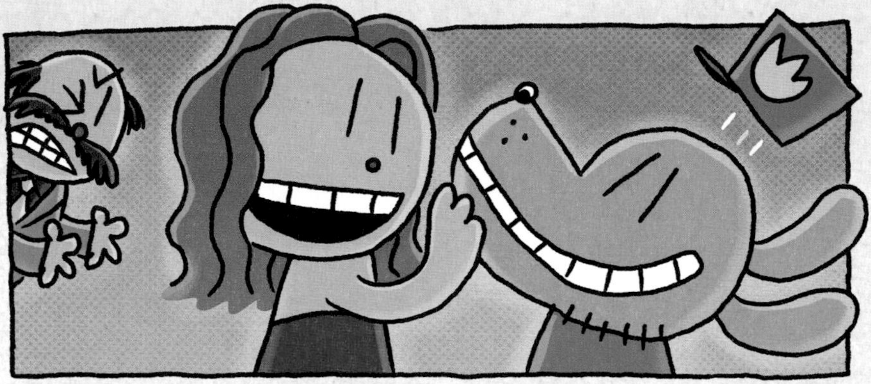

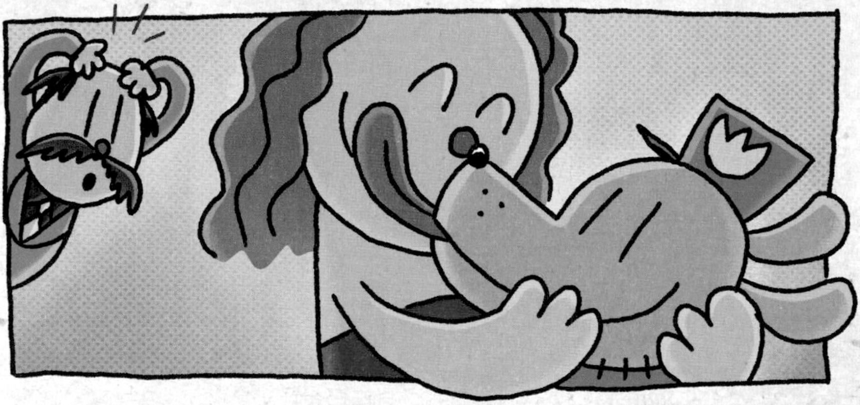

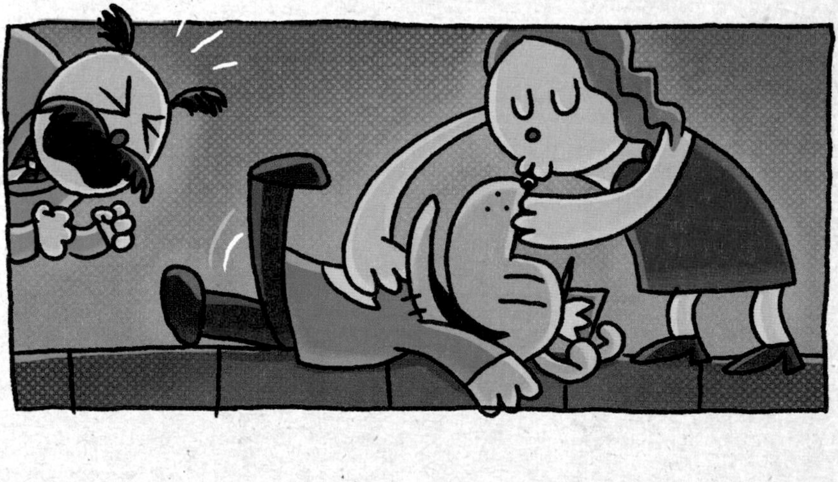

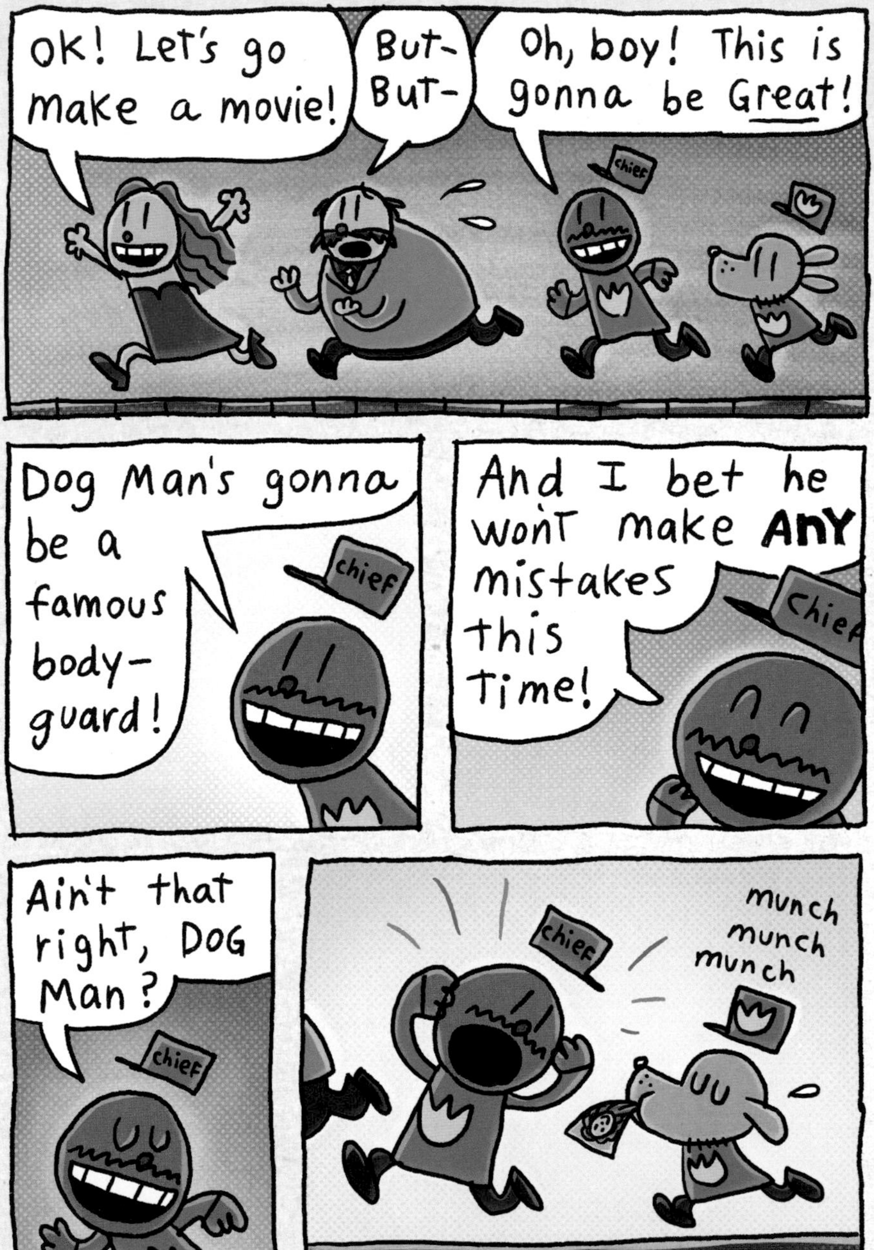
OK! Let's go make a movie!
But- But-
Oh, boy! This is gonna be Great!
chief
Dog Man's gonna be a famous body-guard!
chief
And I bet he won't make ANY mistakes this time!
Chief
Ain't that right, DOG Man?
chief
chief
munch munch munch

Chapter 3

THE TALK

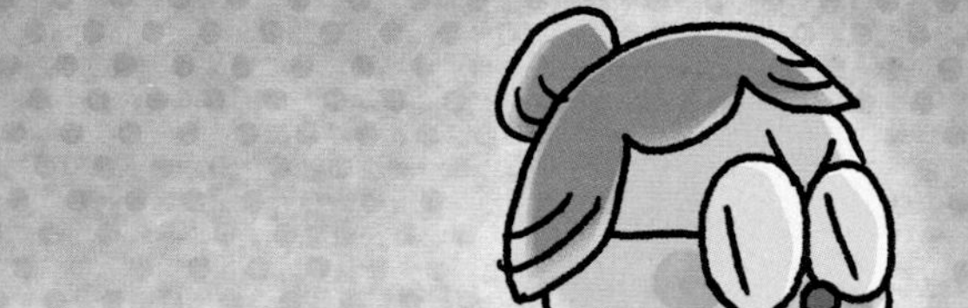

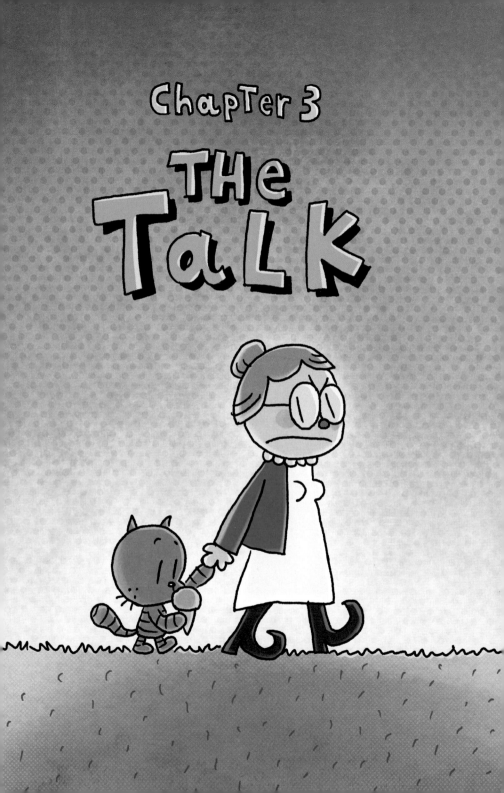

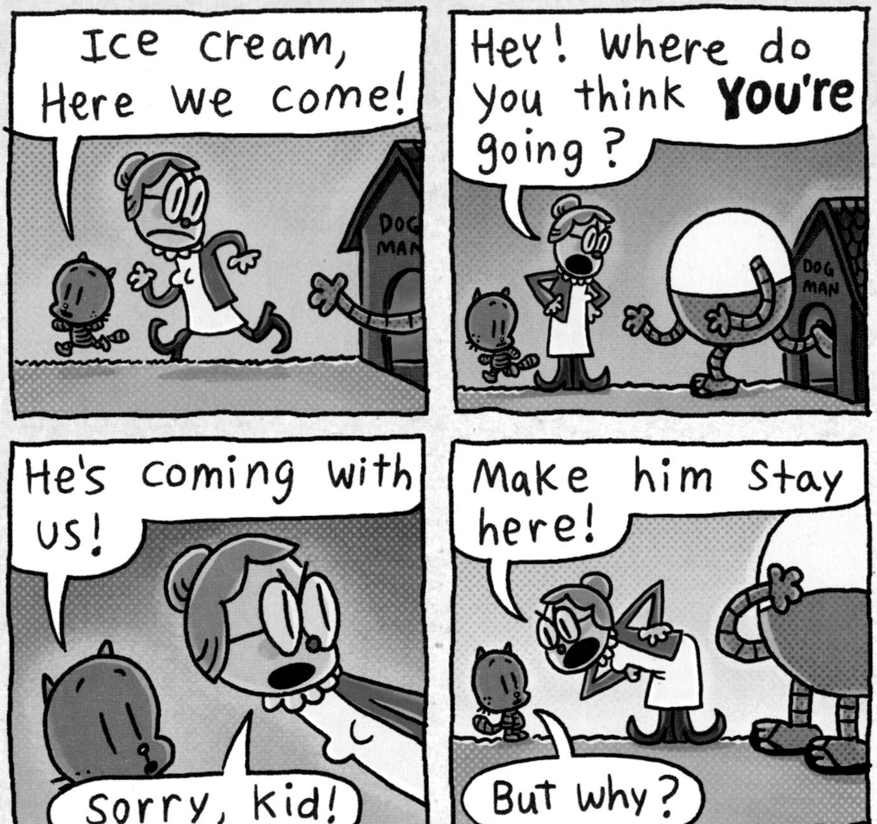
Ice cream, Here we come!
DOG MAN
Hey! Where do you think YOU'RE going?
DOG MAN
He's coming with us!
Sorry, kid!
Make him stay here!
But why?
Just make him stay here--- or NO ICE CREAM!
Wait here for me, 80-HD!

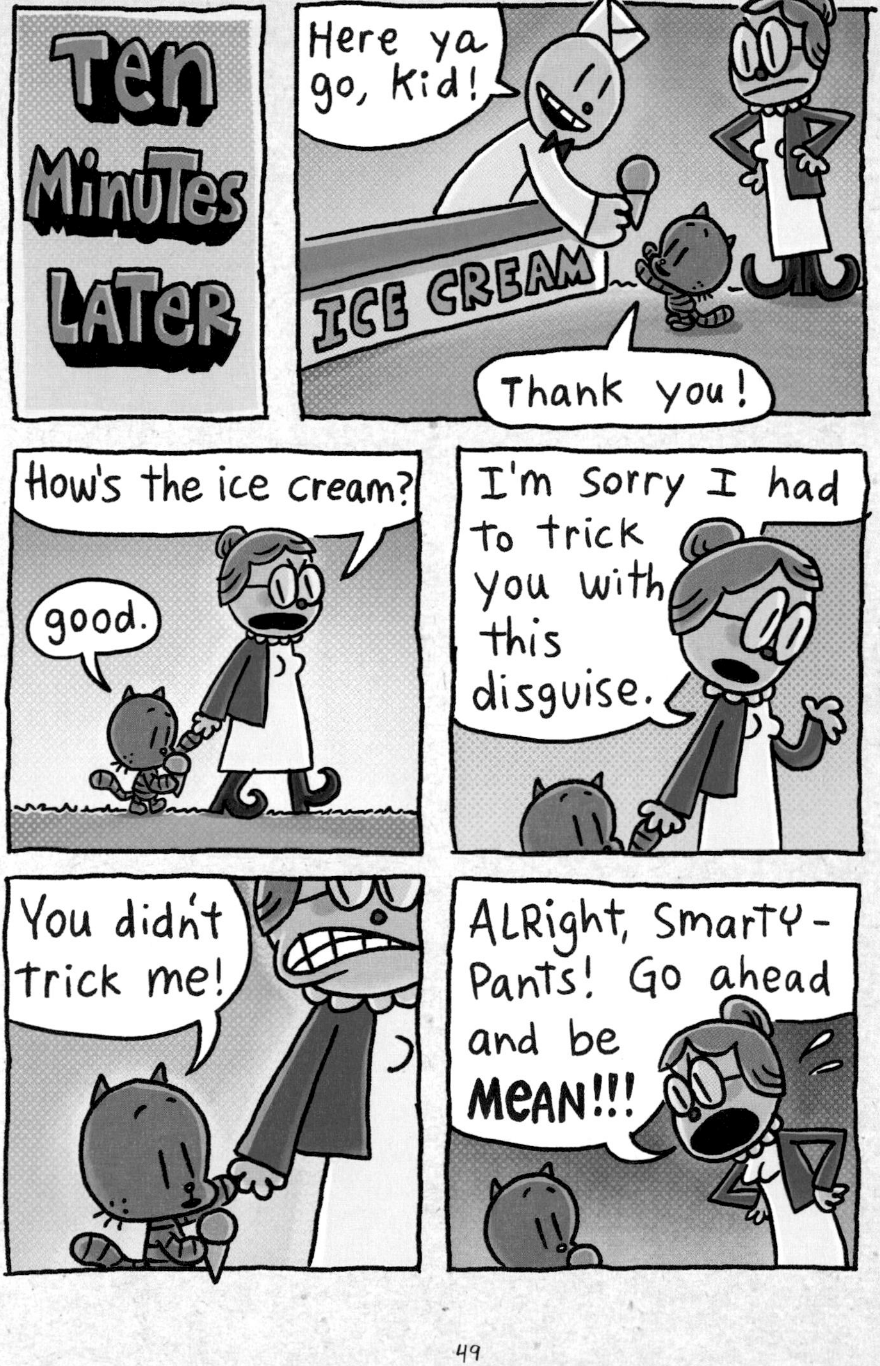
Ten Minutes Later
Here ya go, kid!
ICE CREAM
Thank you!
How's the ice cream?
good.
I'm sorry I had to trick you with this disguise.
You didn't trick me!
ALRight, SmarTY-Pants! Go ahead and be MEAN!!!

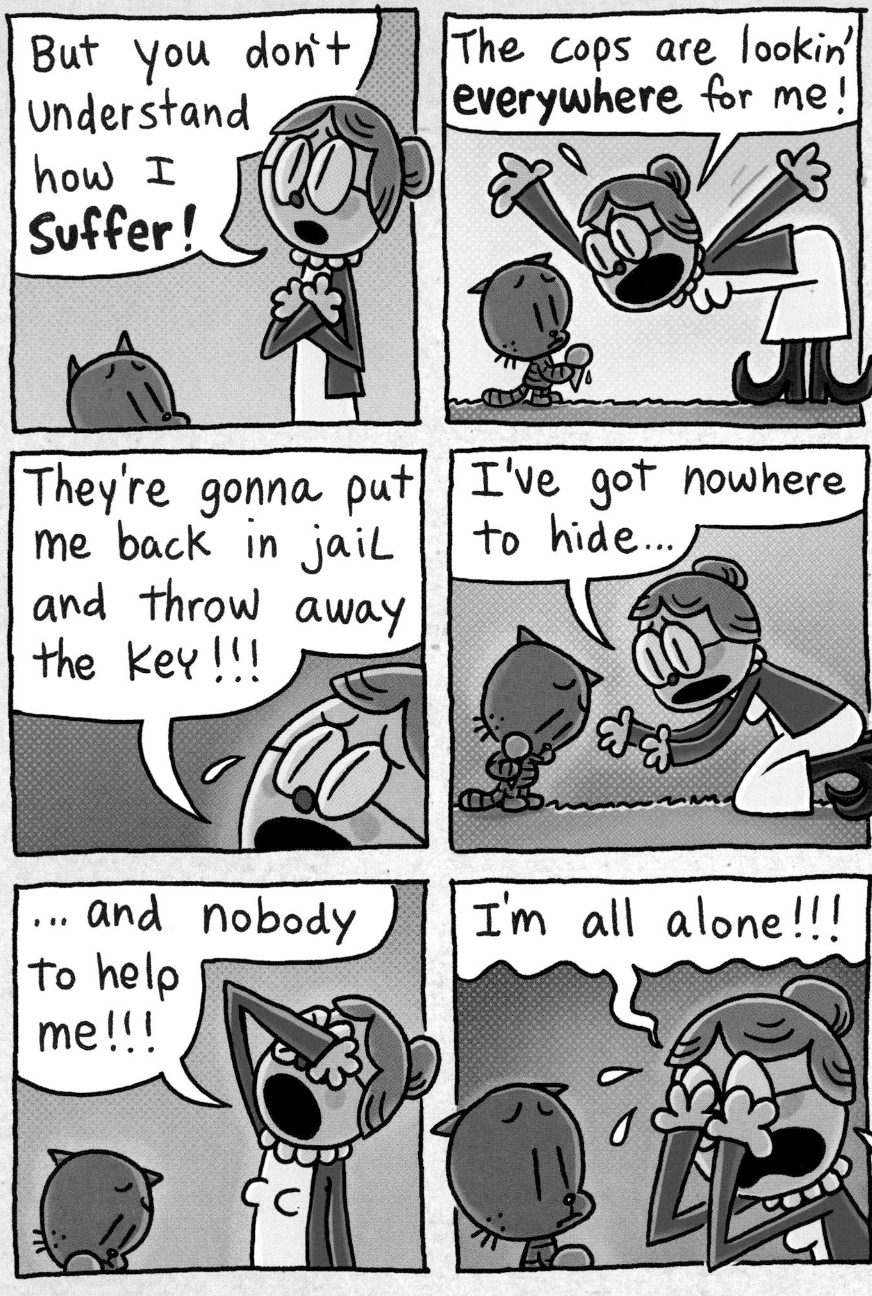
But you don't understand how I Suffer!
The cops are lookin' everywhere for me!
They're gonna put me back in jail and throw away the key!!!
I've got nowhere to hide...
... and nobody to help me!!!
I'm all alone!!!

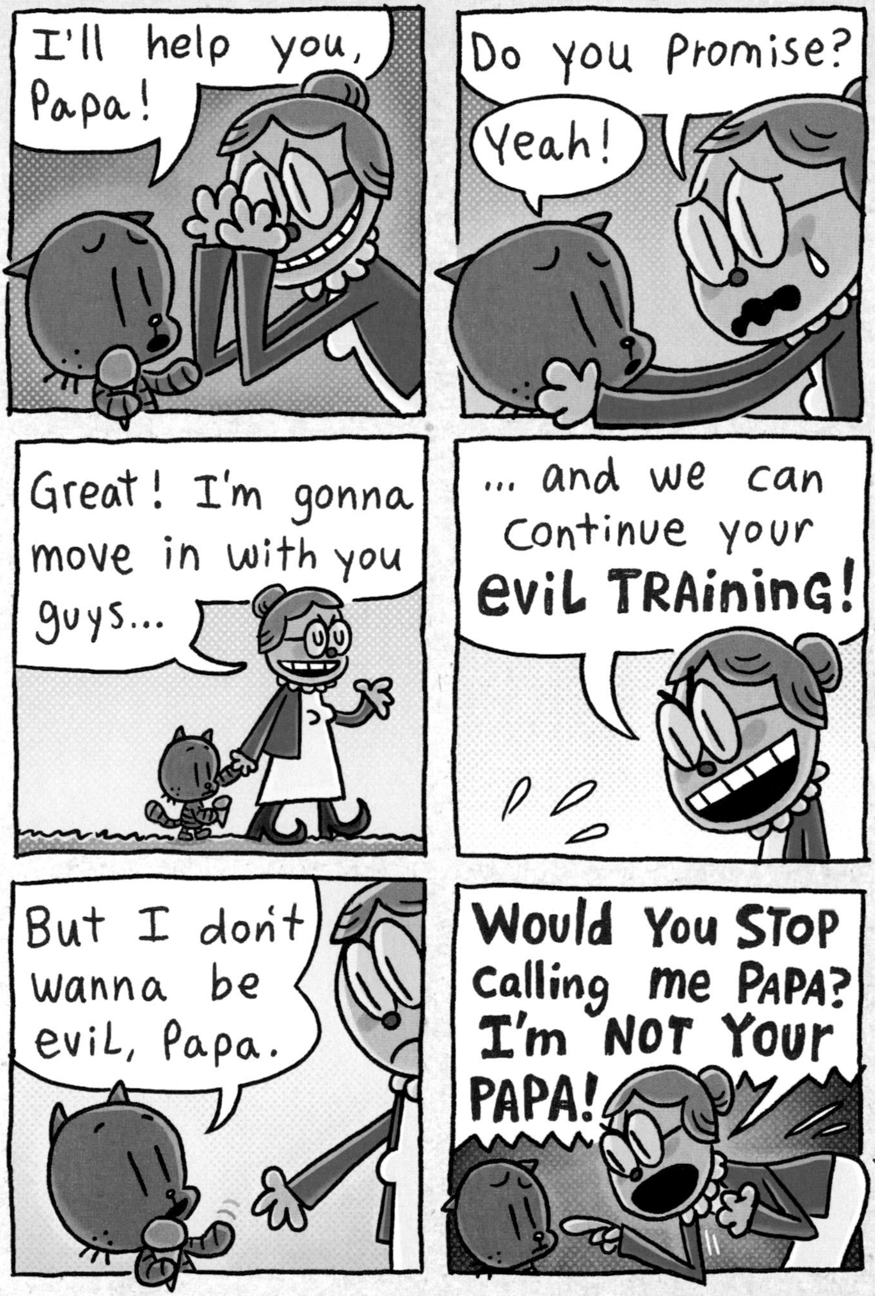
I'll help you, Papa!
Do you Promise?
Yeah!
Great! I'm gonna move in with you guys...
... and we can continue your EVIL TRAINING!
But I don't wanna be evil, Papa.
Would You STOP Calling me PAPA? I'm NOT YOUR PAPA!

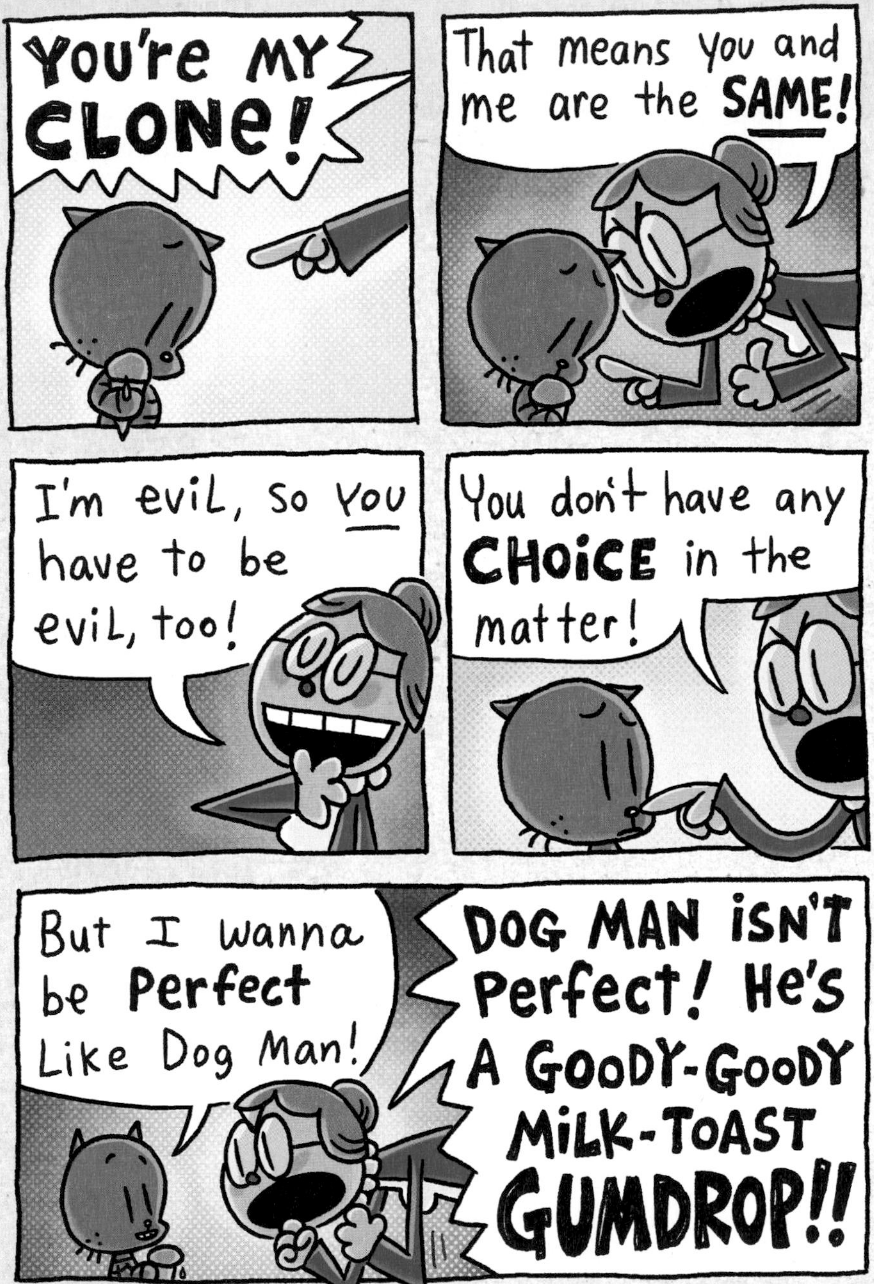
YOU'RE MY CLONE!
That means you and me are the SAME!
I'm evil, so you have to be evil, too!
You don't have any CHOICE in the matter!
But I wanna be Perfect like Dog Man!
DOG MAN ISN'T Perfect! He's A GOODY-GOODY MILK-TOAST GUMDROP!!

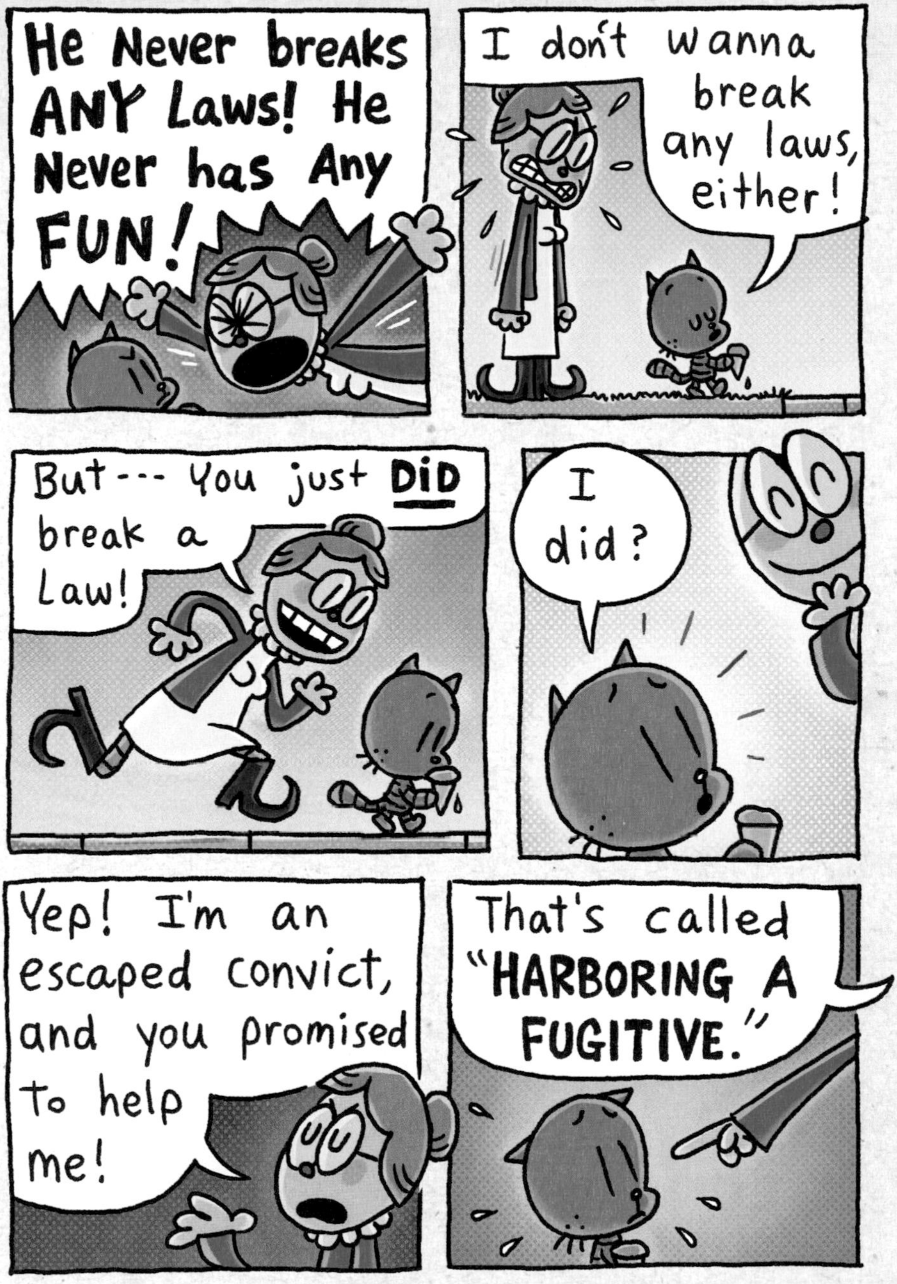
He Never breaks ANY Laws! He Never has Any FUN!
I don't wanna break any laws, either!
But--- You just DID break a Law!
I did?
Yep! I'm an escaped convict, and you promised to help me!
That's called "HARBORING A FUGITIVE."

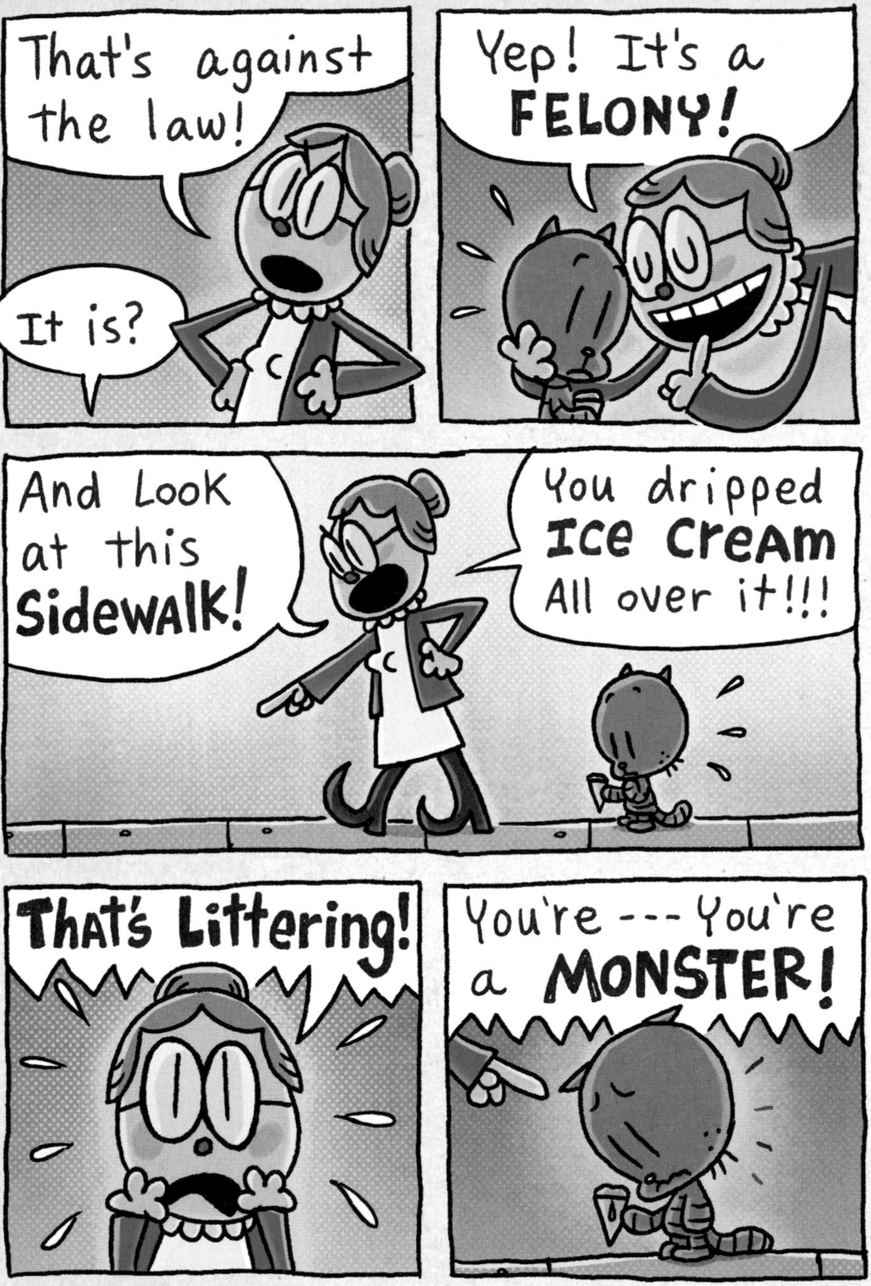
That's against the law!
It is?
Yep! It's a FELONY!
And Look at this SidewAlK!
You dripped Ice CreAm All over it!!!
That's Littering!
You're --- You're a MONSTER!

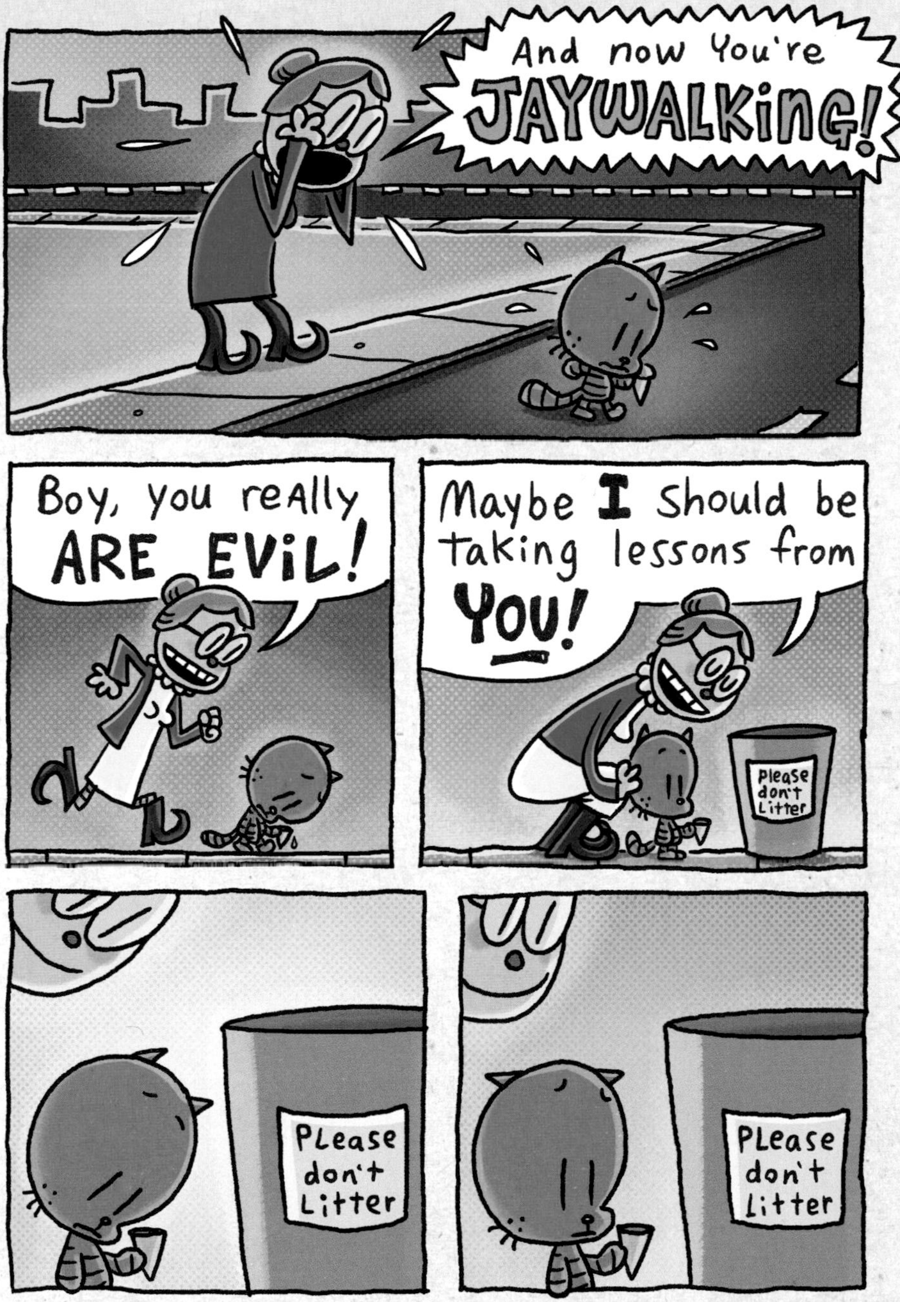
And now You're JAYWALKinG!
Boy, you reAlly ARE EViL!
Maybe I should be taking lessons from YOU!
Please don't Litter
PLease don't Litter
PLease don't Litter

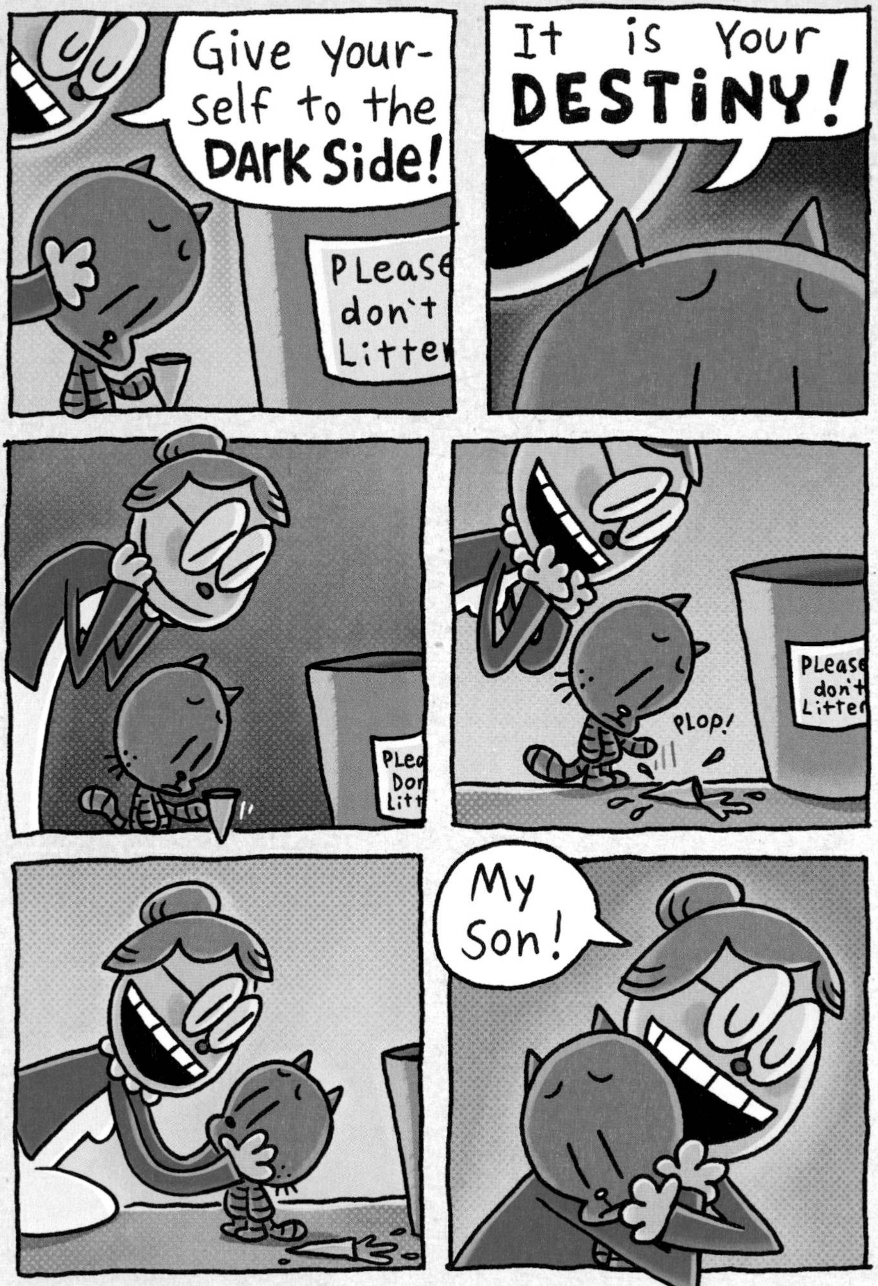
Give your-self to the DARK Side!
Please don't Litter
It is Your DESTINY!
PLea Don Litt
PLOP!
Please don't Litter
My Son!

Chapter 4

An Aching Kind of Growing

By George and Harold

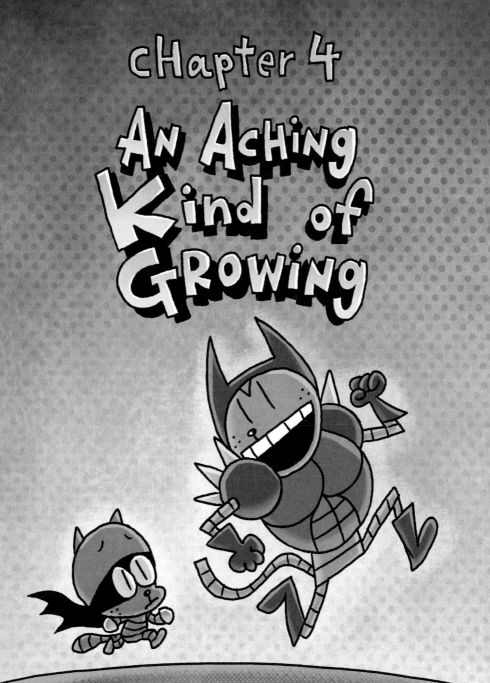

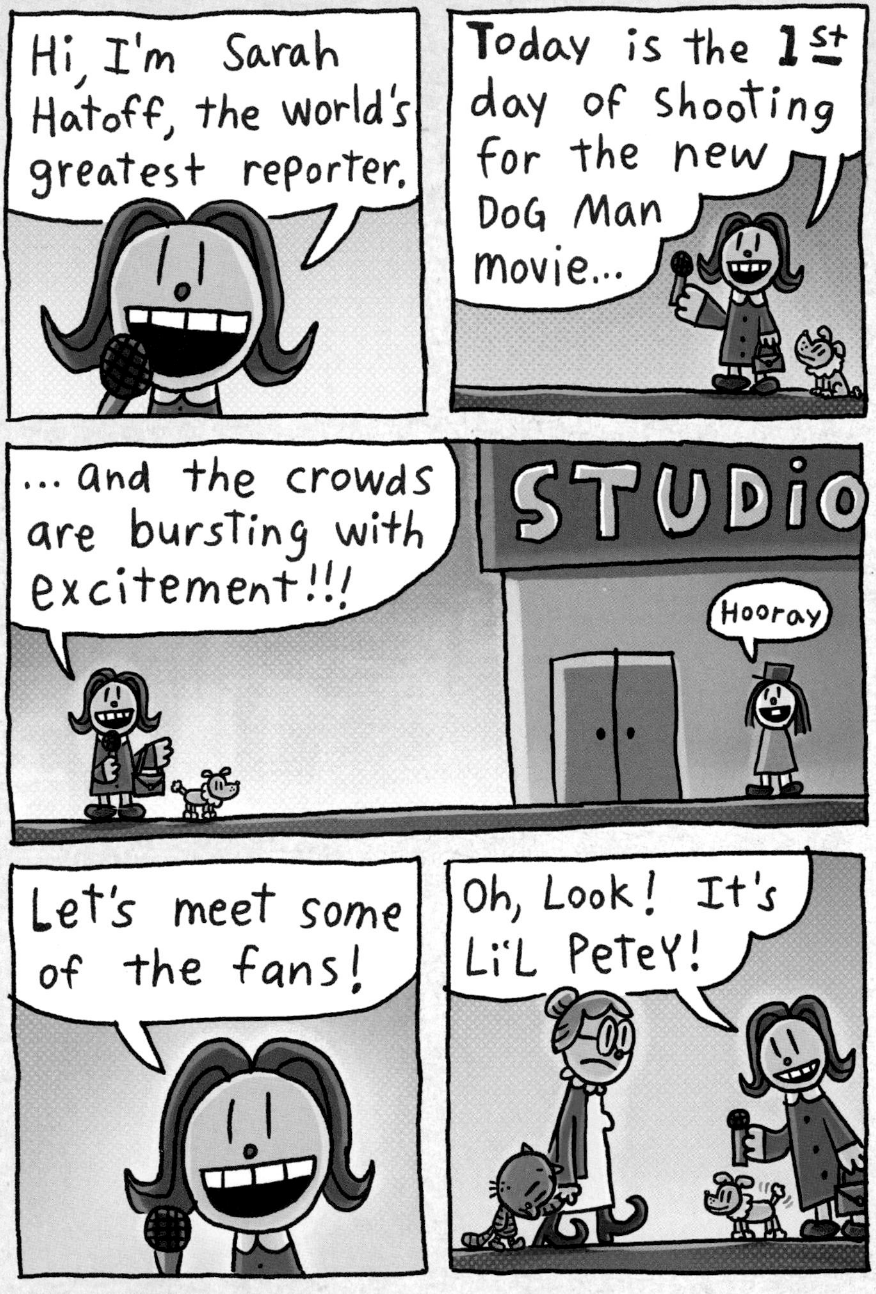
Hi, I'm Sarah Hatoff, the world's greatest reporter.
Today is the 1st day of shooting for the new DOG Man movie...
STUDIO
... and the crowds are bursting with excitement!!!
Hooray
Let's meet some of the fans!
Oh, Look! It's Li'L Petey!

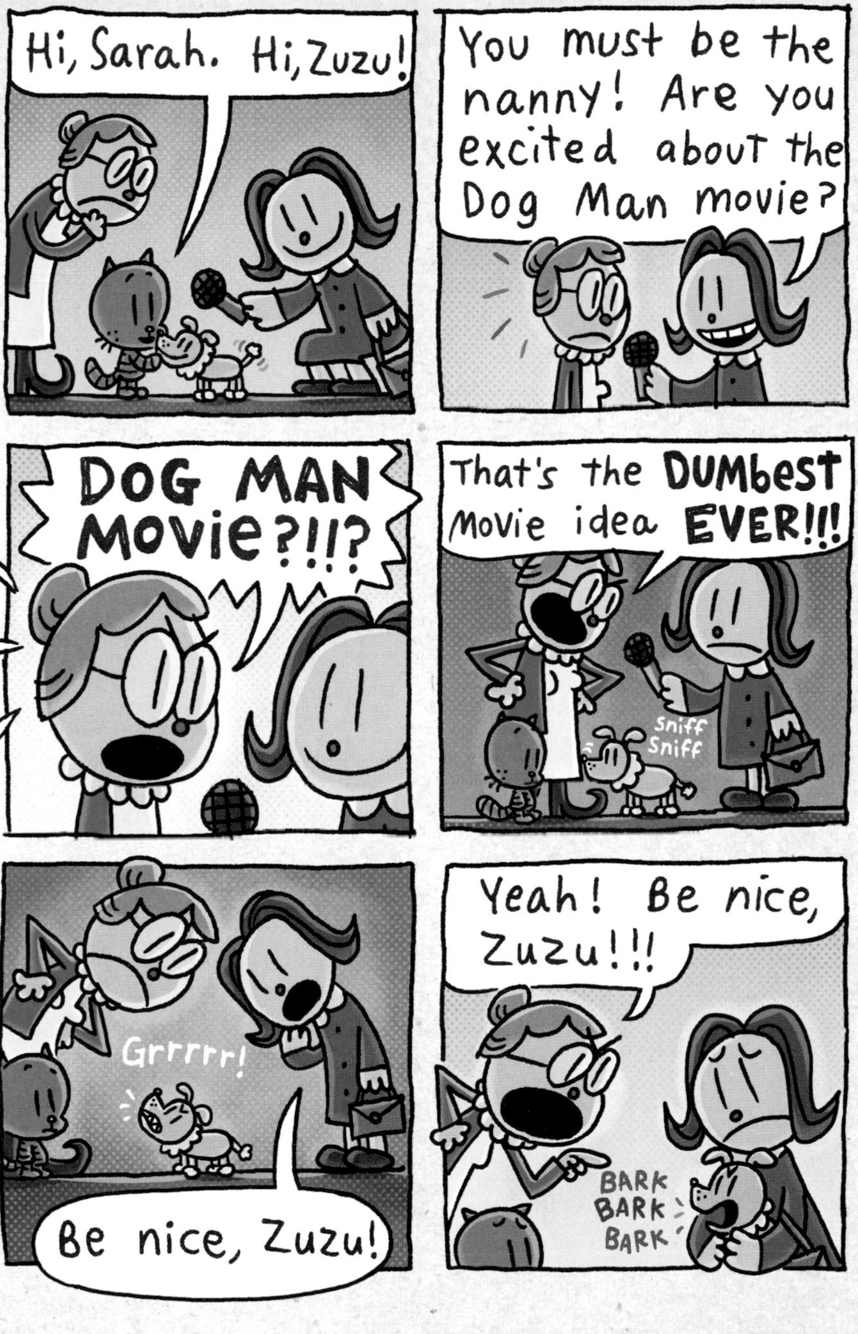
Hi, Sarah. Hi, Zuzu!
You must be the nanny! Are you excited about the Dog Man movie?
DOG MAN MOVIE?!!?
That's the DUMbest Movie idea EVER!!!
Sniff Sniff
Grrrrr!
Be nice, Zuzu!
Yeah! Be nice, Zuzu!!!
BARK BARK BARK

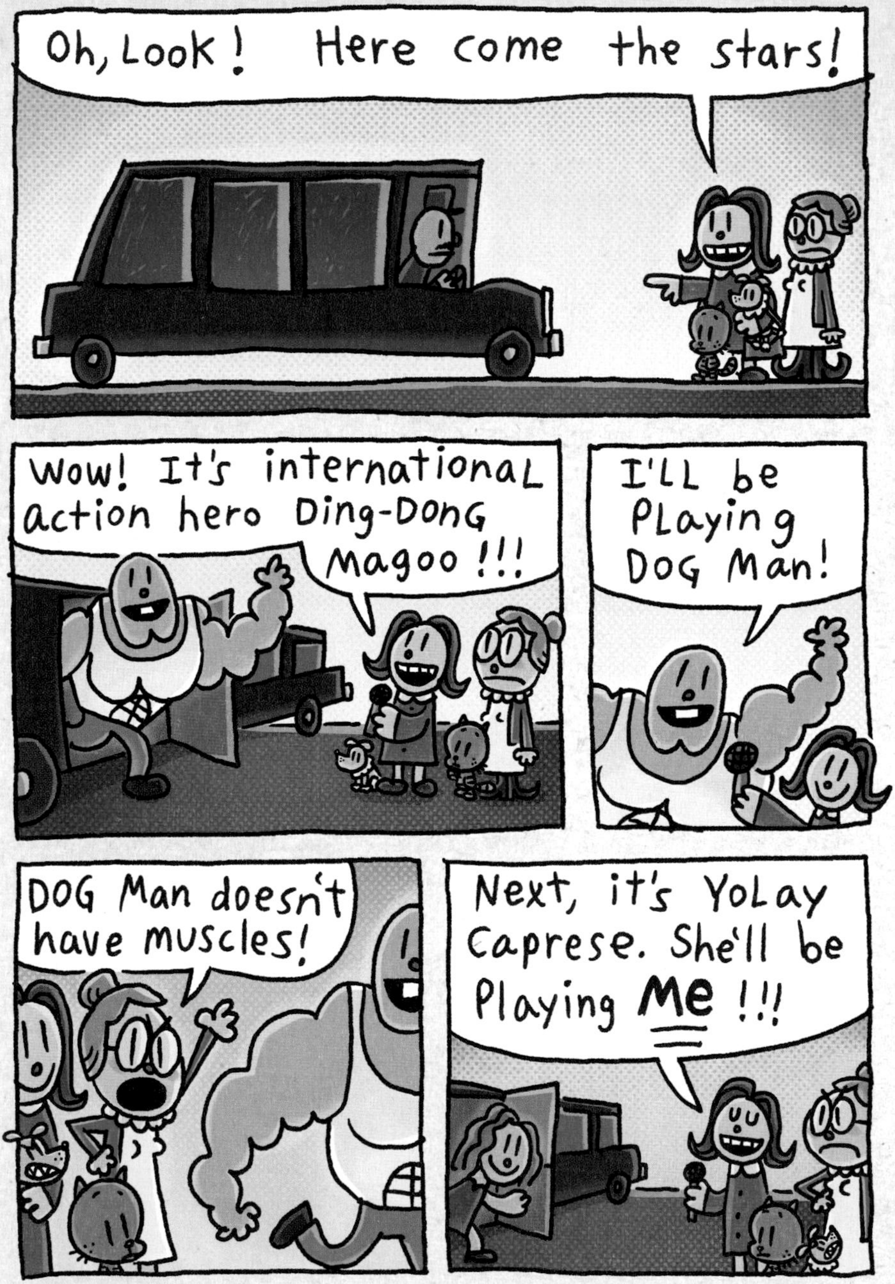
Oh, Look! Here come the stars!
Wow! It's international action hero Ding-Dong Magoo!!!
I'LL be Playing DOG Man!
DOG Man doesn't have muscles!
Next, it's YoLay Caprese. She'll be Playing ME!!!

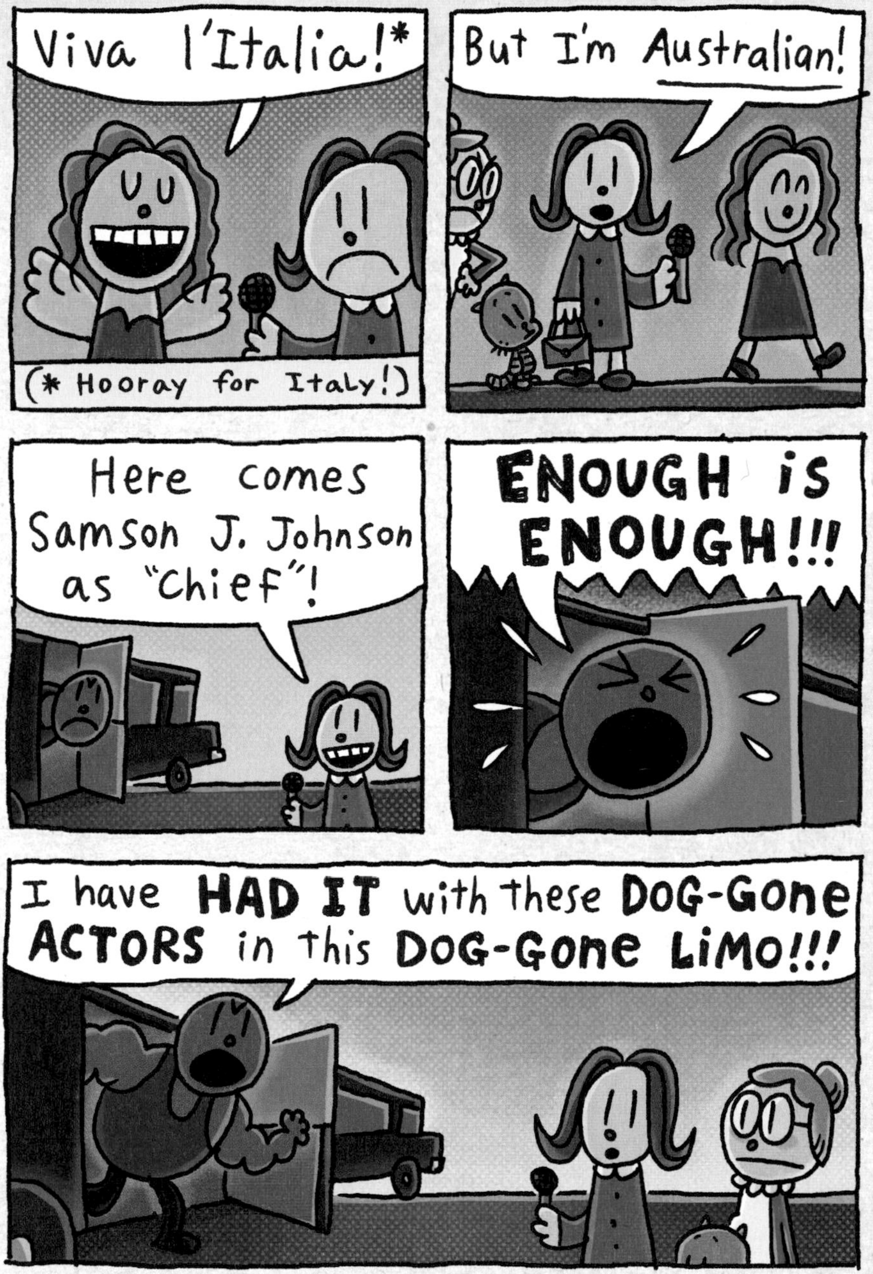

Viva l'Italia!*
(* Hooray for Italy!)
But I'm Australian!
Here comes Samson J. Johnson as "Chief"!
ENOUGH IS ENOUGH!!!
I have HAD IT with these DOG-GONE ACTORS in this DOG-GONE LIMO!!!

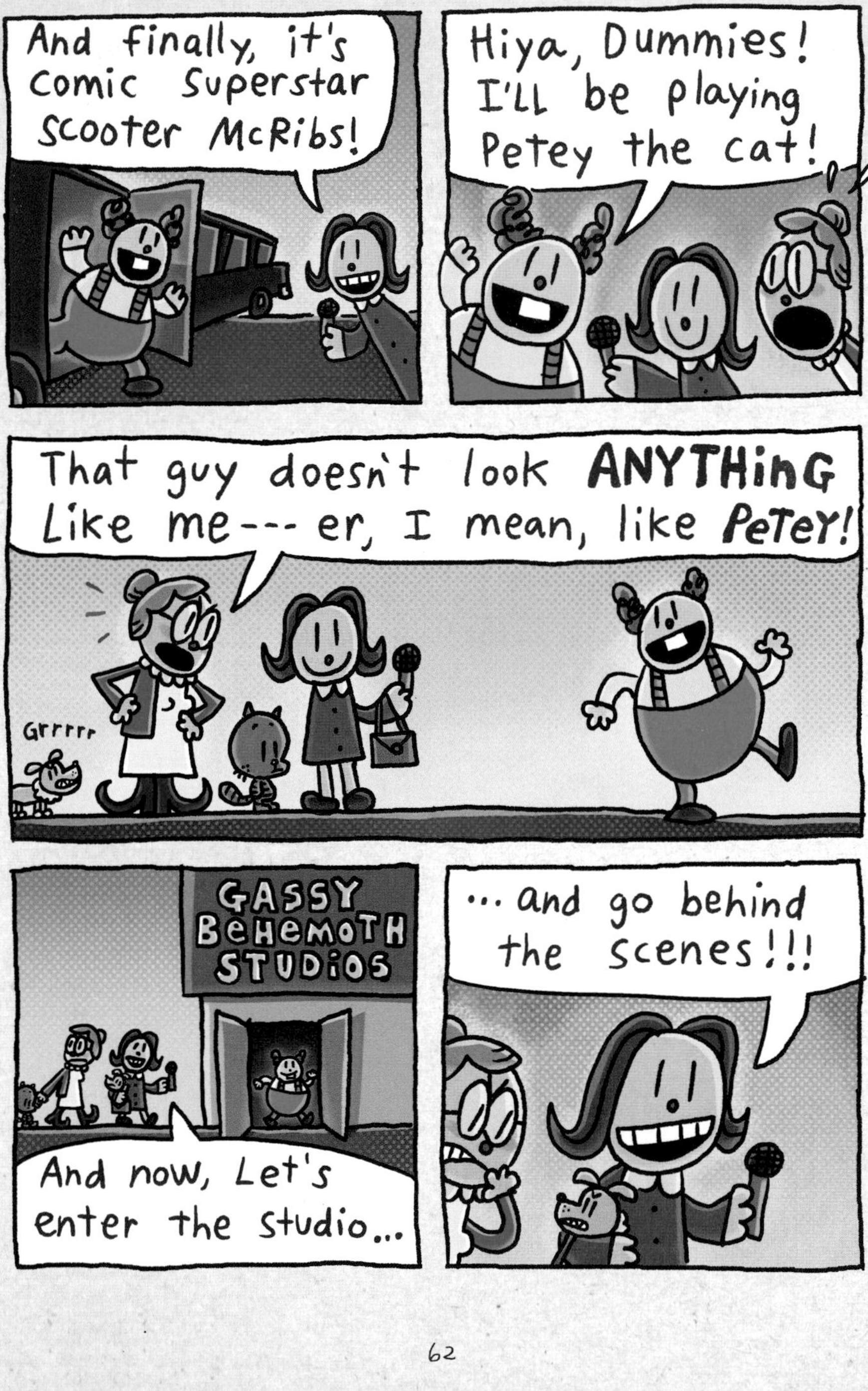
And finally, it's Comic Superstar Scooter McRibs!
Hiya, Dummies! I'LL be playing Petey the cat!
That guy doesn't look ANYTHING Like me--- er, I mean, like PETEY!
Grrrrr
GASSY BEHEMOTH STUDIOS
And now, Let's enter the studio...
...and go behind the scenes!!!

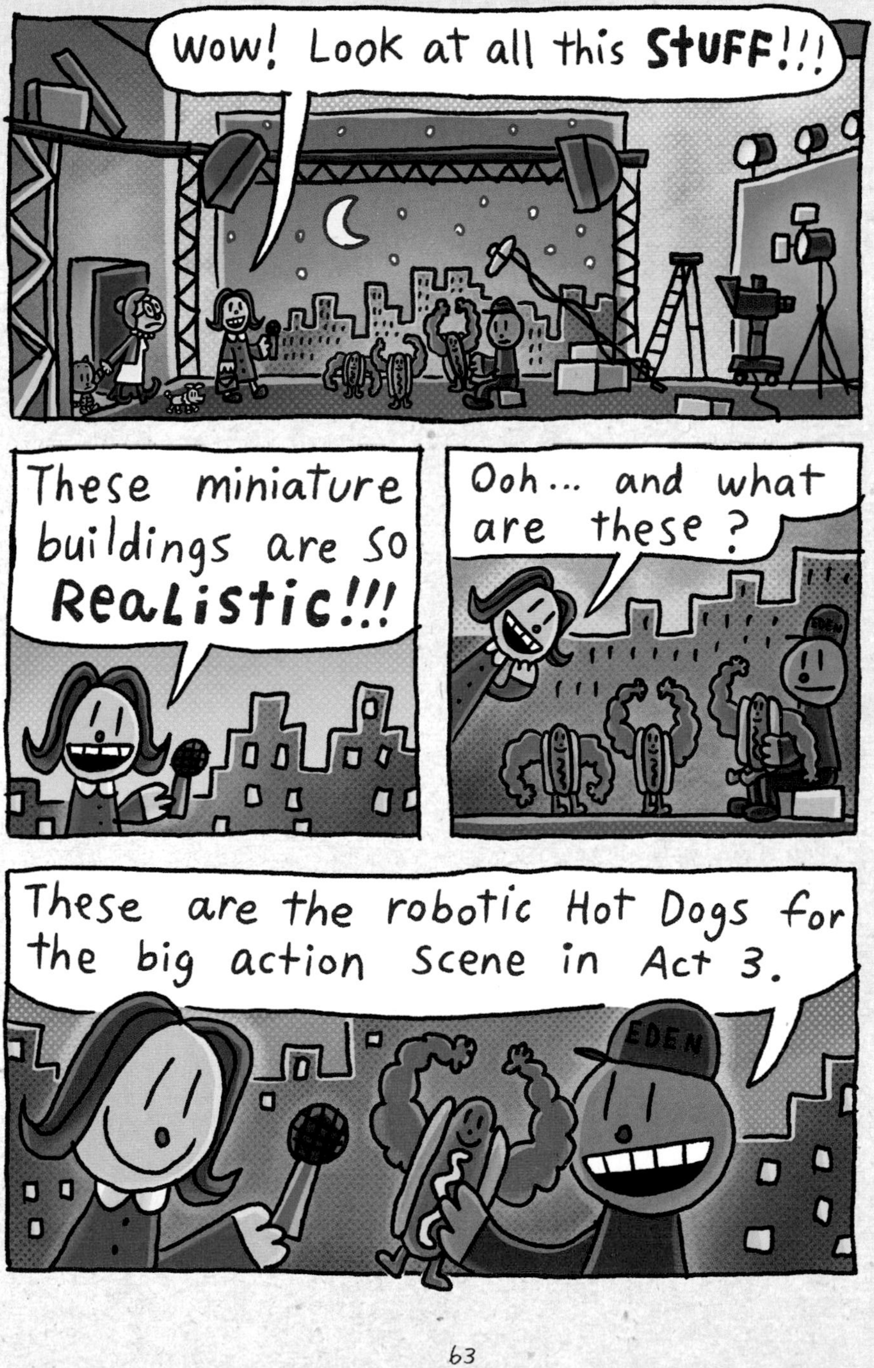
WOW! Look at all this STUFF!!!
These miniature buildings are so REALISTIC!!!
Ooh... and what are these?
These are the robotic Hot Dogs for the big action scene in Act 3.
EDEN
EDEN

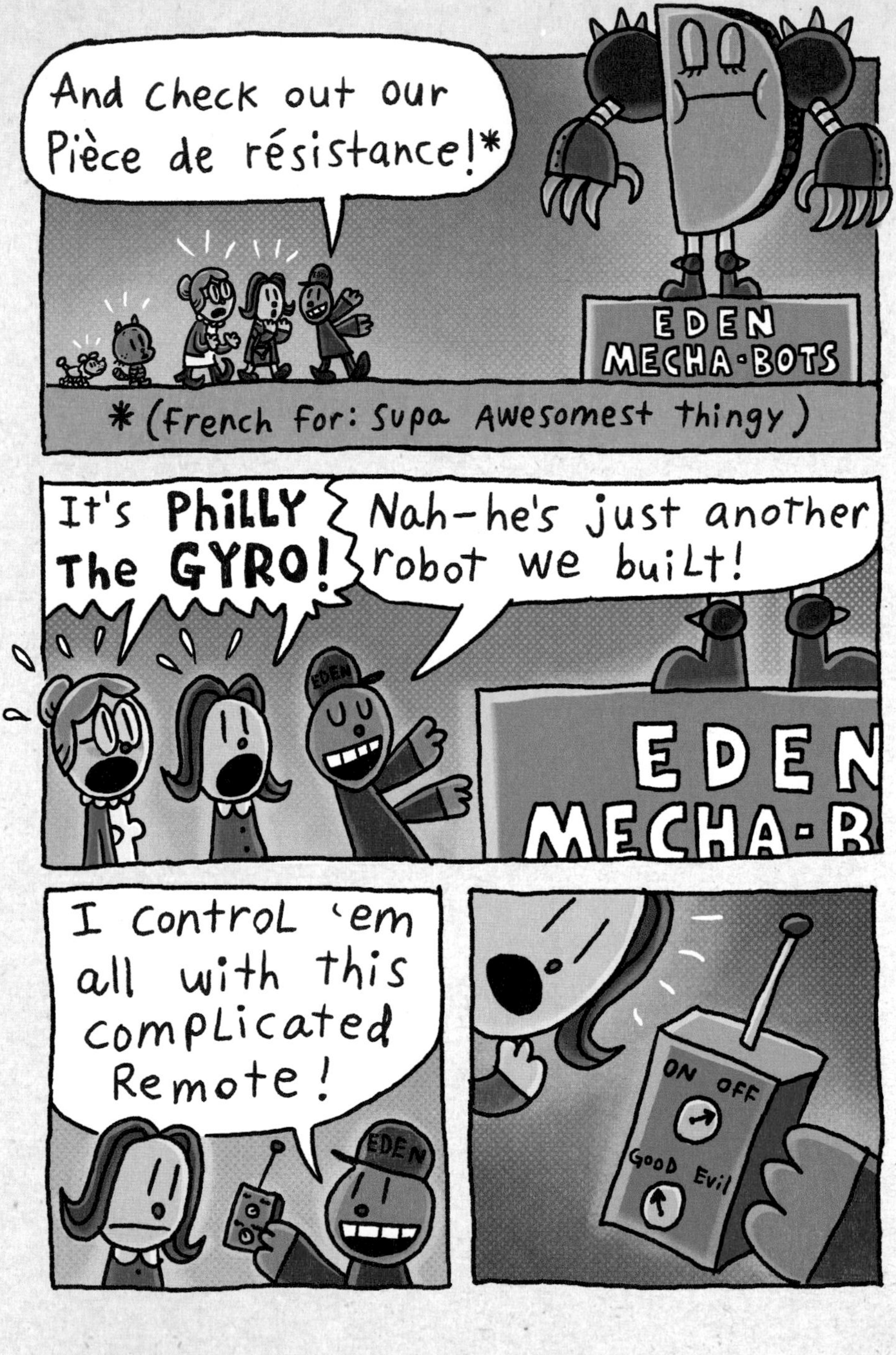

And check out our Pièce de résistance!*
EDEN MECHA-BOTS
*(French for: Supa Awesomest thingy)
It's PHILLY The GYRO!
Nah-he's just another robot we built!
EDEN
EDEN MECHA-B
I control 'em all with this complicated Remote!
EDEN
ON OFF
GOOD Evil

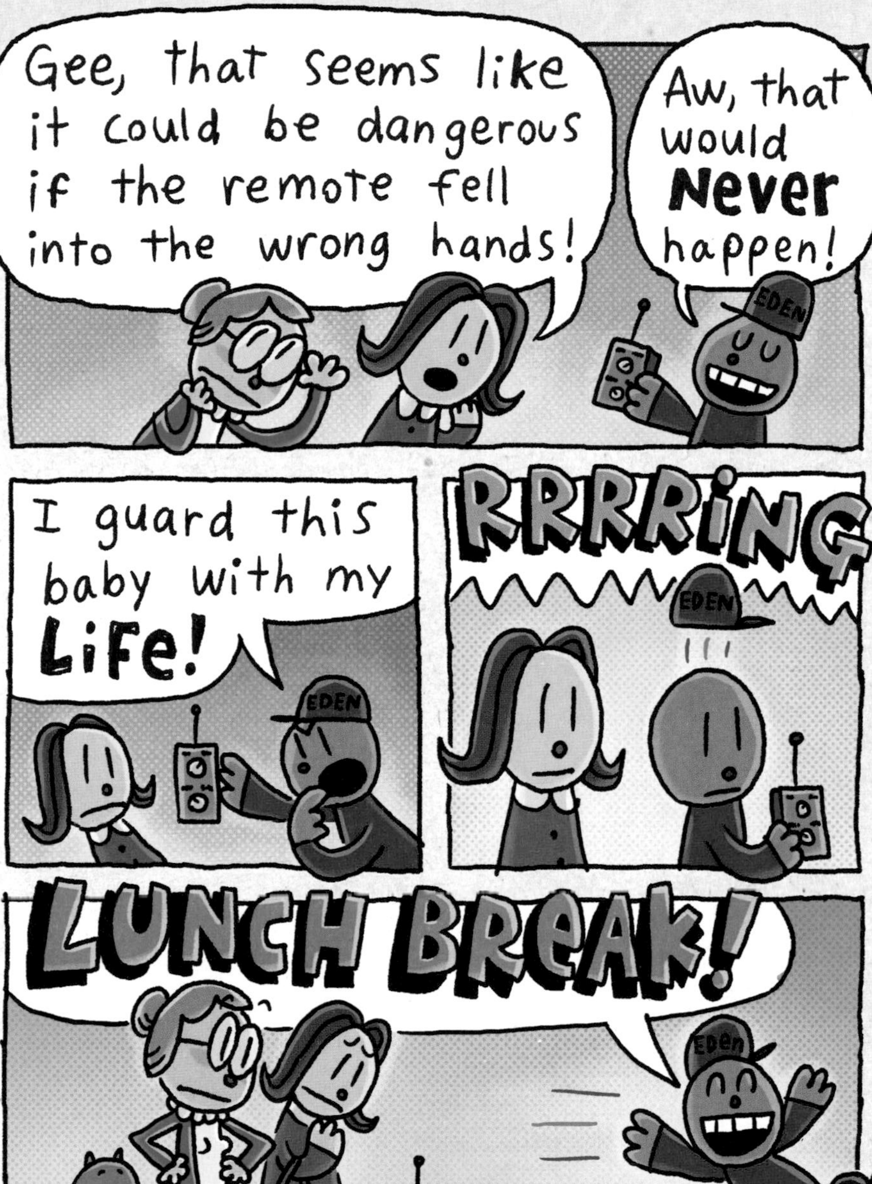
Gee, that seems like it could be dangerous if the remote fell into the wrong hands!
Aw, that would **Never** happen!
I guard this baby with my **LiFe!**
RRRRiNG
EDEN
LUNCH BReAK!

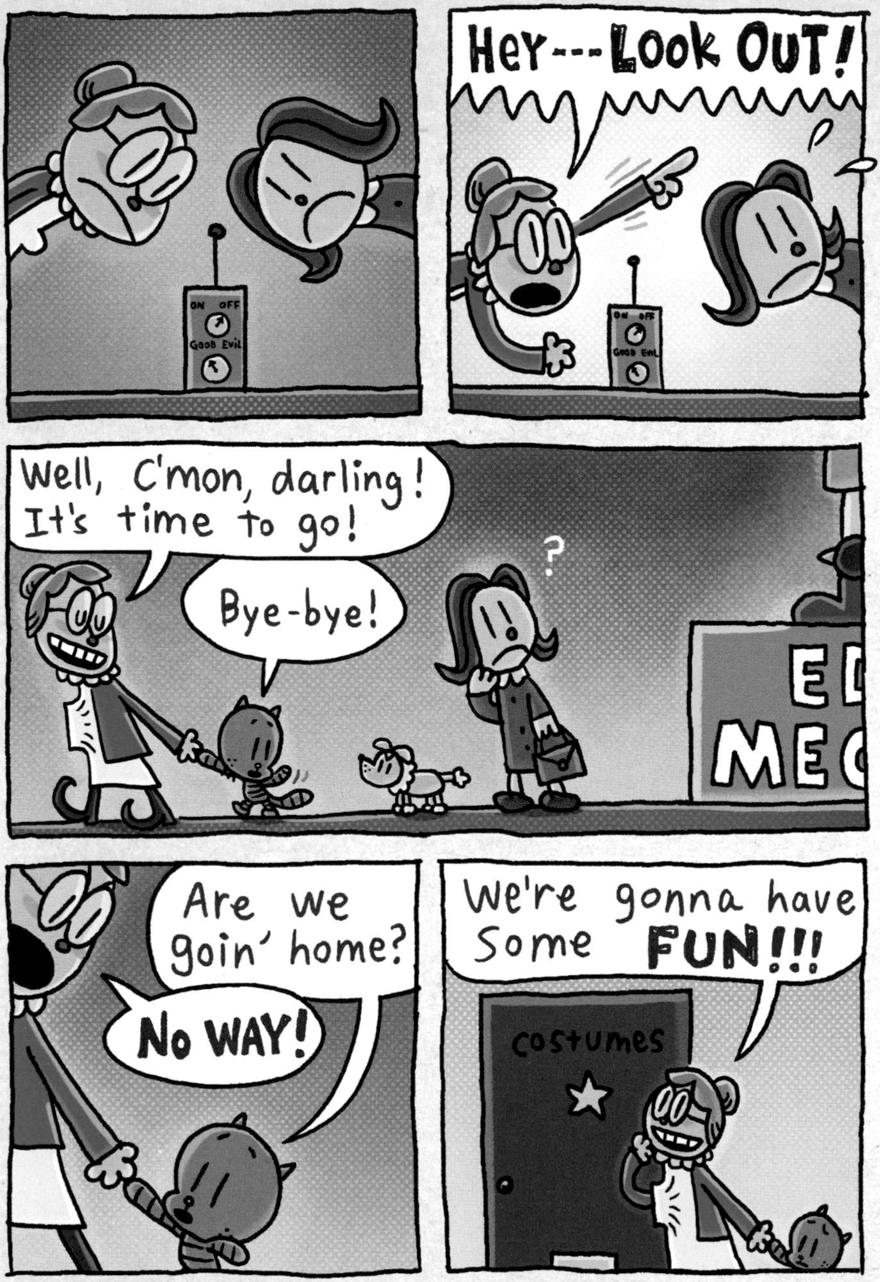
ON OFF
GOOD EVIL
HEY---LOOK OUT!
ON OFF
GOOD EVIL
Well, C'mon, darling! It's time to go!
Bye-bye!
?
Are we goin' home?
NO WAY!
We're gonna have Some FUN!!!
costumes

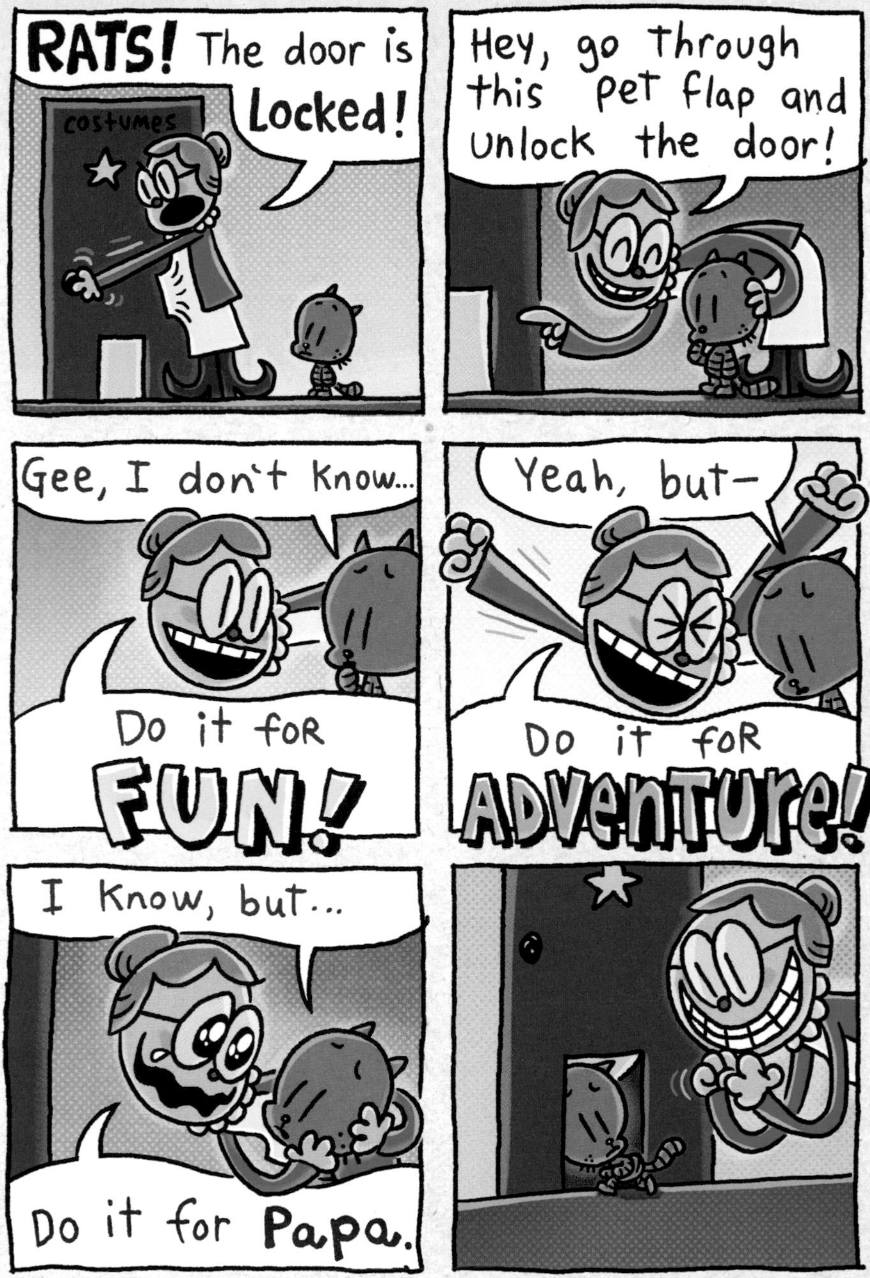
RATS! The door is Locked!
COSTUMES
Hey, go through this pet flap and unlock the door!
Gee, I don't know...
Do it for FUN!
Yeah, but—
Do it for ADVENTURE!
I know, but...
Do it for Papa.

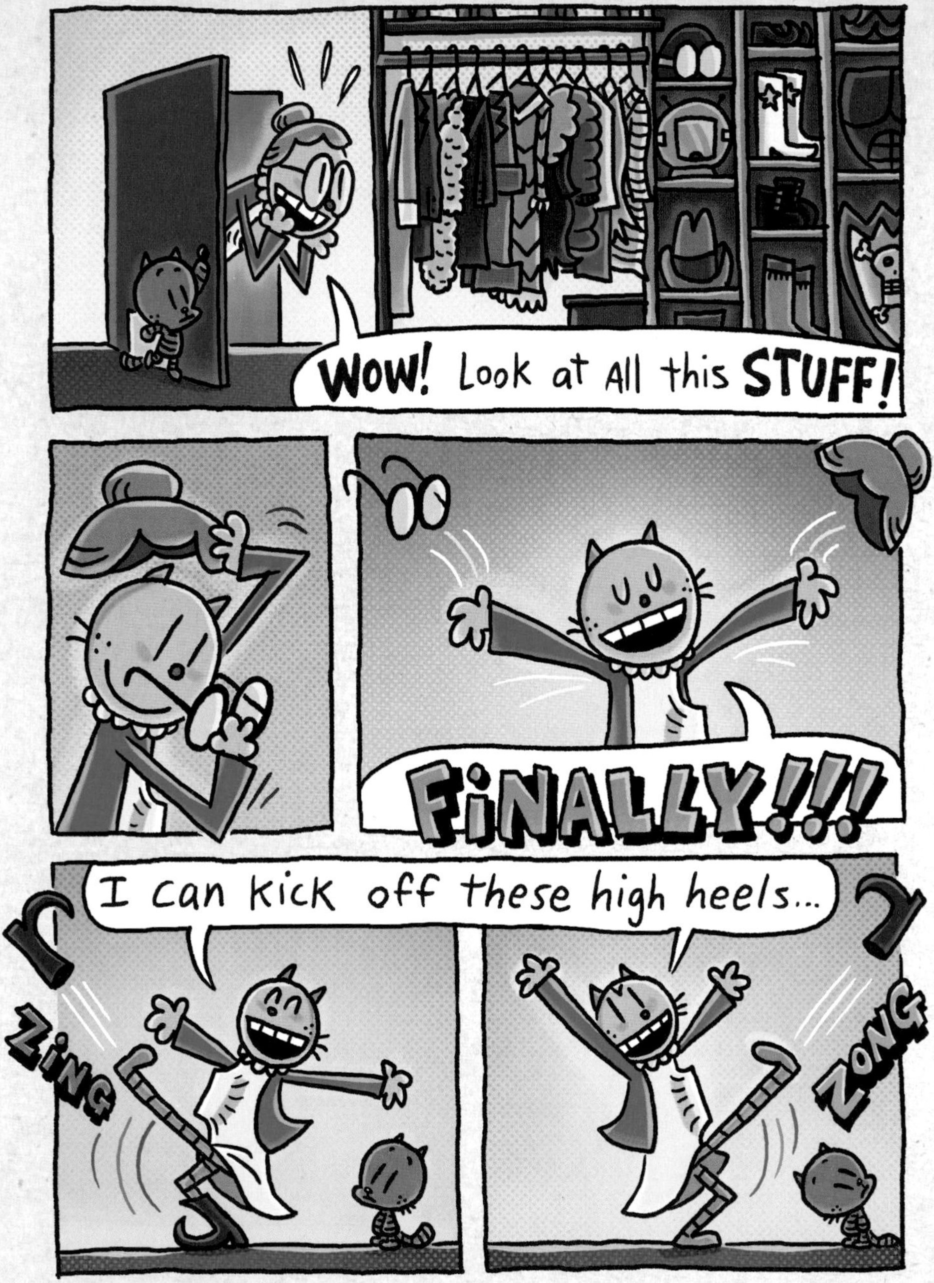
WOW! Look at All this STUFF!
FINALLY!!!
I can kick off these high heels...
ZING
ZONG

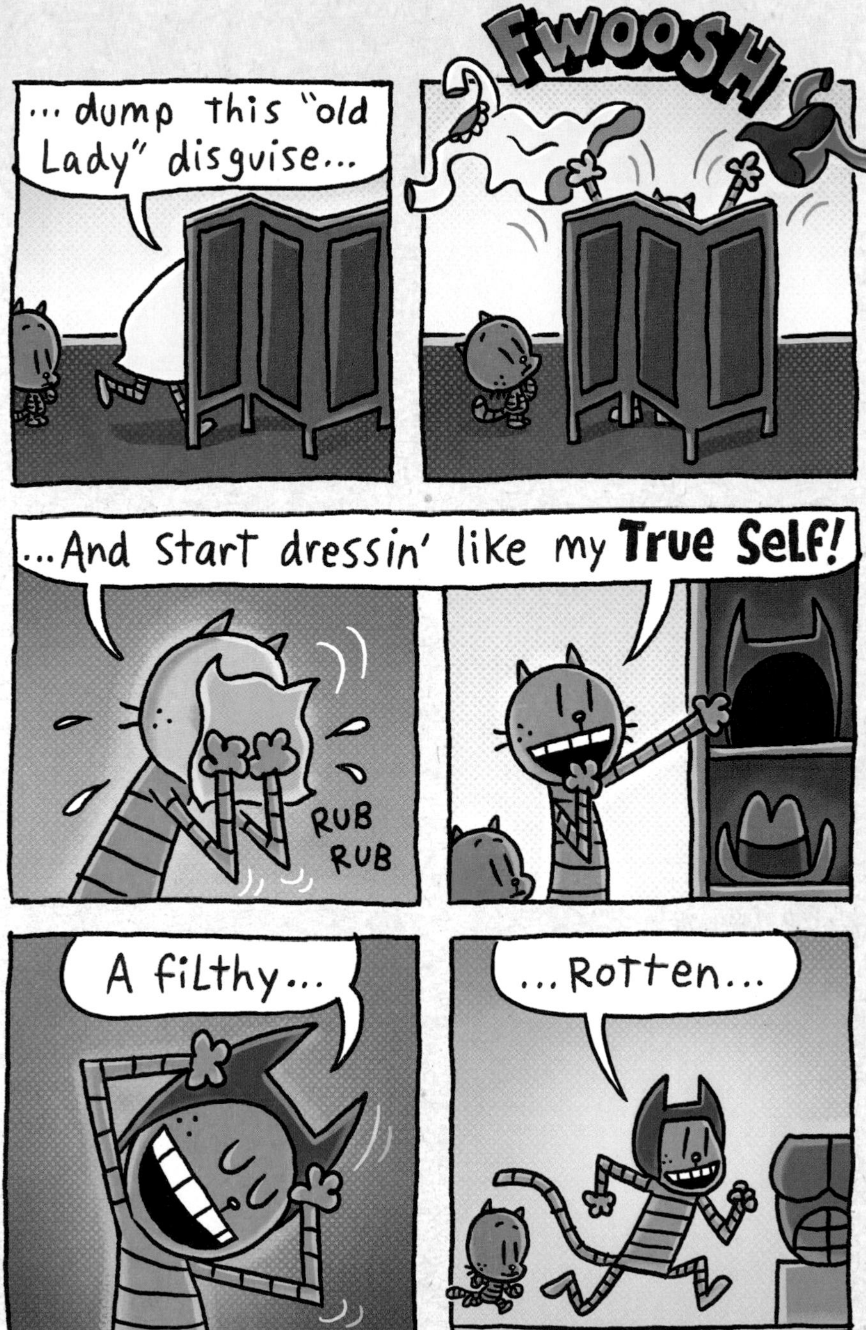
...dump this "old Lady" disguise...
FWOOSH
...And start dressin' like my True Self!
RUB RUB
A filthy...
...Rotten...

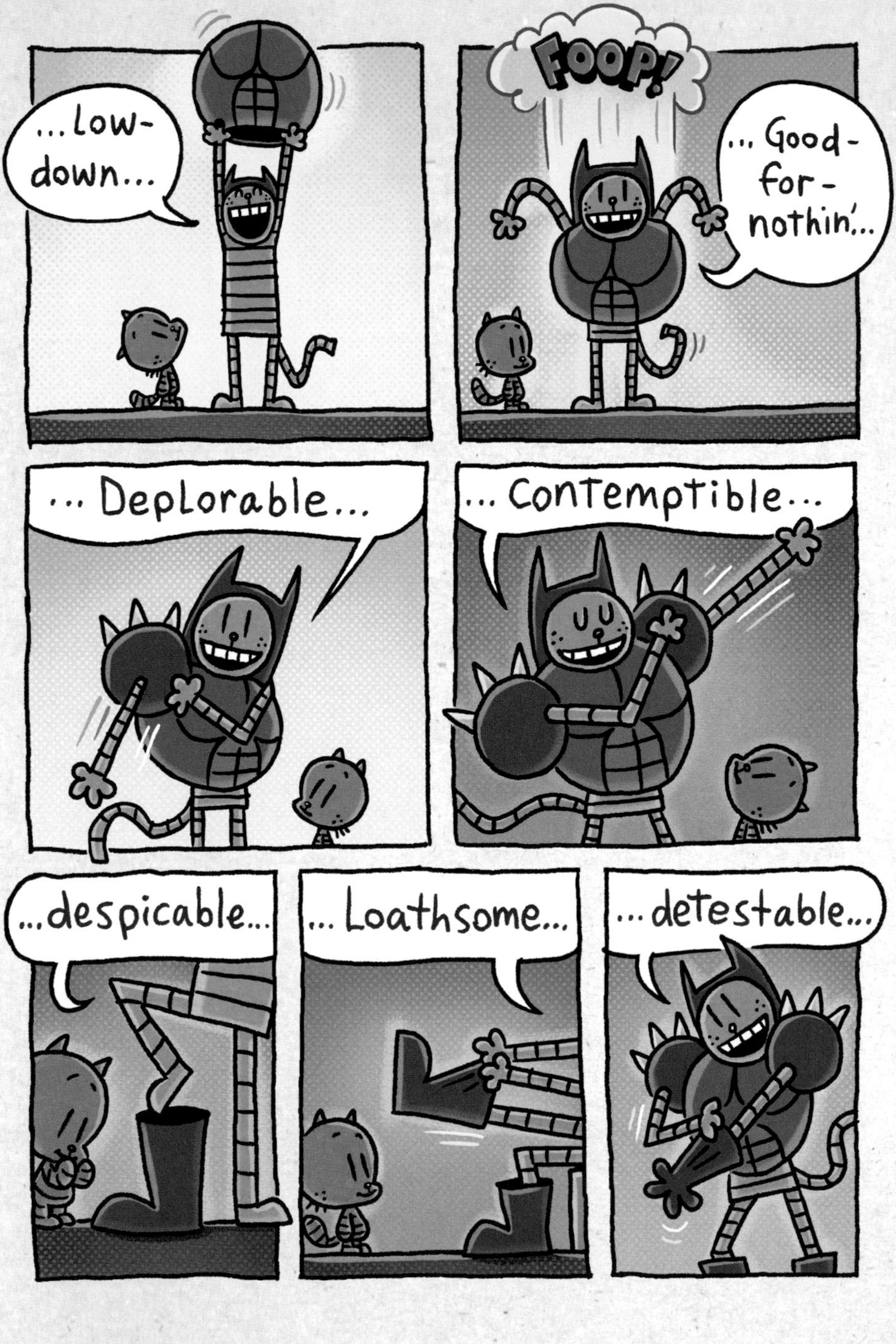
...Low-down...
FOOP!
...Good-for-nothin'...
...Deplorable...
...Contemptible...
...despicable...
...Loathsome...
...detestable...

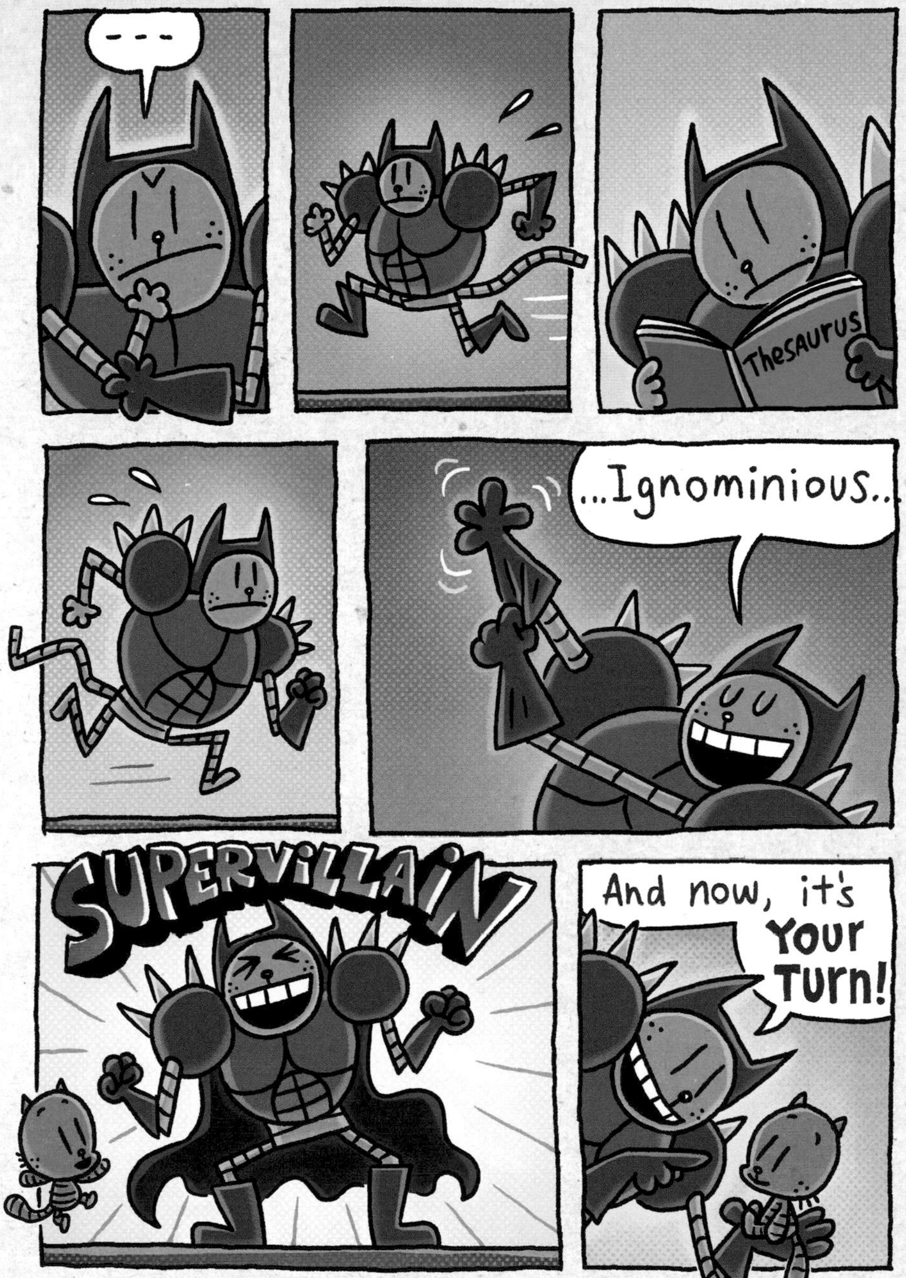
. . .
Thesaurus
...Ignominious...
SUPERVILLAIN
And now, it's YOUR TURN!

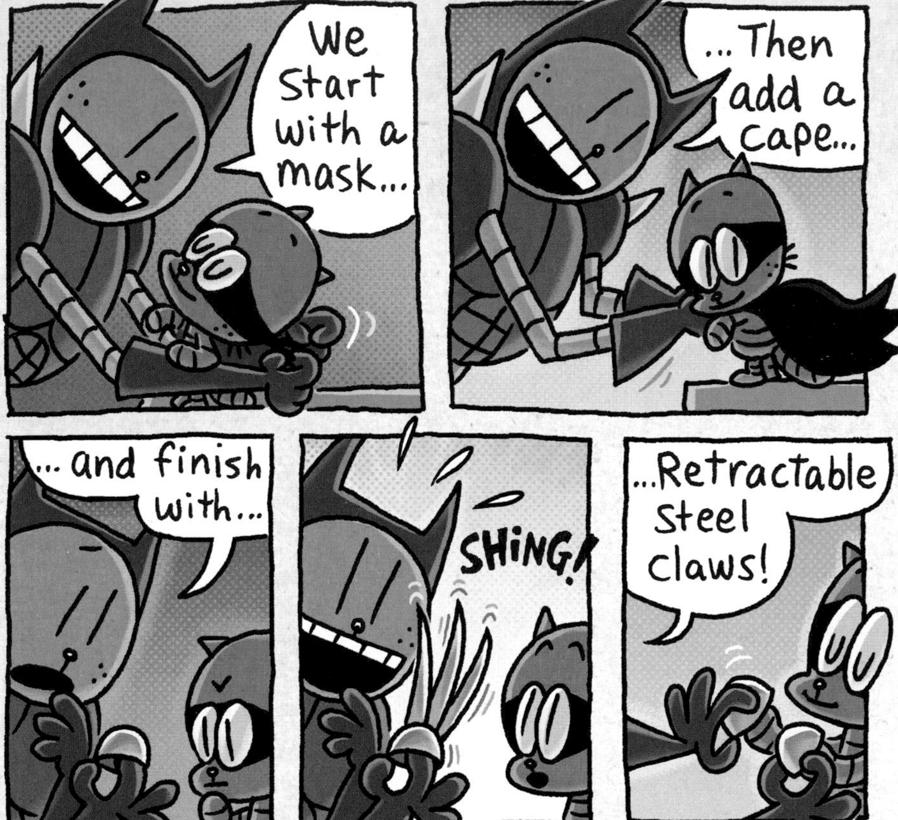
We Start with a mask...
...Then add a cape...
...and finish with...
SHING!
...Retractable Steel Claws!
SHING

TRIPLE FLIP-O-RAMA

Left hand here.

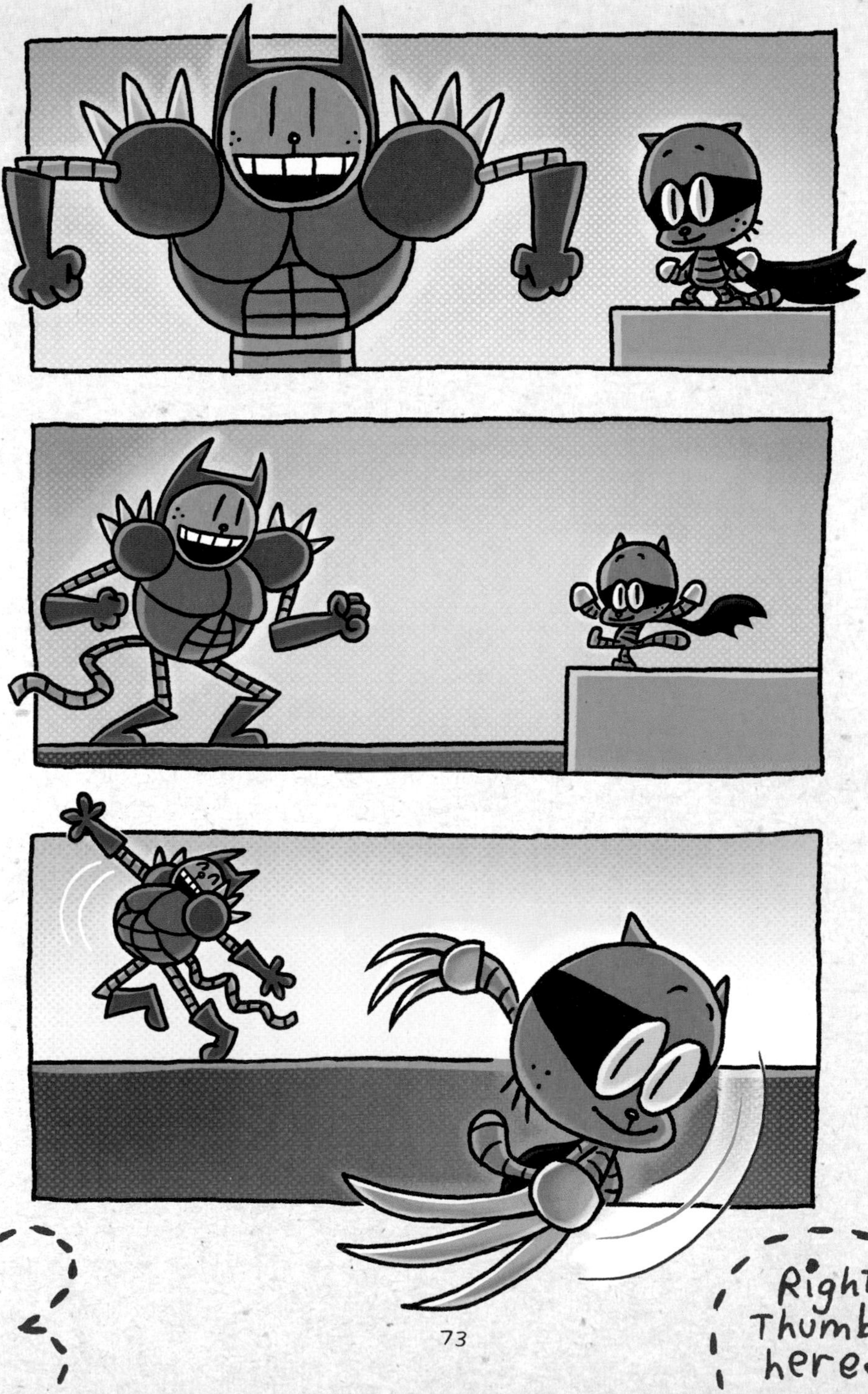

Right
Thumb
here.

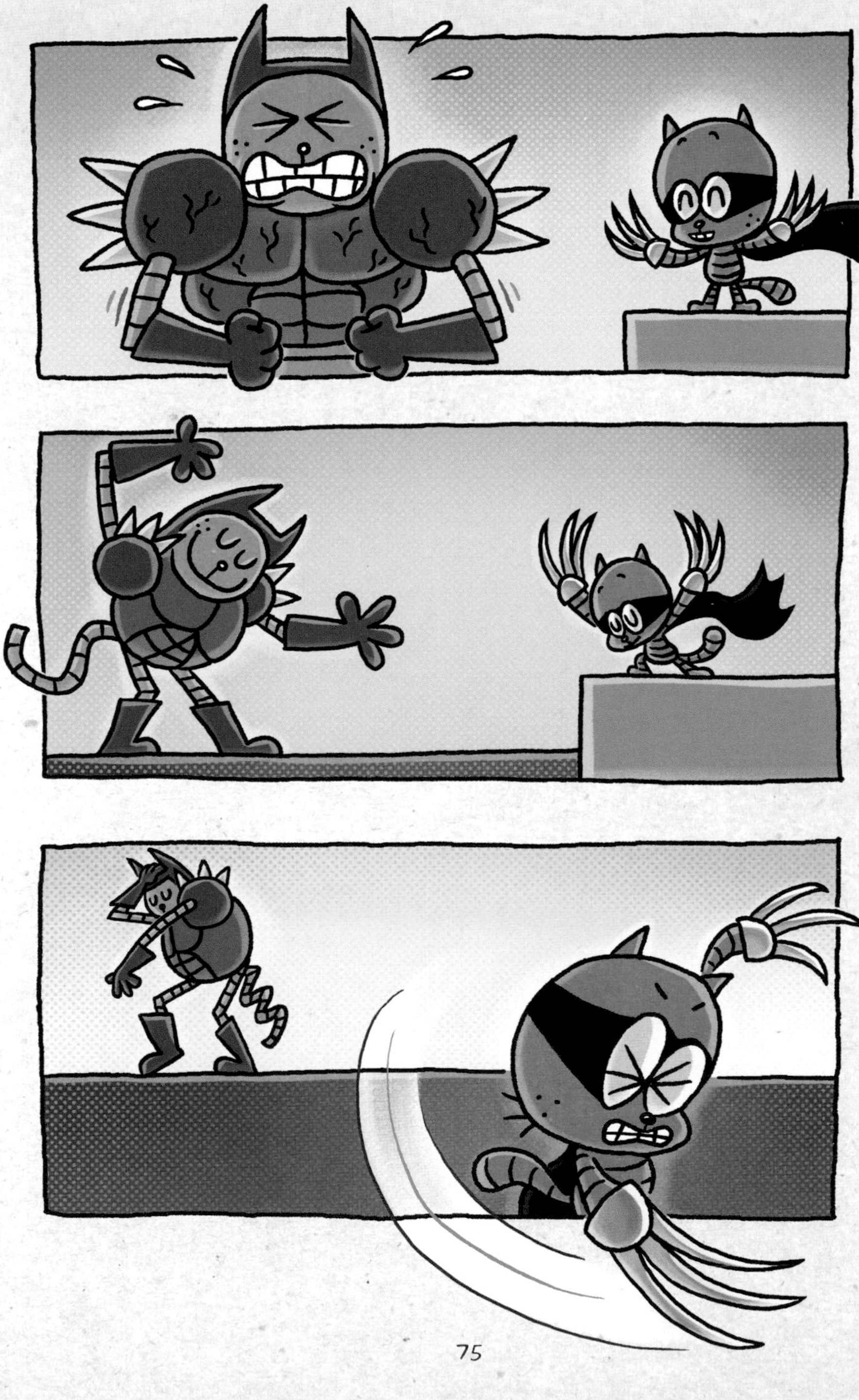

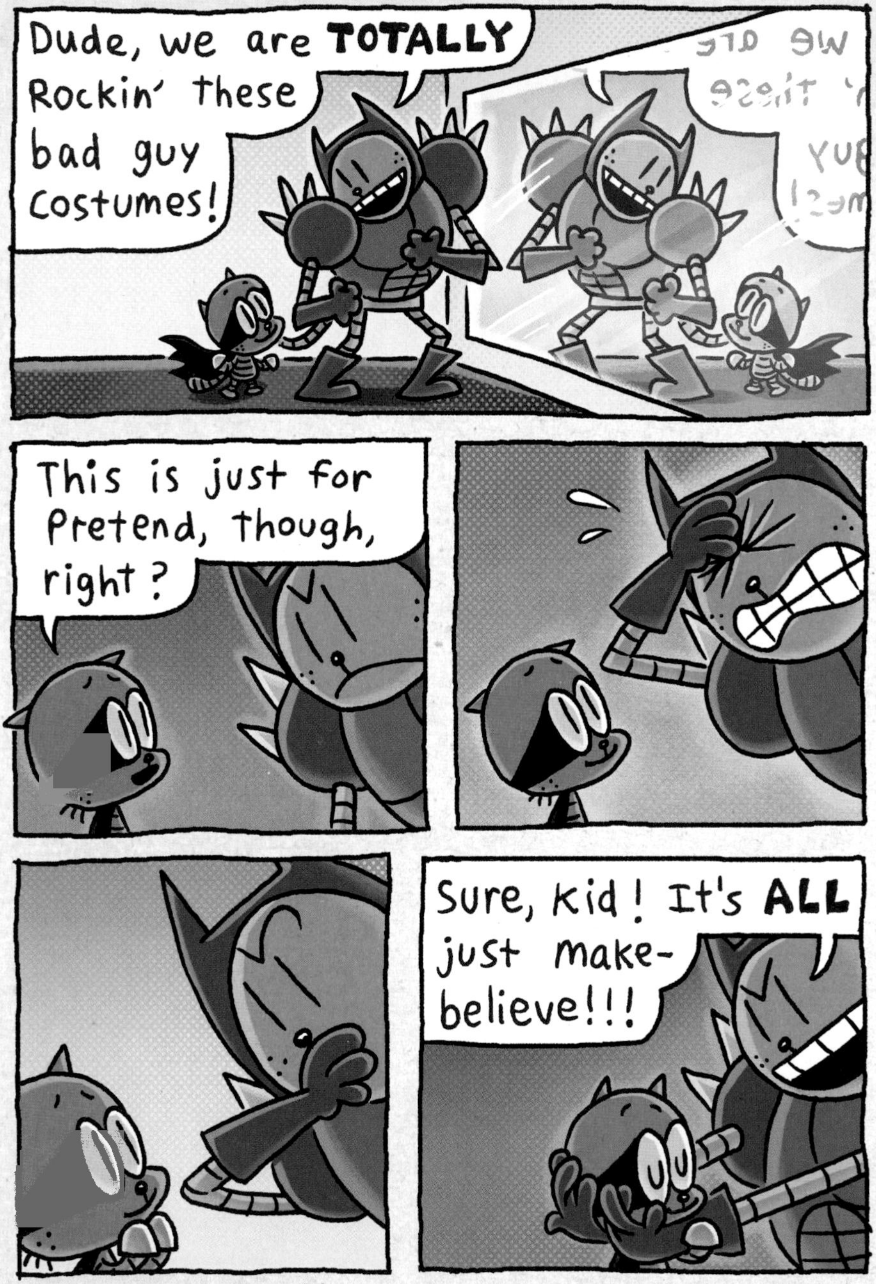
Dude, we are TOTALLY Rockin' these bad guy costumes!
This is just for Pretend, though, right?
Sure, kid! It's ALL just make-believe!!!

CHAPTER 5

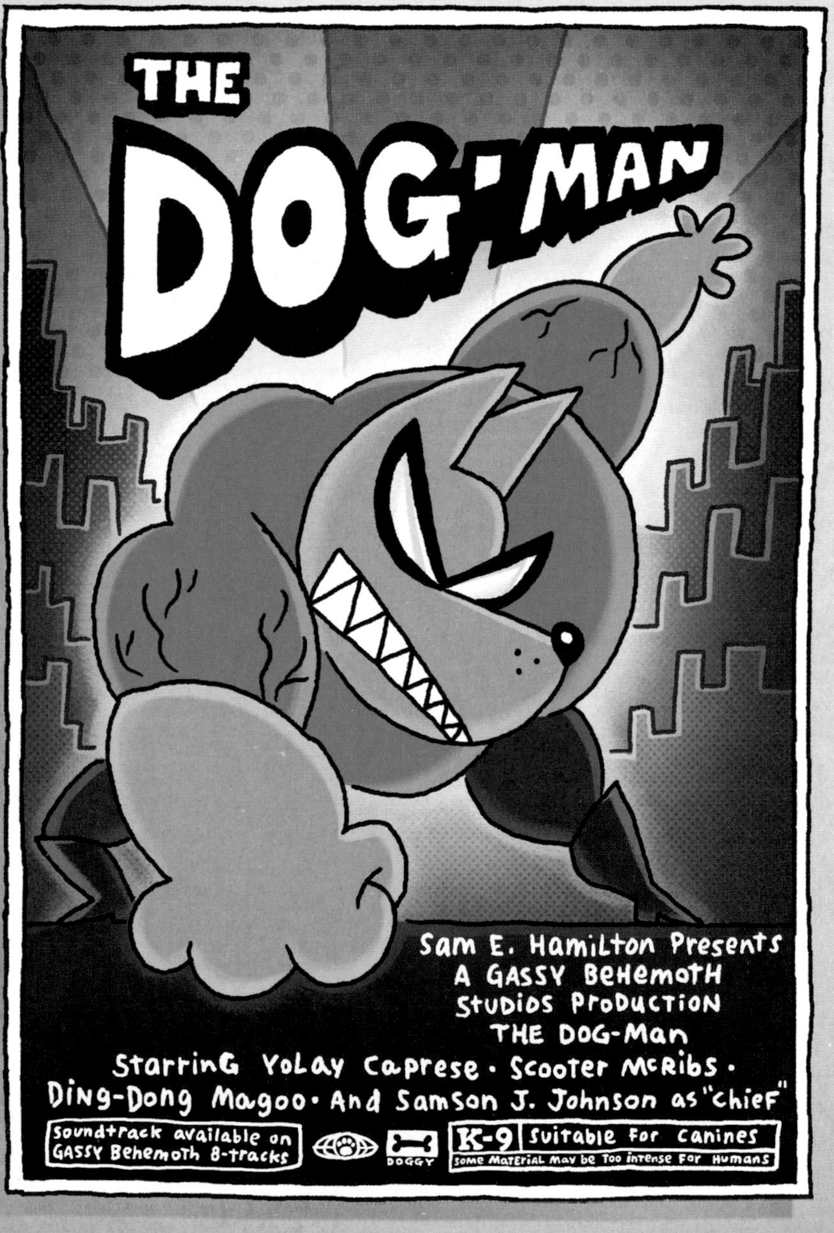
THE DOG-MAN
Sam E. Hamilton Presents
A GASSY Behemoth
Studios Production
THE DOG-Man
Starring Yolay Caprese • Scooter McRibs •
Ding-Dong Magoo • And Samson J. Johnson as "Chief"
Soundtrack available on
GASSY Behemoth 8-tracks
DOGGY
K-9 Suitable For Canines
Some Material May be Too intense For Humans

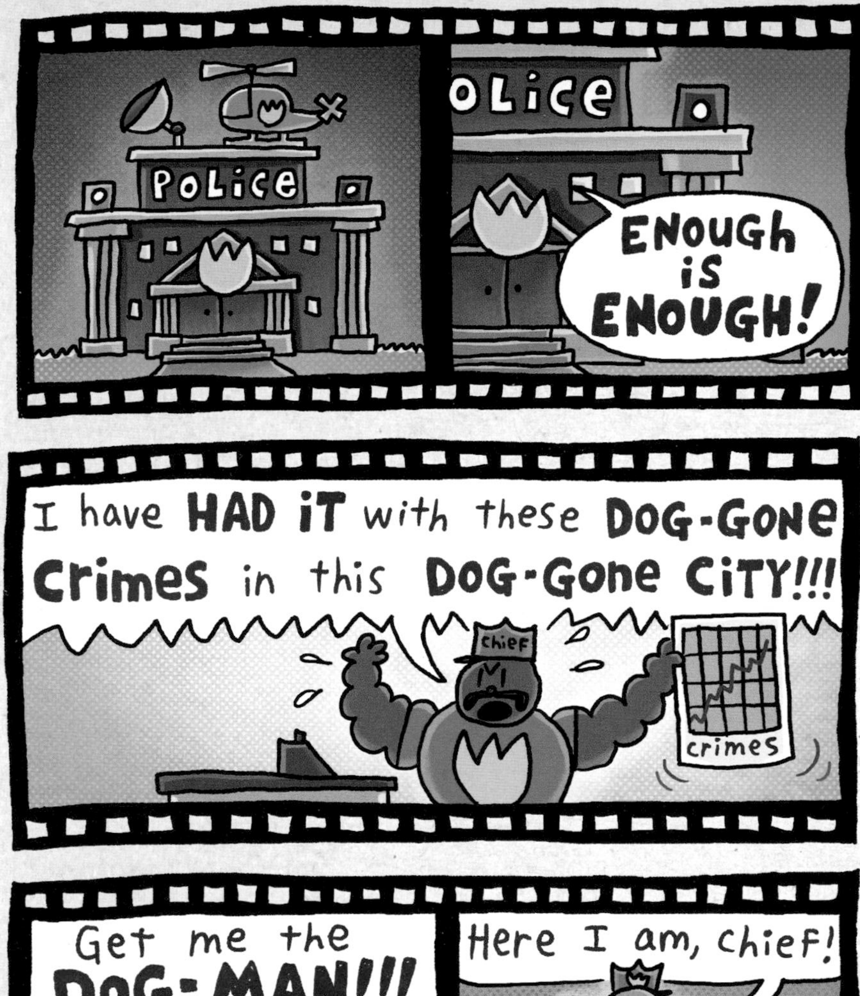
POLICE
OLICE
ENOUGH IS ENOUGH!
I have HAD iT with these DOG-GONE Crimes in this DOG-Gone CITY!!!
chief
crimes
Get me the DOG-MAN!!!
chief
Here I am, chief!

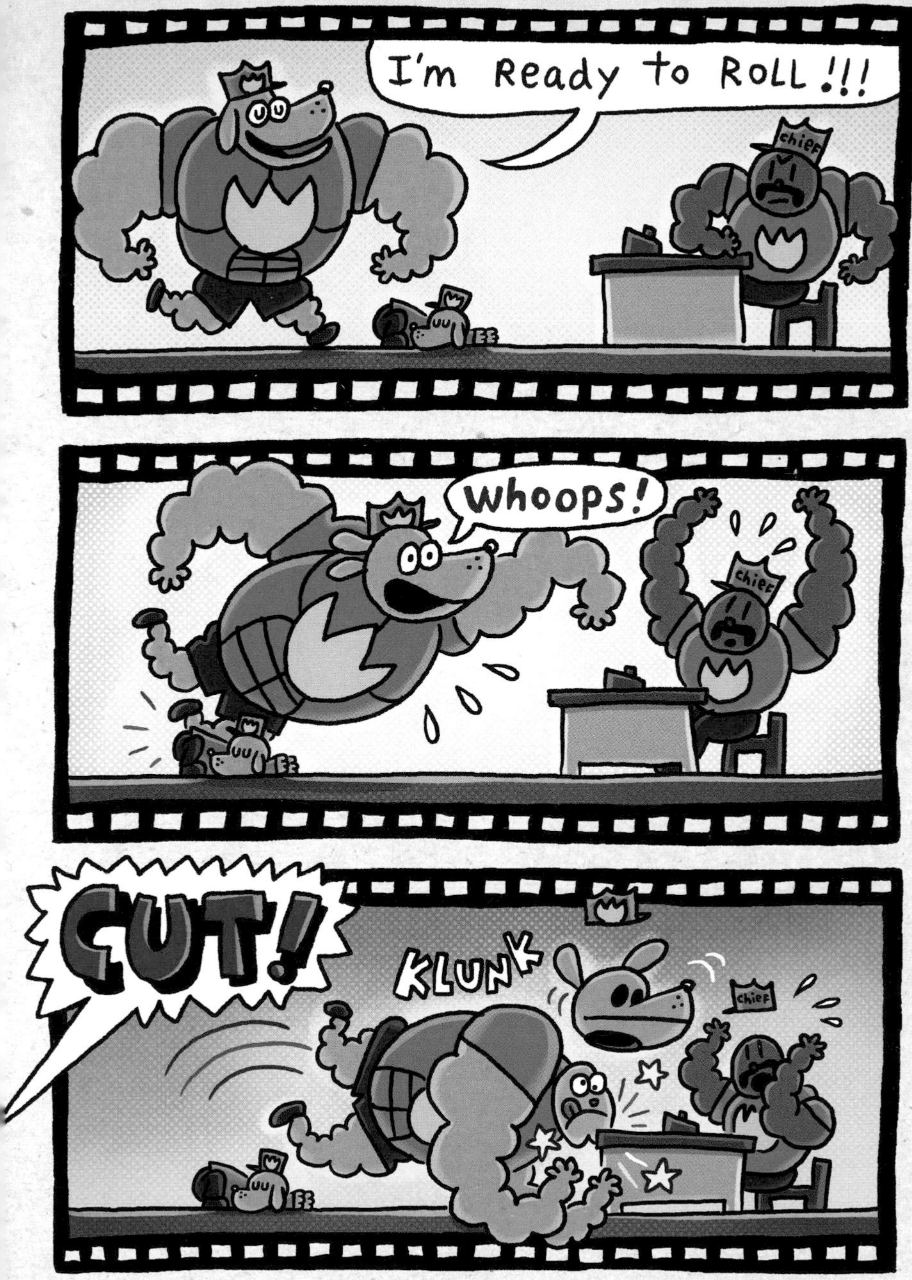
I'm Ready to ROLL!!!
chief
Whoops!
chief
CUT!
KLUNK
chief

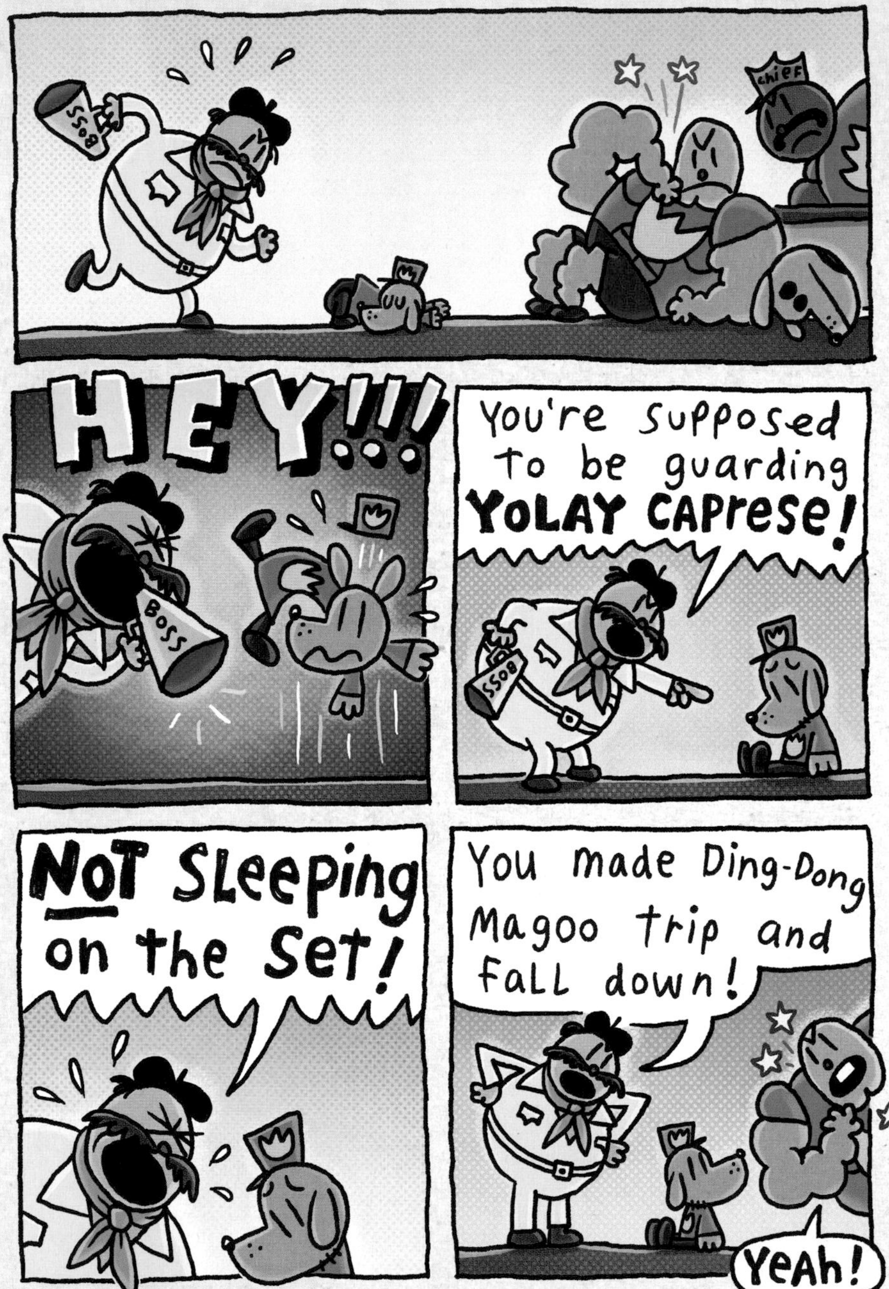
BOSS
CHIEF
HEY!!!
BOSS
You're supposed to be guarding YOLAY CAPRESE!
BOSS
NOT SLEEPING on the SET!
You made Ding-Dong Magoo trip and fall down!
YEAh!

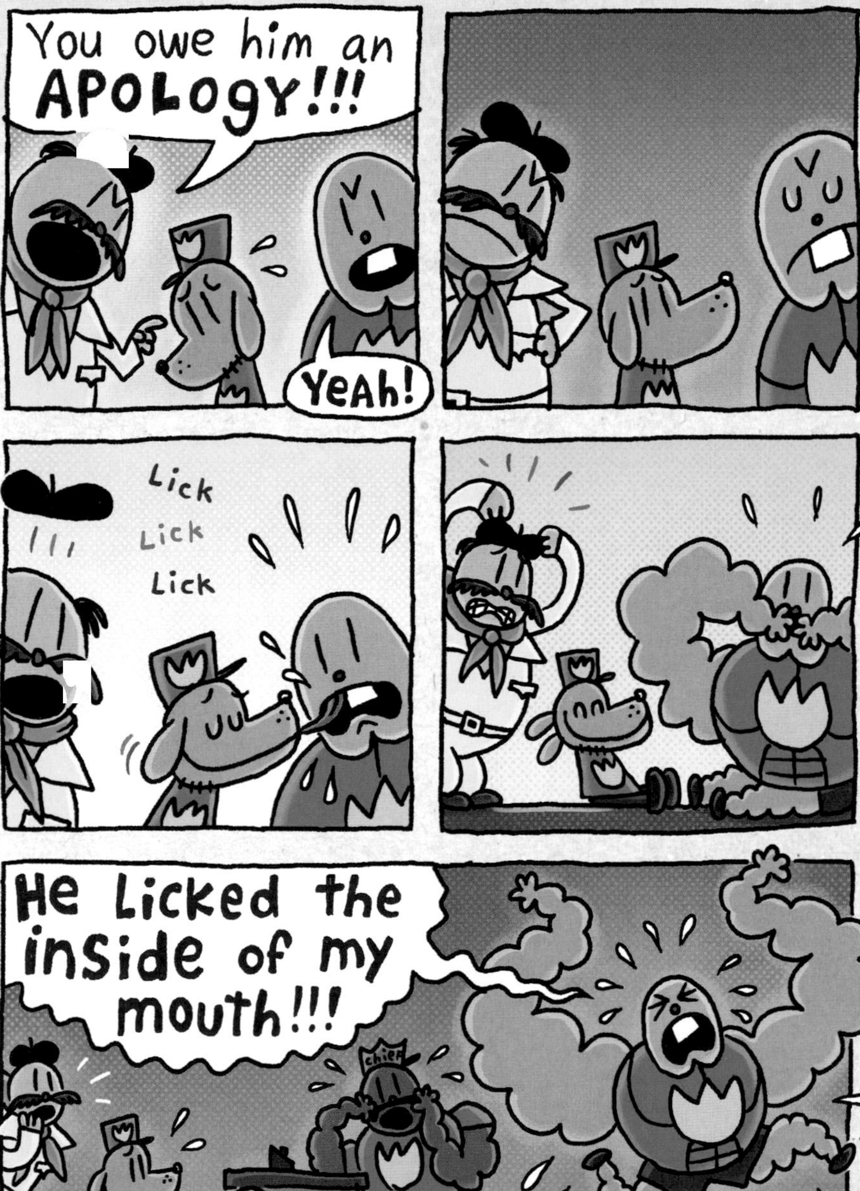
You owe him an APOLOGY!!!
YEAH!
Lick
Lick
Lick
He Licked the inside of my mouth!!!
chief

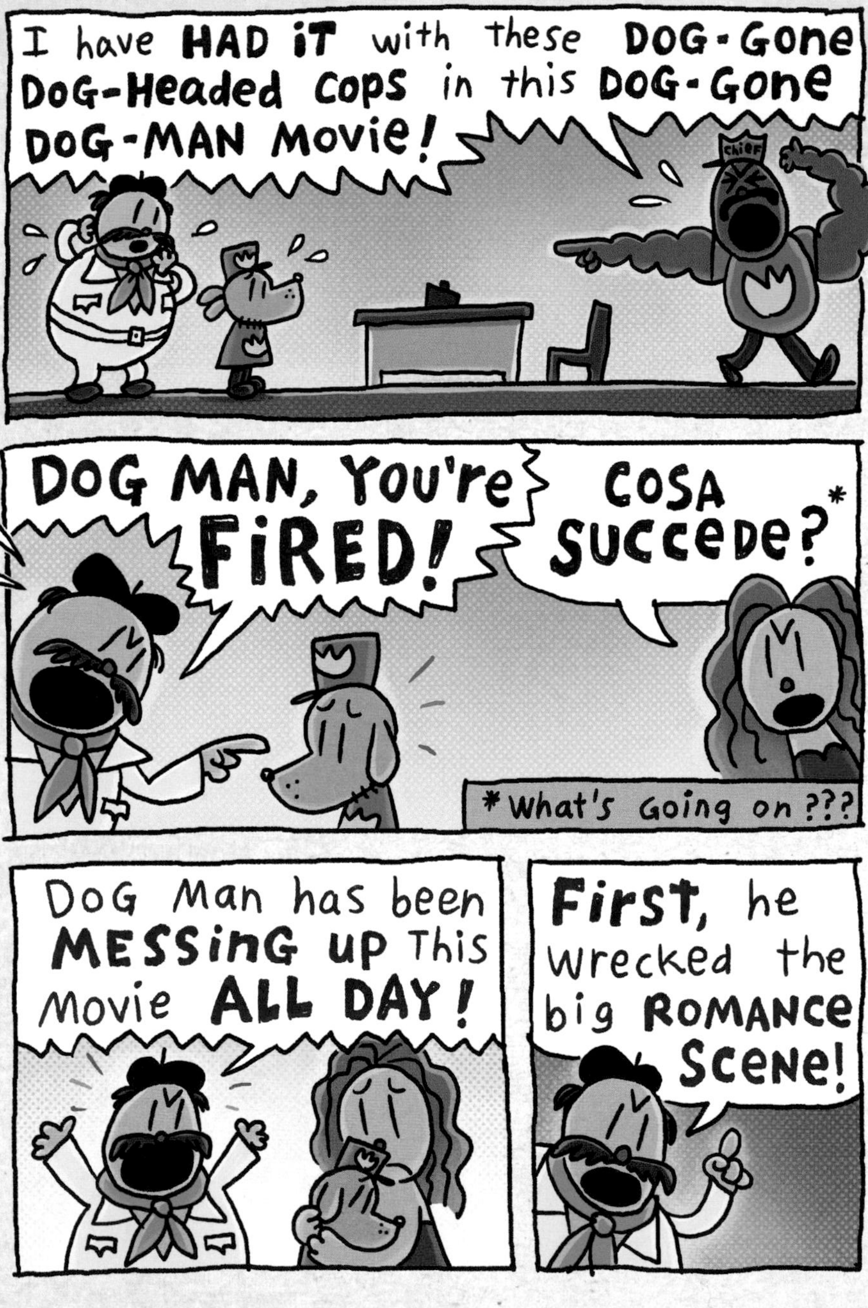
I have HAD IT with these DOG-Gone DOG-Headed Cops in this DOG-Gone DOG-MAN Movie!
DOG MAN, You're FIRED!
COSA SUCCEDE?*
*What's Going on???
DOG Man has been MESSING UP This Movie ALL DAY!
First, he wrecked the big ROMANCE SCENE!

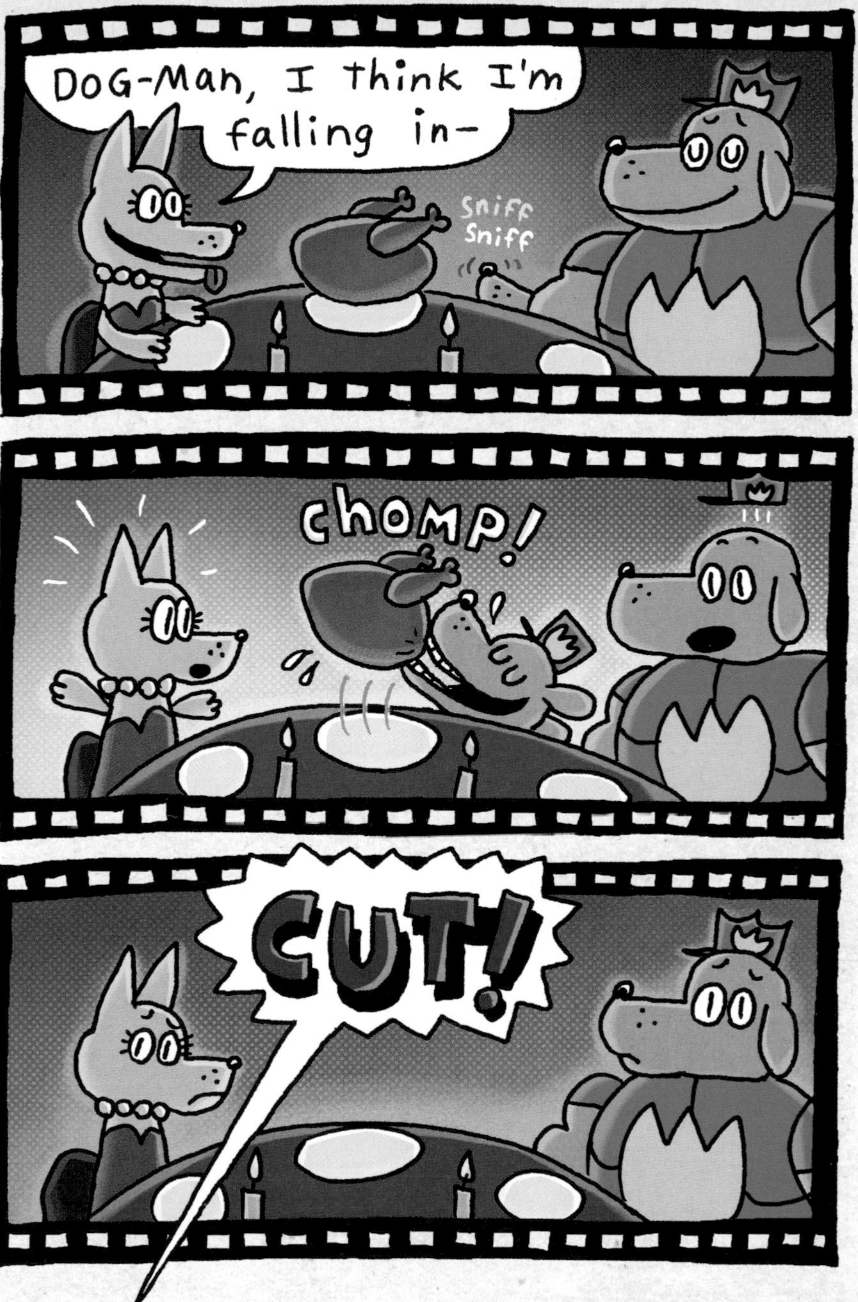
DOG-Man, I think I'm falling in-
Sniff Sniff
chomp!
CUT!

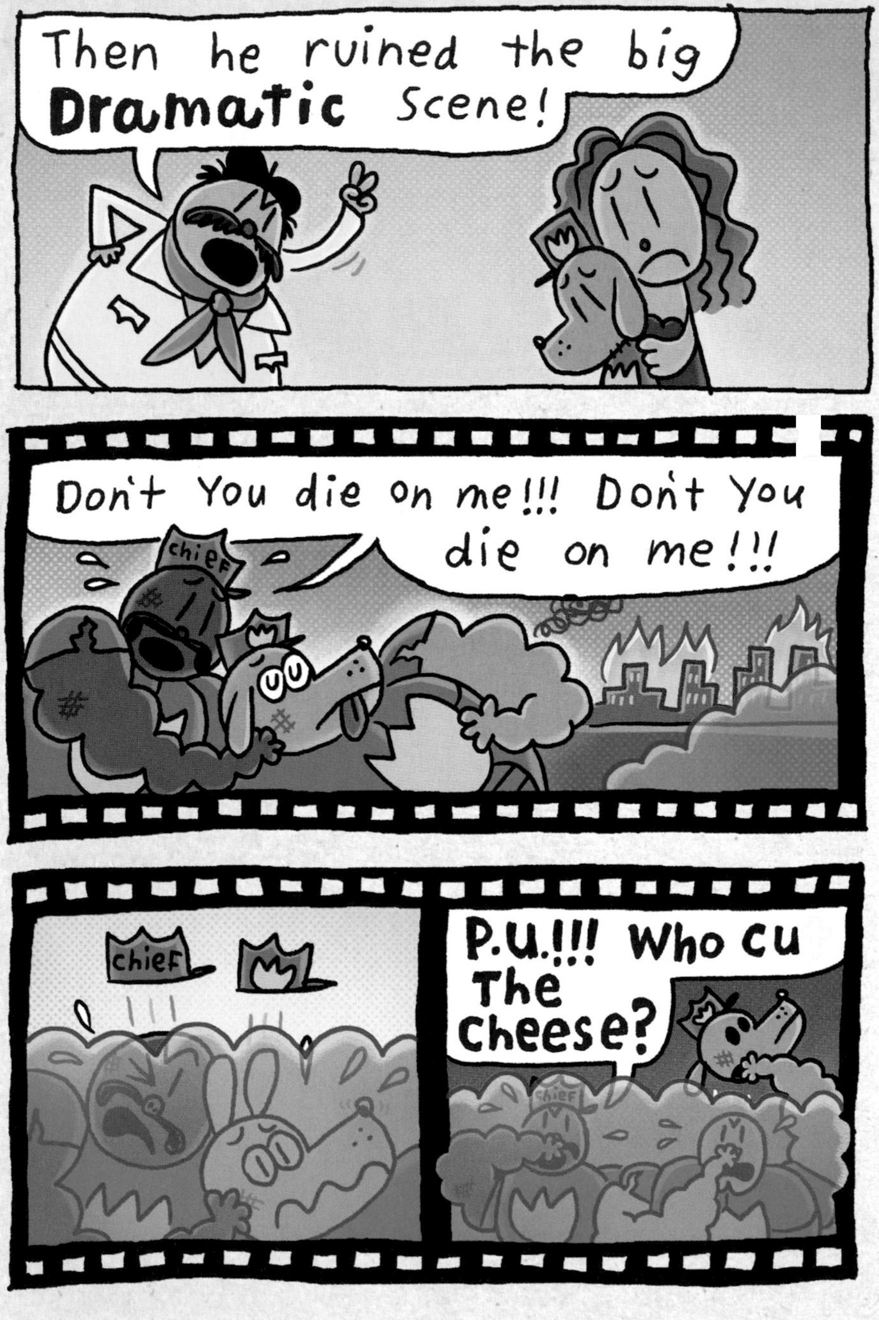
Then he ruined the big **Dramatic** Scene!
Don't You die on me!!! Don't You die on me!!!
chief
chief
P.U.!!! Who cu The cheese?
chief

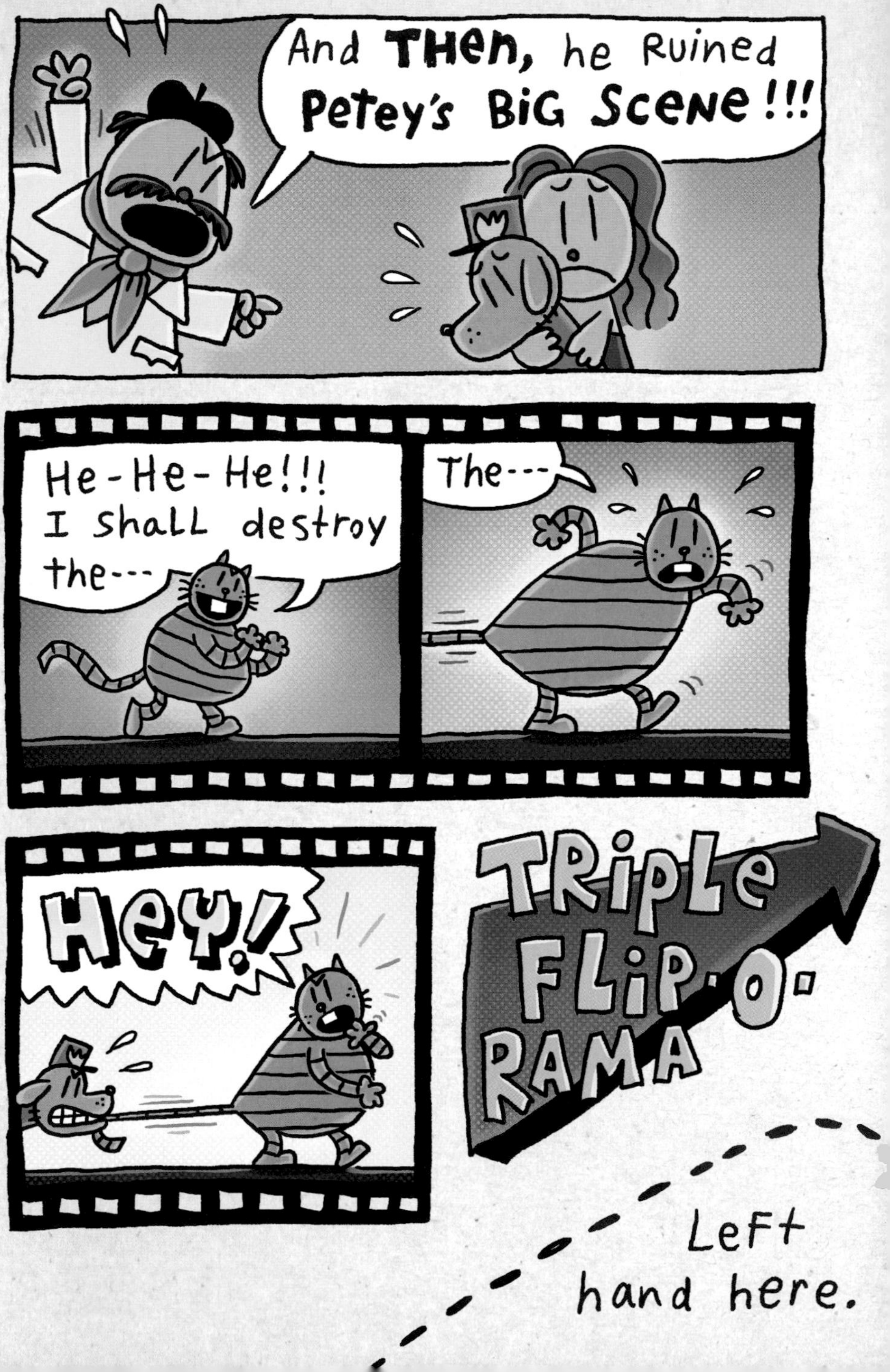
And THEn, he Ruined Petey's BIG SCENE!!!
He-He-He!!! I shall destroy the---
The---
HEY!
TRIPLE FLIP-O-RAMA
Left hand here.

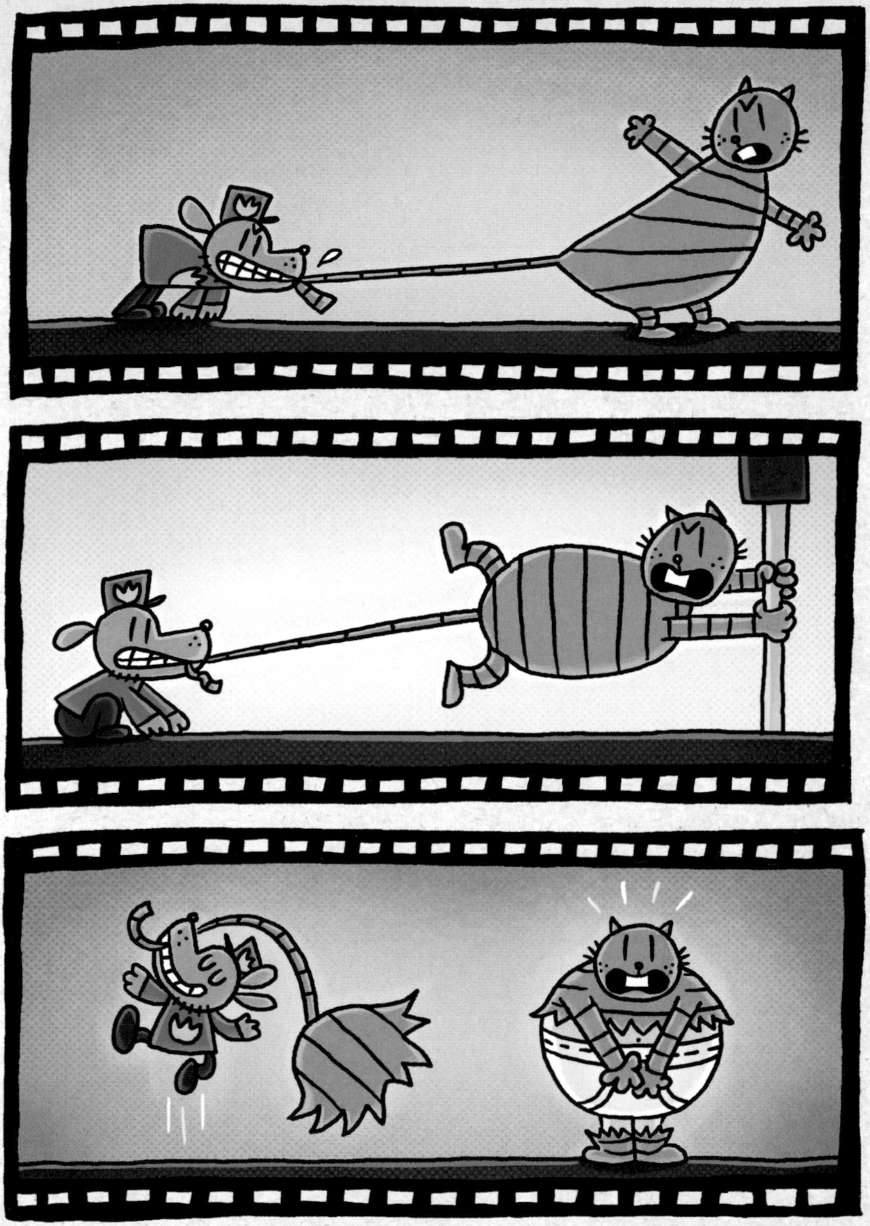

Right
Thumb
here.

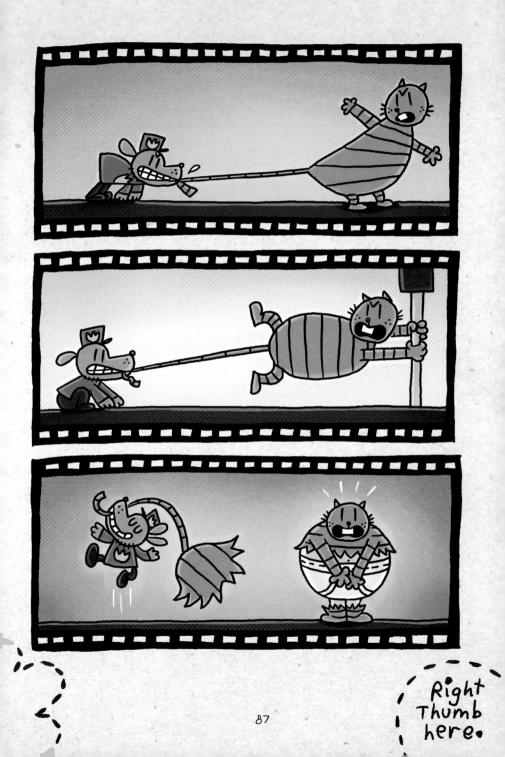

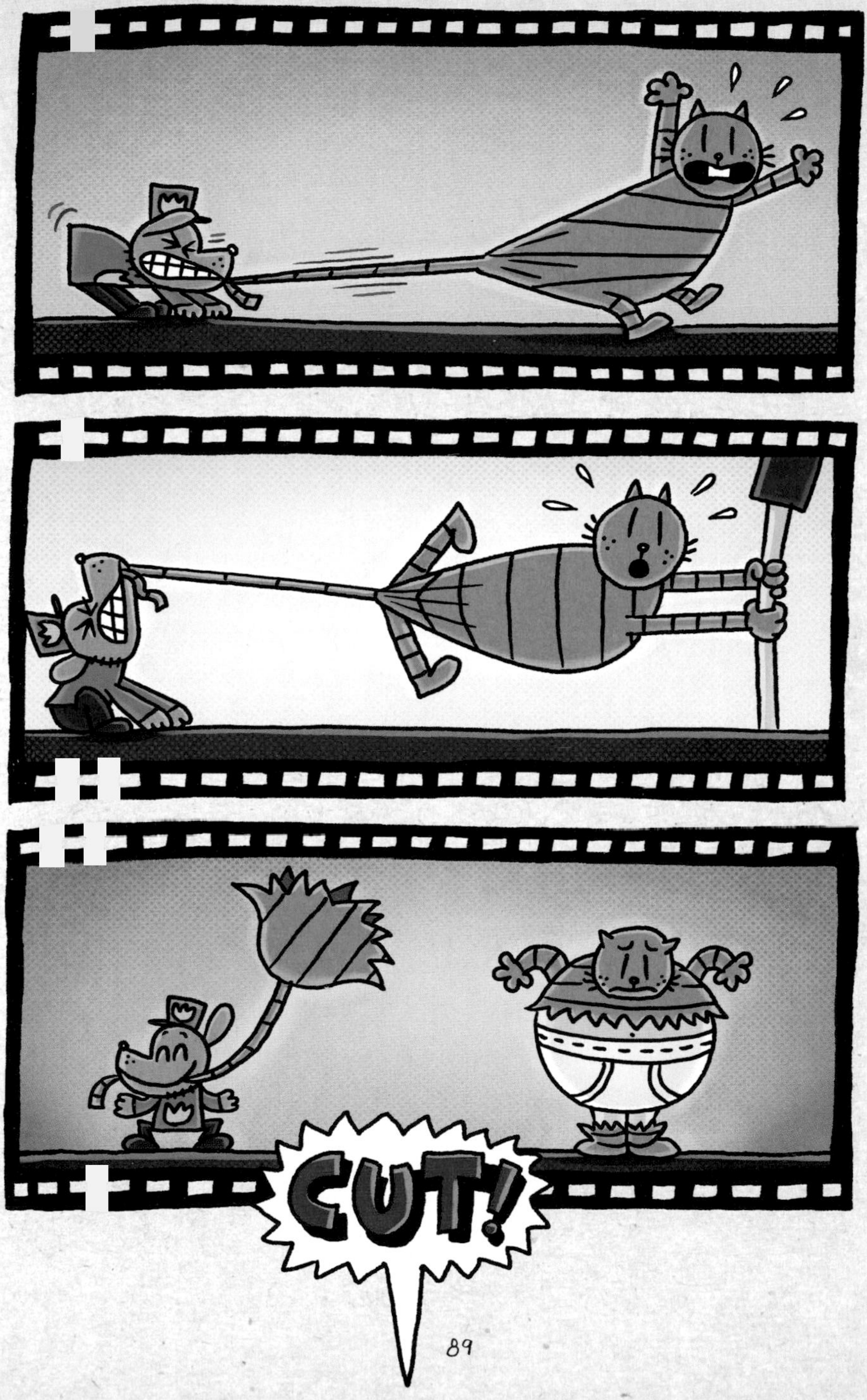
CUT!

Chapter 6

THE BARK KNIGHT RISES

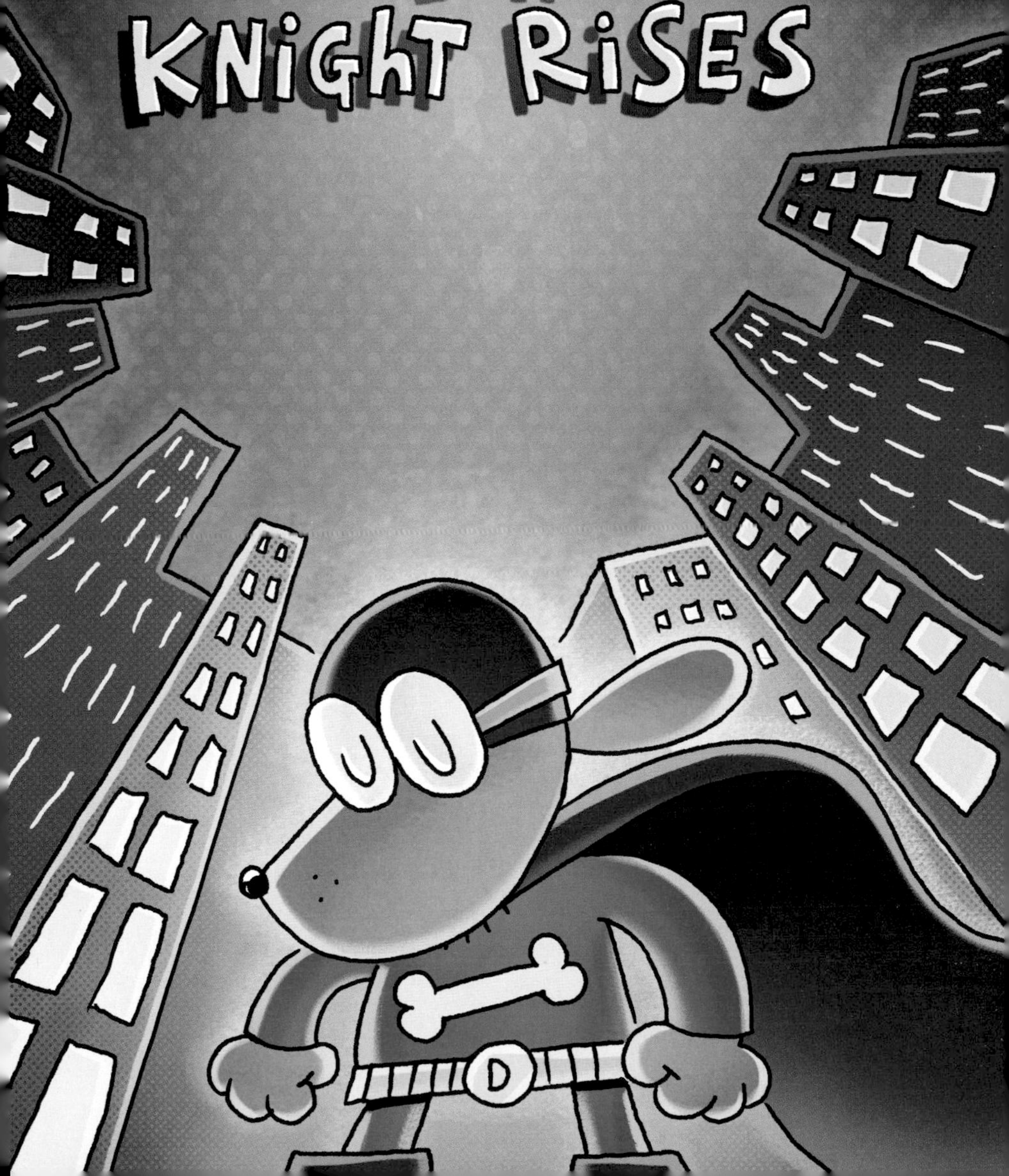
D

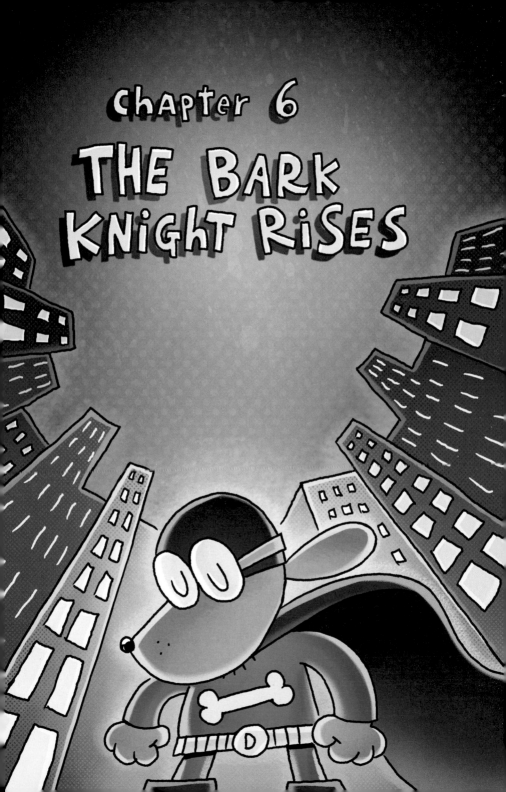

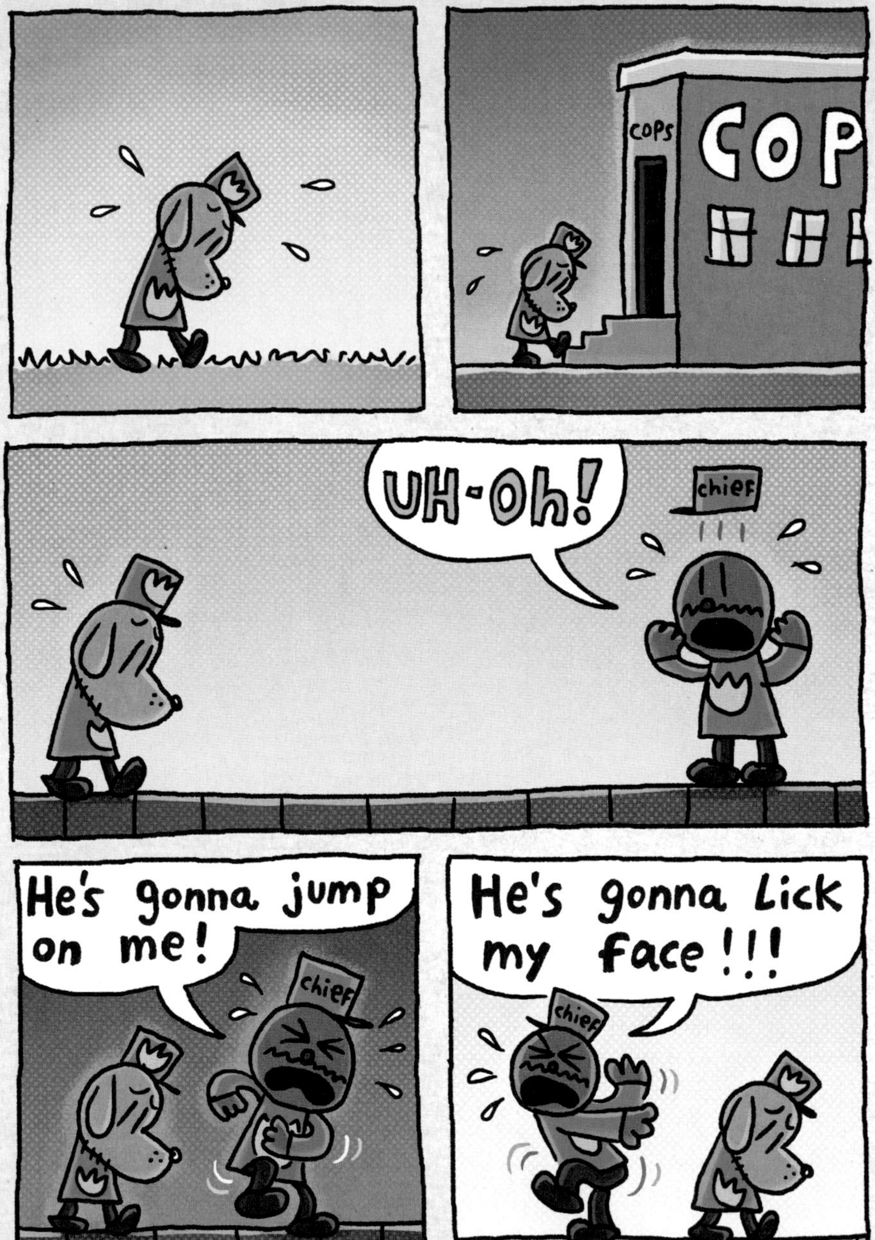
COPS
COP
UH-Oh!
chief
He's gonna jump on me!
chief
He's gonna Lick my face!!!
chief

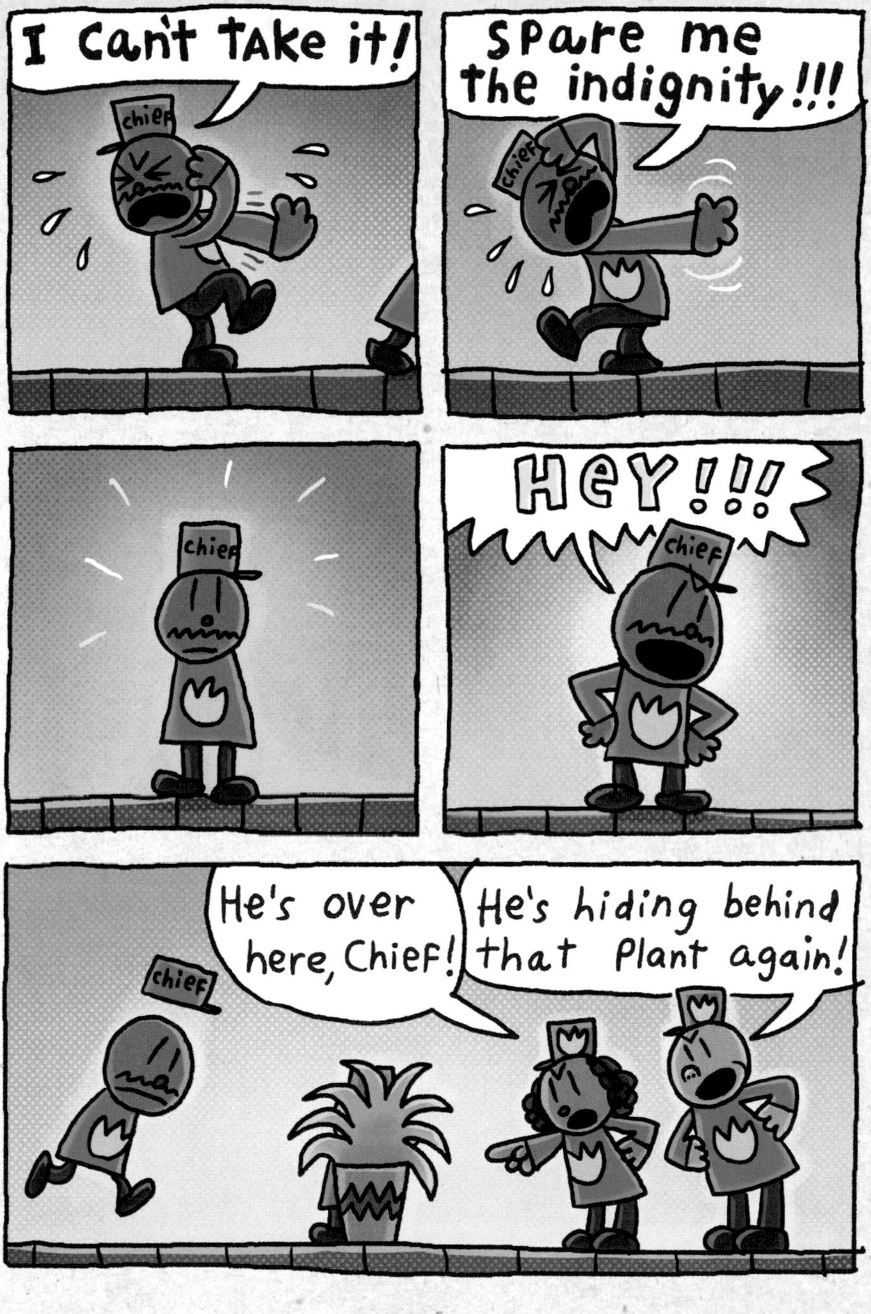
I can't take it!
chief
Spare me the indignity!!!
chief
chief
HEY!!!
chief
chief
He's over here, Chief!
He's hiding behind that Plant again!

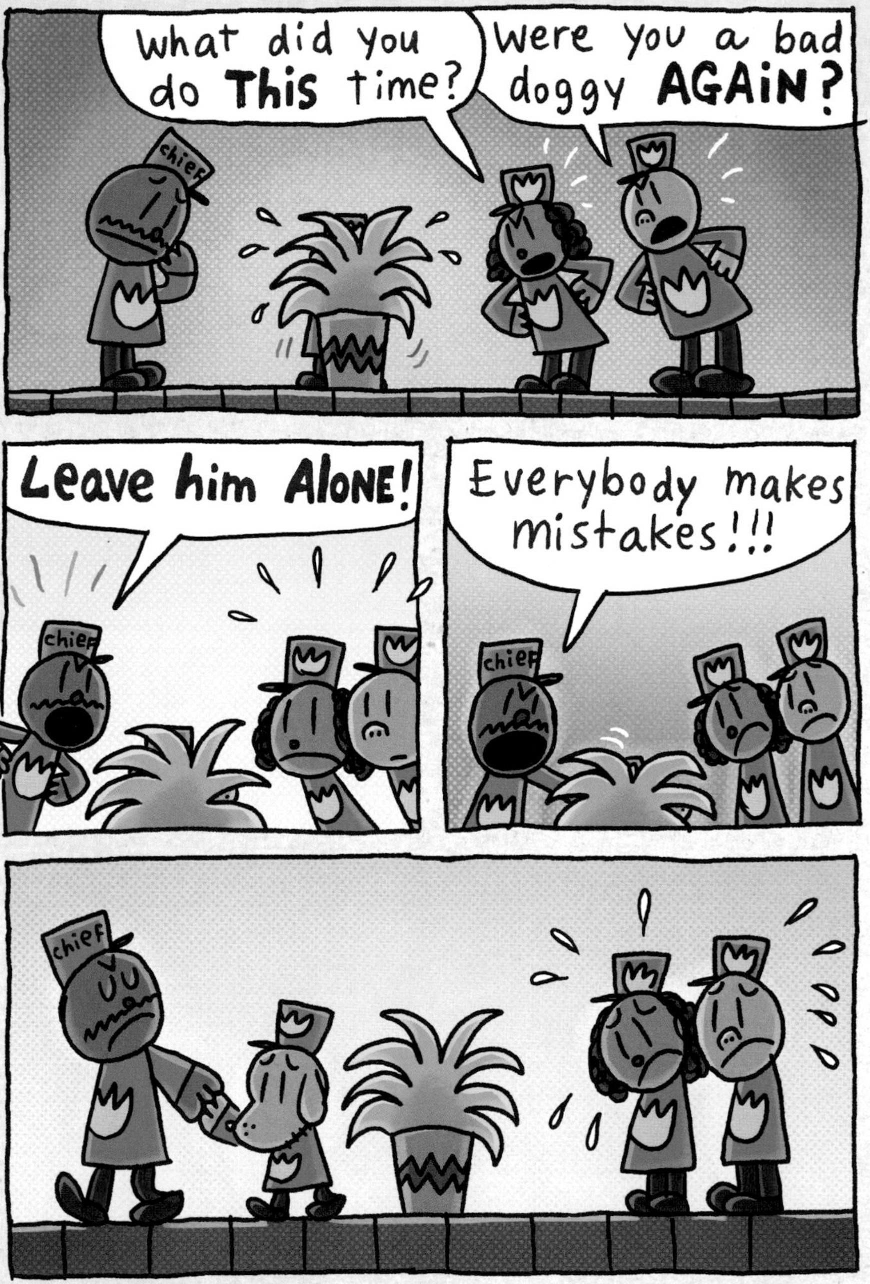
What did you do **THIS** time?
Were you a bad doggy **AGAIN?**
chief
Leave him ALONE!
chief
Everybody makes mistakes!!!
chief
chief

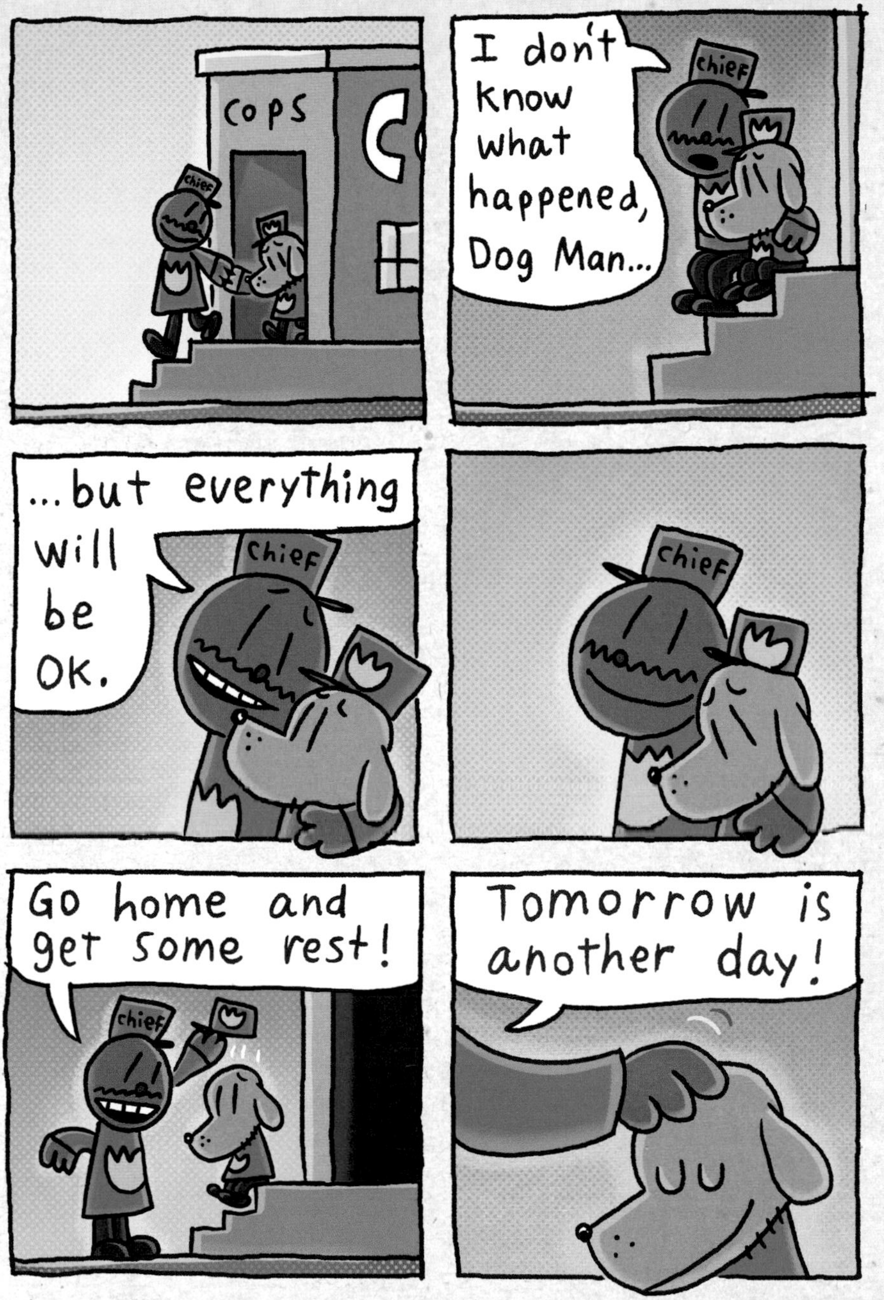
COPS
CHIEF
I don't know what happened, Dog Man...
...but everything will be OK.
Go home and get some rest!
Tomorrow is another day!

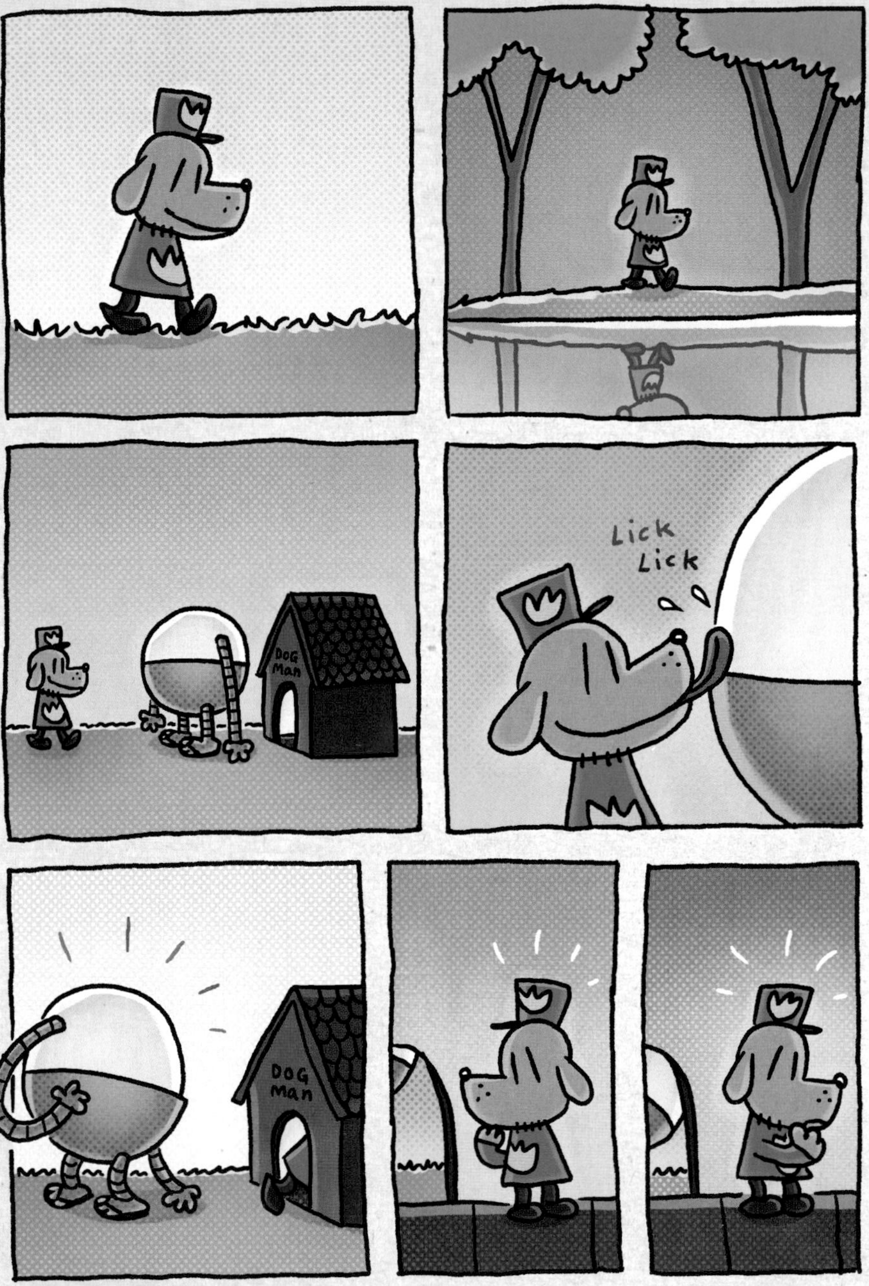
Lick
Lick
DOG Man
DOG Man

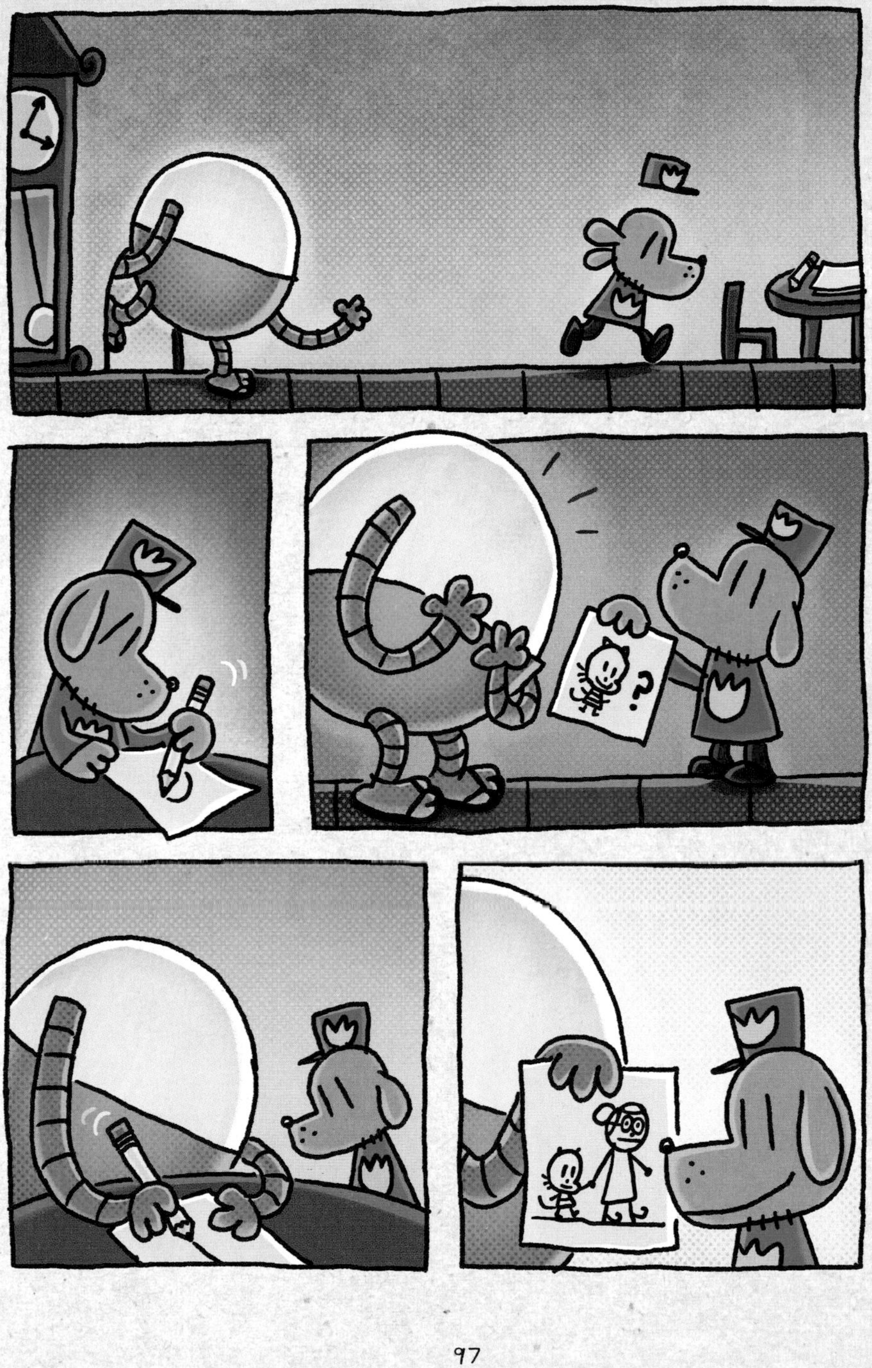

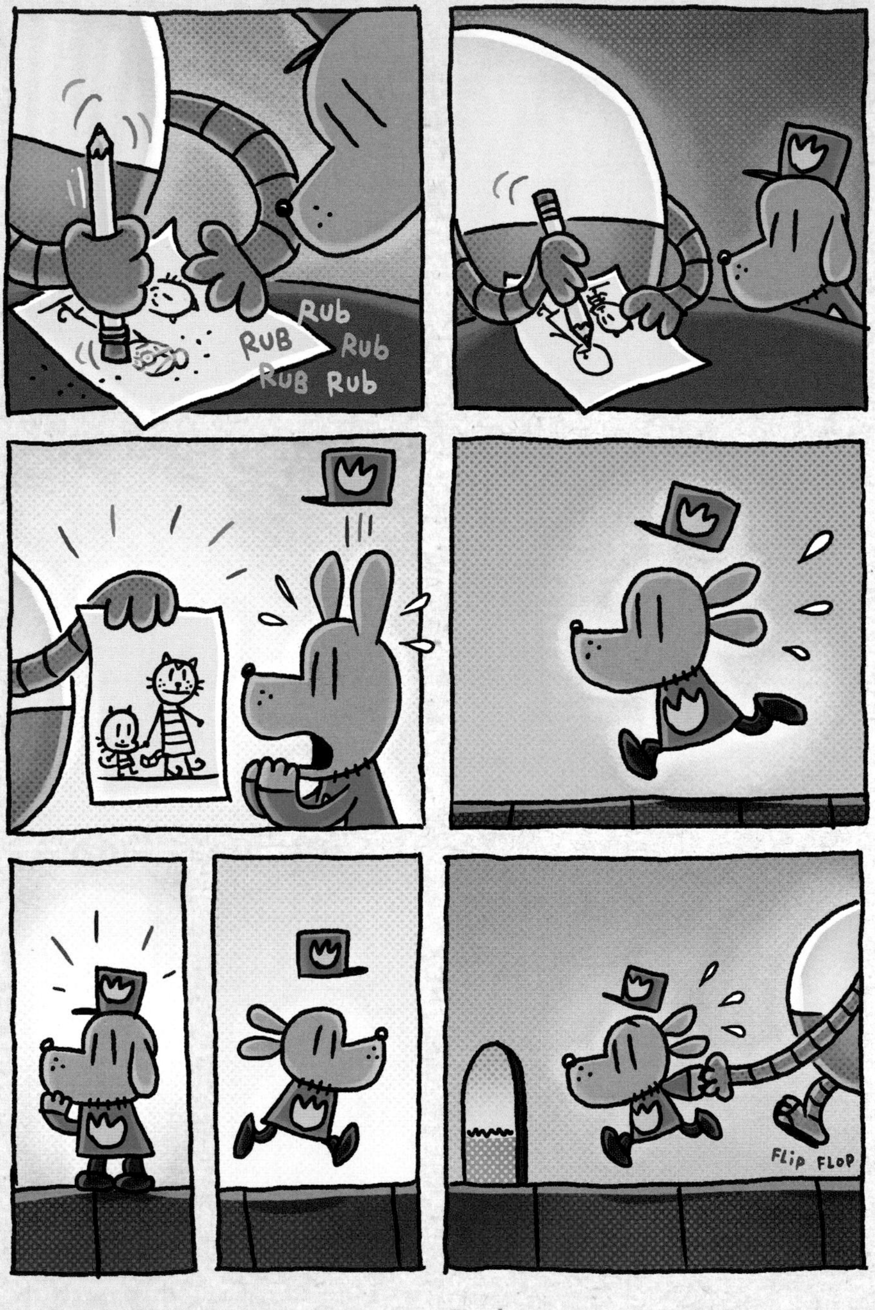
RUB
Rub
RUB
Rub
RUB
Rub
FLIP FLOP

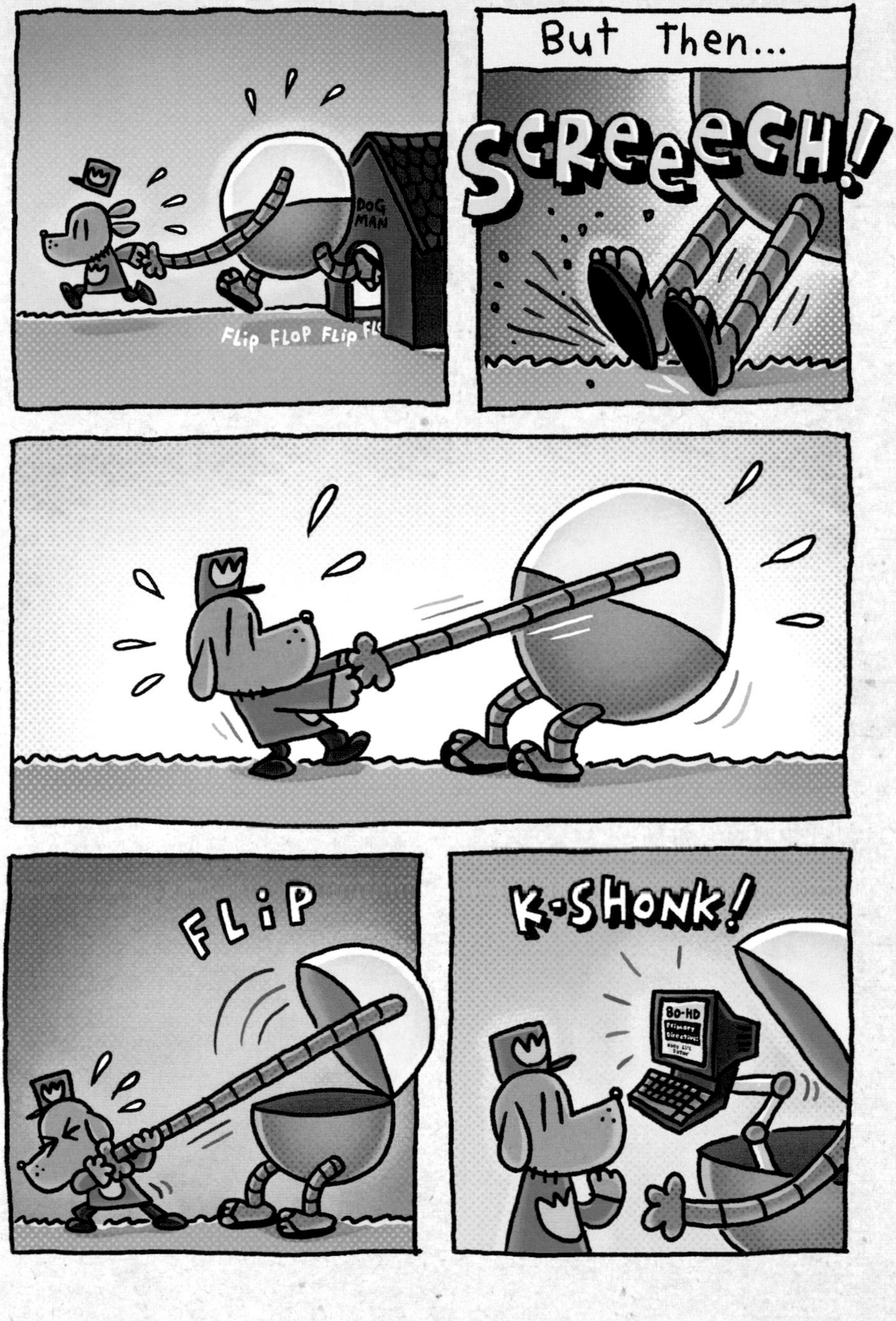
DOG MAN
FLip FLOP FLip
But Then...
SCREEECH!
FLiP
K-SHONK!
80-HD
Primary Directive:

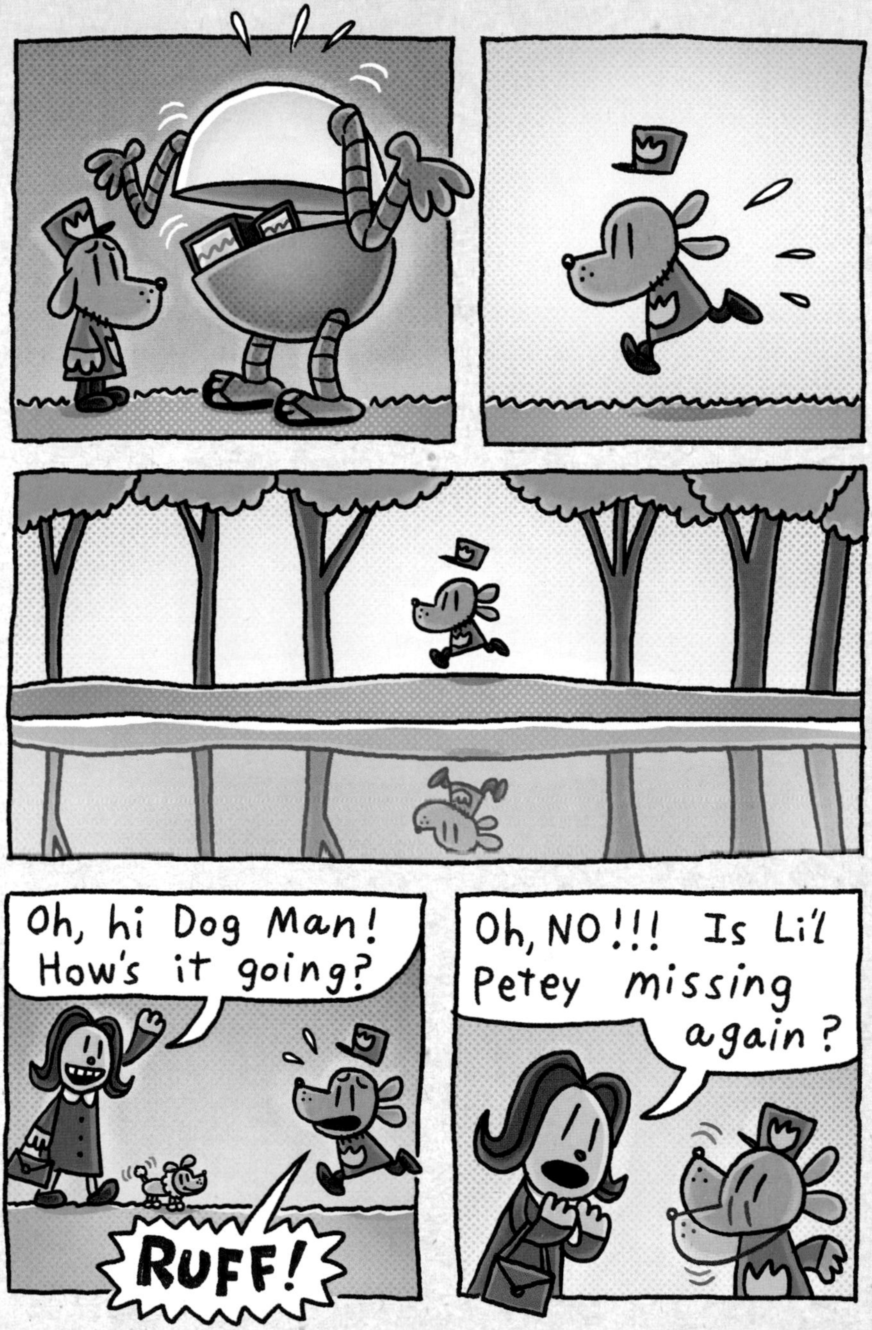
Oh, hi Dog Man! How's it going?
RUFF!
Oh, NO!!! Is Li'l Petey missing again?

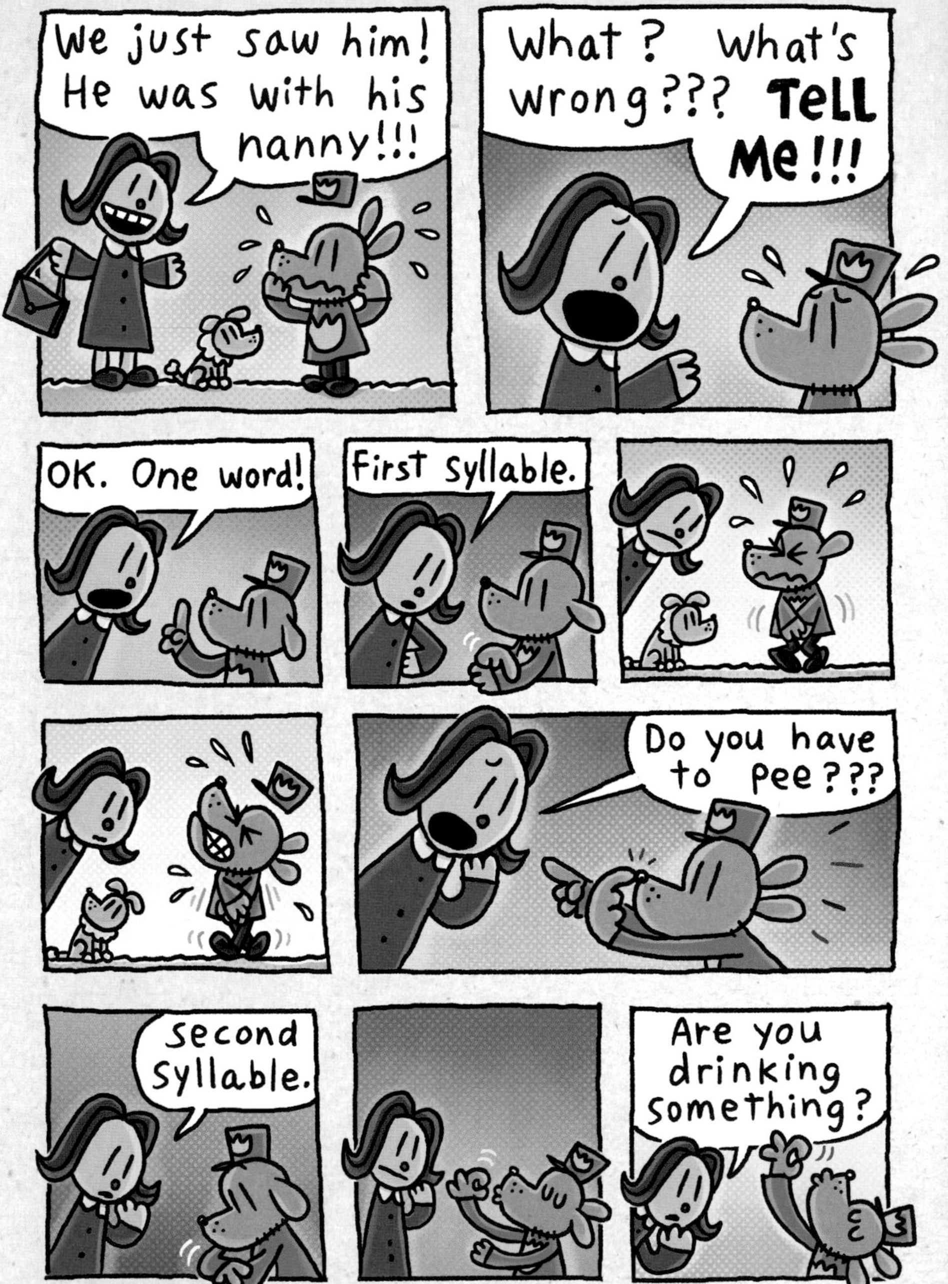
We just saw him! He was with his nanny!!!
What? What's wrong??? TELL ME!!!
OK. One word!
First syllable.
Do you have to pee???
Second syllable.
Are you drinking something?

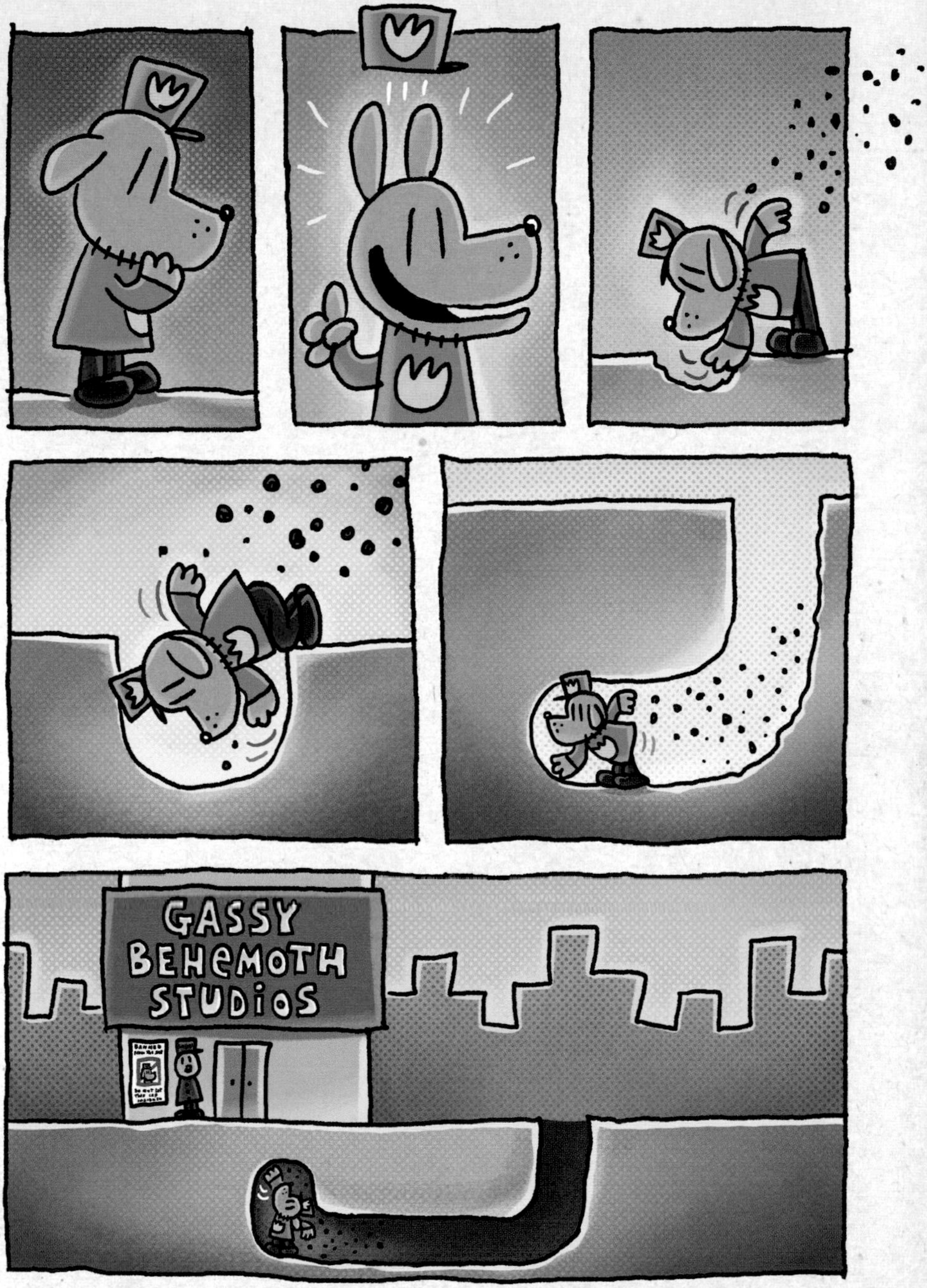
GASSY BEHEMOTH STUDIOS

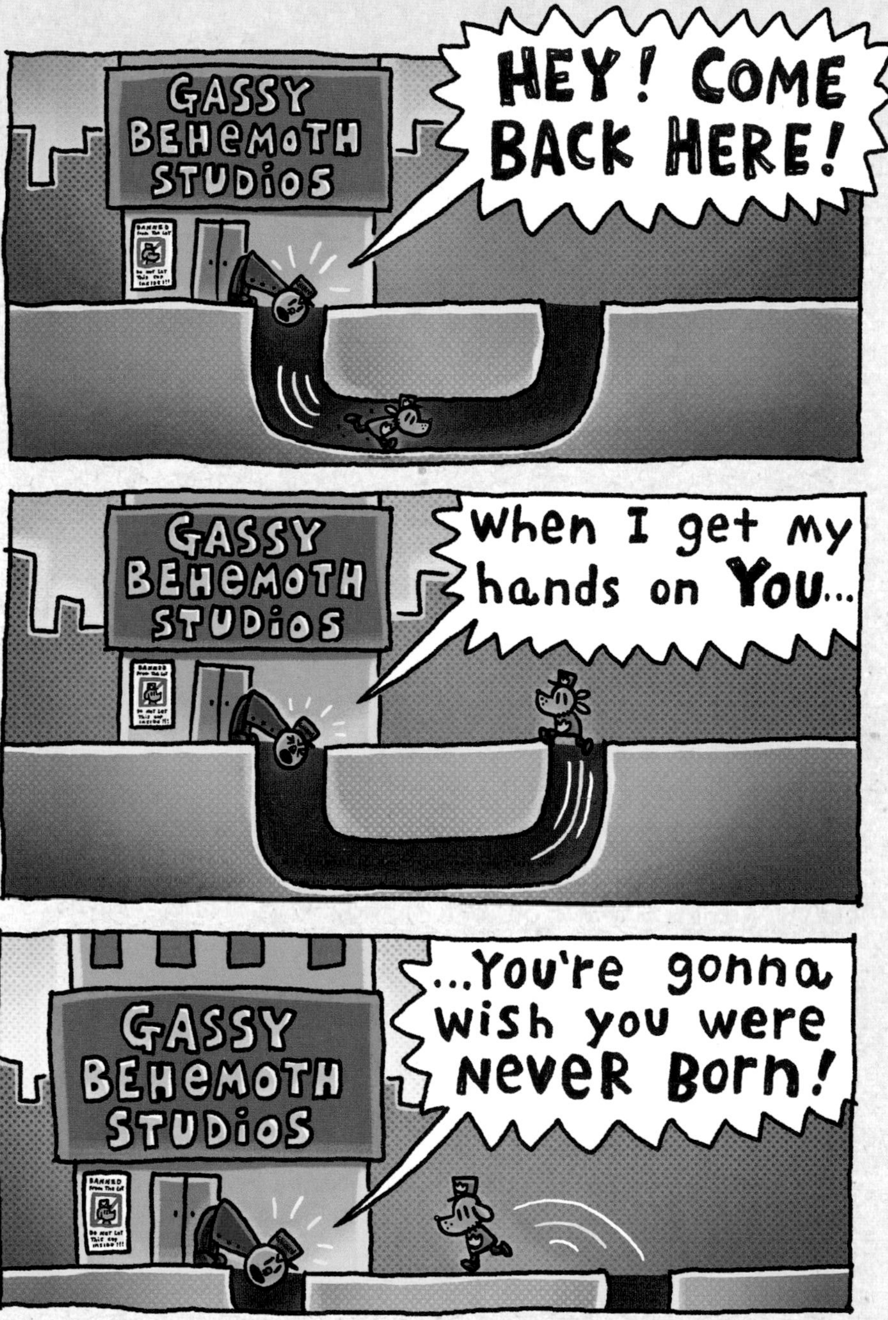
GASSY BEHEMOTH STUDIOS
HEY! COME BACK HERE!
GASSY BEHEMOTH STUDIOS
When I get my hands on YOU...
GASSY BEHEMOTH STUDIOS
...You're gonna wish you were NEVER Born!

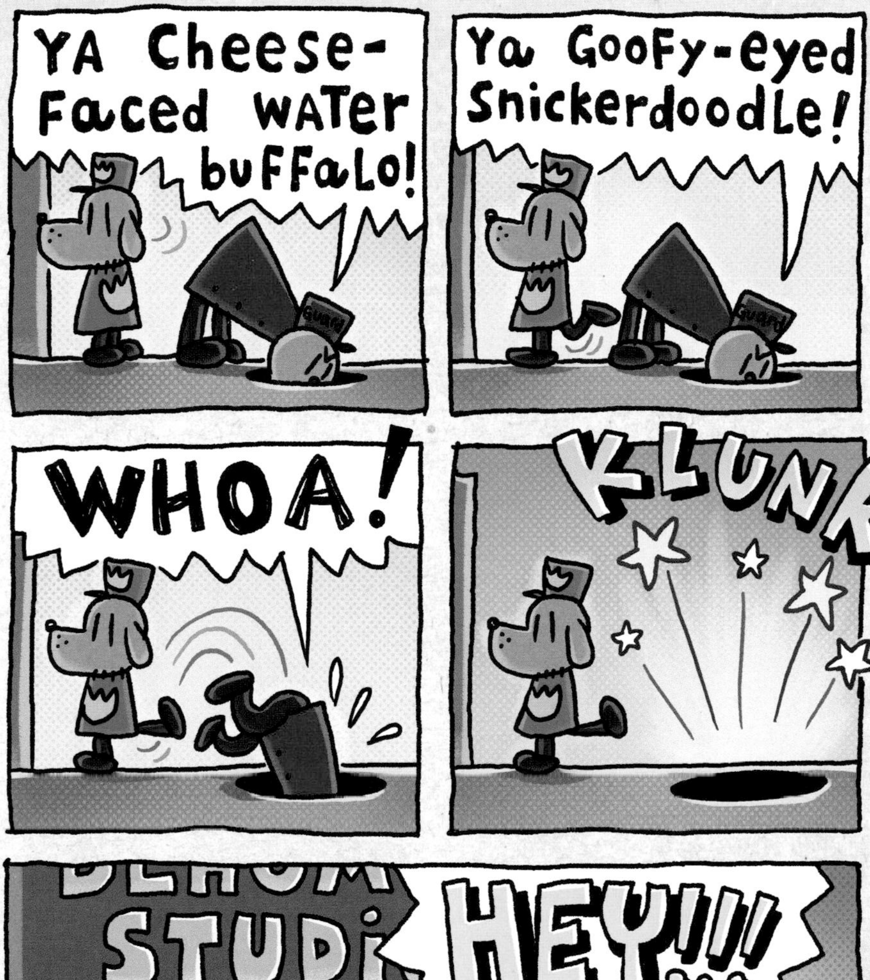
YA Cheese-Faced WATER buFFaLo!
Ya GooFy-eyed Snickerdoodle!
Guard
WHOA!
KLUNK
STUDi
HEY!!!!
BANNED From The LoT
DO NOT LET This cop inSiDE!!!

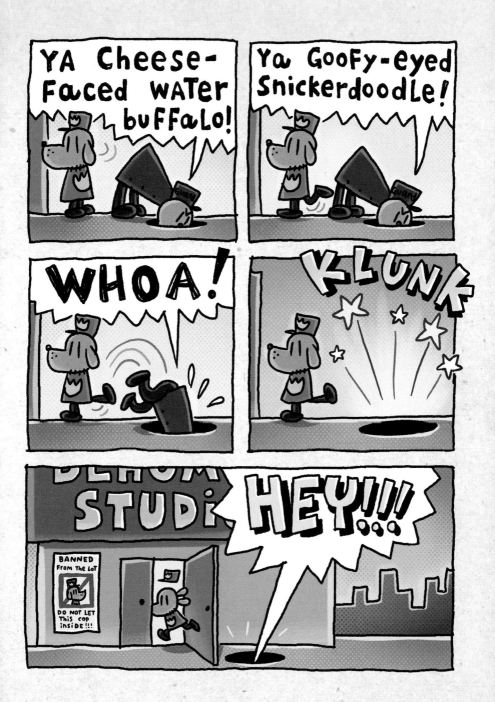

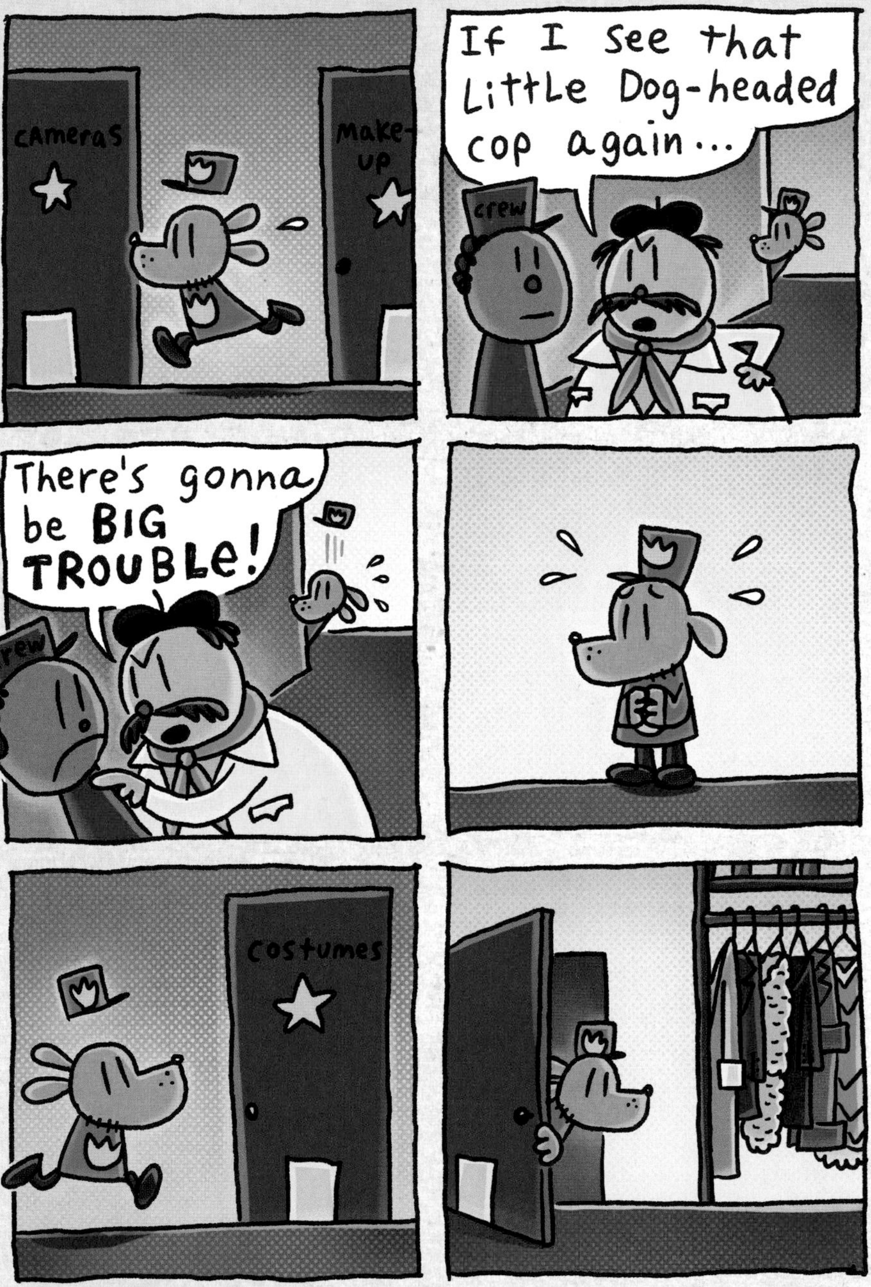
cameras
make-up
If I see that Little Dog-headed cop again...
crew
There's gonna be BIG TROUBLE!
crew
costumes

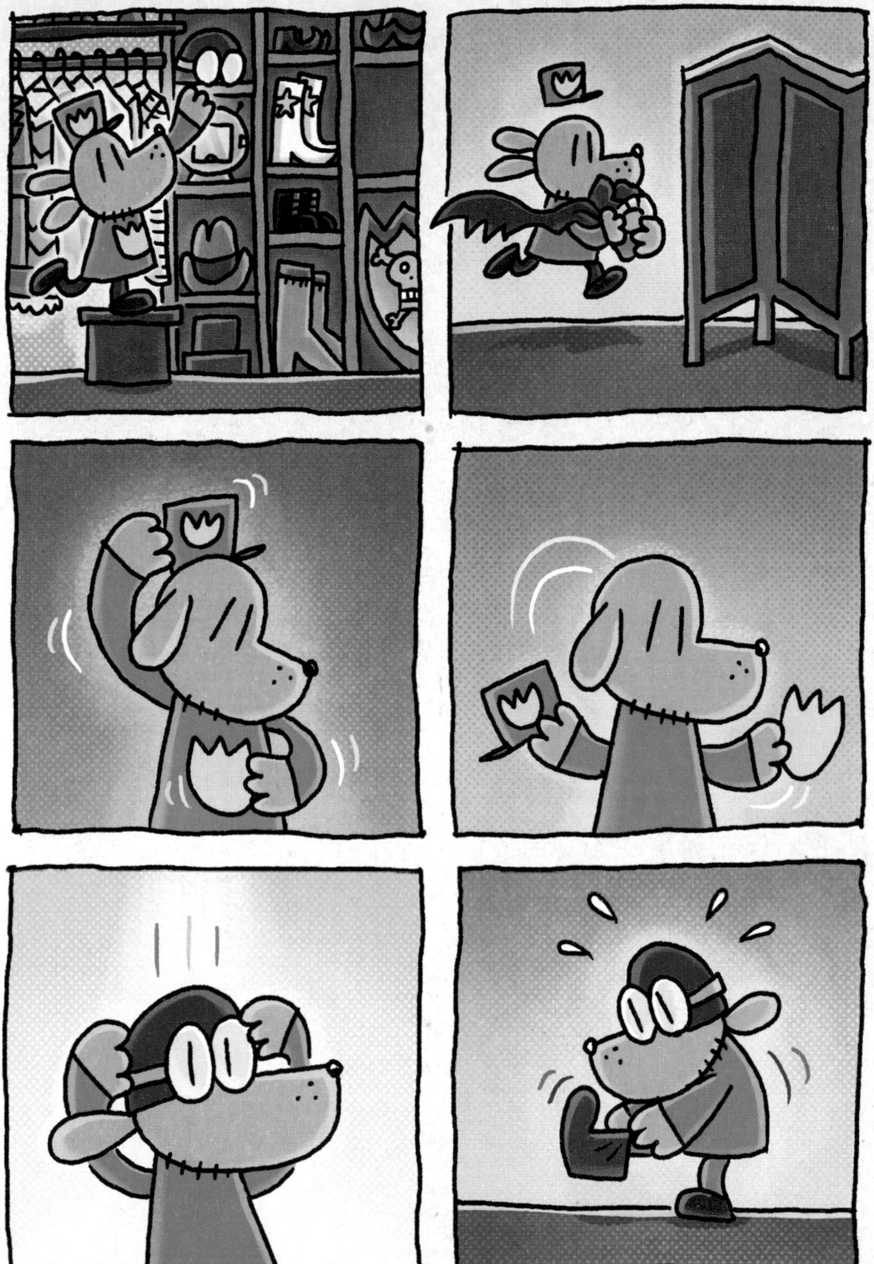

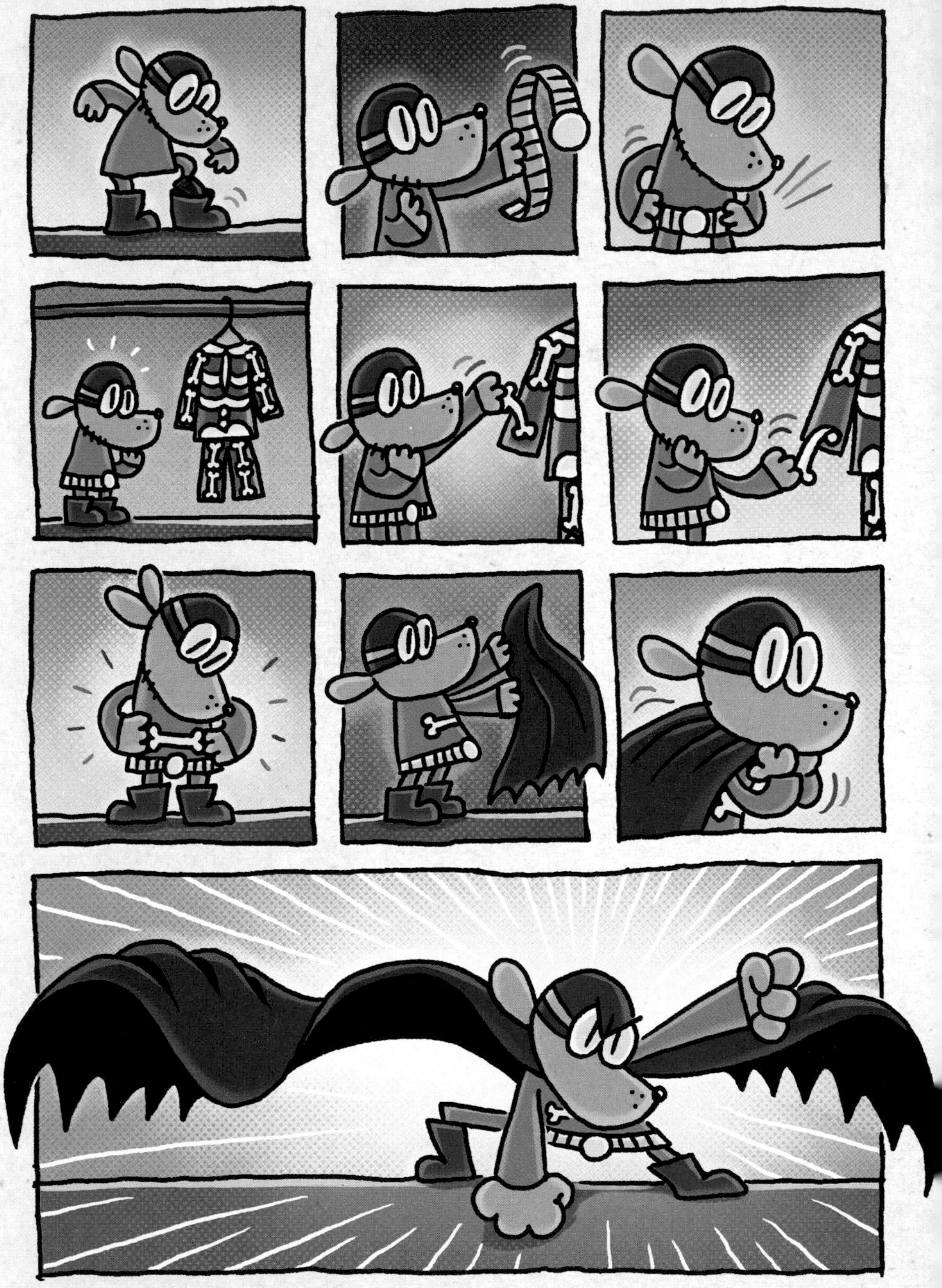

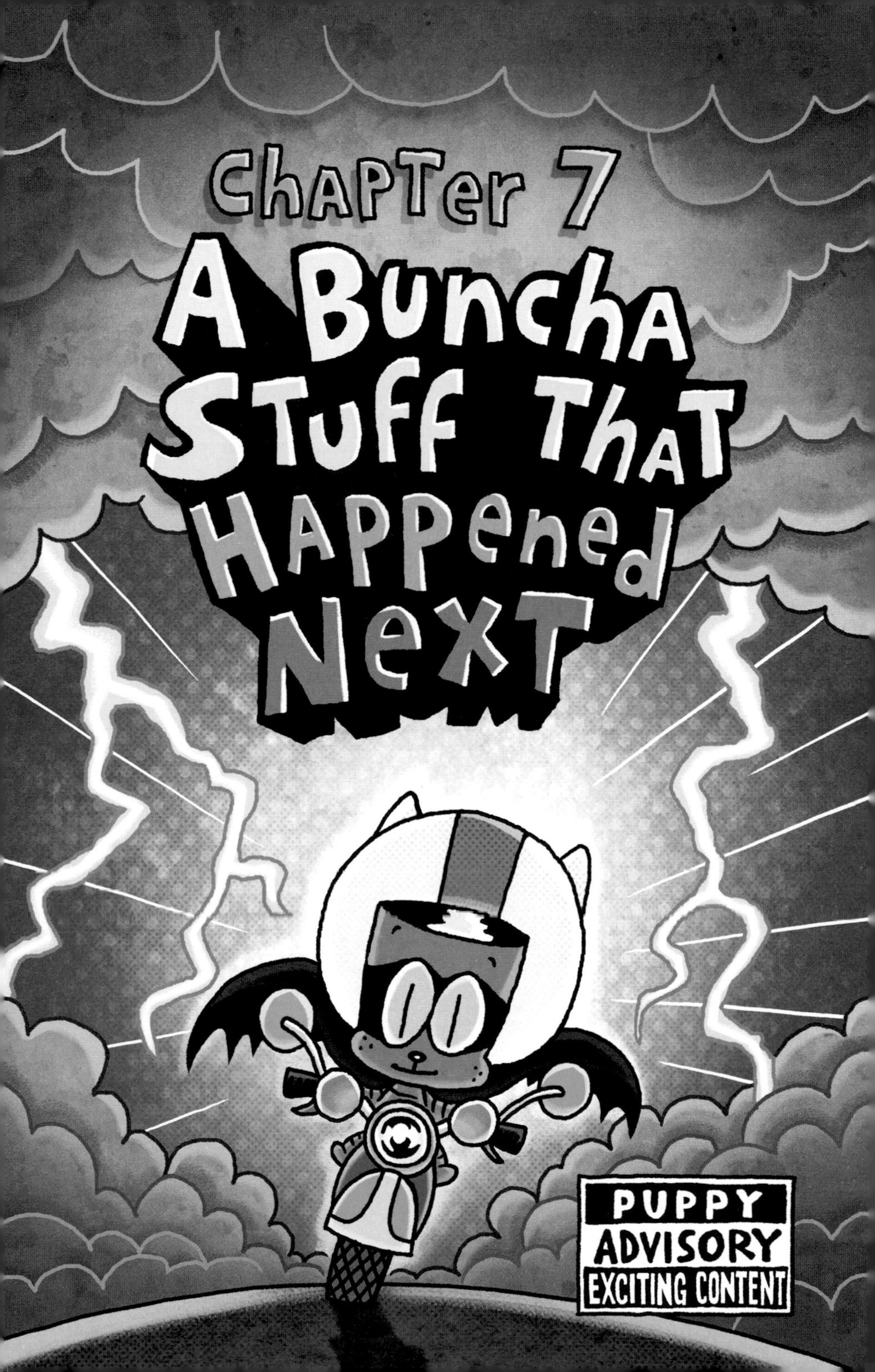
ChapTer 7
A Buncha Stuff That Happened Next
PUPPY
ADVISORY
EXCITING CONTENT

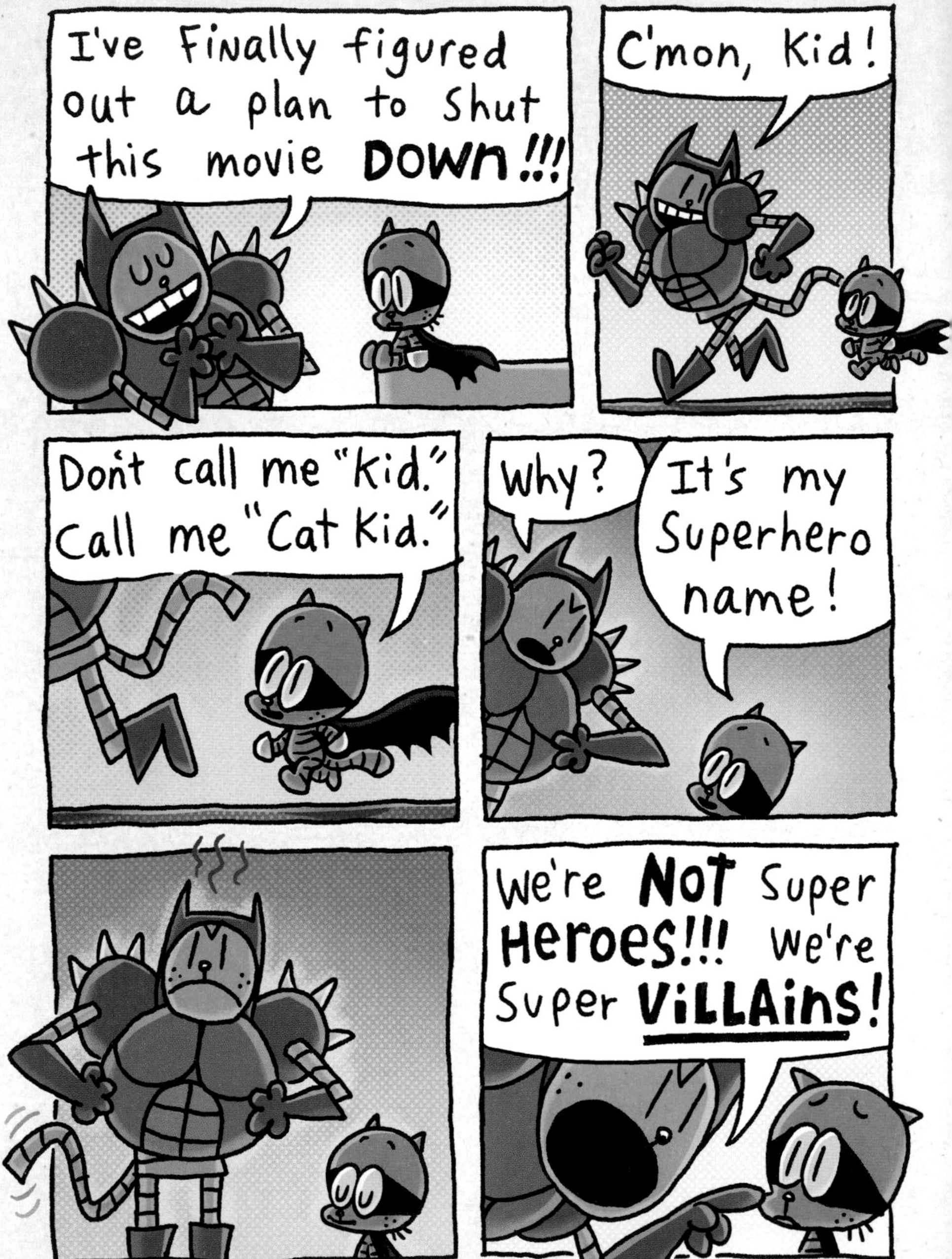
I've Finally figured out a plan to Shut this movie DOWN!!!
C'mon, Kid!
Don't call me "kid." Call me "Cat Kid."
Why?
It's my Superhero name!
We're NOT Super HEROES!!! We're Super VILLAINS!

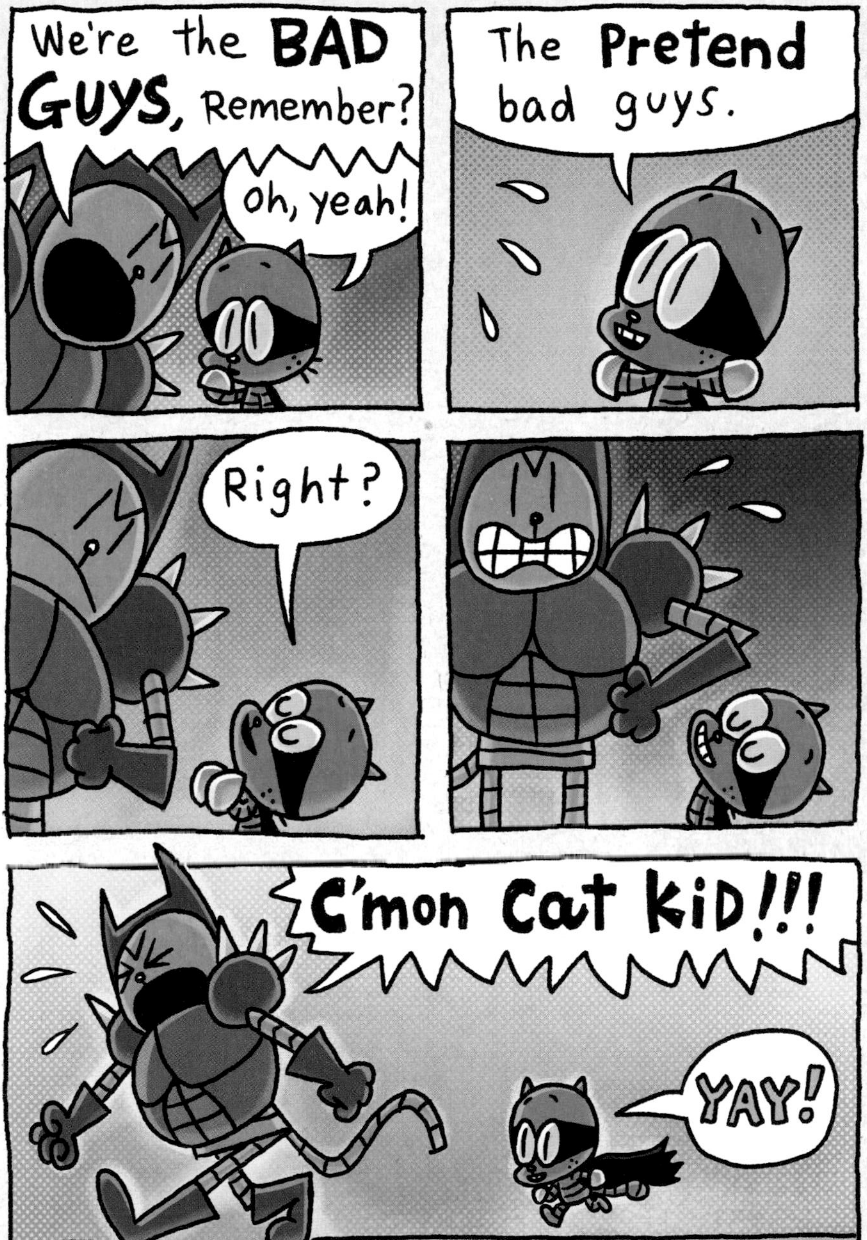
We're the BAD GUYS, Remember?
Oh, yeah!
The Pretend bad guys.
Right?
C'mon Cat KiD!!!
YAY!

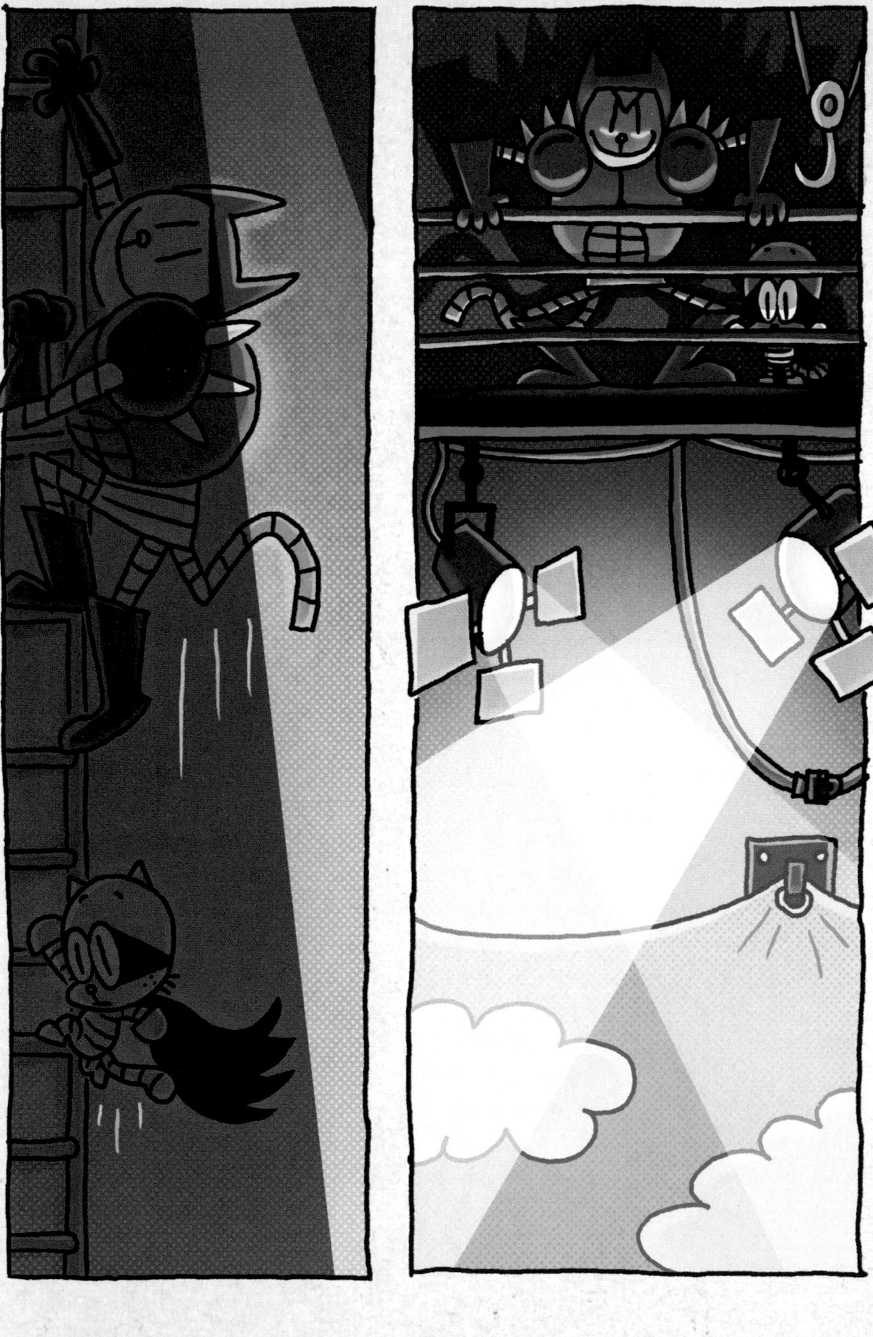

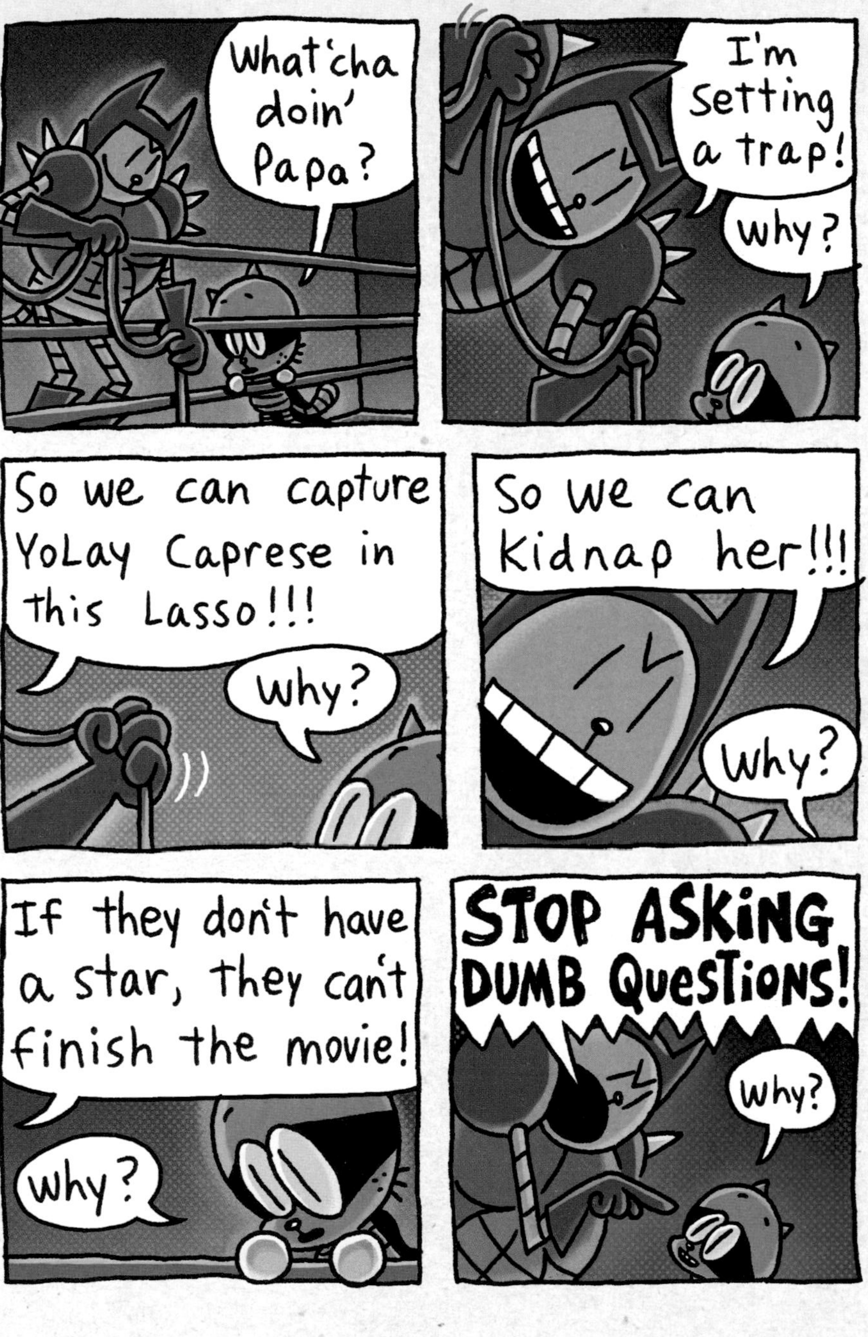
What'cha doin' Papa?
I'm setting a trap!
Why?
So we can capture YoLay Caprese in this Lasso!!!
Why?
So we can Kidnap her!!!
Why?
If they don't have a star, they can't finish the movie!
Why?
STOP ASKING DUMB QUESTIONS!
Why?

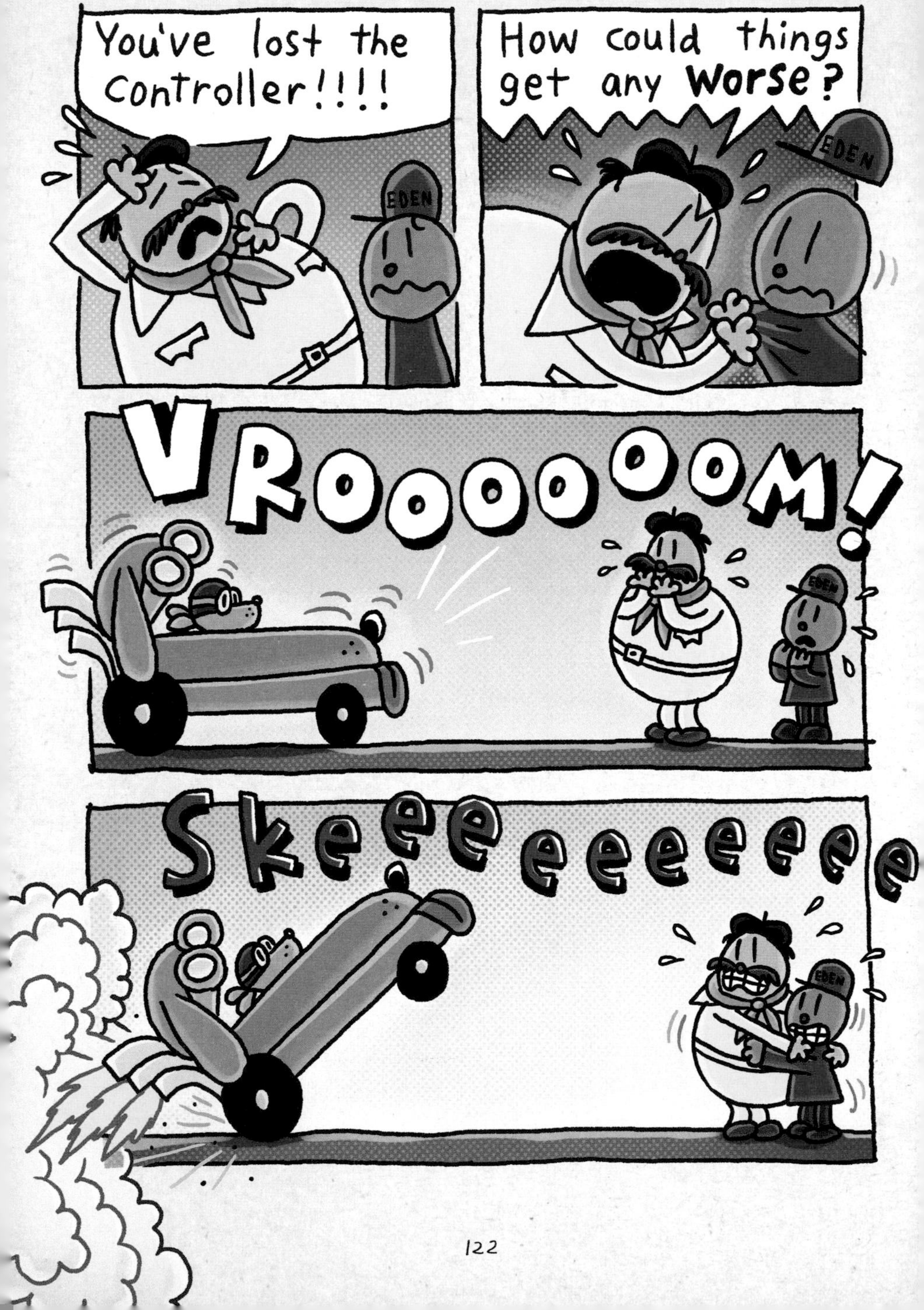
You've lost the controller!!!!
EDEN
How could things get any **worse**?
EDEN
VROOOOOOM!
EDEN
Skeeeeeeeeee
EDEN

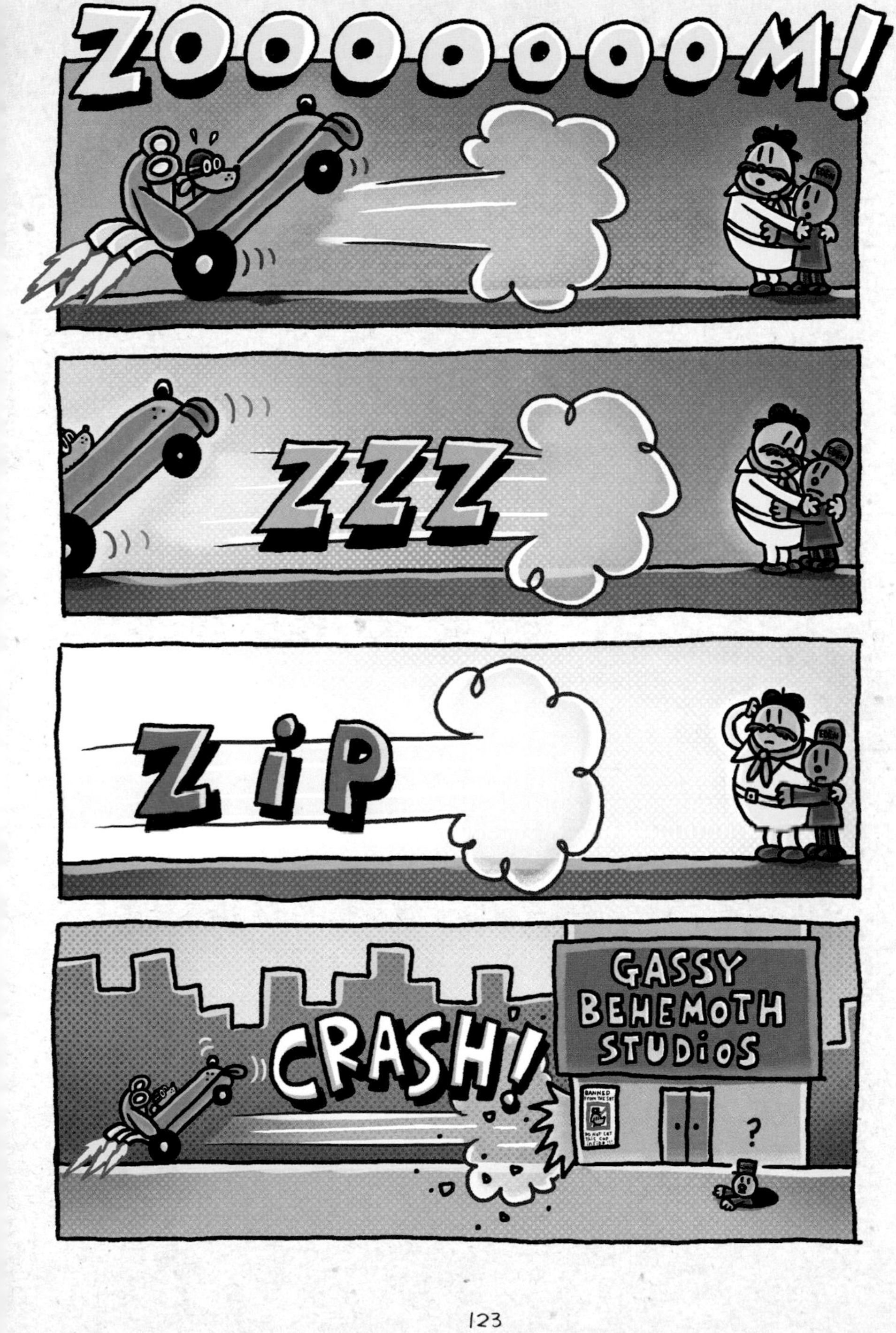
ZOOOOOOOM!
ZZZ
ZiP
CRASH!
GASSY BEHEMOTH STUDIOS
BANNED FROM THE SET
DO NOT LET THIS COP INSIDE!!!
?

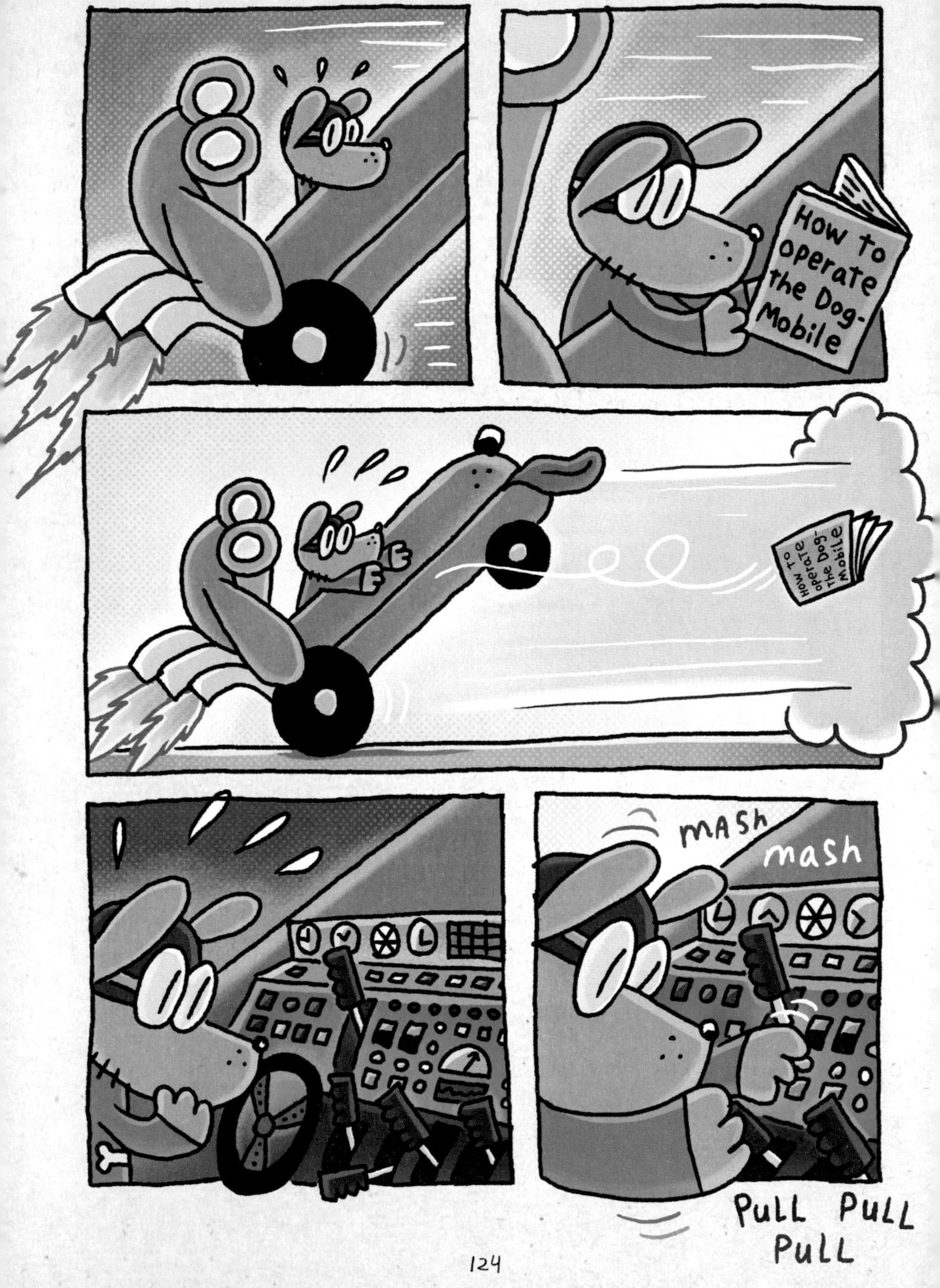
How to operate the Dog-Mobile
How to operate the Dog-Mobile
MASh
mash
PULL PULL
PULL

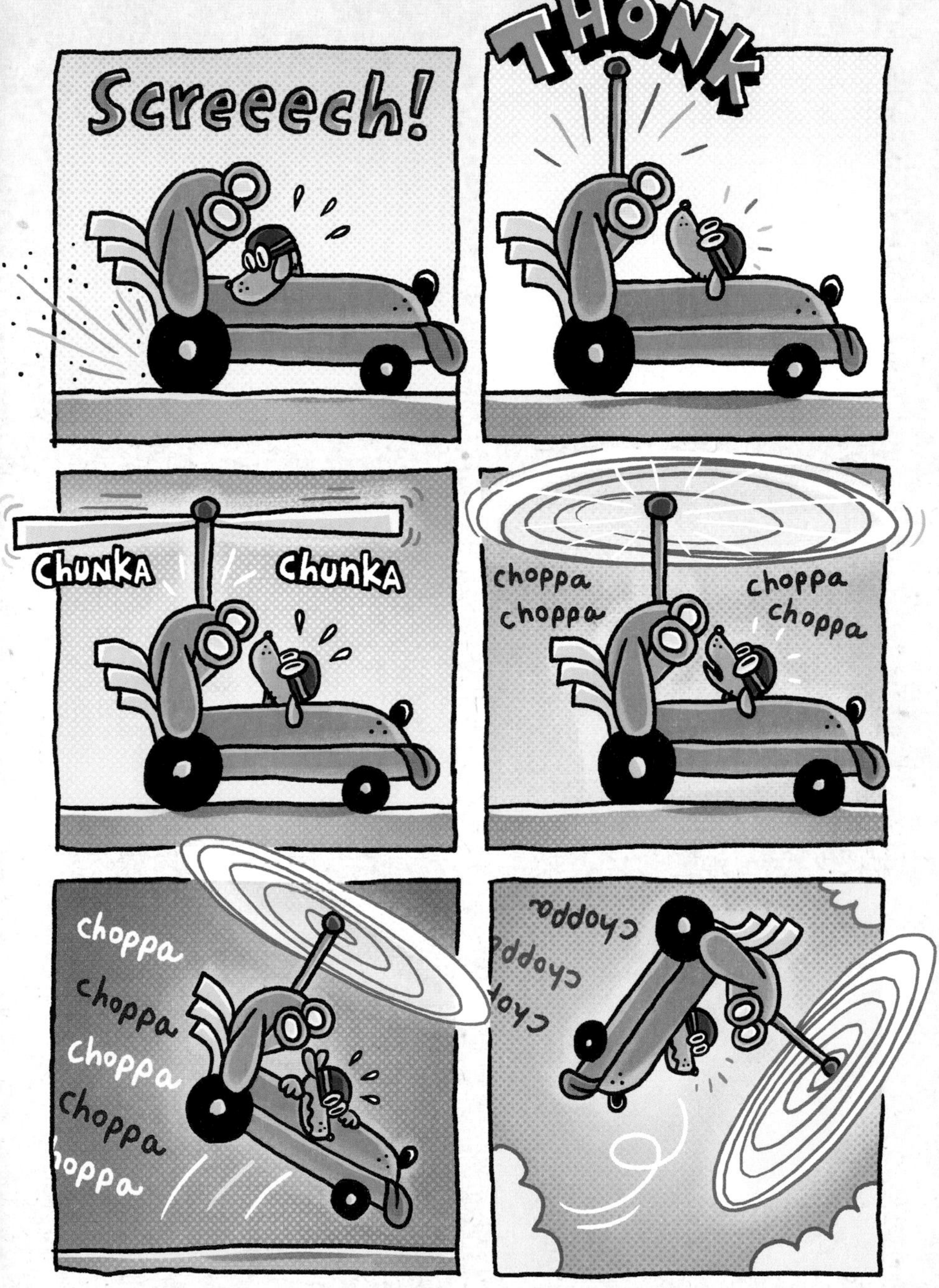
Screeech!
THONK
CHUNKA
CHUNKA
choppa
choppa
choppa
choppa
choppa
choppa
choppa
choppa
choppa
hoppa
choppa
choppa
chop

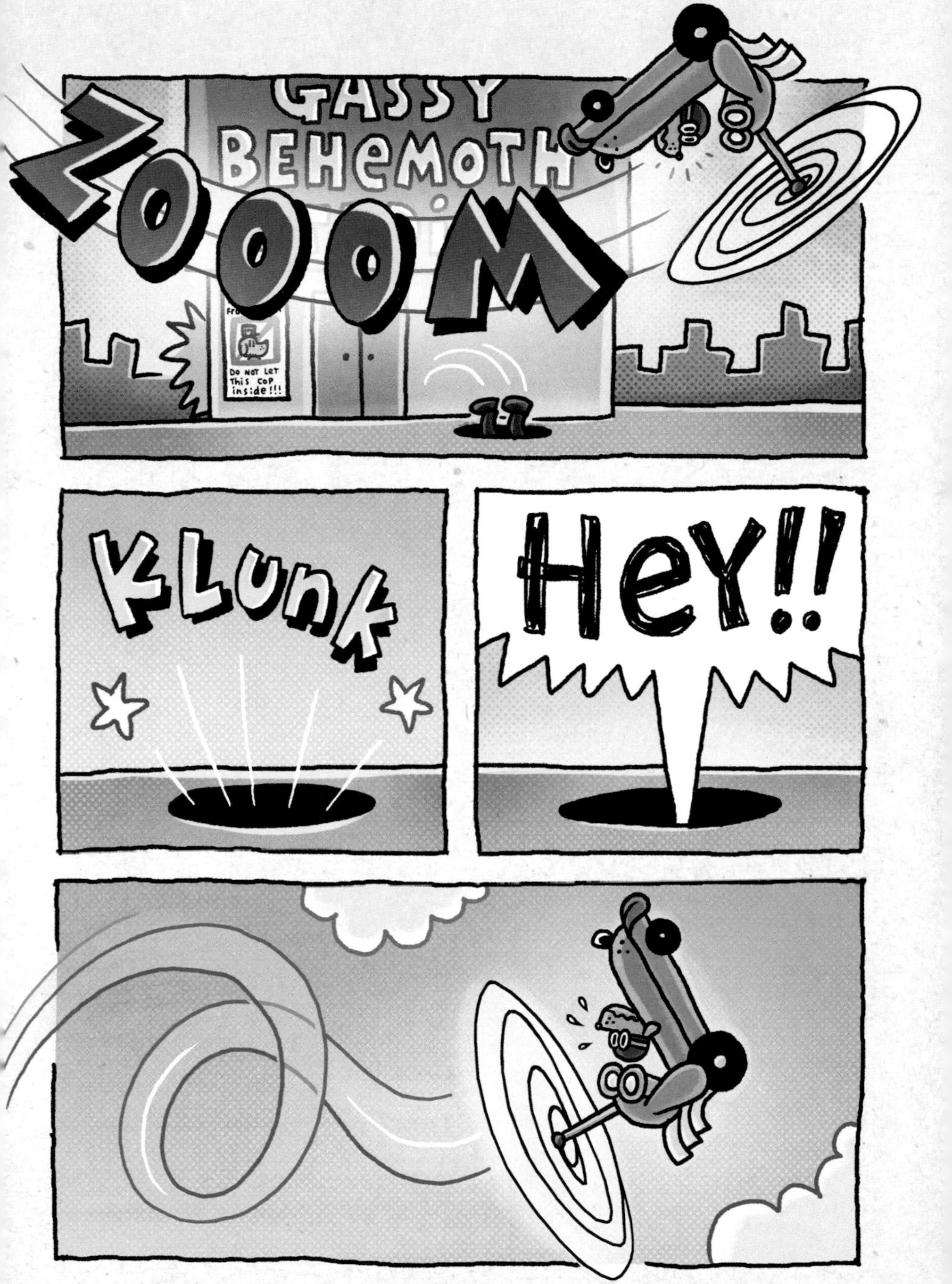
GASSY
BEHEMOTH
ZOOOM
DO NOT LET THIS COP inside!!!
KLUNK
HEY!!

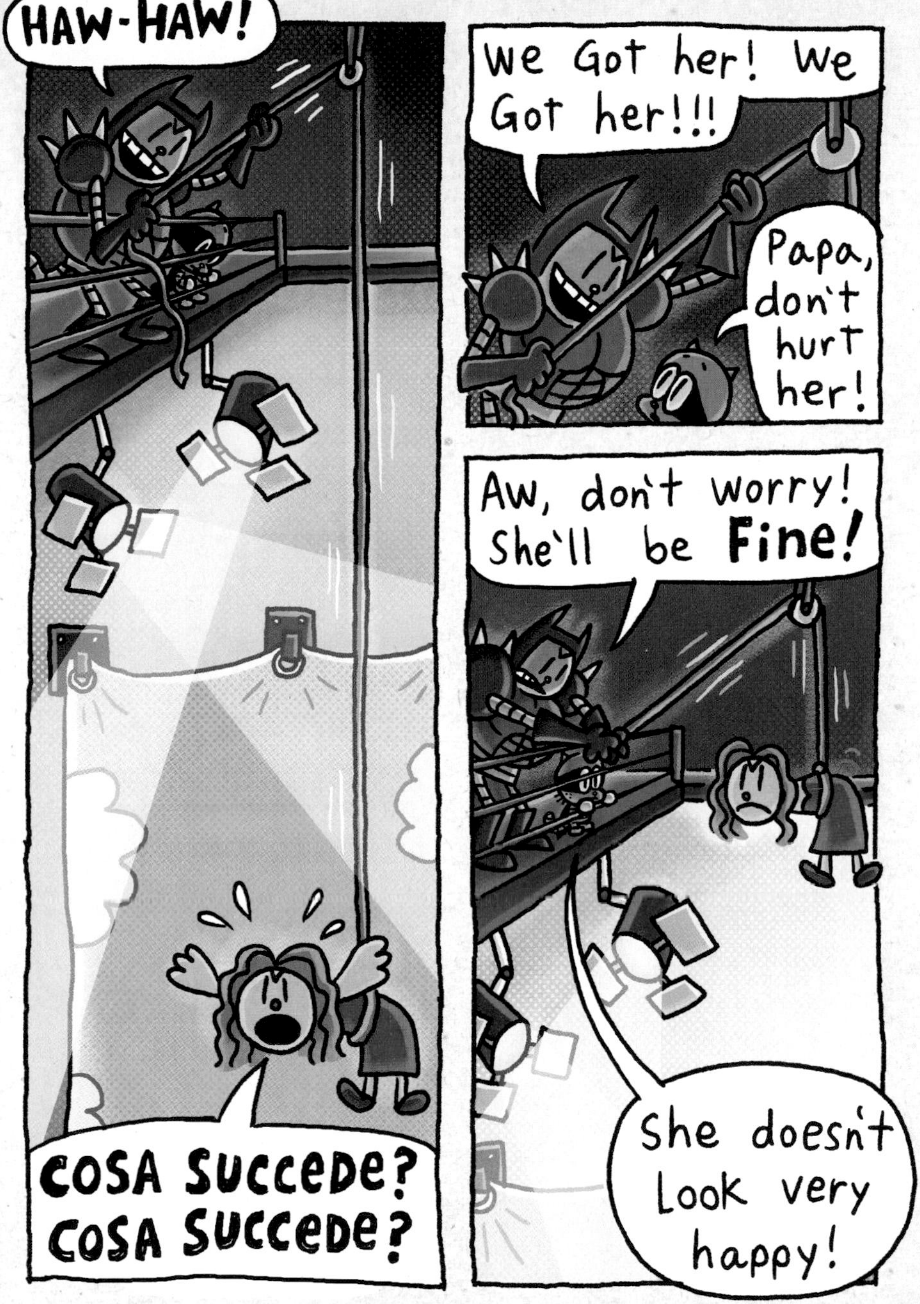
HAW-HAW!
COSA SUCCEDE? COSA SUCCEDE?
We Got her! We Got her!!!
Papa, don't hurt her!
Aw, don't worry! She'll be Fine!
She doesn't Look very happy!

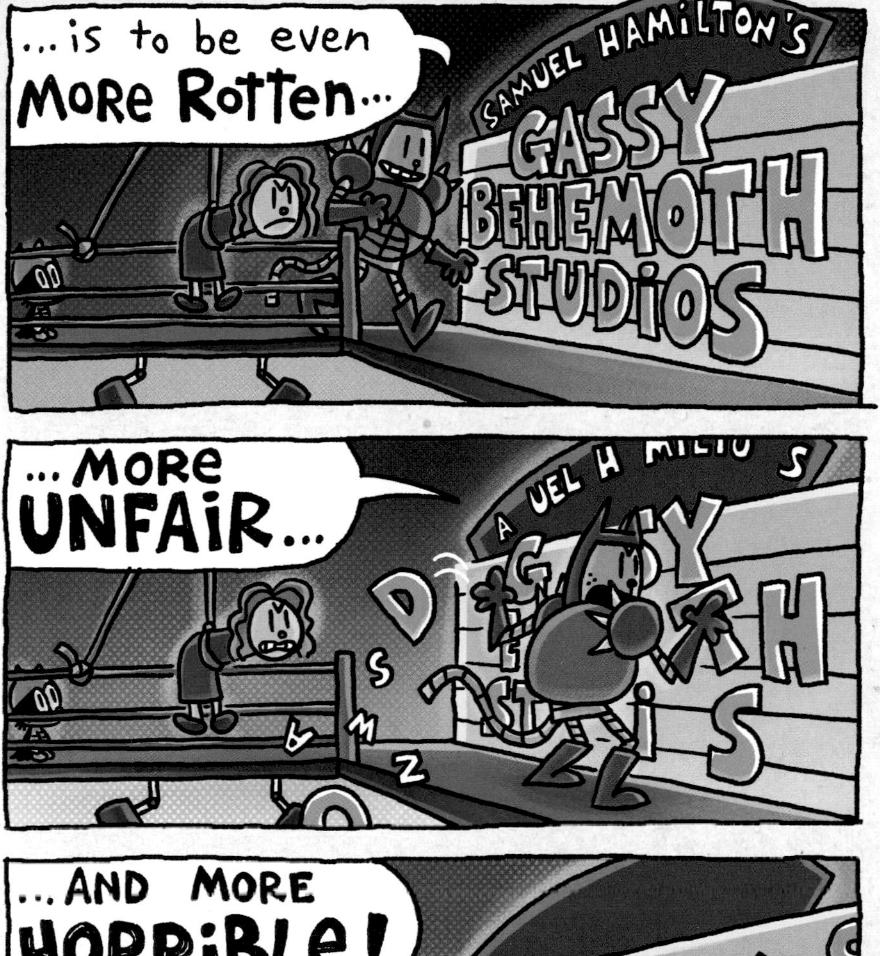
...is to be even MORE ROTTEN...
SAMUEL HAMILTON'S
GASSY BEHEMOTH STUDIOS
...MORE UNFAIR...
...AND MORE HORRIBLE!

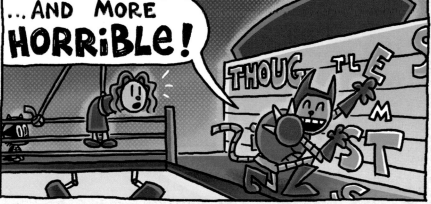

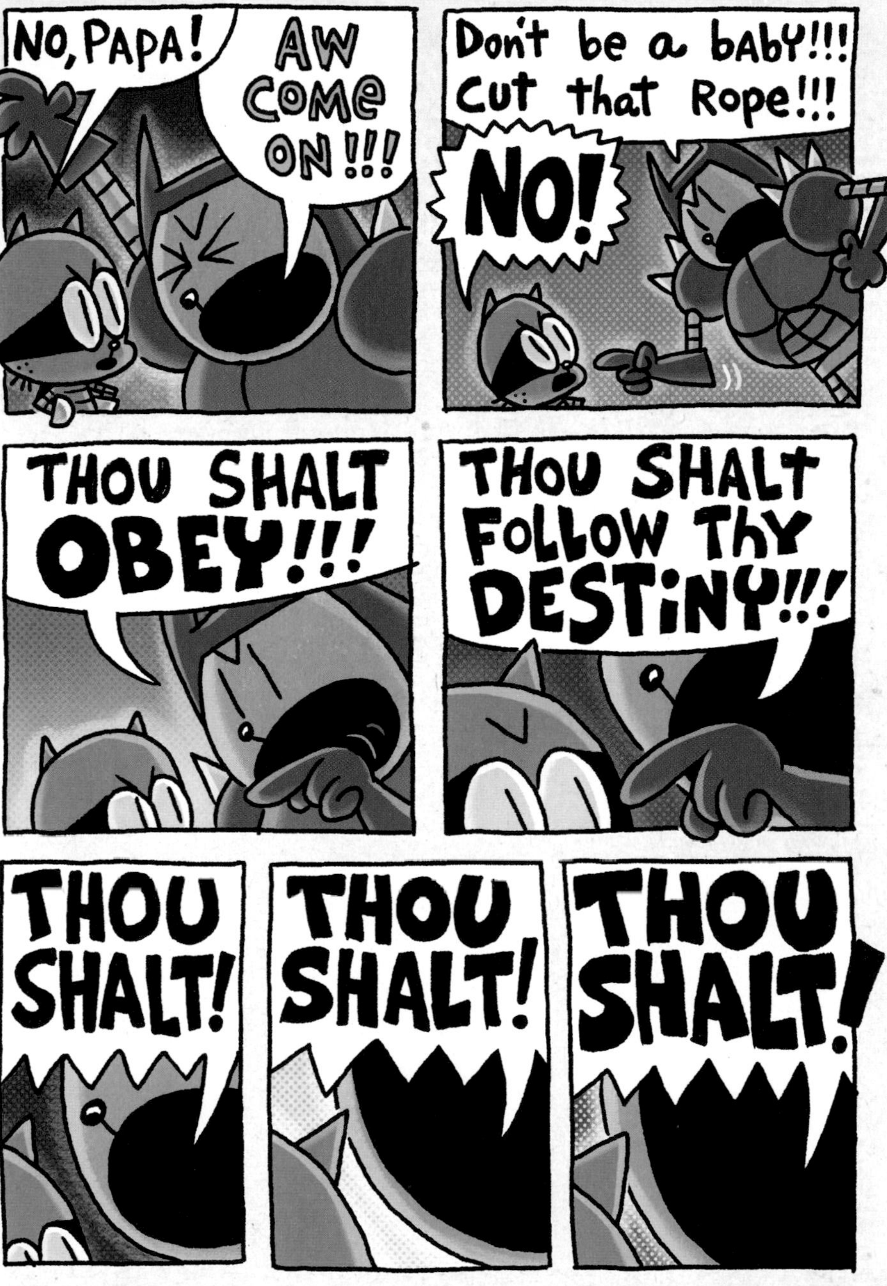
NO, PAPA!
AW COME ON!!!
Don't be a baby!!! Cut that Rope!!!
NO!
THOU SHALT OBEY!!!
THOU SHALT FOLLOW THY DESTINY!!!
THOU SHALT!
THOU SHALT!
THOU SHALT!

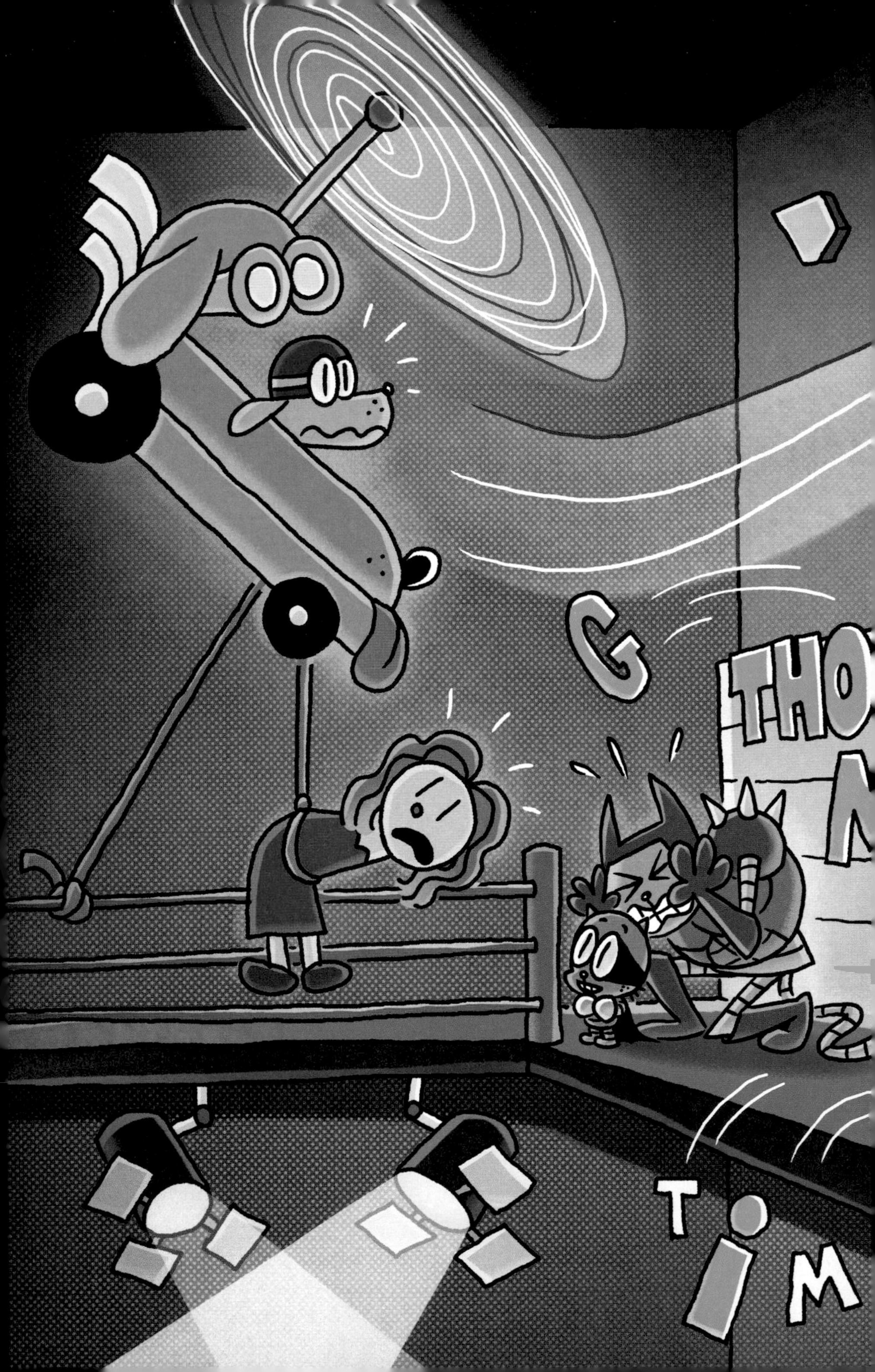
G
THO
M
T
i
M

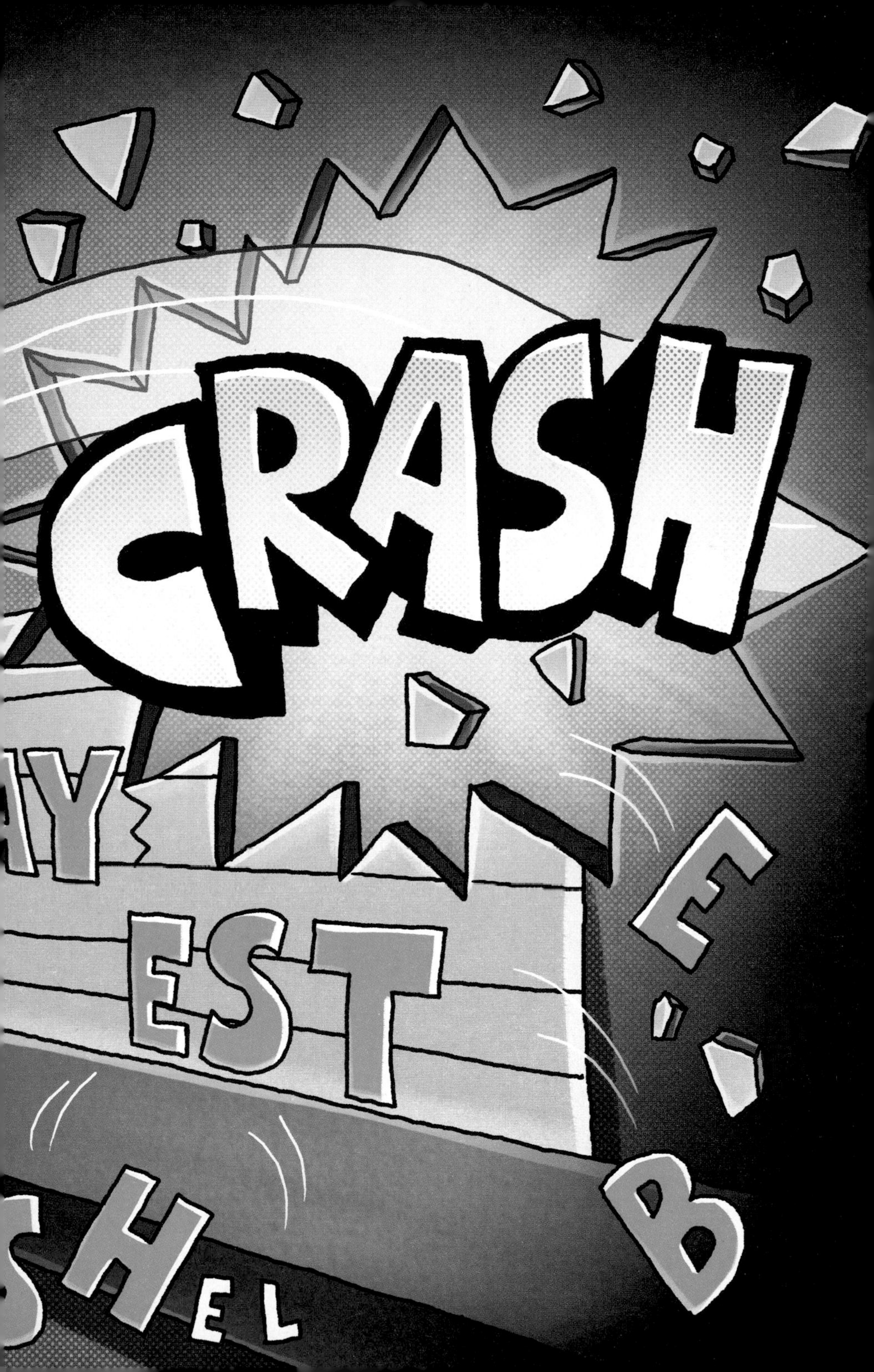
CRASH
AY
EST
E
B
SHEL

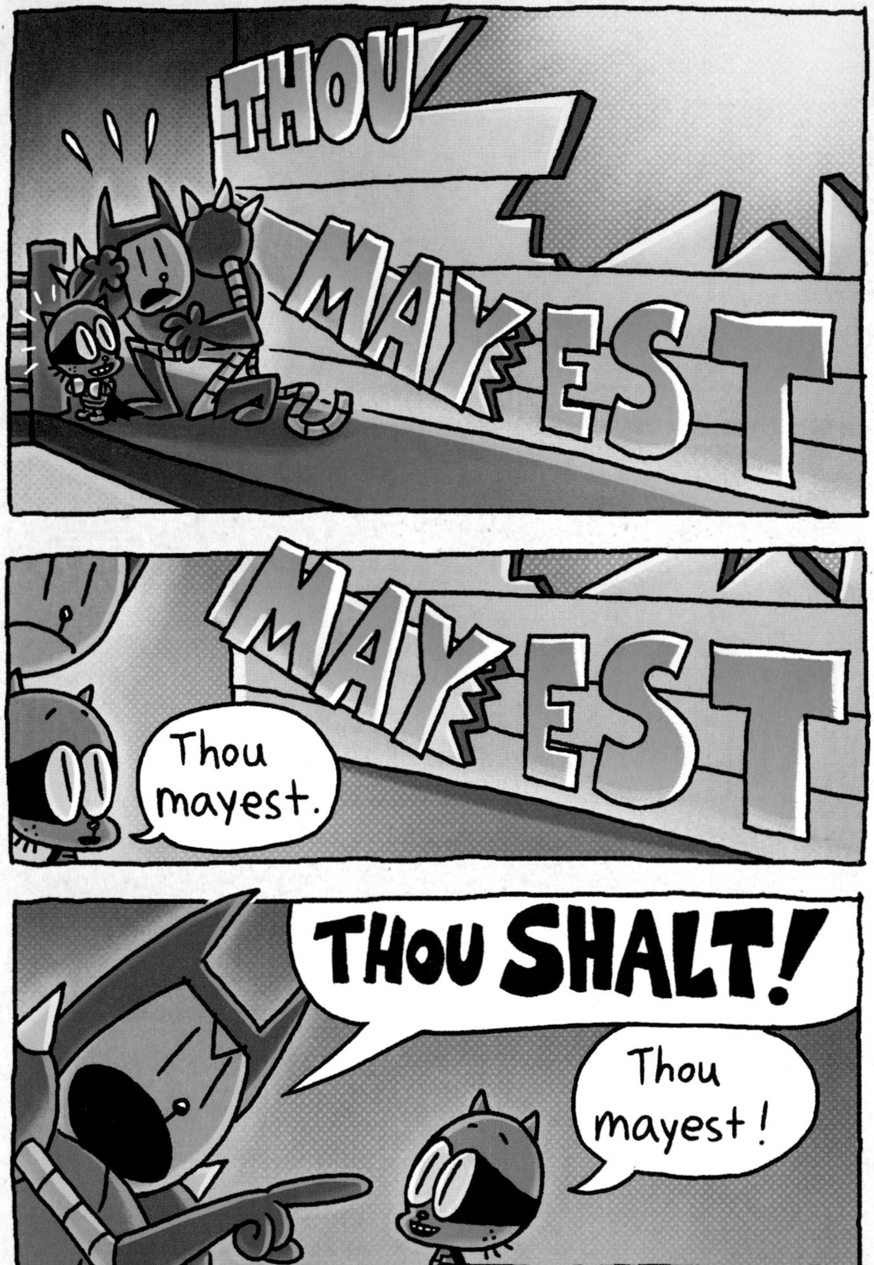
THOU
MAYEST
MAYEST
Thou mayest.
THOU SHALT!
Thou mayest!

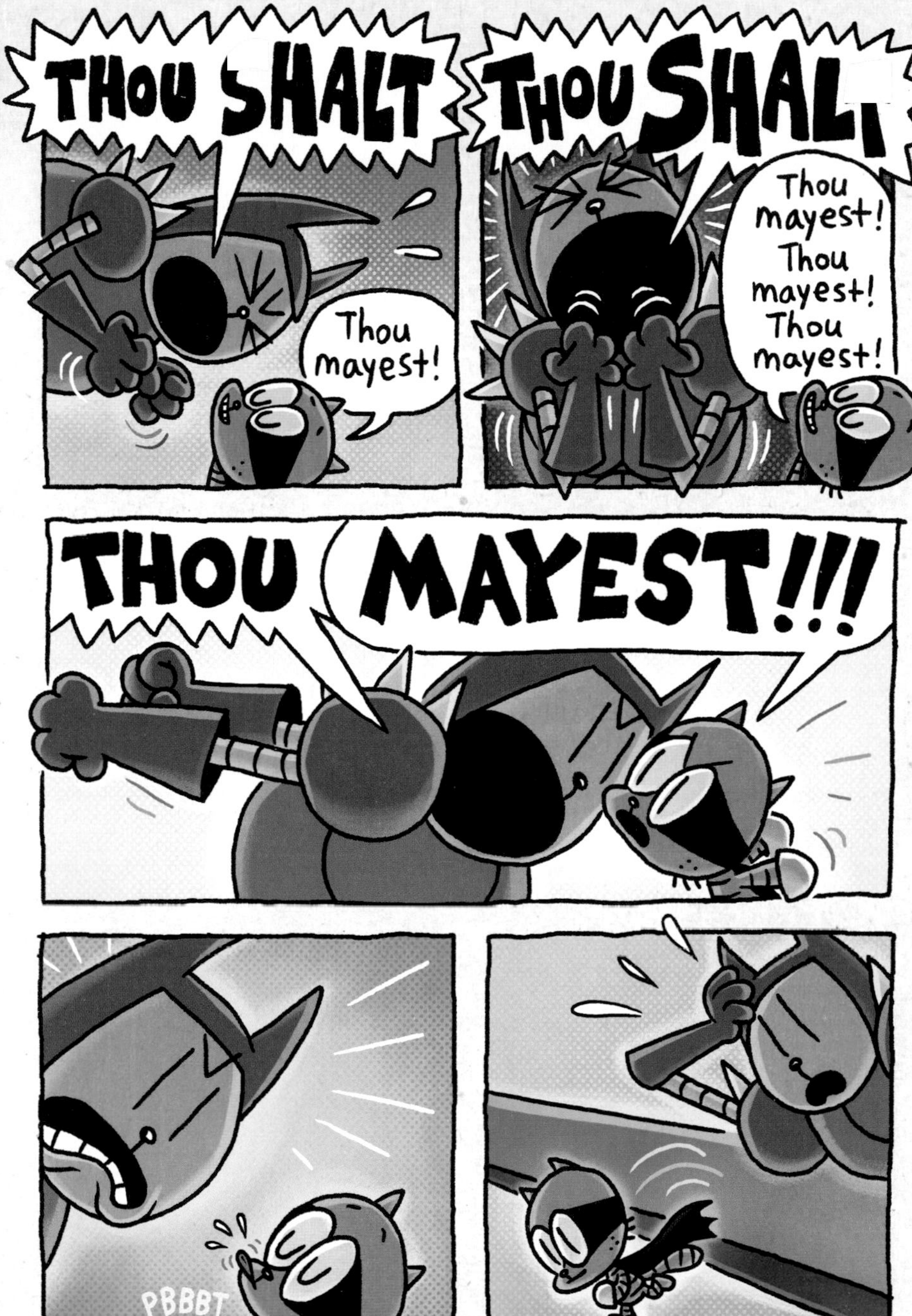
THOU SHALT
Thou mayest!
THOU SHALT
Thou mayest! Thou mayest! Thou mayest!
THOU MAYEST!!!
PBBBT

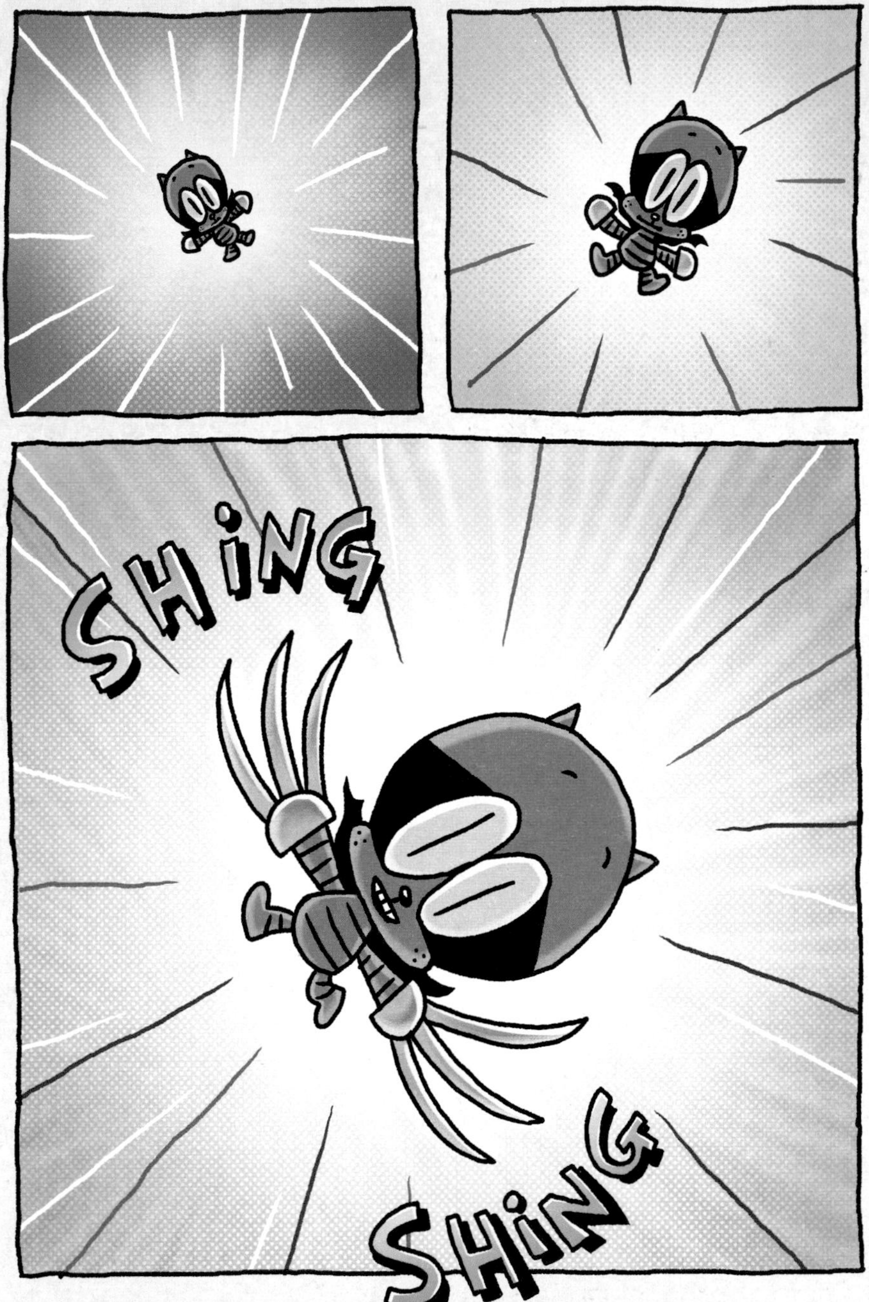
SHiNG
SHiNG

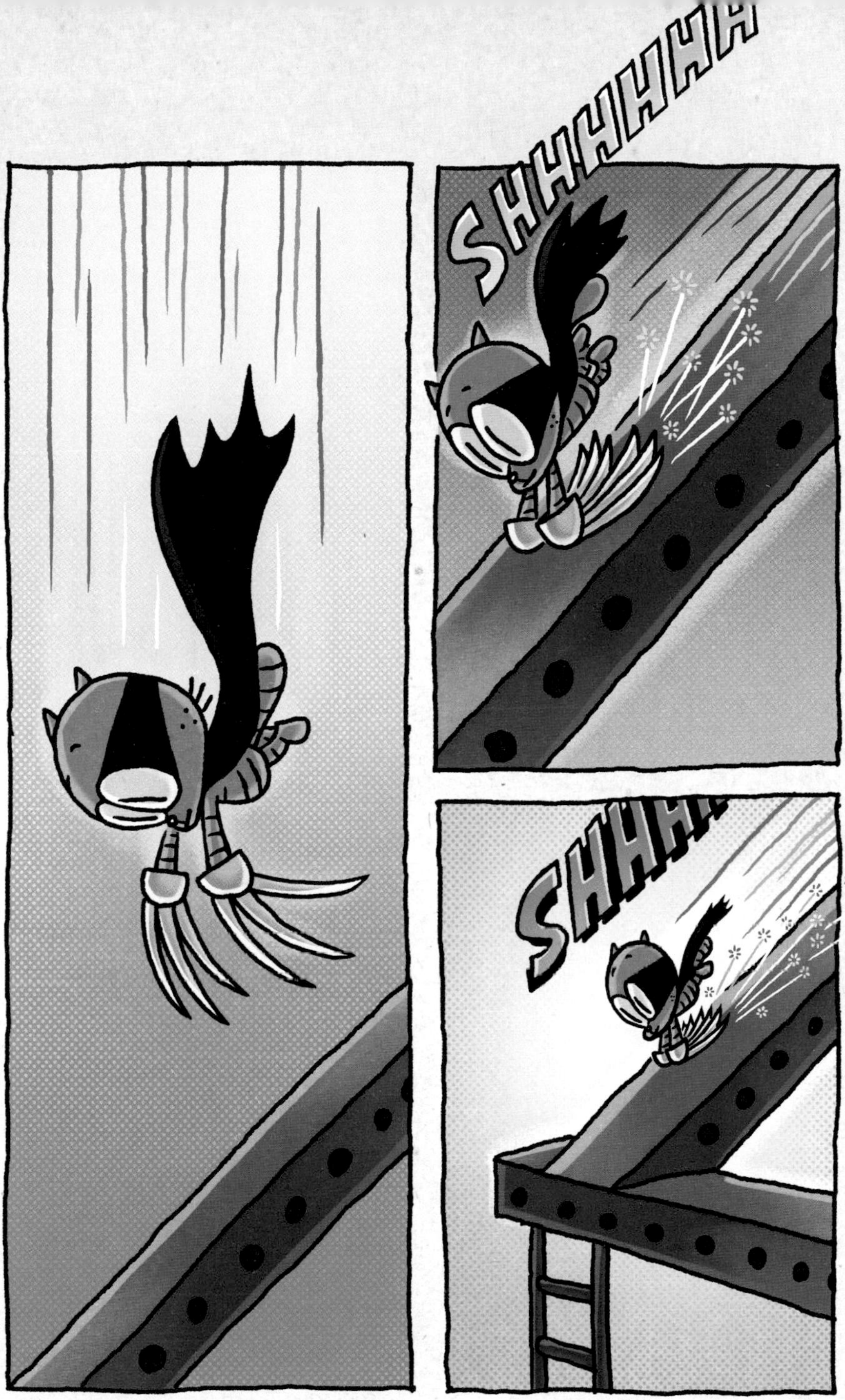
SHHHHHHA
SHHH

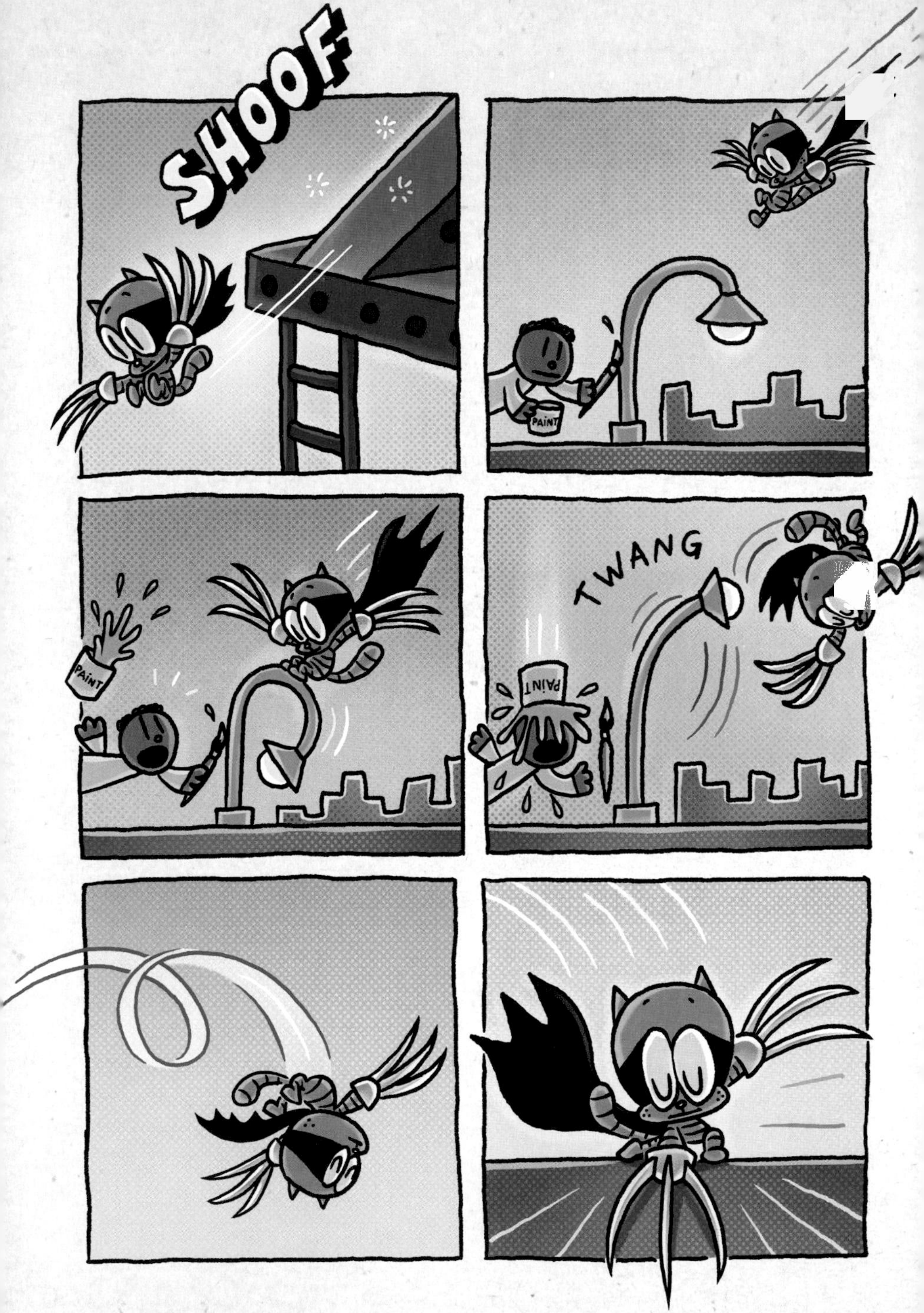
SHOOF
PAINT
PAINT
TWANG
PAINT

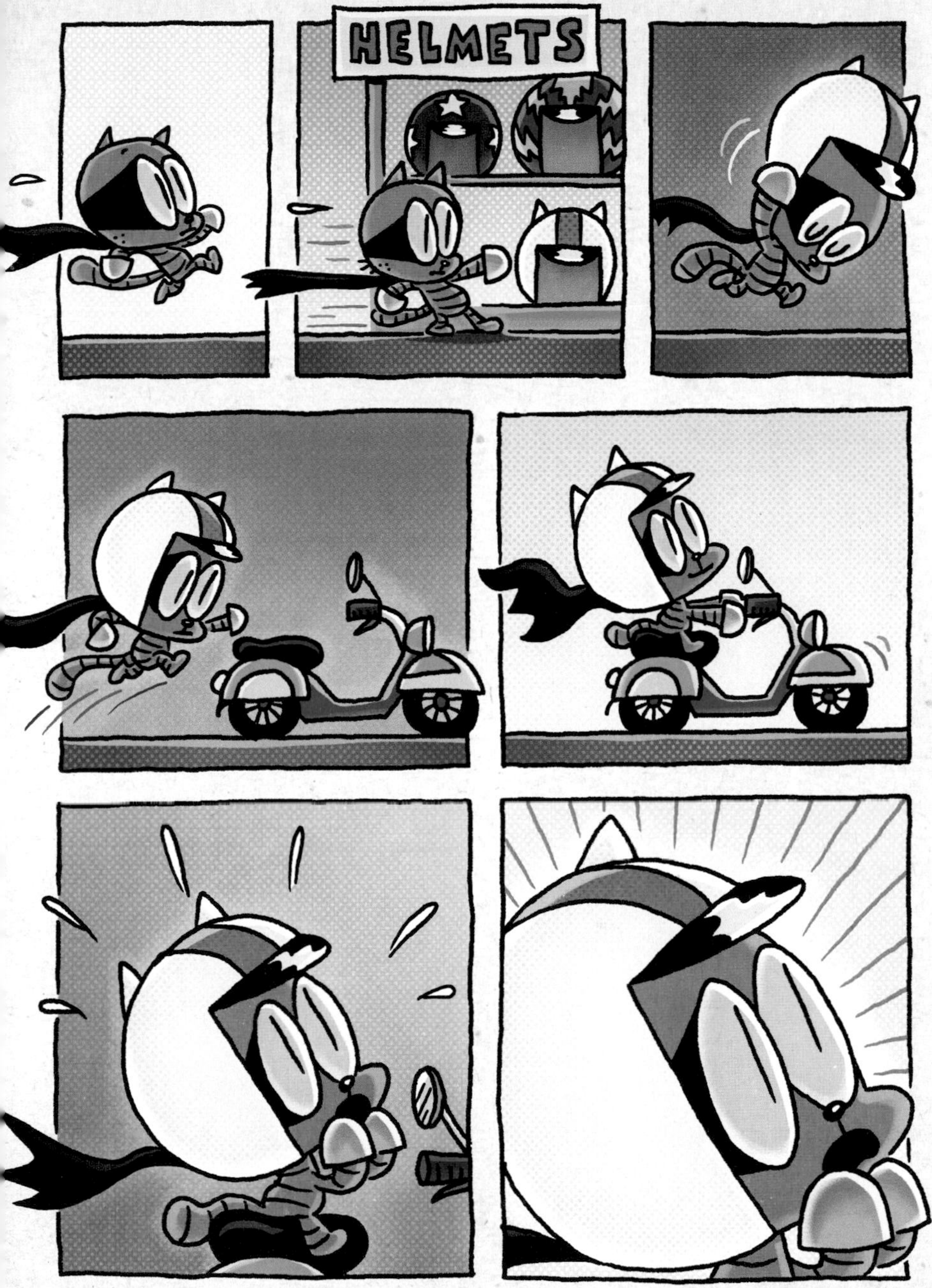
HELMETS

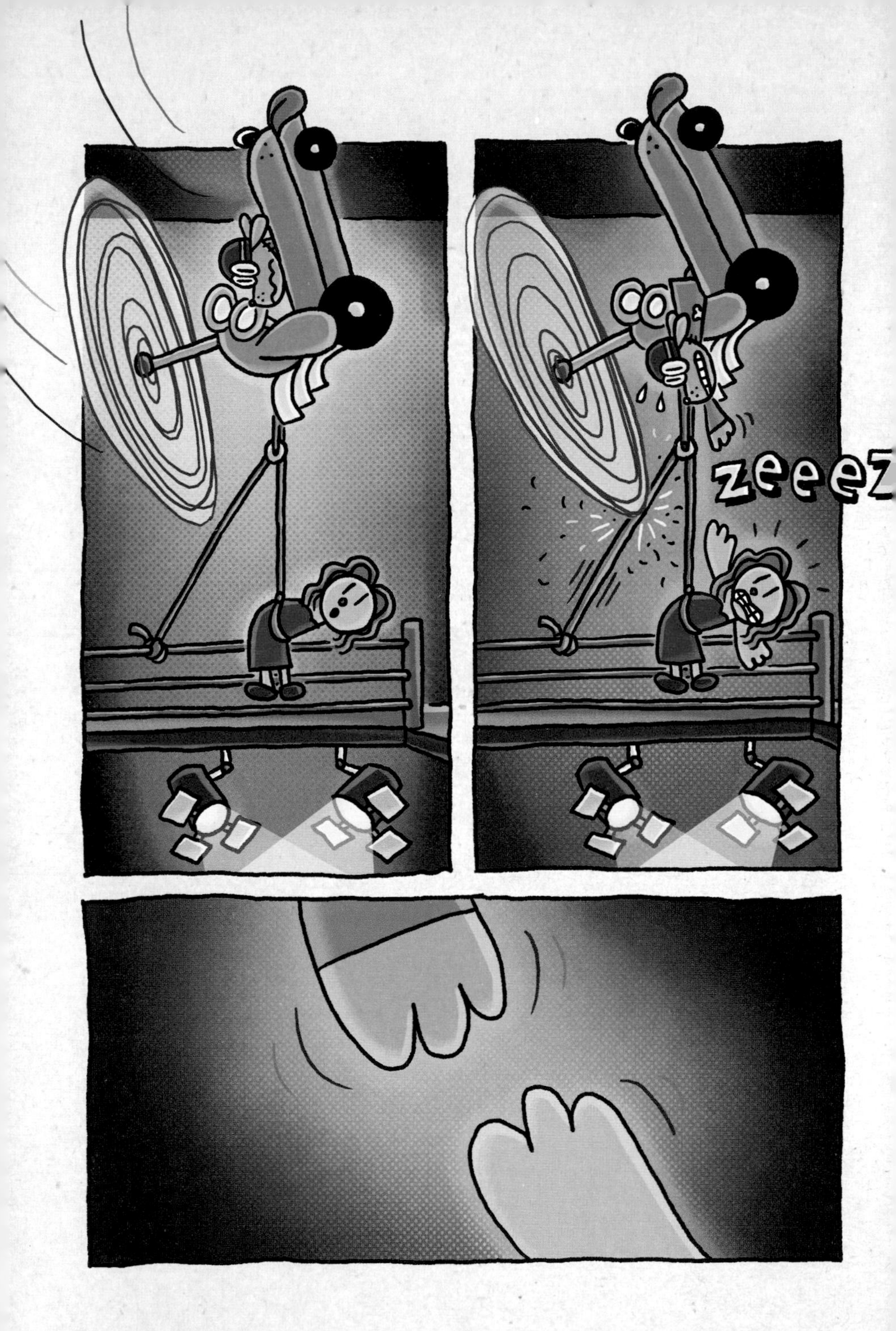
zeeez

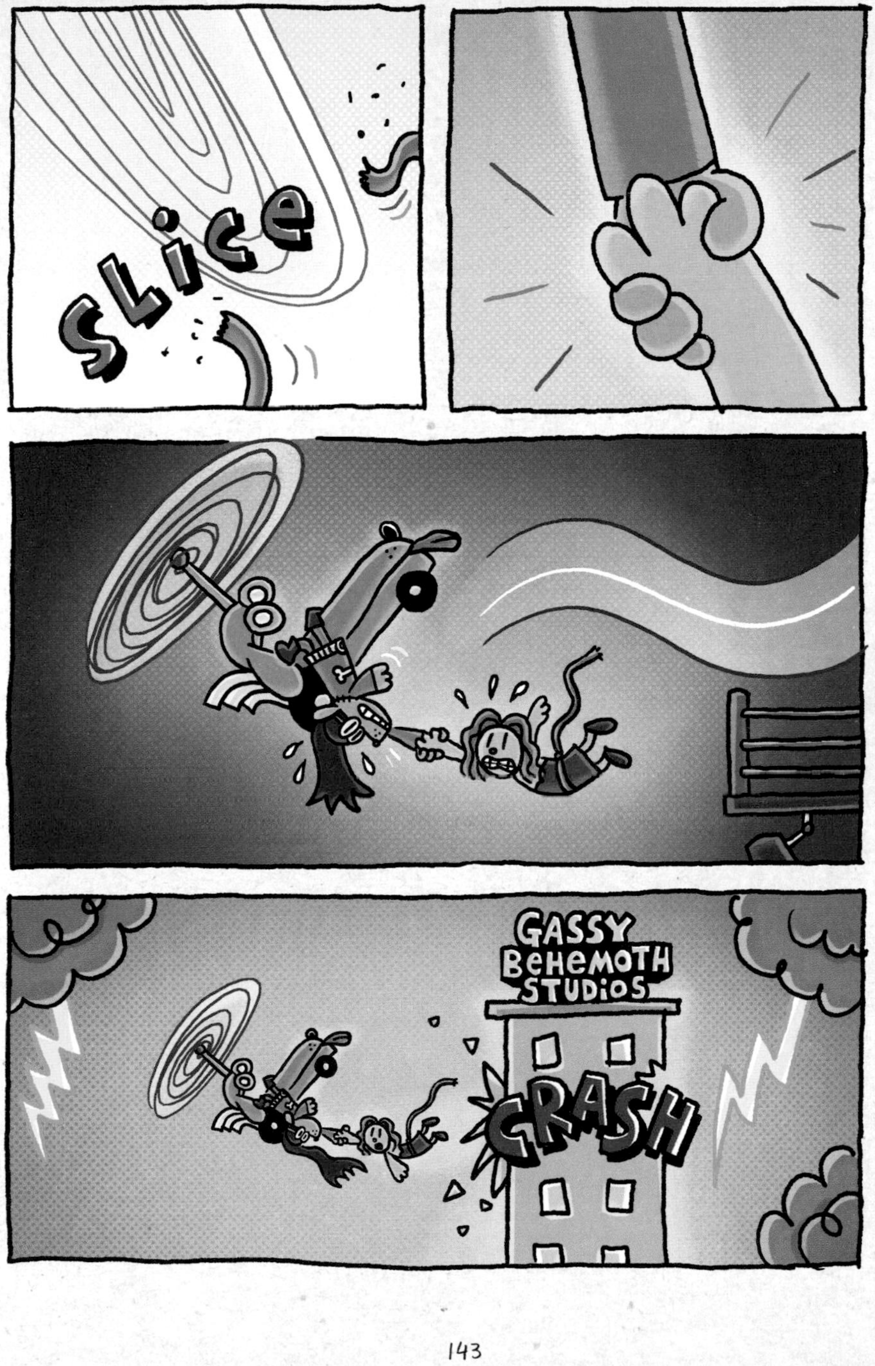
SLICE
GASSY BEHEMOTH STUDIOS
CRASH

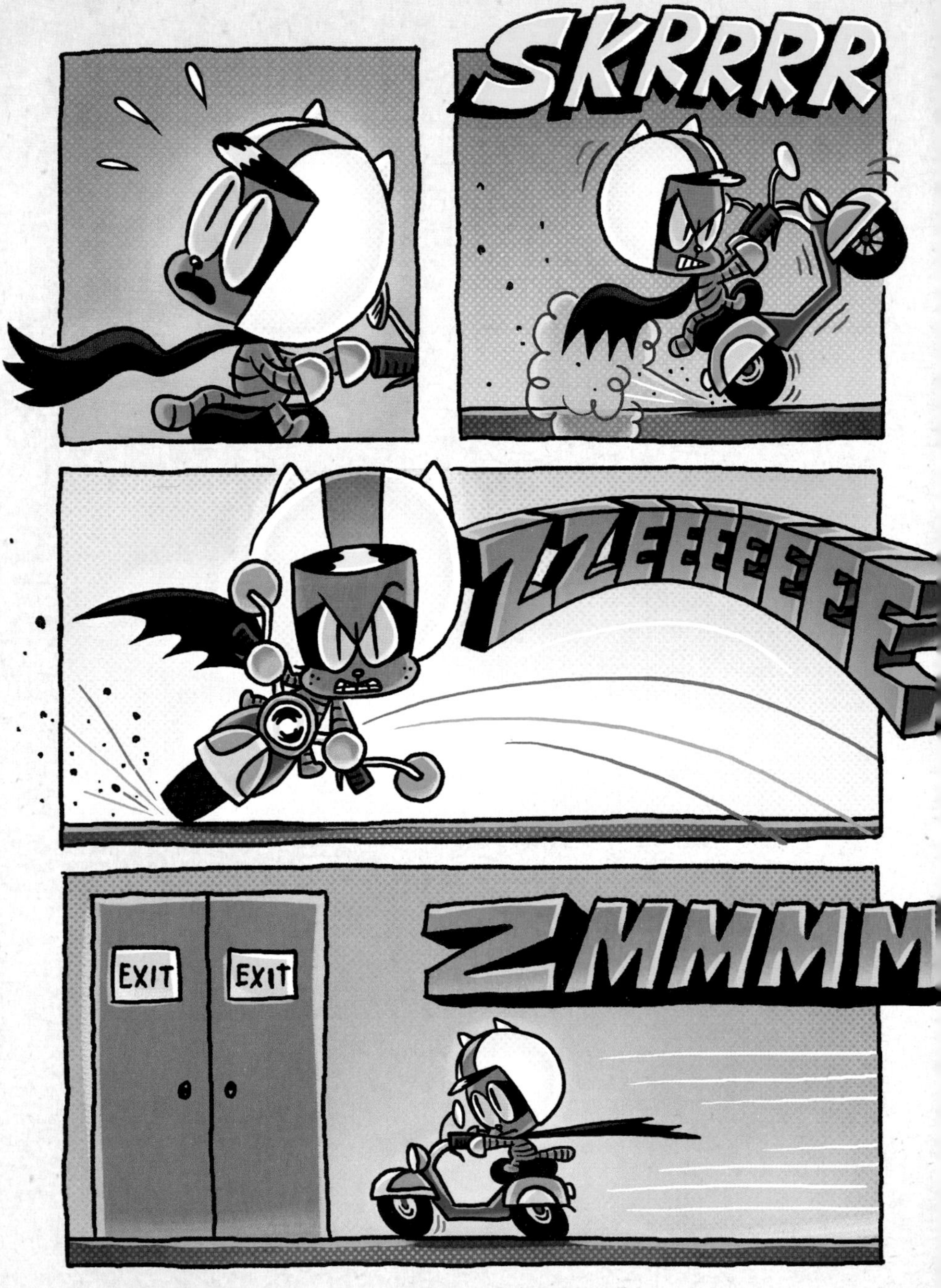
SKRRRR
ZZEEEEEEE
EXIT
EXIT
ZMMMMM

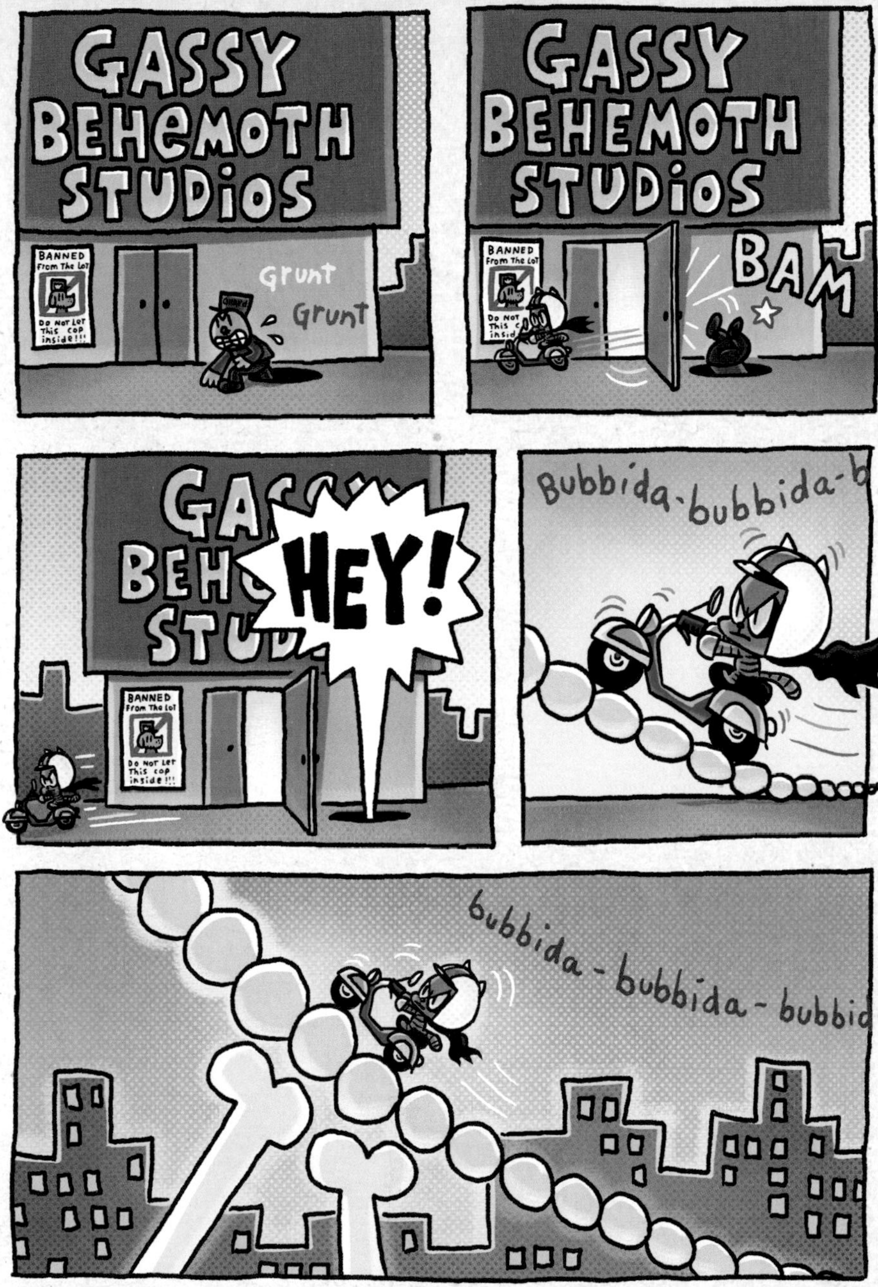
GASSY BEHEMOTH STUDIOS
BANNED From The Lot
Do Not Let This cop inside!!!
Grunt
Grunt
GASSY BEHEMOTH STUDIOS
BAM
HEY!
Bubbida-bubbida-b
bubbida-bubbida-bubbid

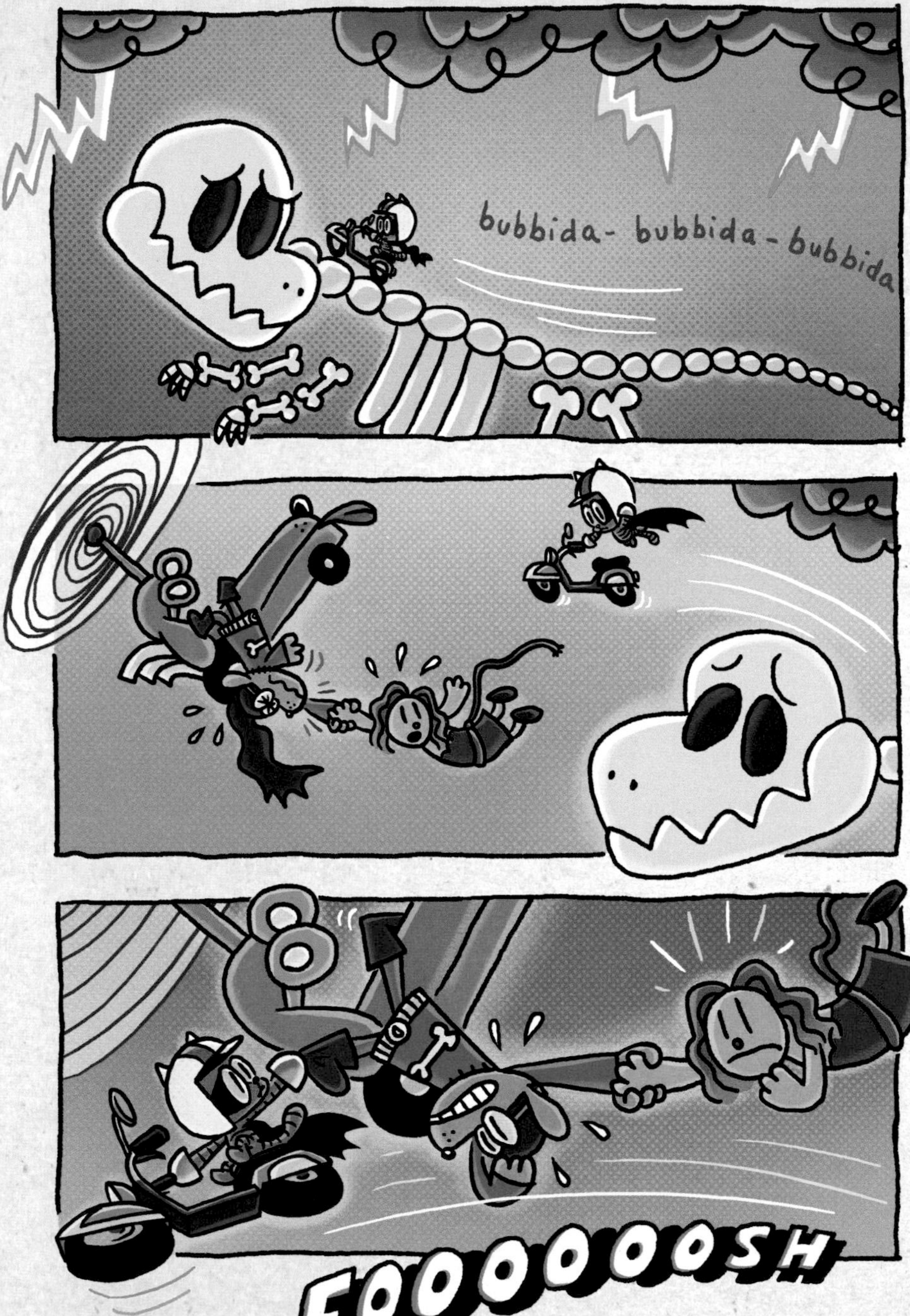
bubbida- bubbida-bubbida
FOOOOOOOSH

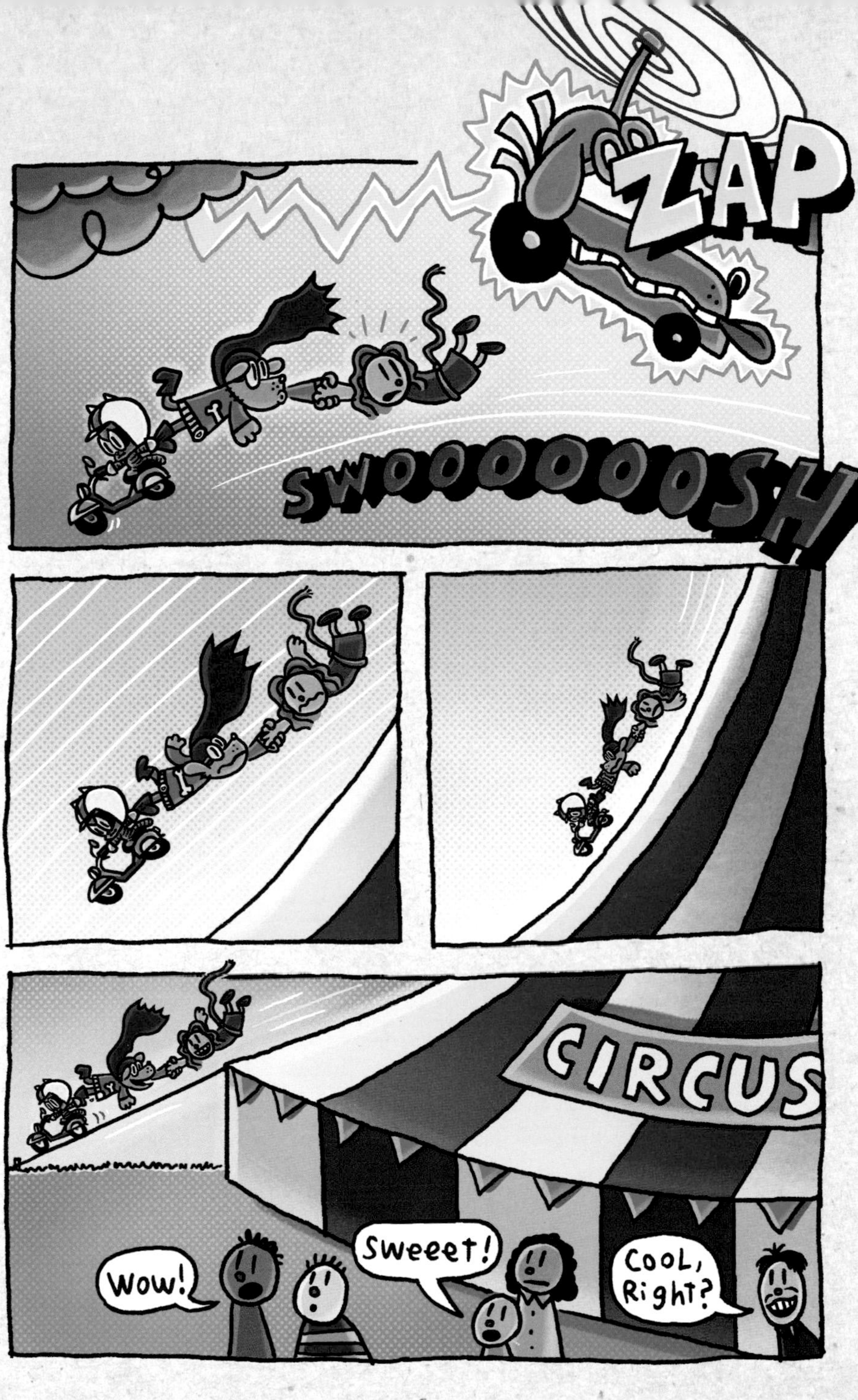
ZAP
SWOOOOOOOSH
CIRCUS
WOW!
SWEEET!
COOL, RIGHT?

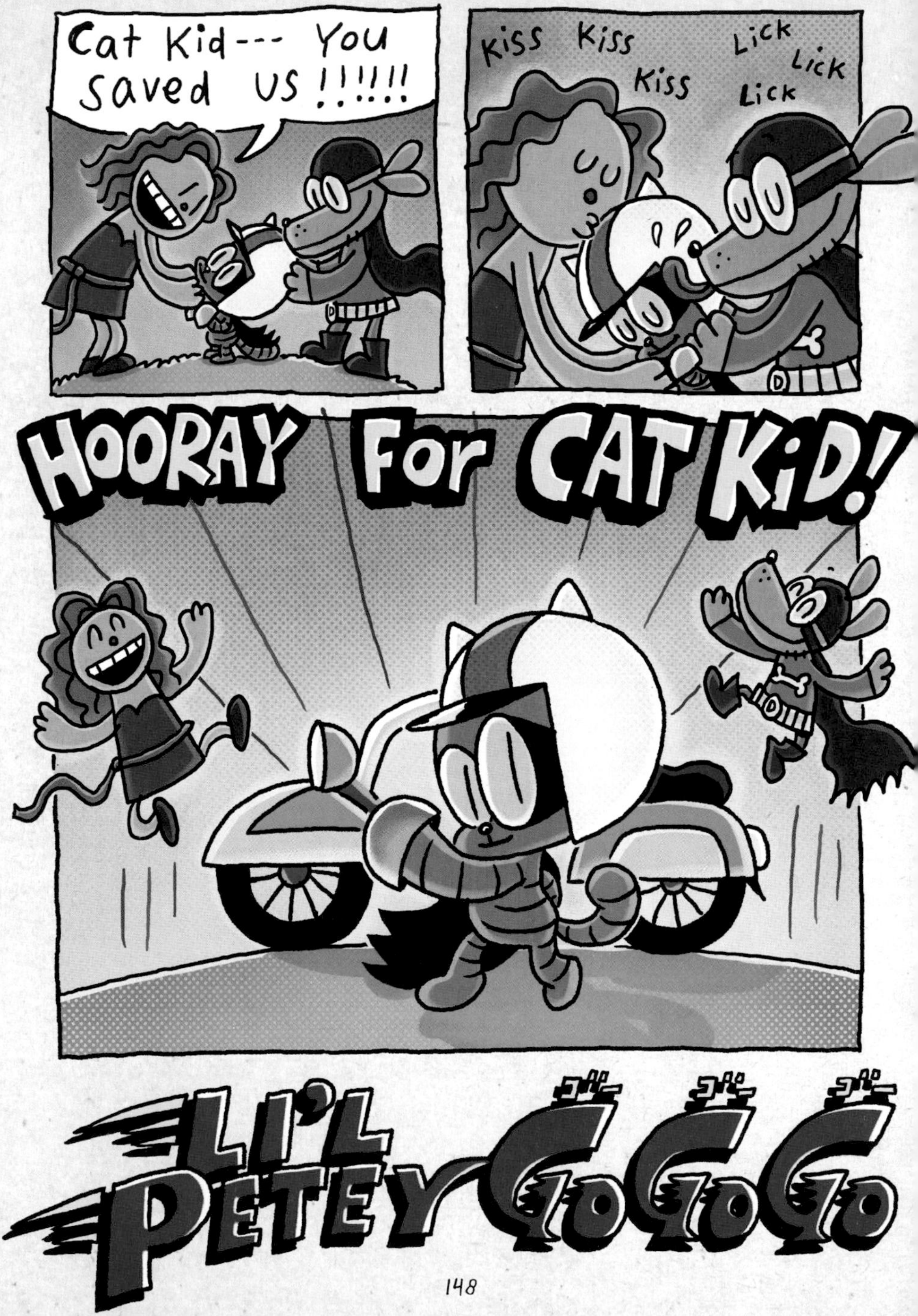

Cat Kid--- You saved US!!!!!!
Kiss Kiss Kiss
Lick Lick Lick
HOORAY For CAT KiD!
LI'L PETEY GoGoGo

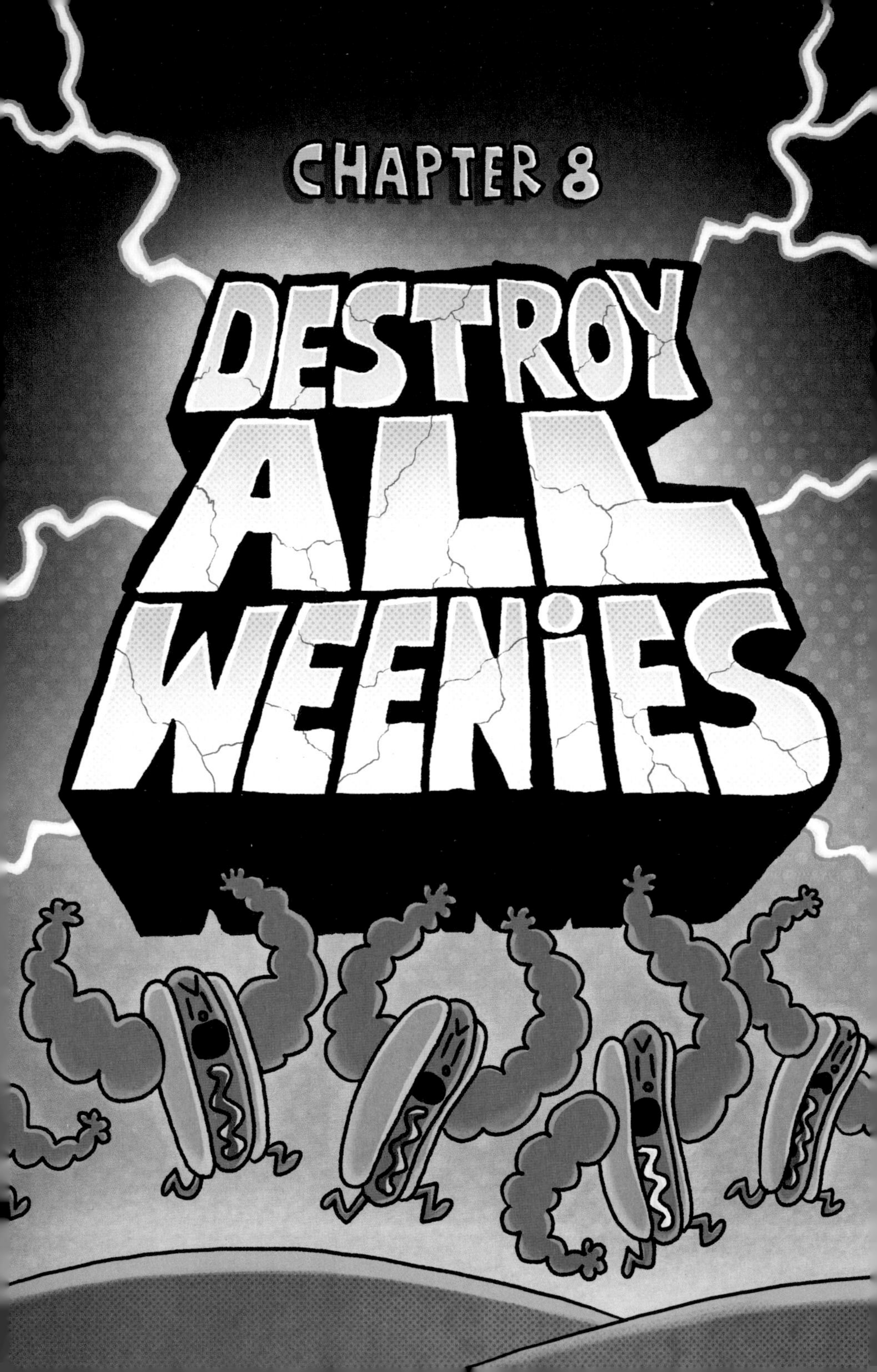
CHAPTER 8
DESTROY ALL WEENiES

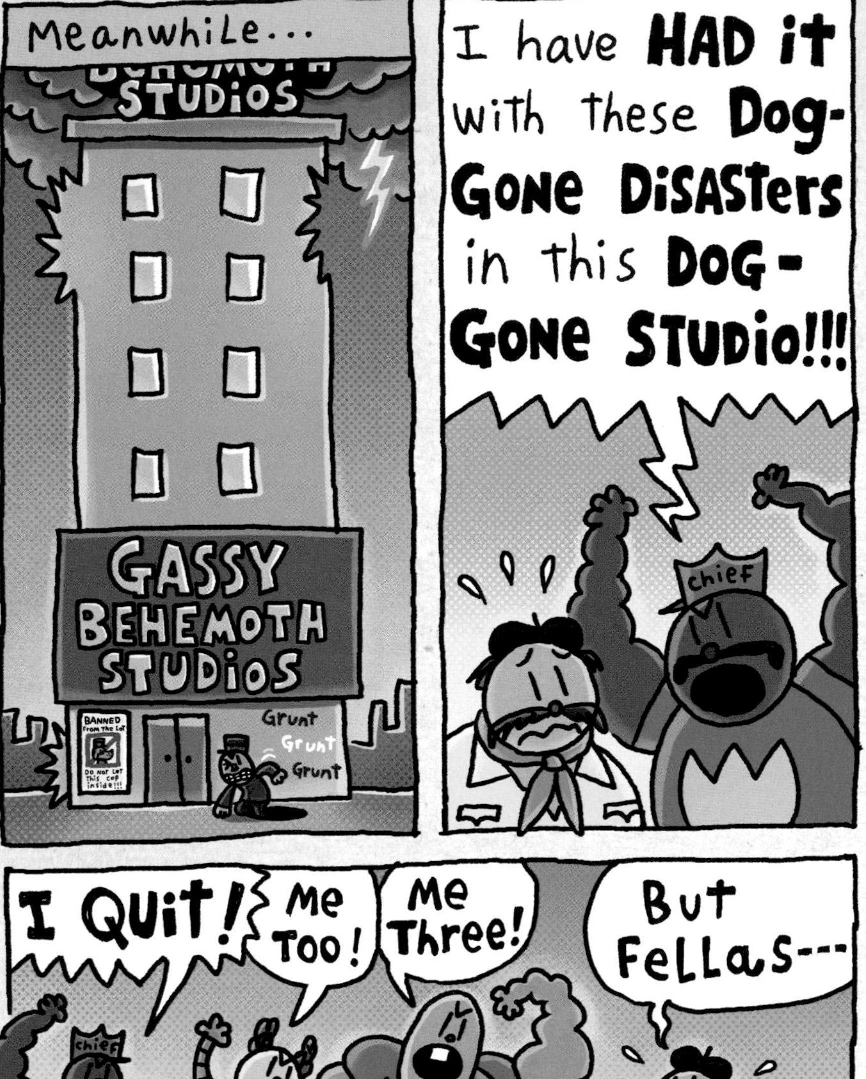
Meanwhile...
STUDIOS
GASSY BEHEMOTH STUDIOS
BANNED From the Lot
Do Not Let This cop inside!!!
Grunt
Grunt
Grunt
I have HAD it with these Dog-Gone DiSASTers in this DOG-Gone STUDIO!!!
chief
I QUIT!
Me Too!
Me Three!
But Fellas---
chief

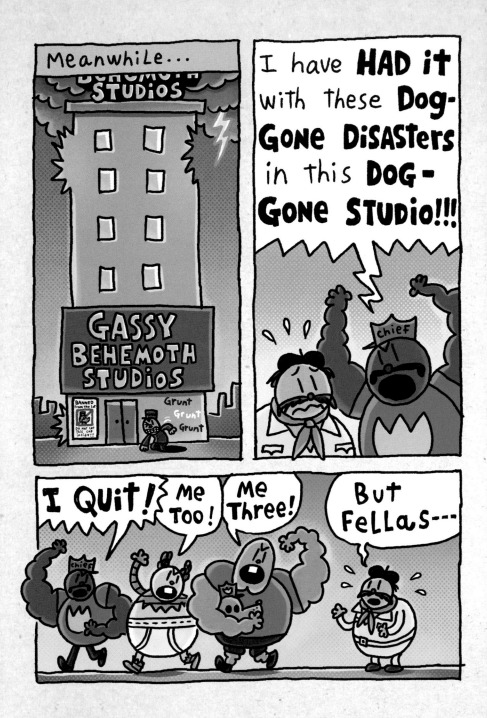

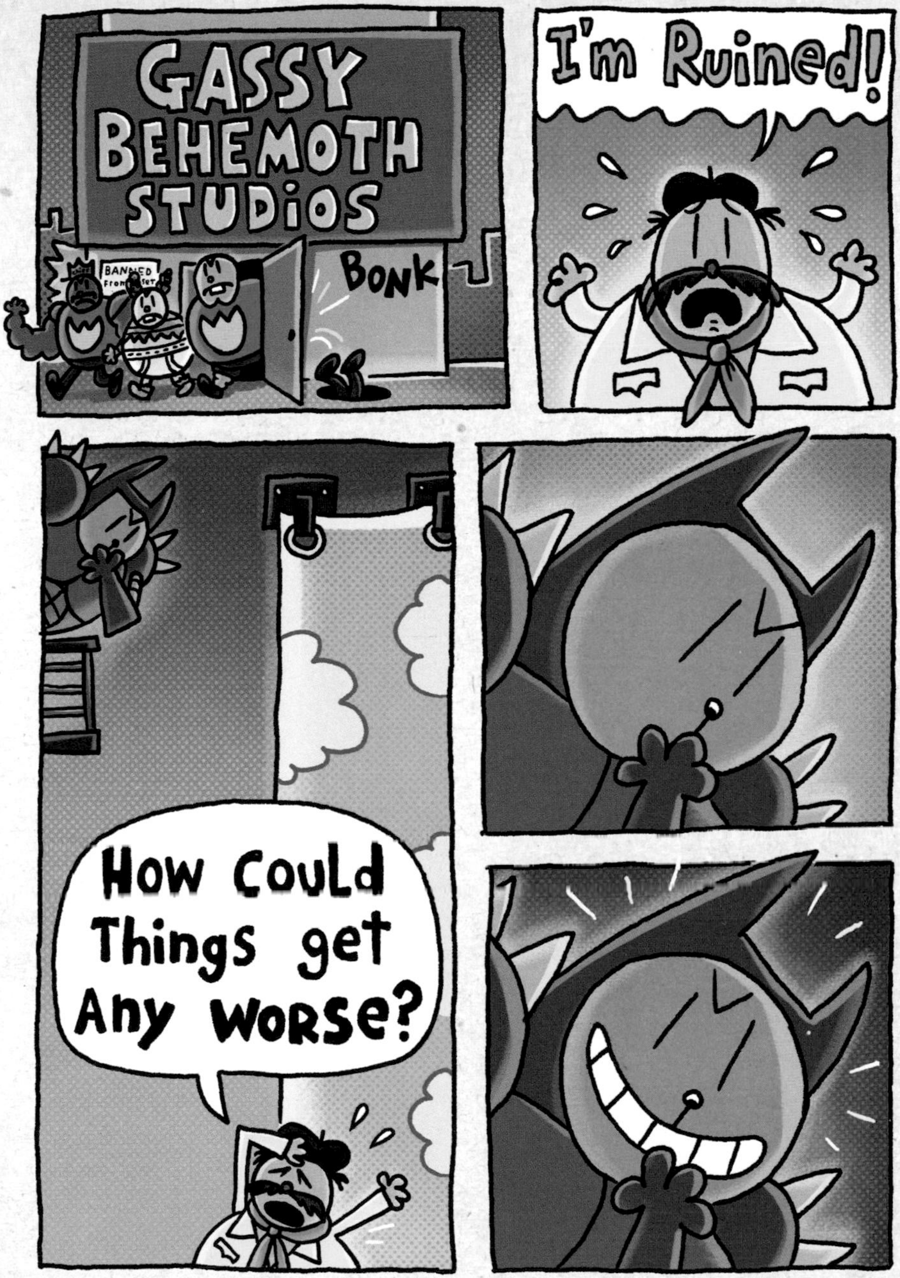
GASSY
BEHEMOTH
STUDIOS
BANNED From set
BONK
I'm Ruined!
How Could Things get Any WORSE?

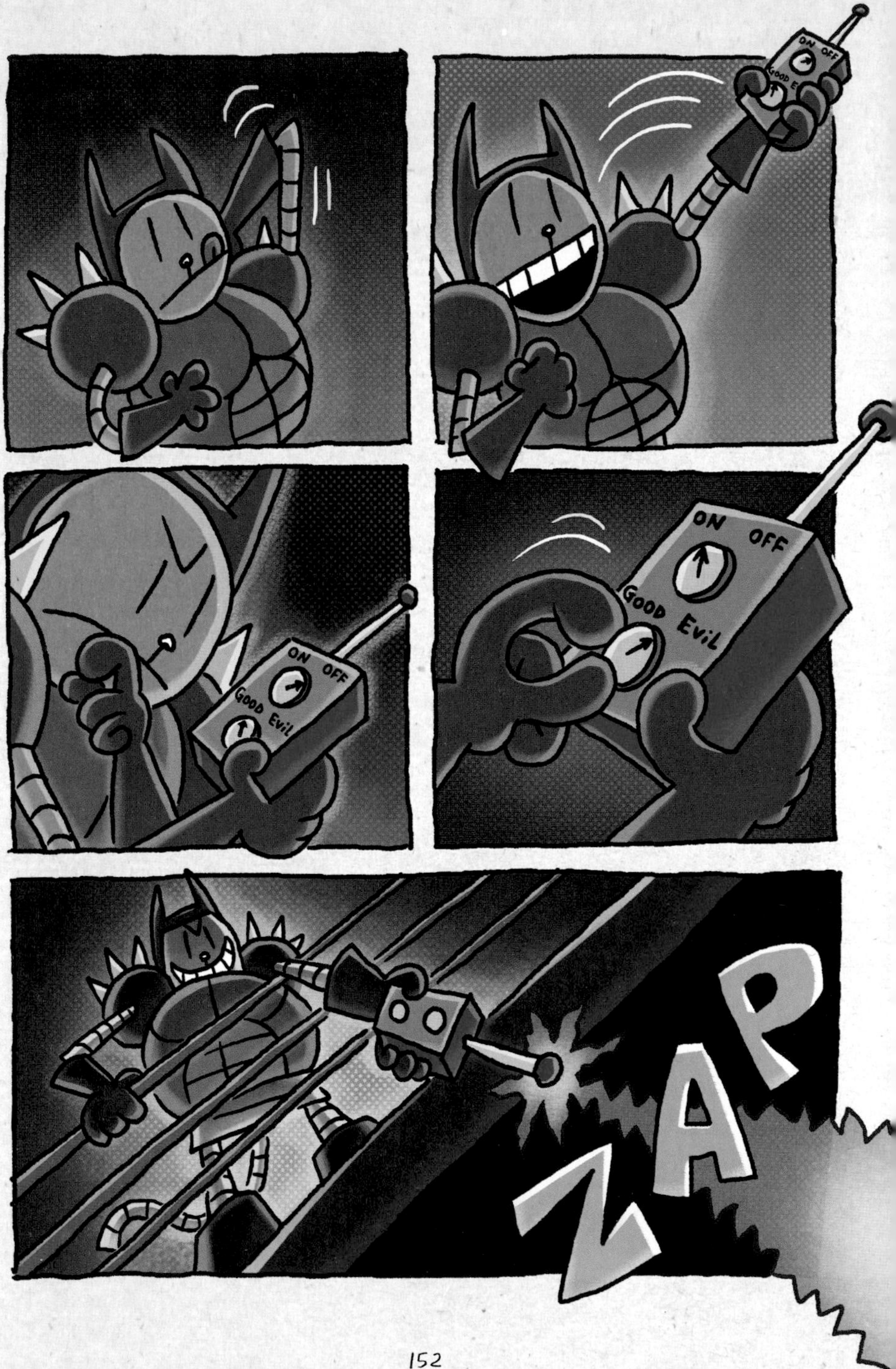
ON OFF
GOOD E
ON OFF
GOOD Evil
ON OFF
GOOD EviL
ZAP

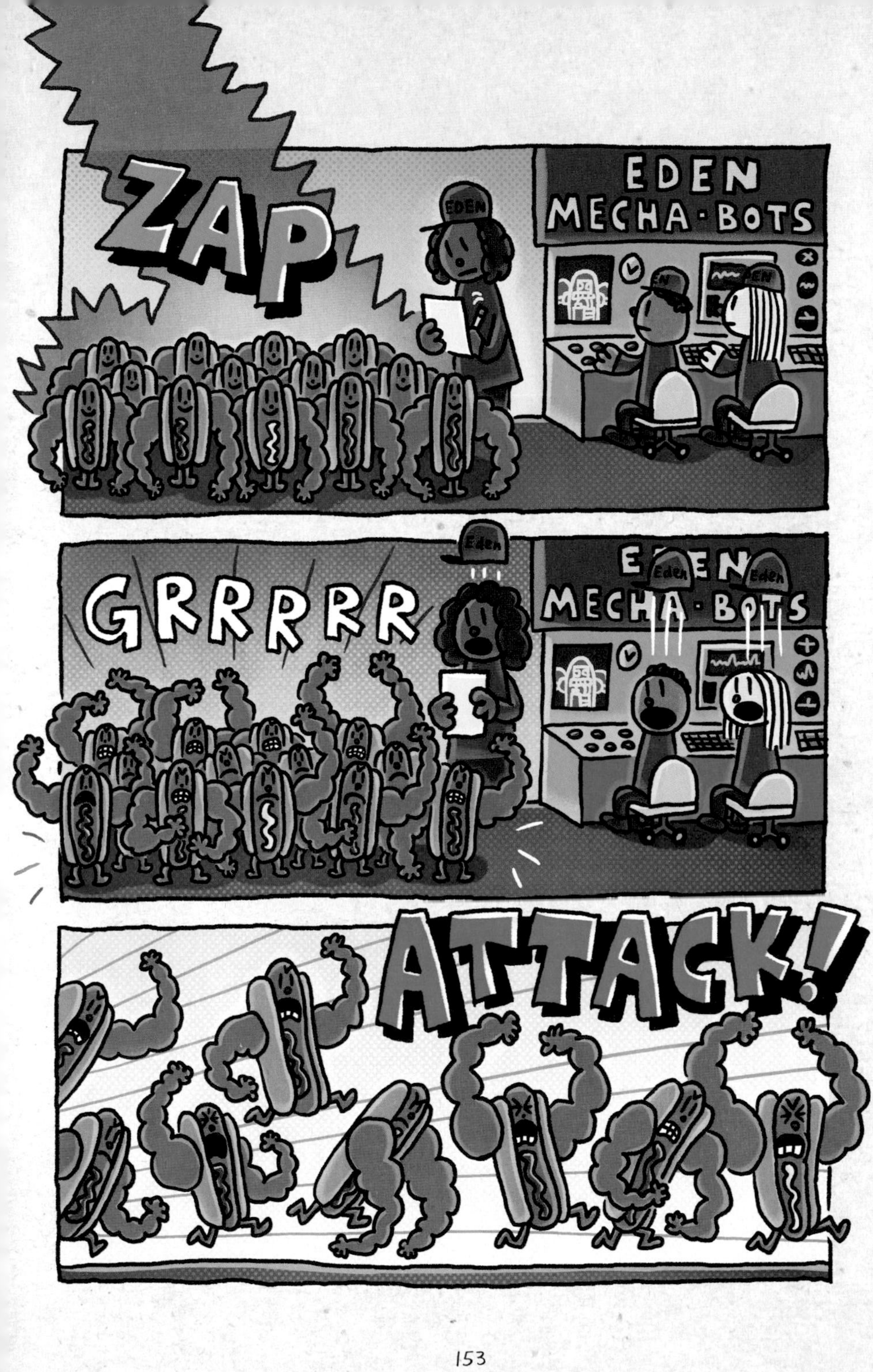
ZAP
EDEN
EDEN
MECHA-BOTS
GRRRRR
Eden
Eden
Eden
EDEN
MECHA-BOTS
ATTACK!

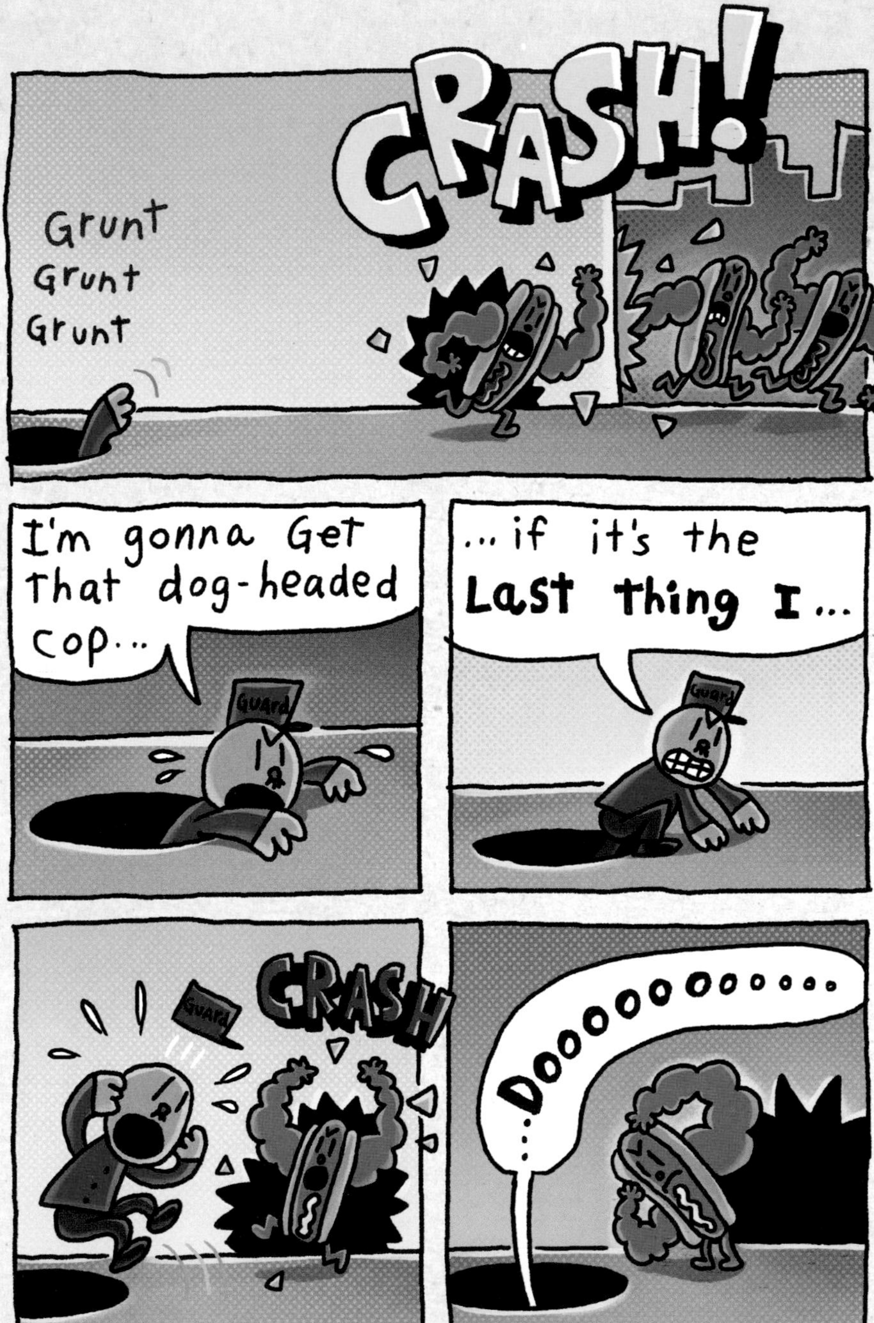
CRASH!
Grunt
Grunt
Grunt
I'm gonna Get That dog-headed cop...
...if it's the **LAST thing I...**
CRASH
Guard
Doooooooooooo...

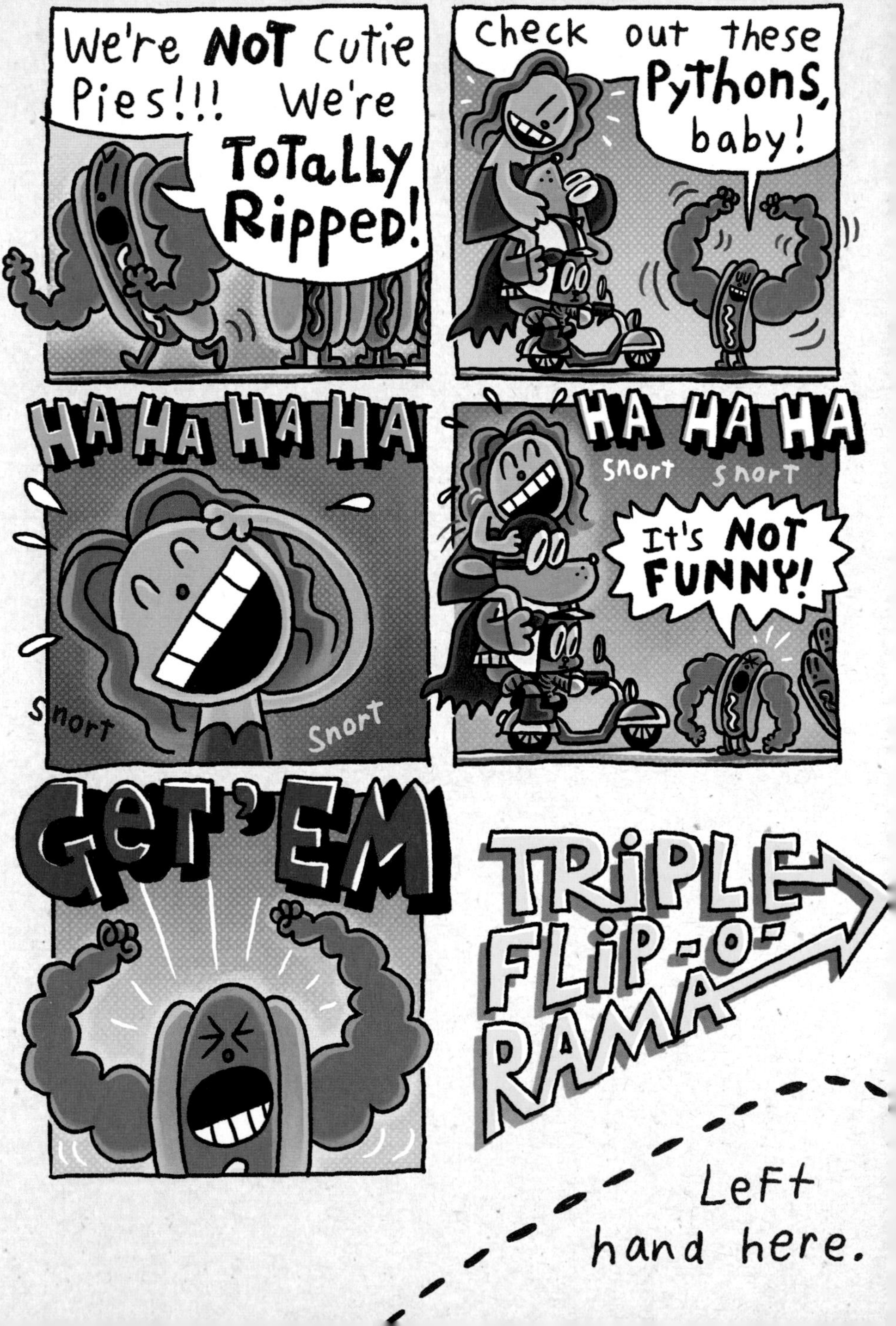
We're NOT cutie Pies!!! We're TOTALLY RIPPED!
Check out these Pythons, baby!
HA HA HA HA HA
Snort
Snort
HA HA HA
Snort
Snort
It's NOT FUNNY!
GET 'EM
TRIPLE FLIP-O-RAMA
Left hand here.

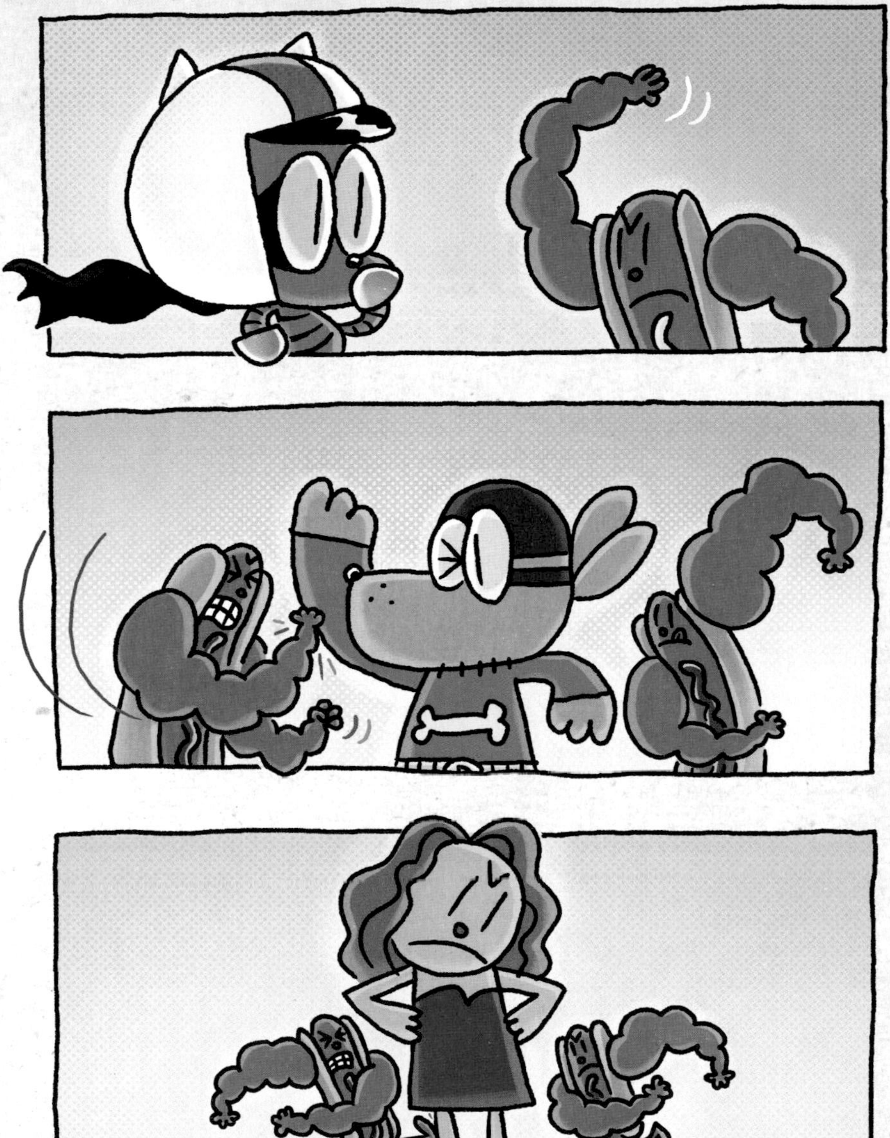

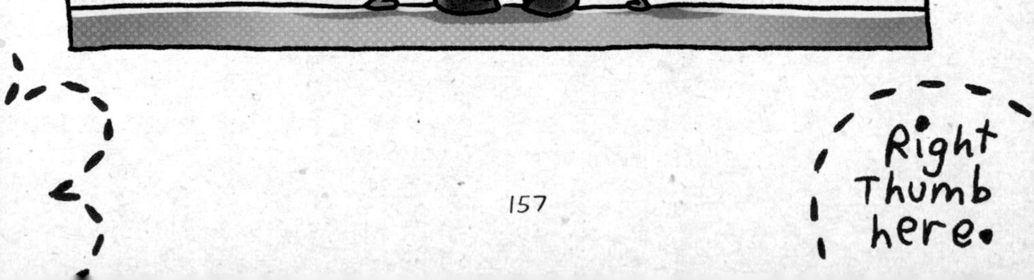
Right Thumb here.

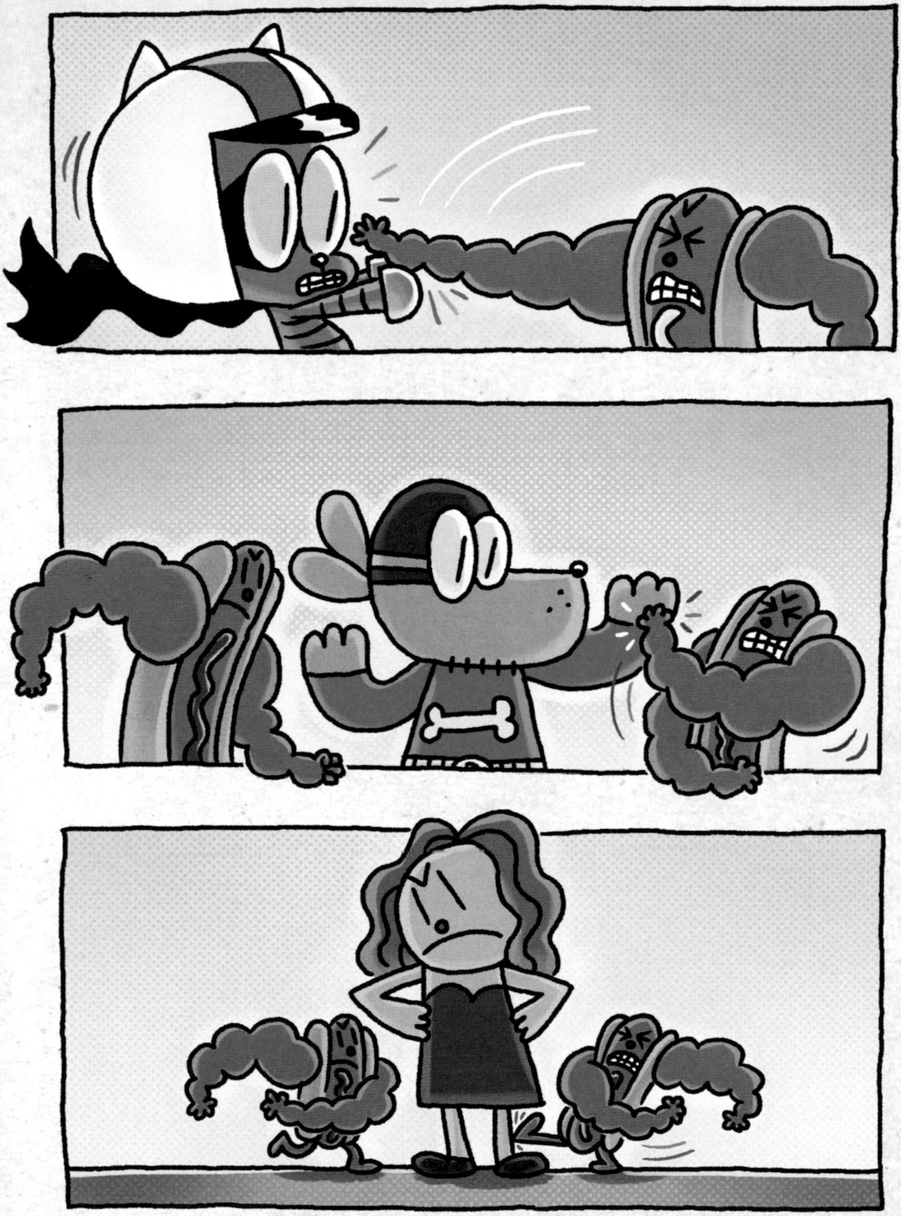

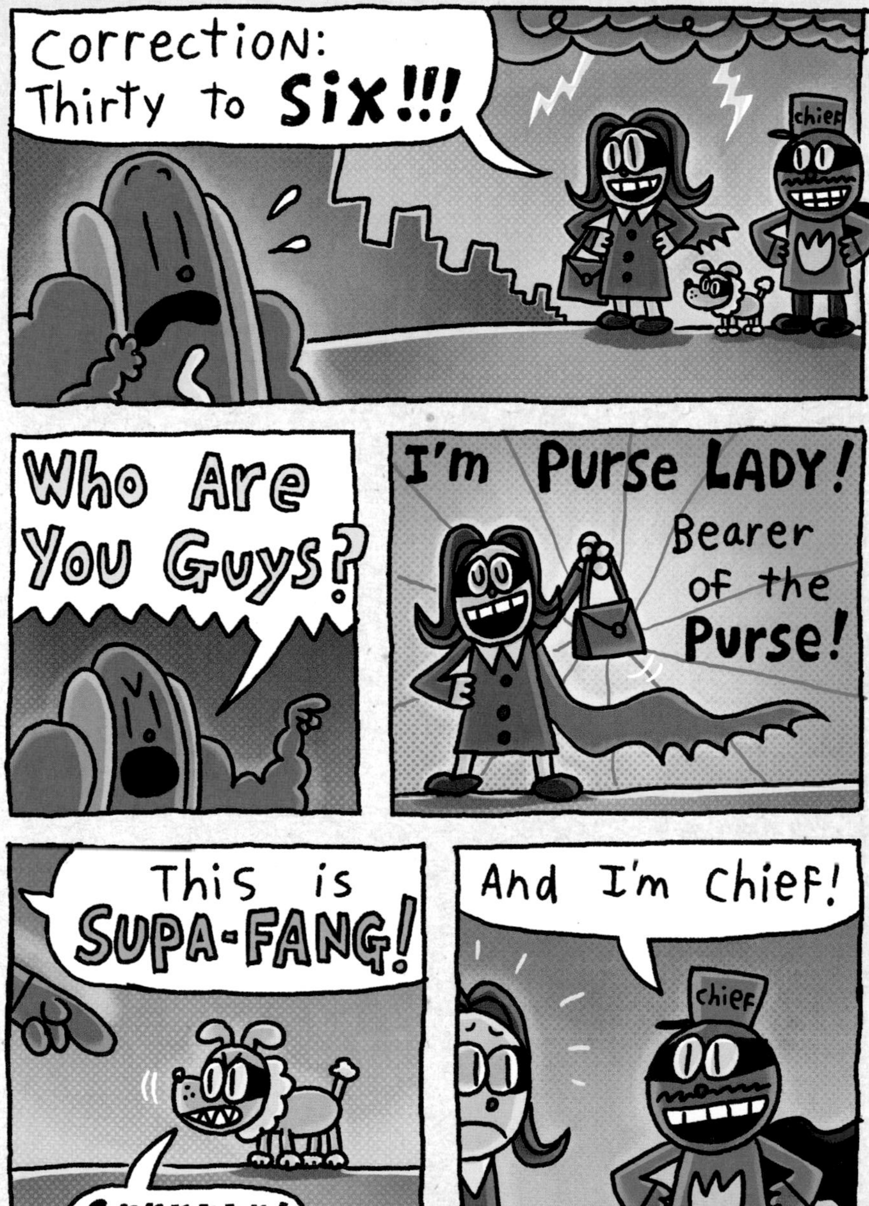
Correction: Thirty to SIX!!!
chief
Who Are You Guys?
I'm Purse LADY!
Bearer of the Purse!
This is SUPA-FANG!
Grrrrrr!
And I'm Chief!
chief

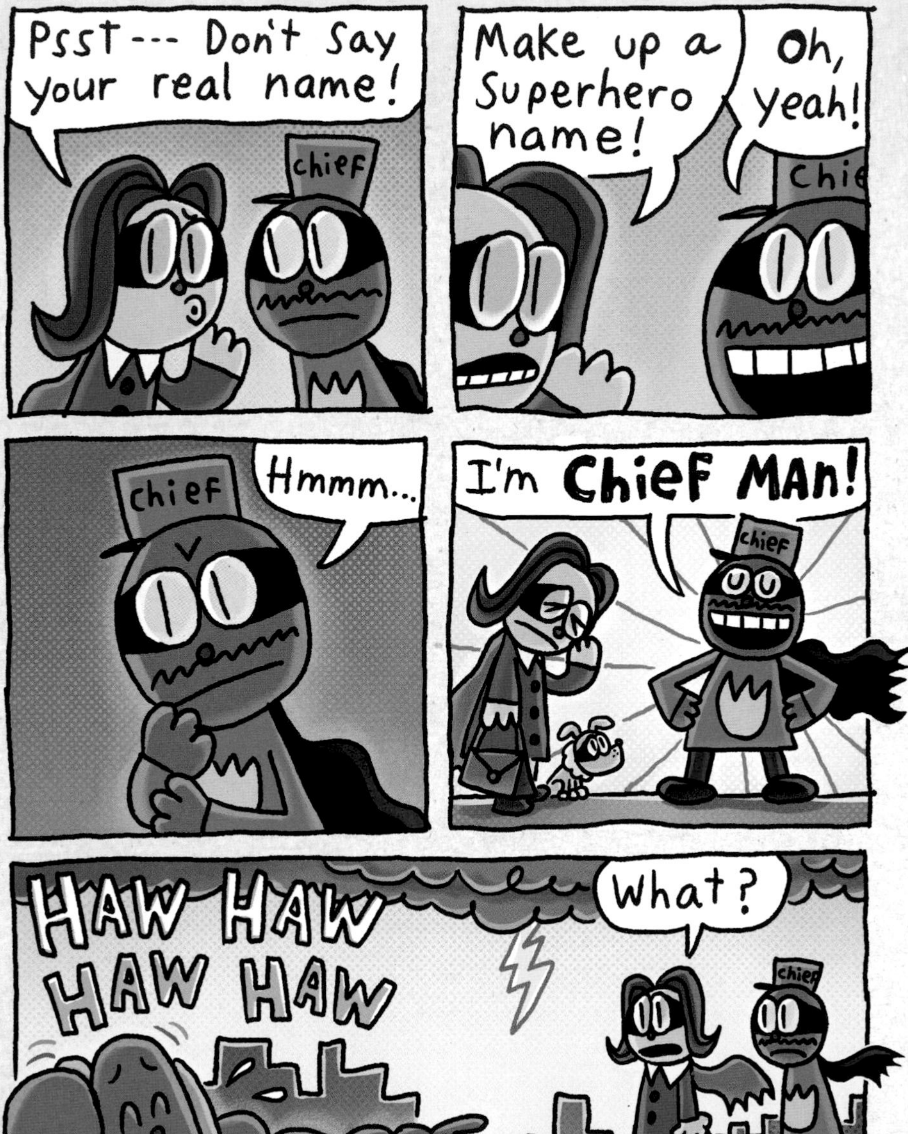
Psst--- Don't Say your real name!
chief
Make up a Superhero name!
Oh, yeah!
Chie
chief
Hmmm...
I'm CHIEF MAN!
chief
HAW HAW HAW HAW
What?
chief

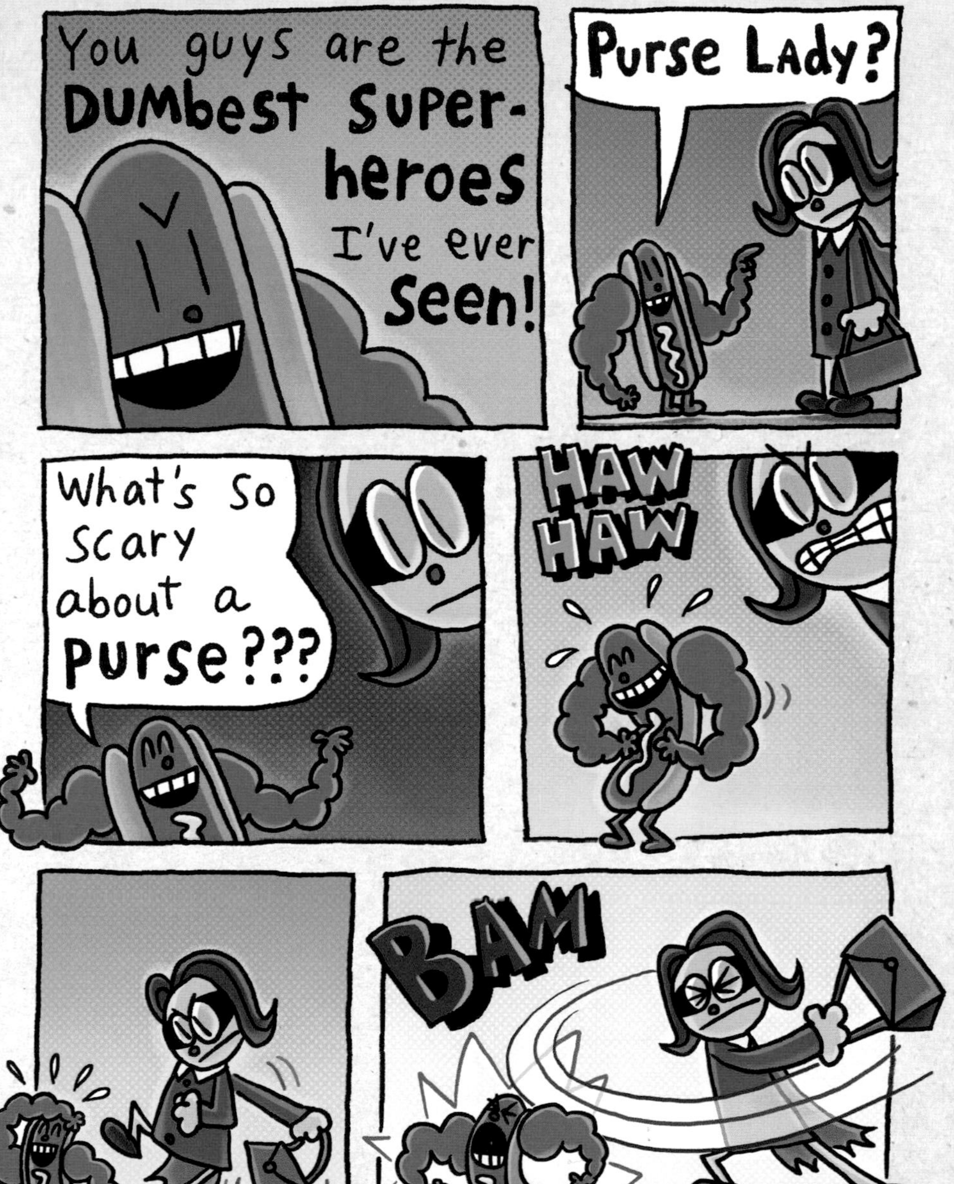
You guys are the DUMbest Super-heroes I've ever Seen!
Purse LAdy?
What's So scary about a Purse???
HAW HAW
BAM

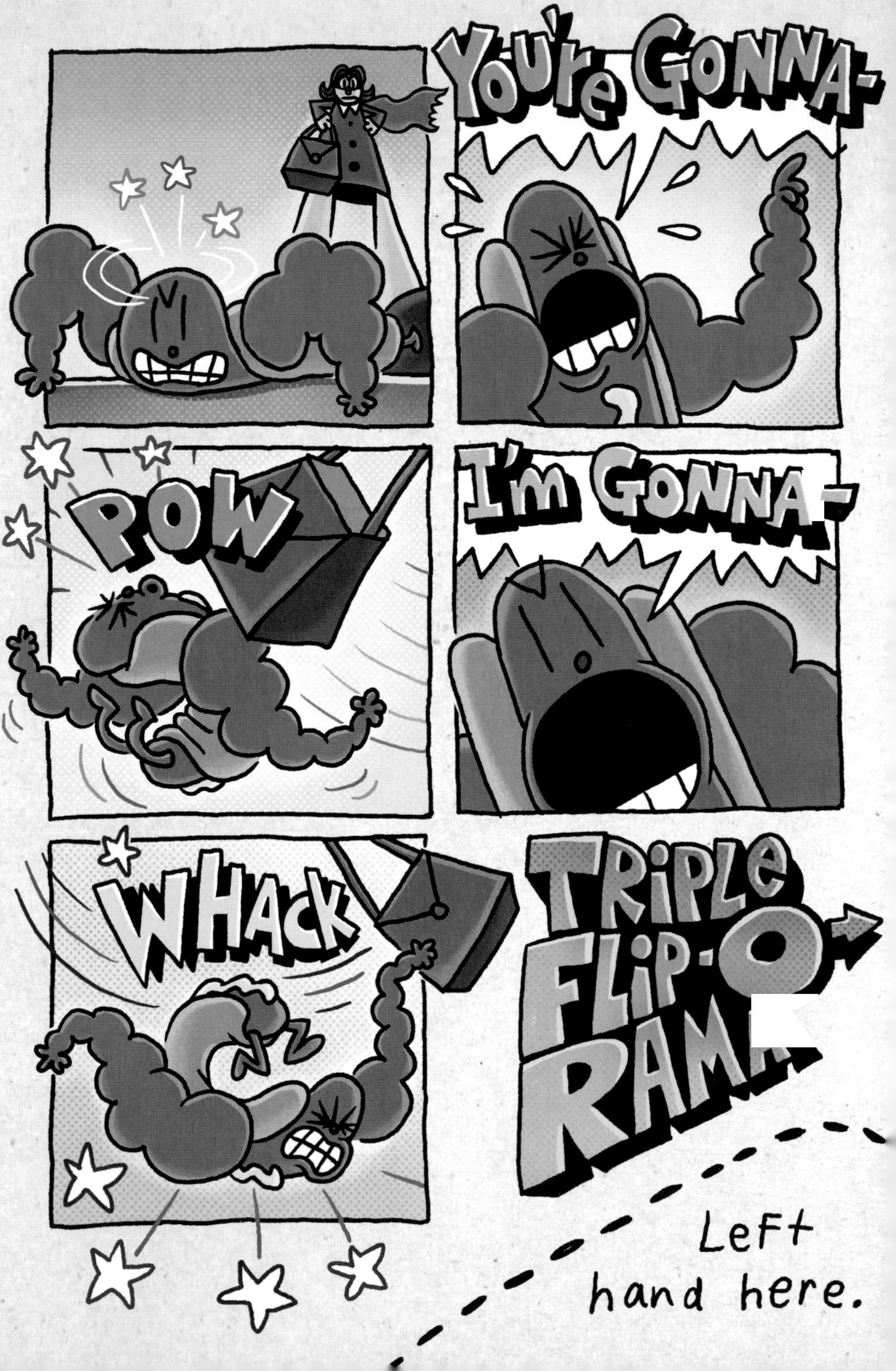
YOU'RE GONNA-
POW
I'M GONNA-
WHACK
TRIPLE
FLIP-O-
RAM
Left hand here.

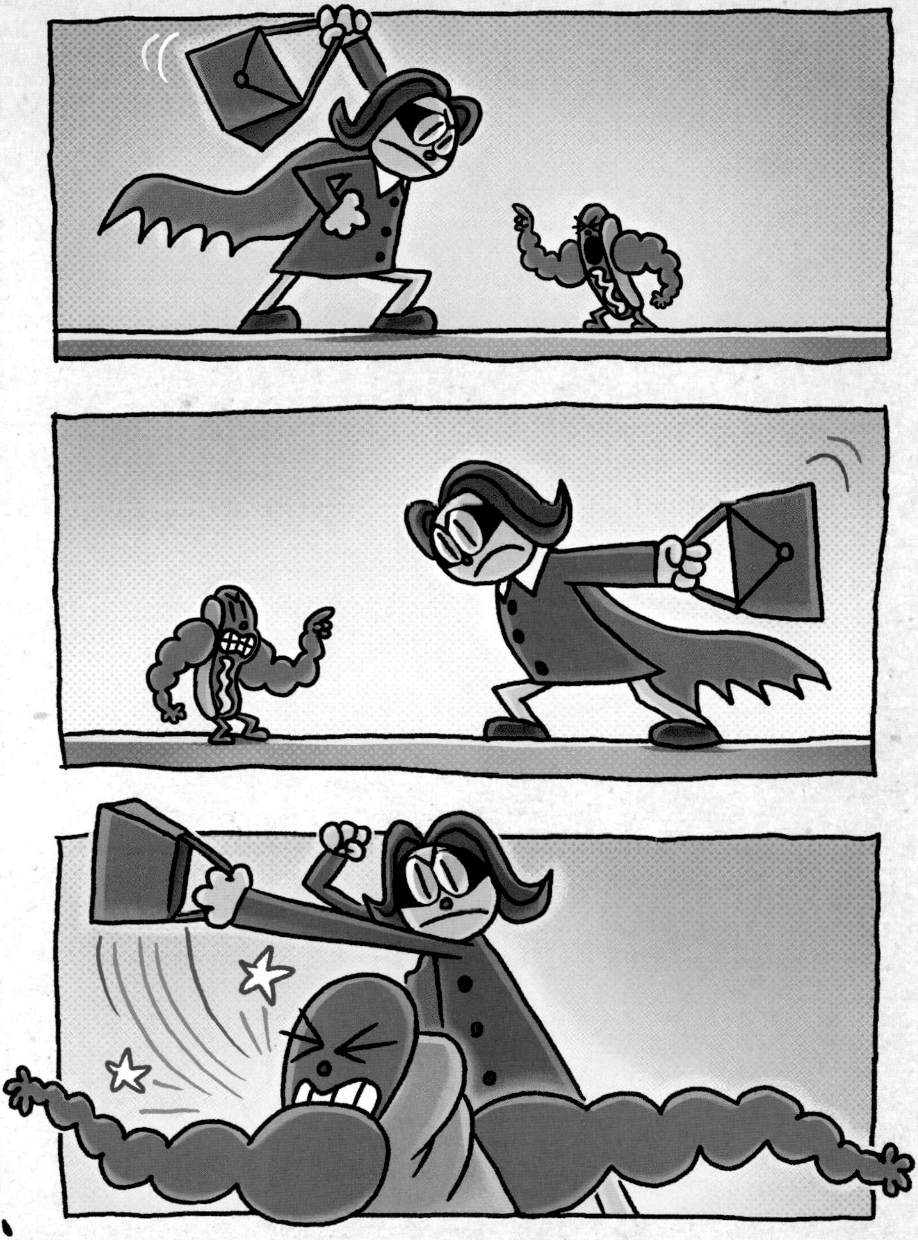

Right Thumb here.

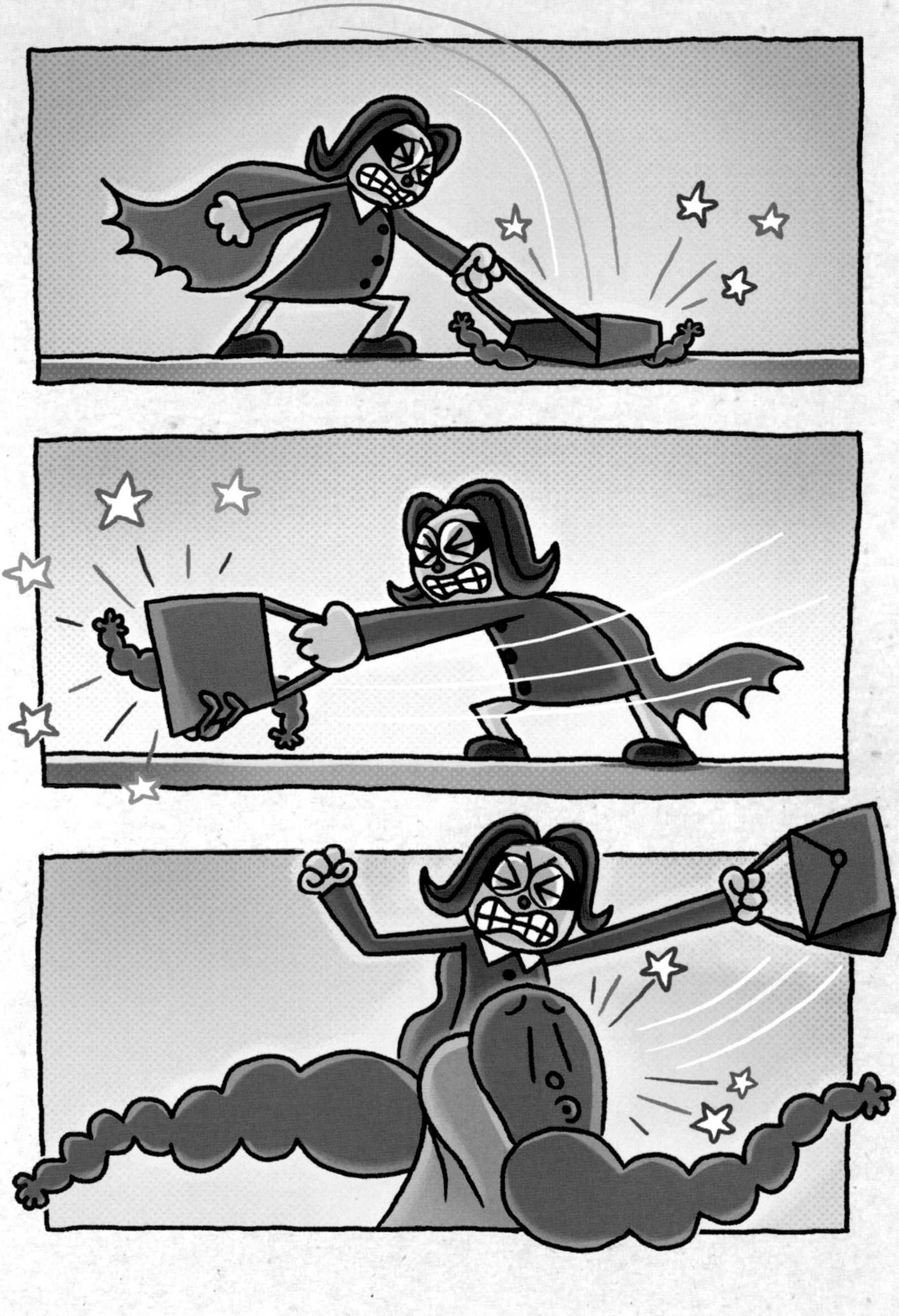

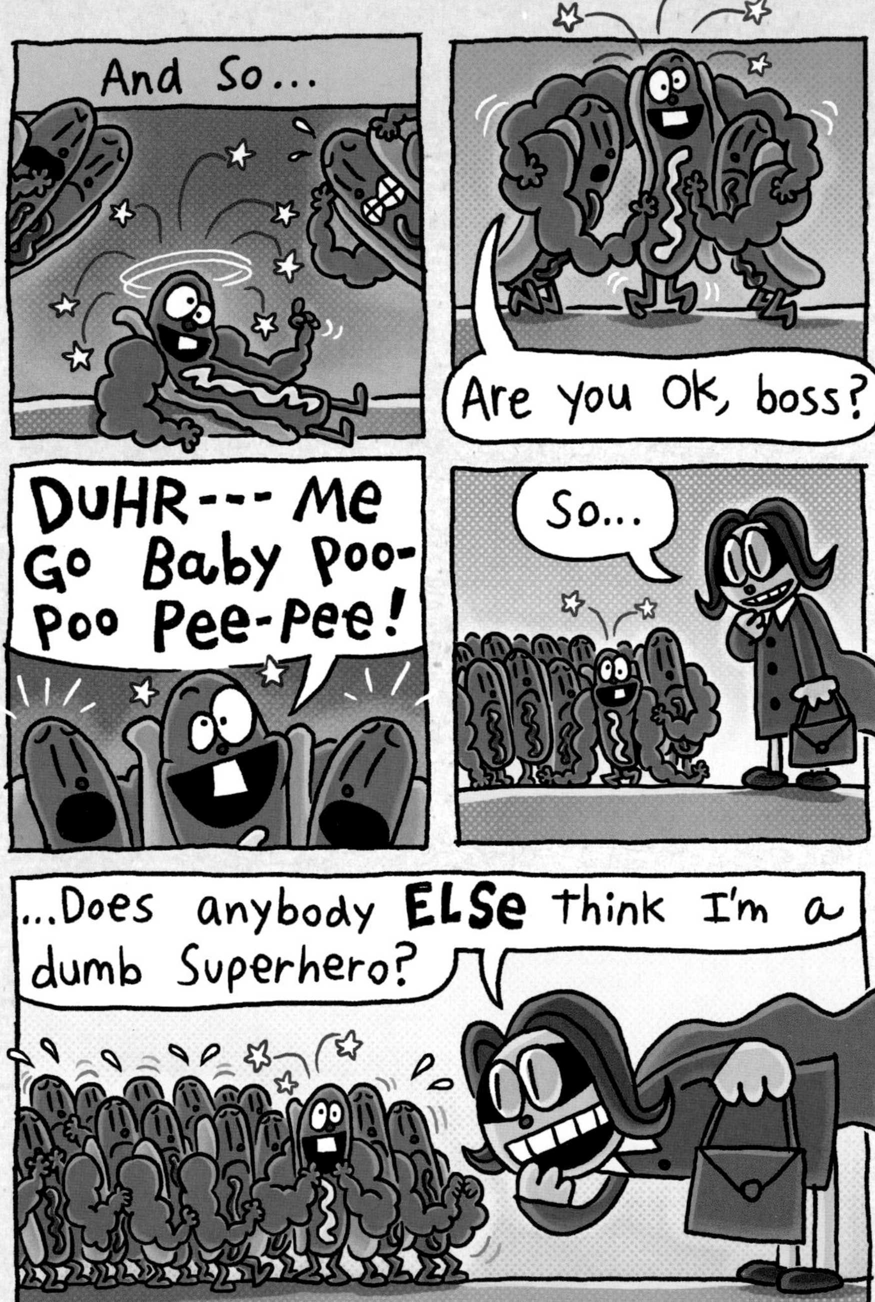
And So...
Are you OK, boss?
DUHR--- Me Go Baby Poo-Poo Pee-Pee!
So...
...Does anybody ELSe think I'm a dumb Superhero?

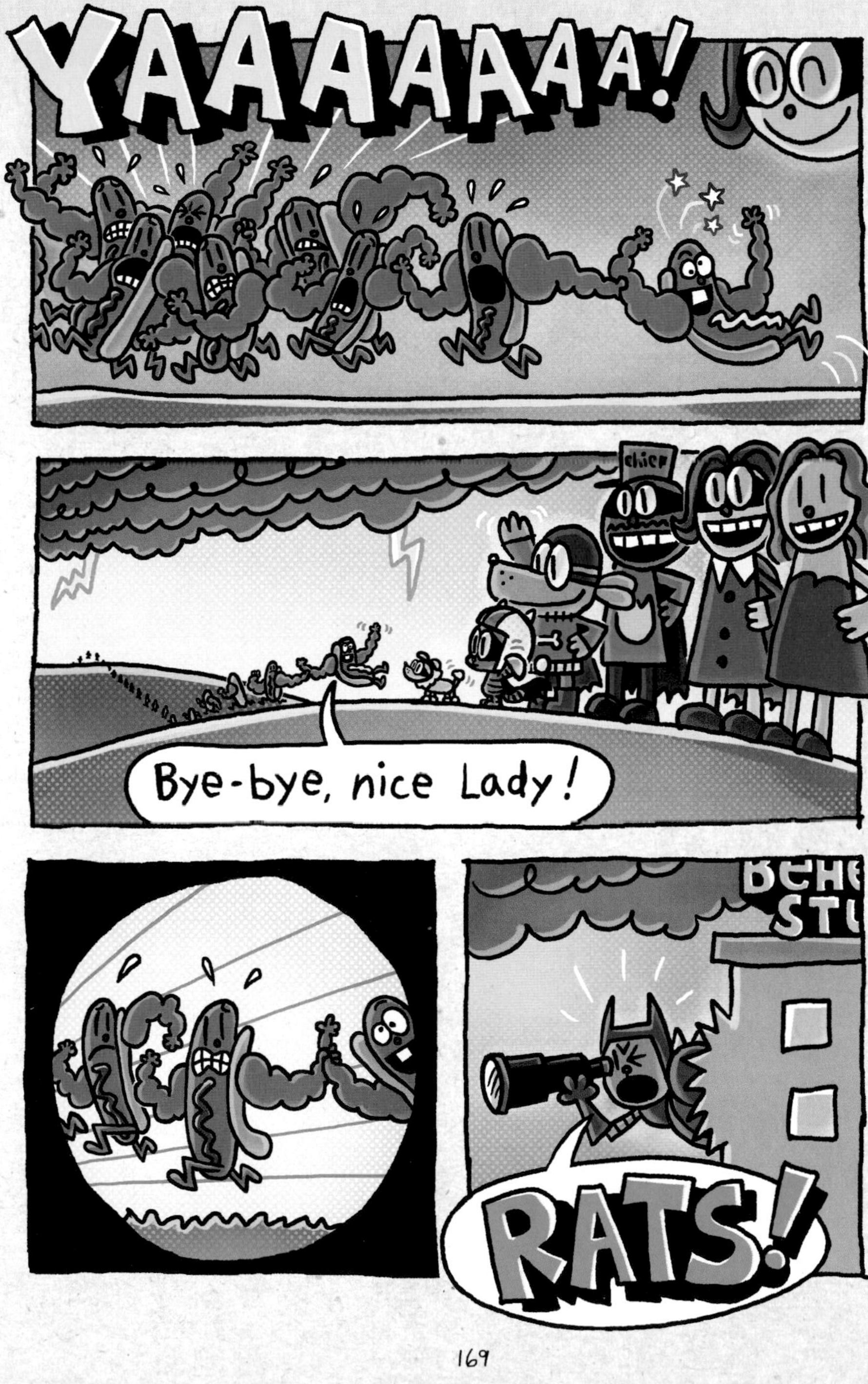
YAAAAAAA!
chief
Bye-bye, nice Lady!
BEHE
STU
RATS!

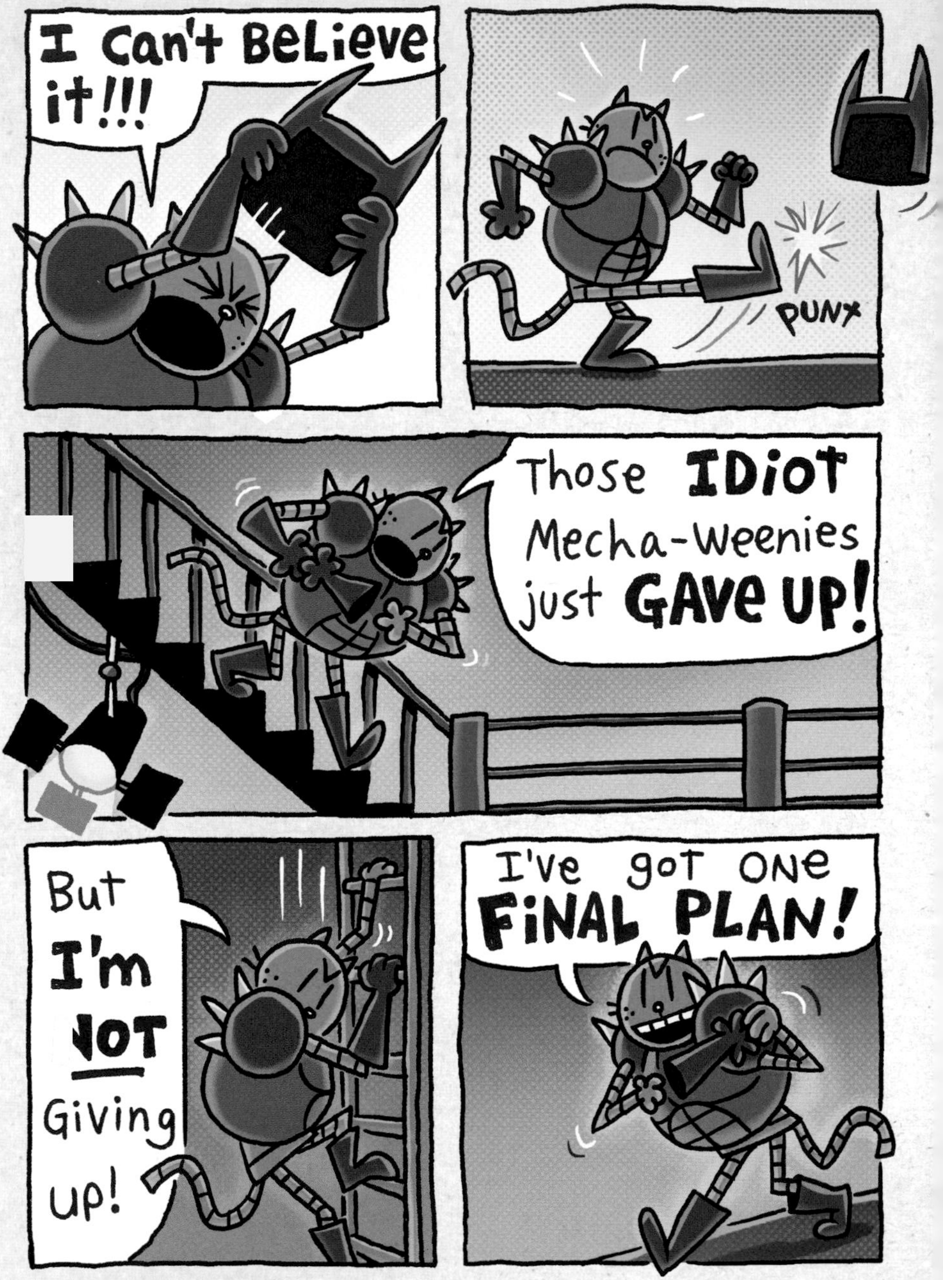
I Can't BeLieve it!!!
PUNT
Those IDIOT Mecha-Weenies just GAVE UP!
But I'm NOT Giving up!
I've got ONE FiNAL PLAN!

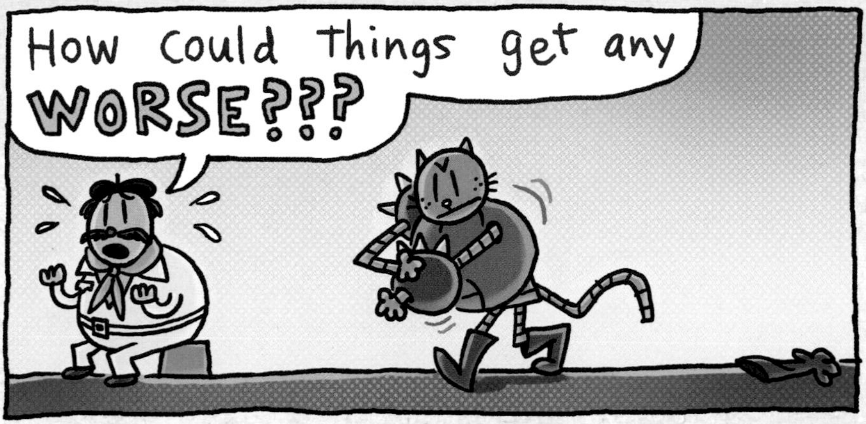
How could things get any WORSE???

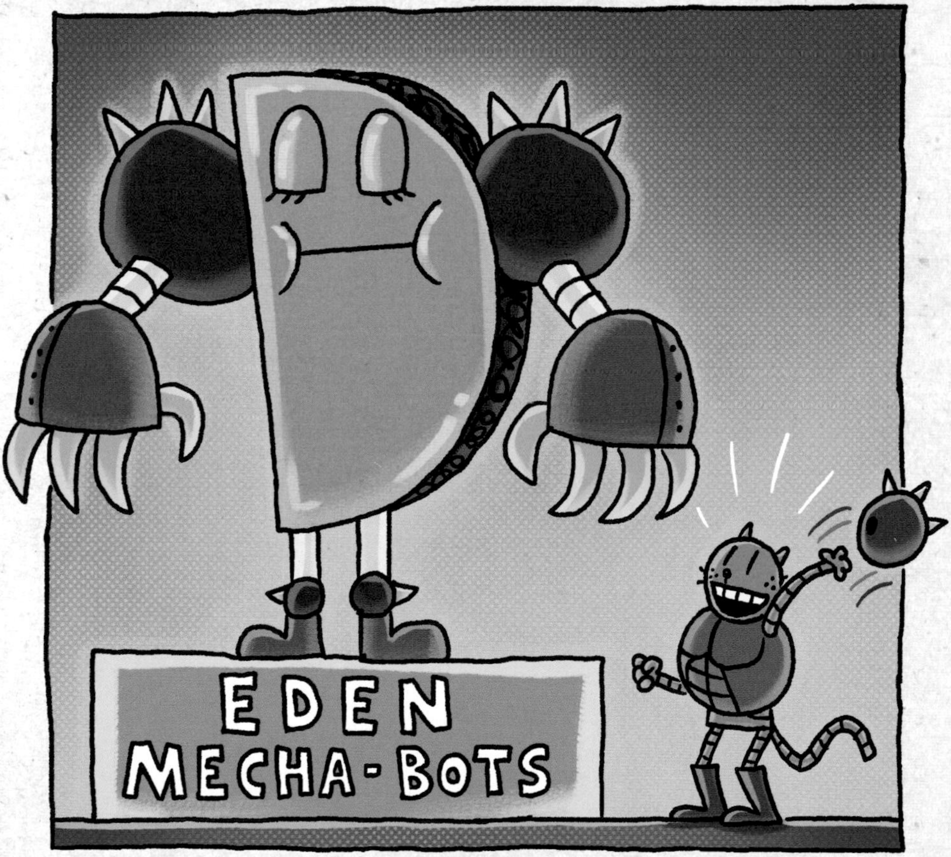
EDEN
MECHA-BOTS

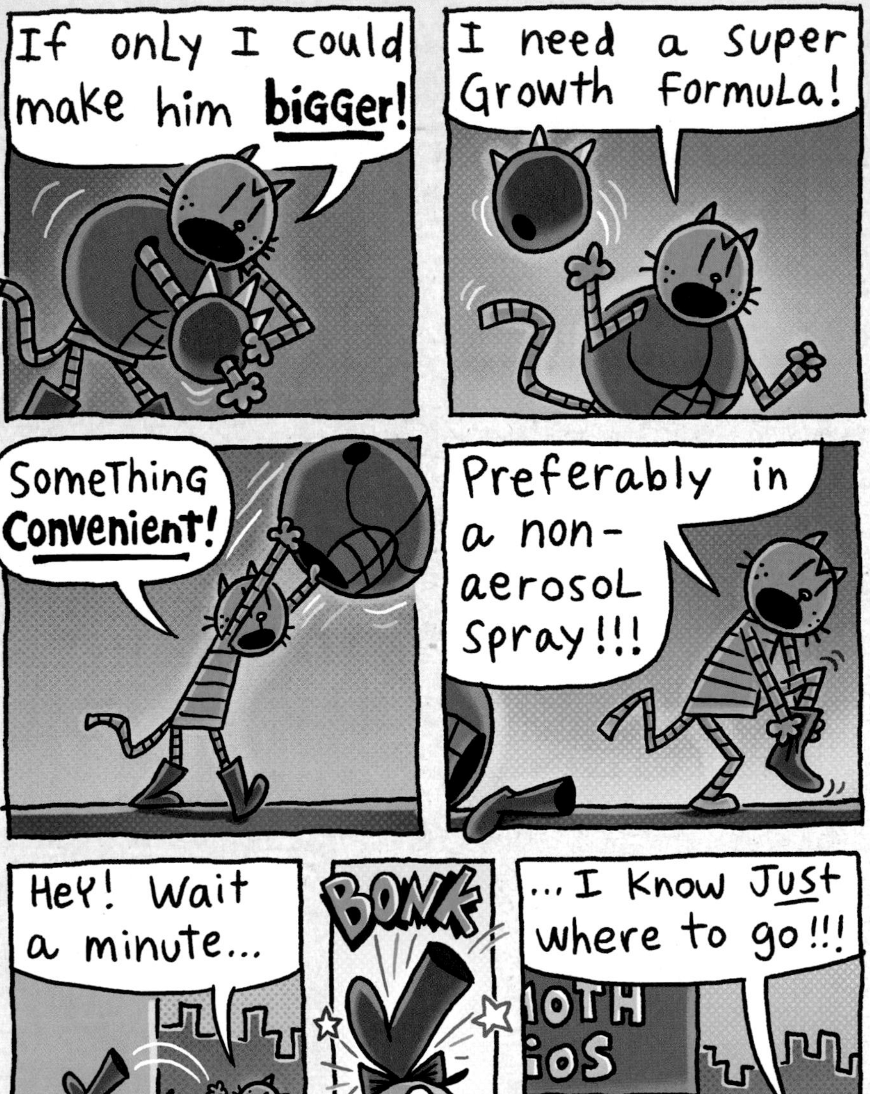
If only I could make him bigger!
I need a Super Growth Formula!
Something Convenient!
Preferably in a non-aerosol Spray!!!
Hey! Wait a minute...
BONK
...I Know JUST where to go!!!

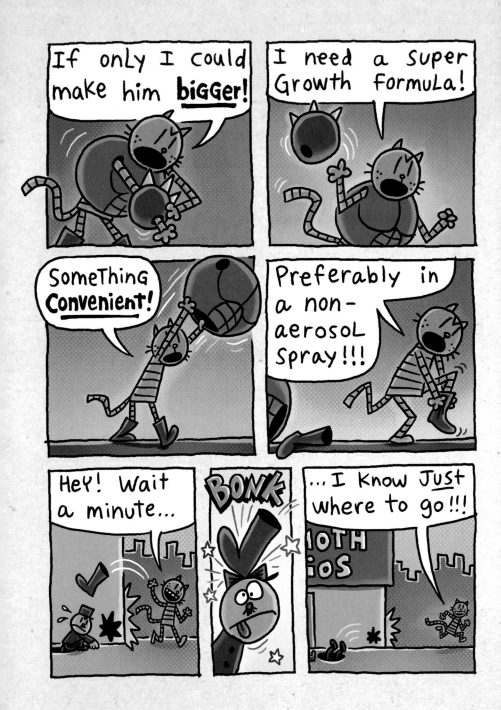

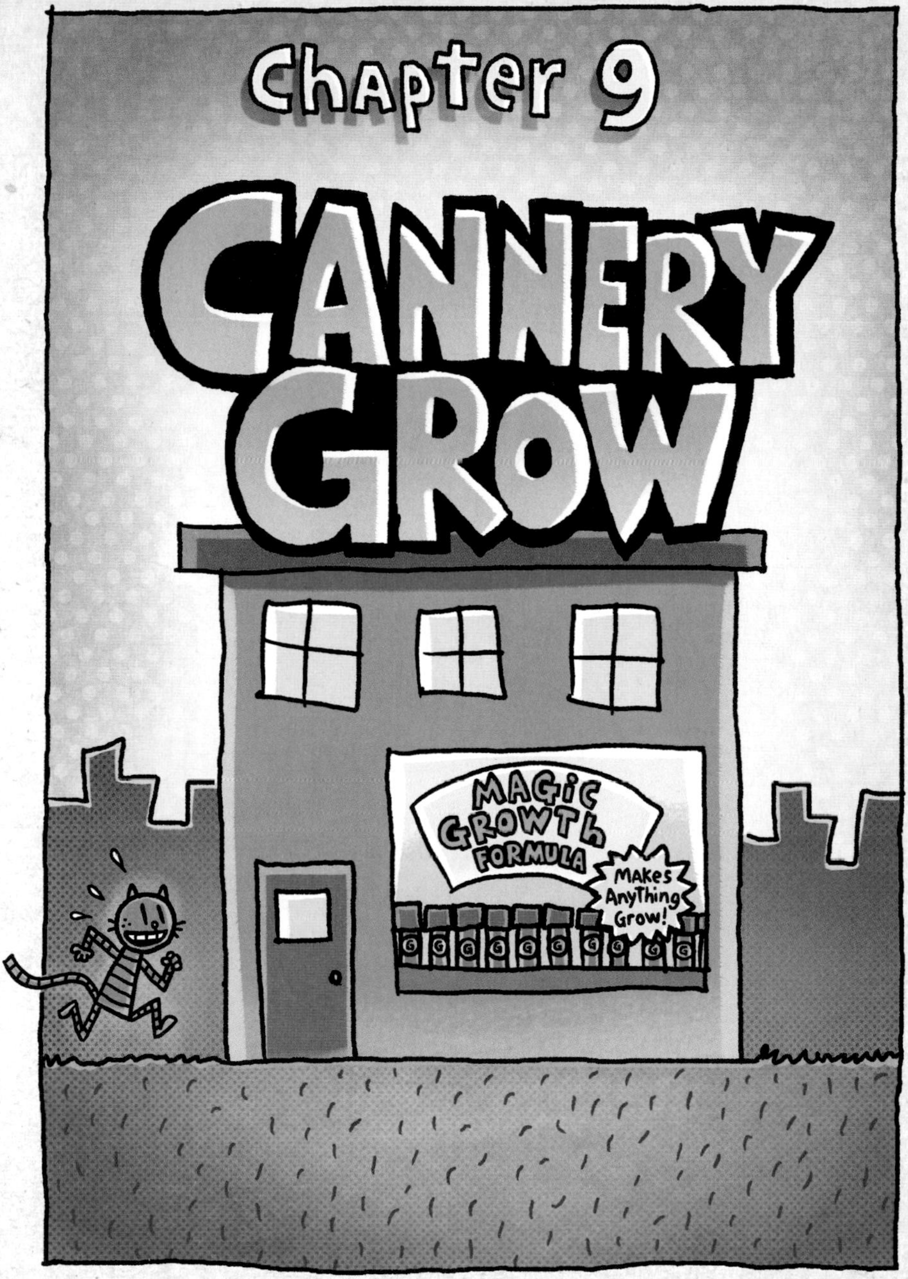
Chapter 9
CANNERY GROW
MAGIC GROWTH FORMULA
Makes Anything Grow!

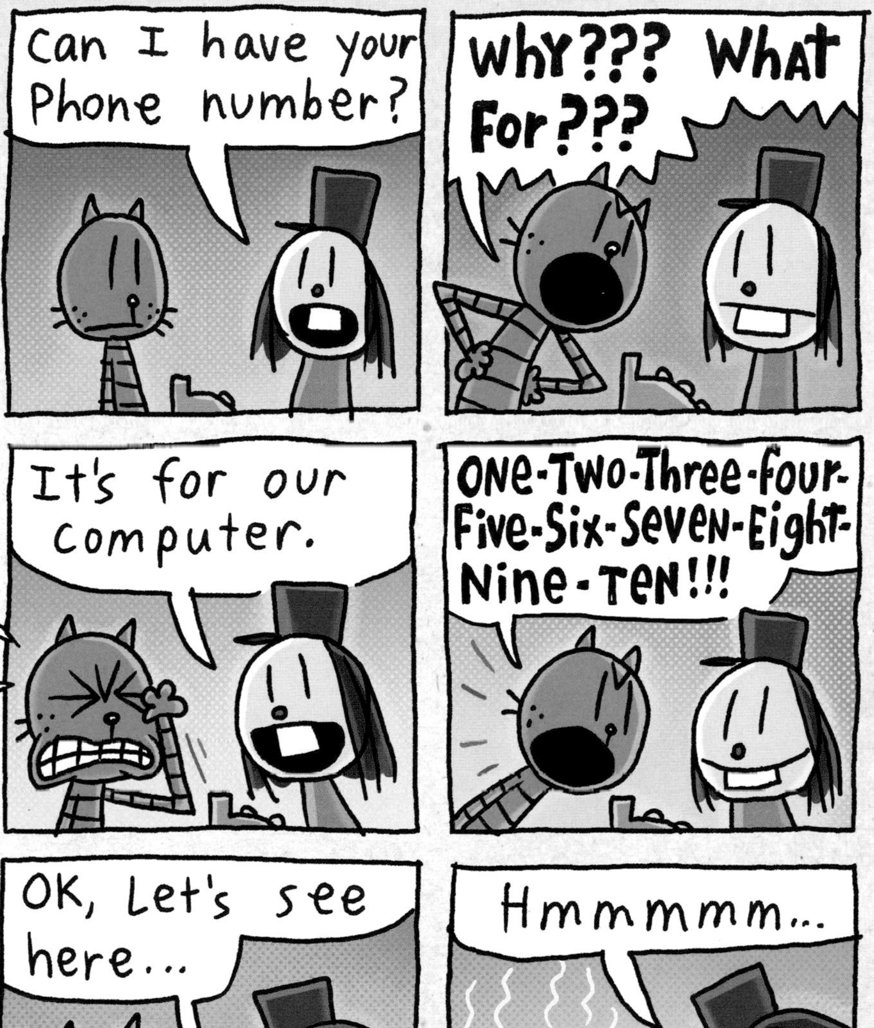
Can I have your Phone number?
WHY??? WHAT For???
It's for our computer.
ONE-Two-Three-four-Five-Six-SeVEN-Eight-Nine-TEN!!!
OK, Let's see here...
Hmmmmmm...

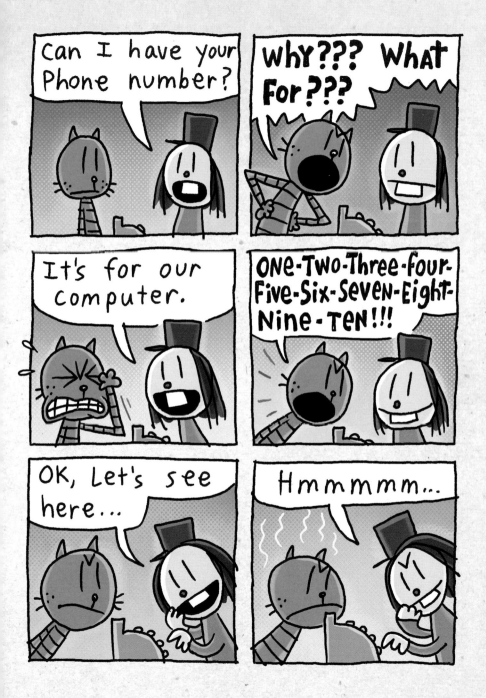

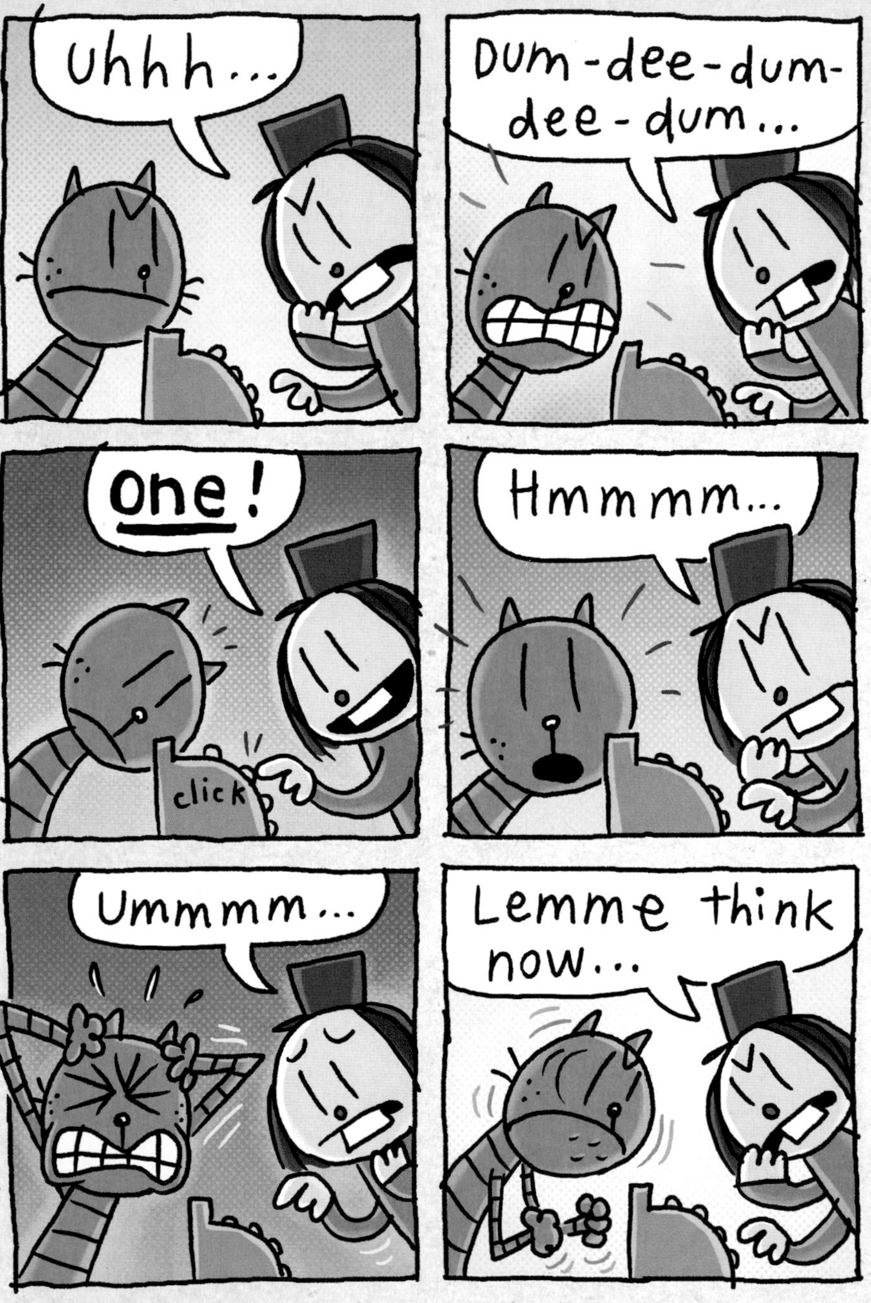
Uhhh...
Dum-dee-dum-dee-dum...
One!
click
Hmmmm...
Ummmm...
Lemme think now...

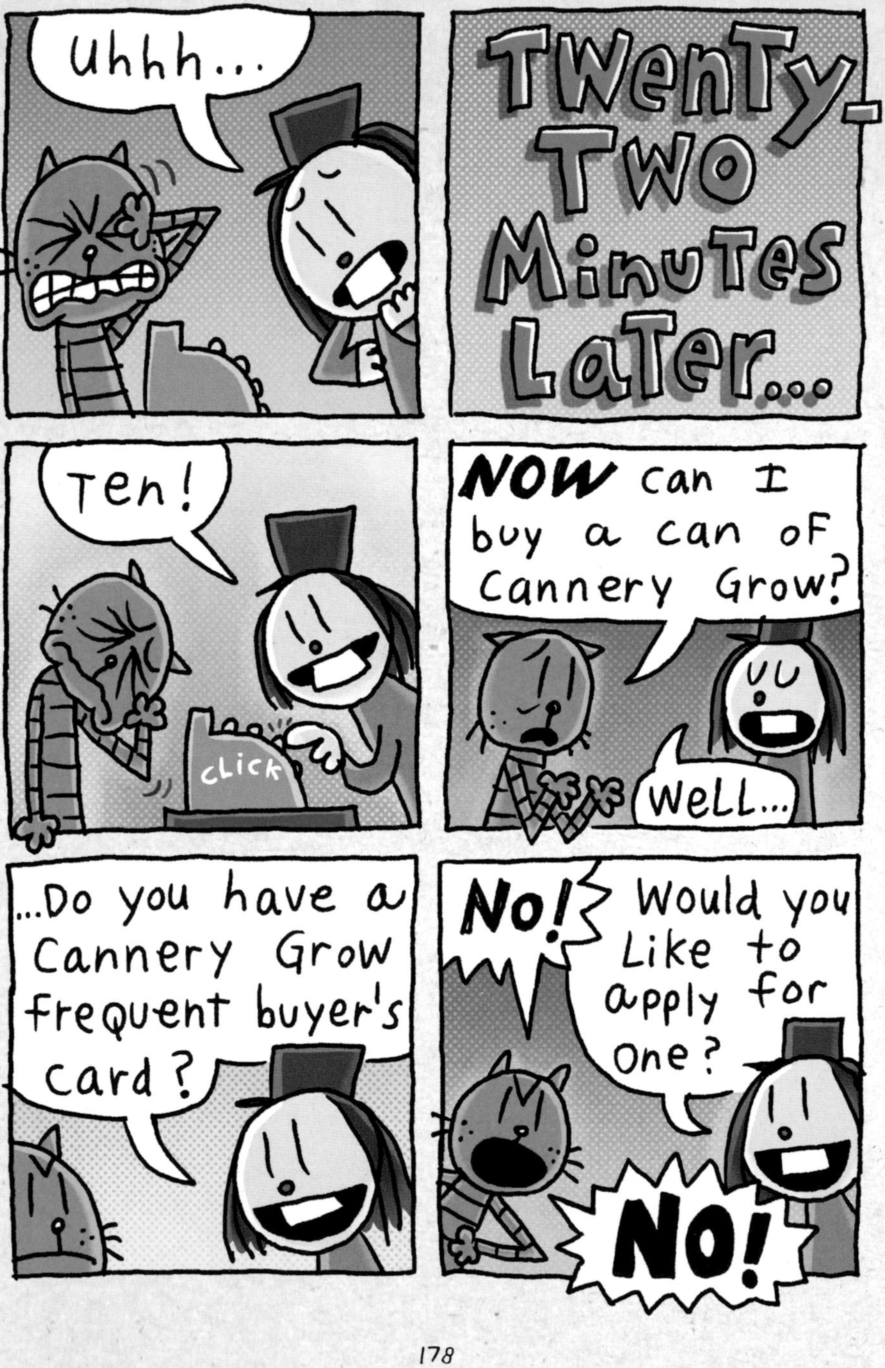
Uhhh...
TwenTy-Two MinuTes LaTer...
Ten!
CLICK
NOW can I buy a can of Cannery Grow?
WeLL...
...Do you have a Cannery Grow frequent buyer's card?
No!
Would you Like to apply for one?
NO!

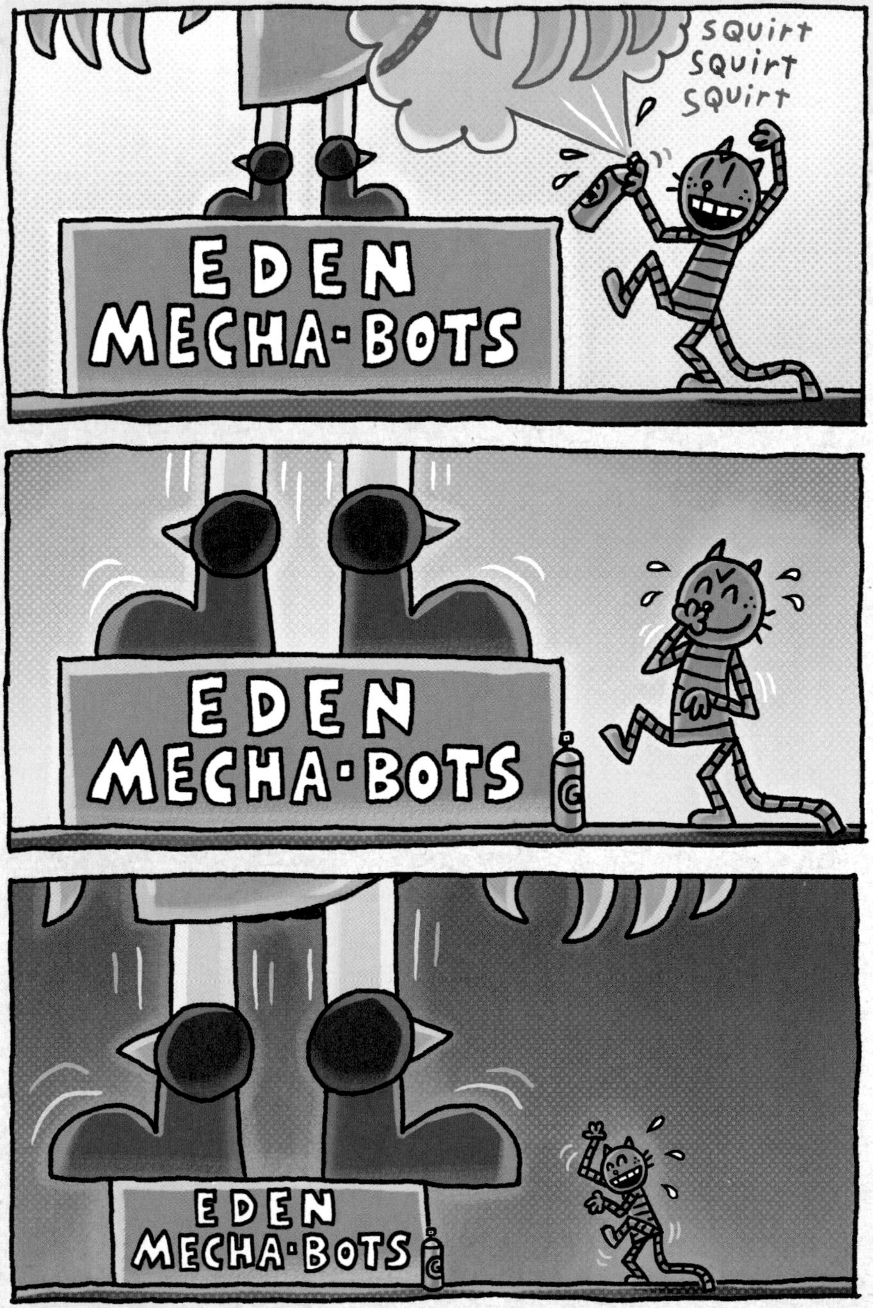
SQUIRT
SQUIRT
SQUIRT
EDEN
MECHA-BOTS
EDEN
MECHA-BOTS
EDEN
MECHA-BOTS

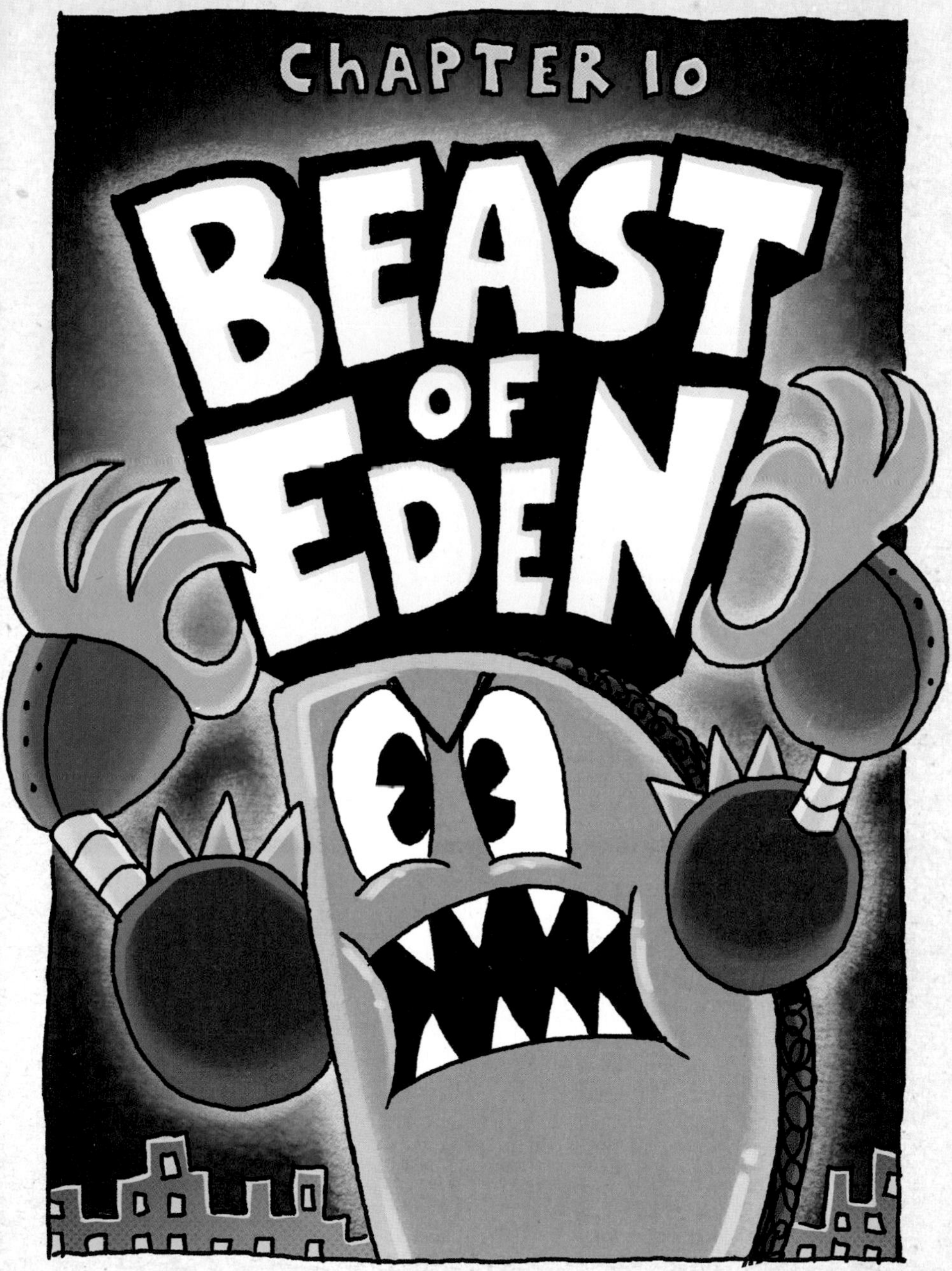
CHAPTER 10
BEAST OF EDEN

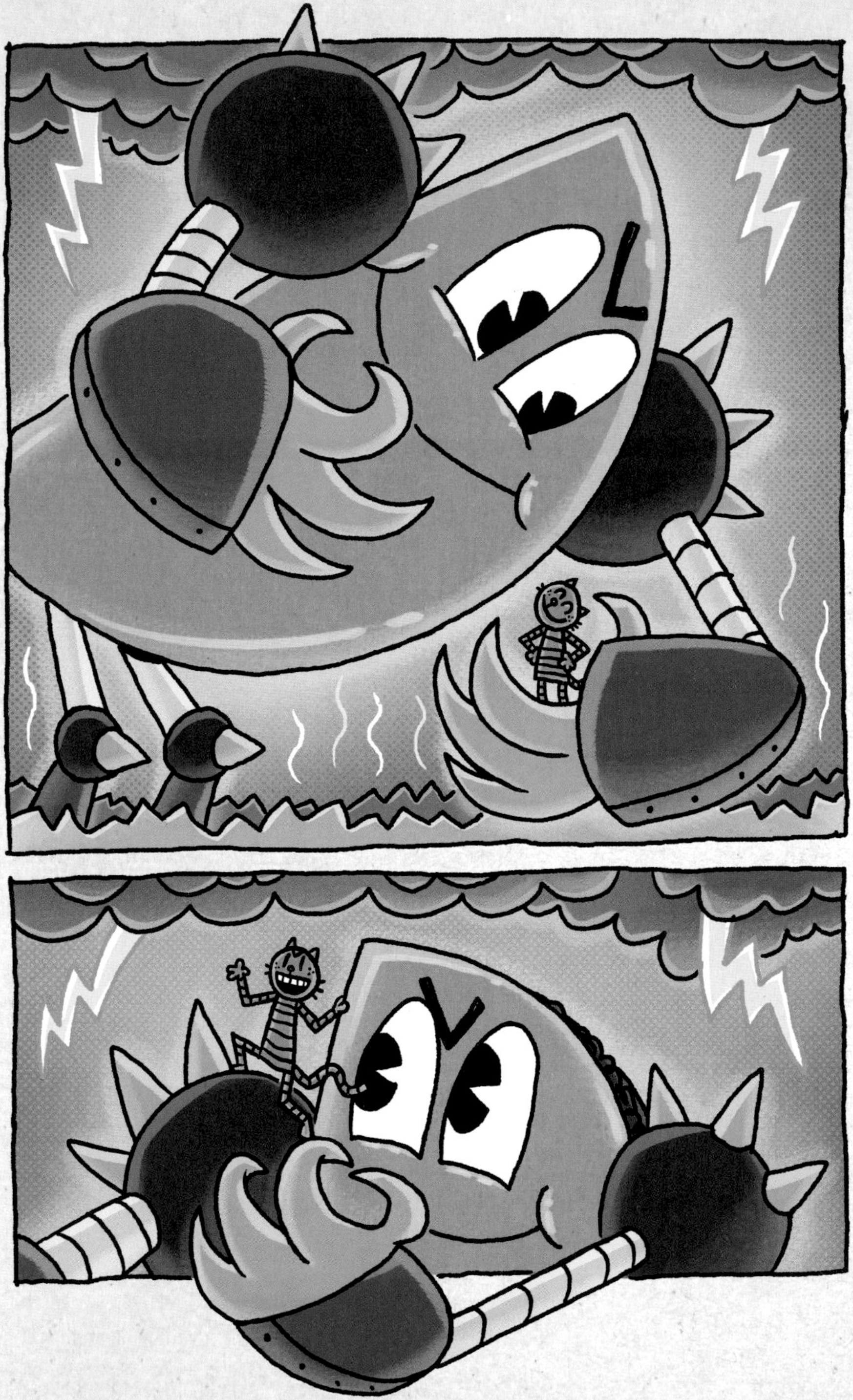

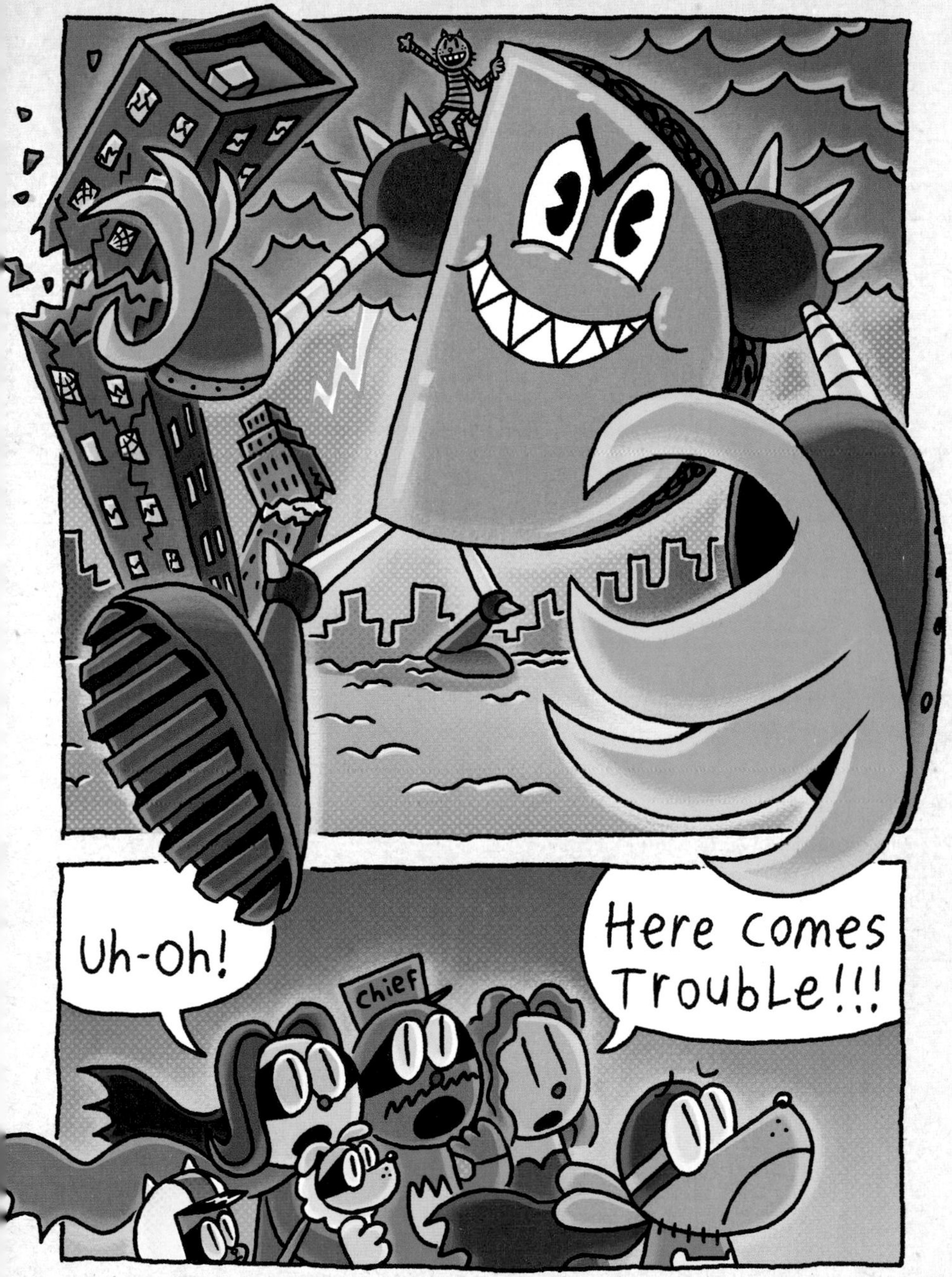

Uh-Oh!
chief
Here comes Trouble!!!

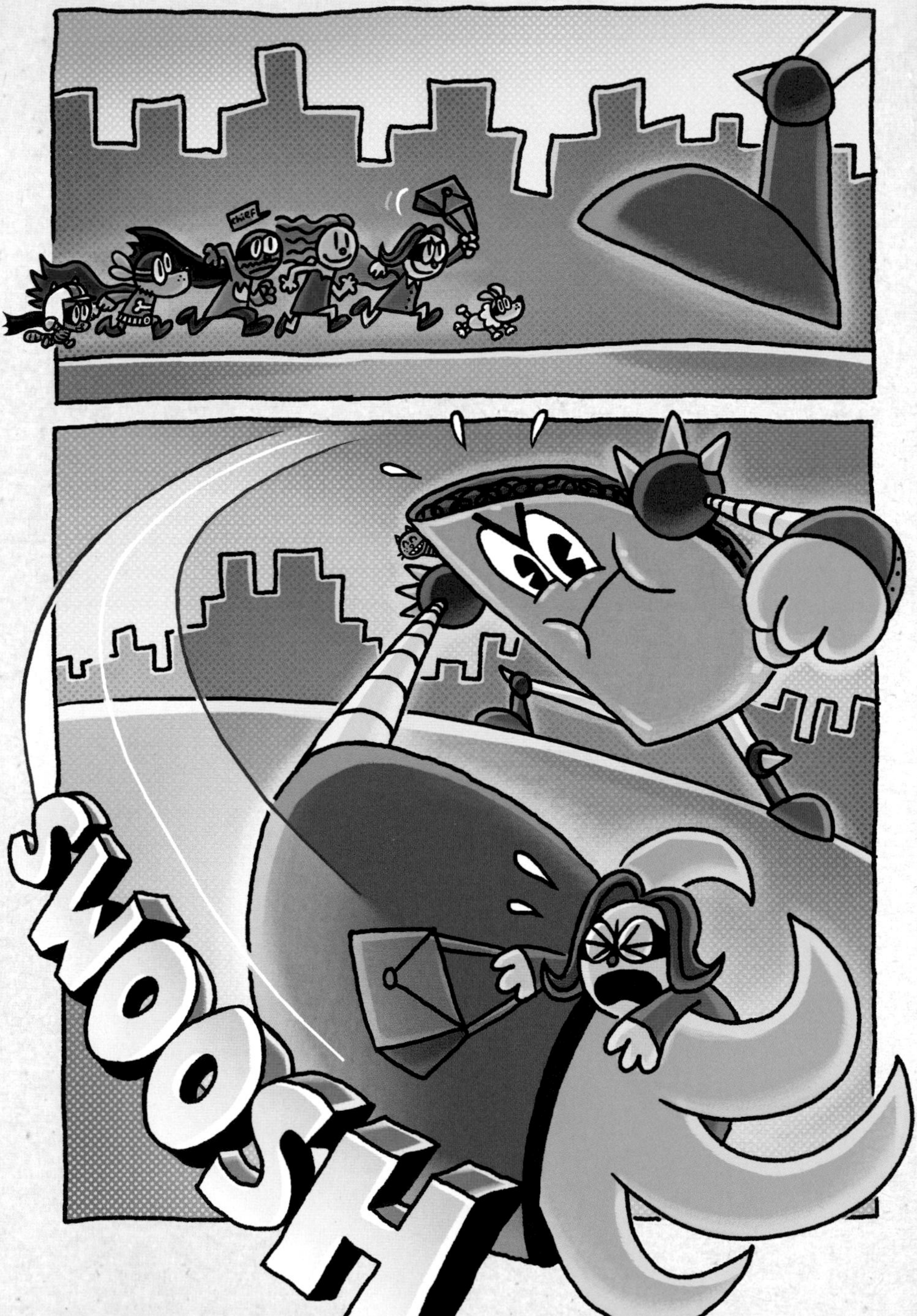
chief
SWOOSH

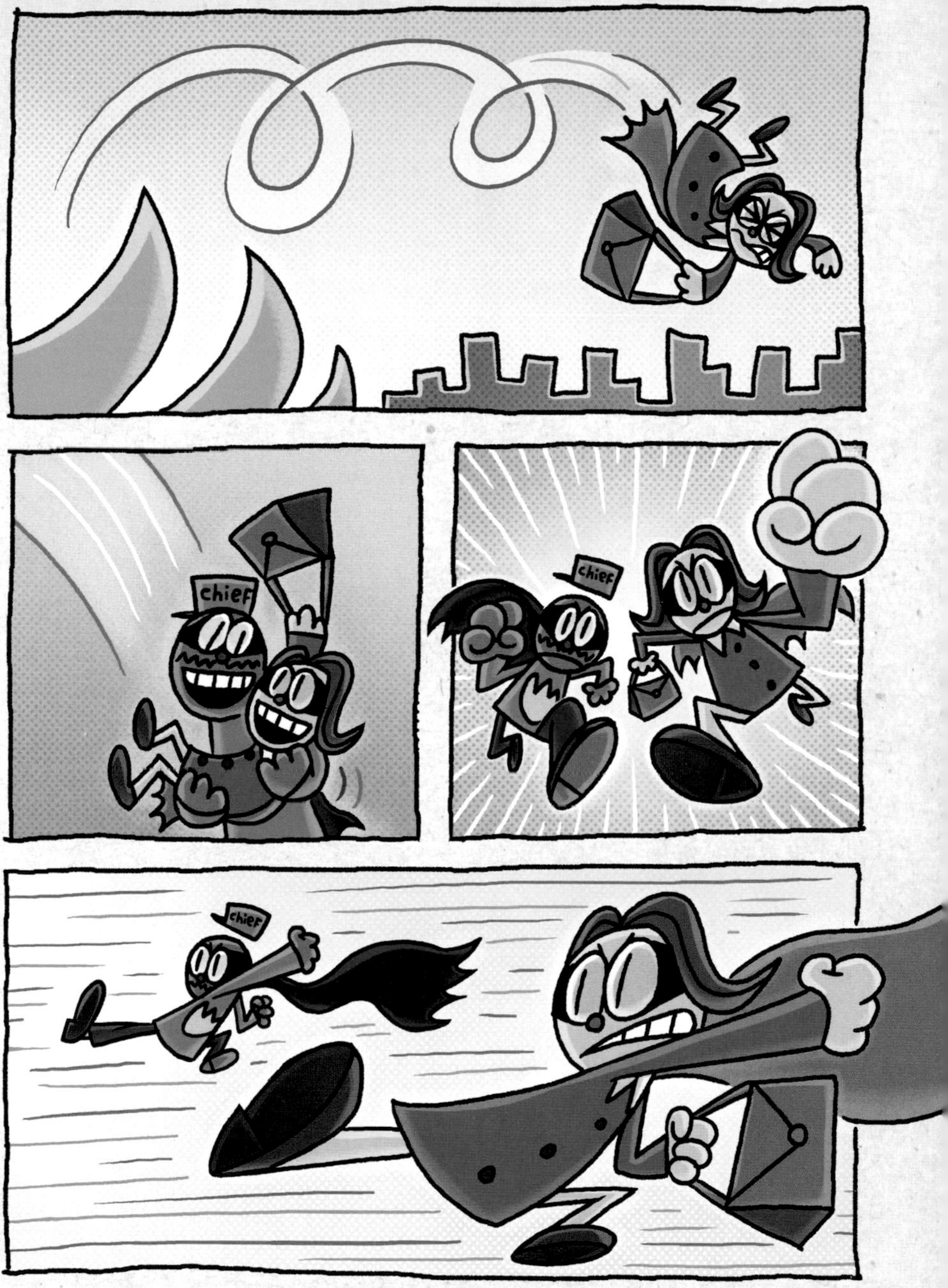
chief
chief
chief

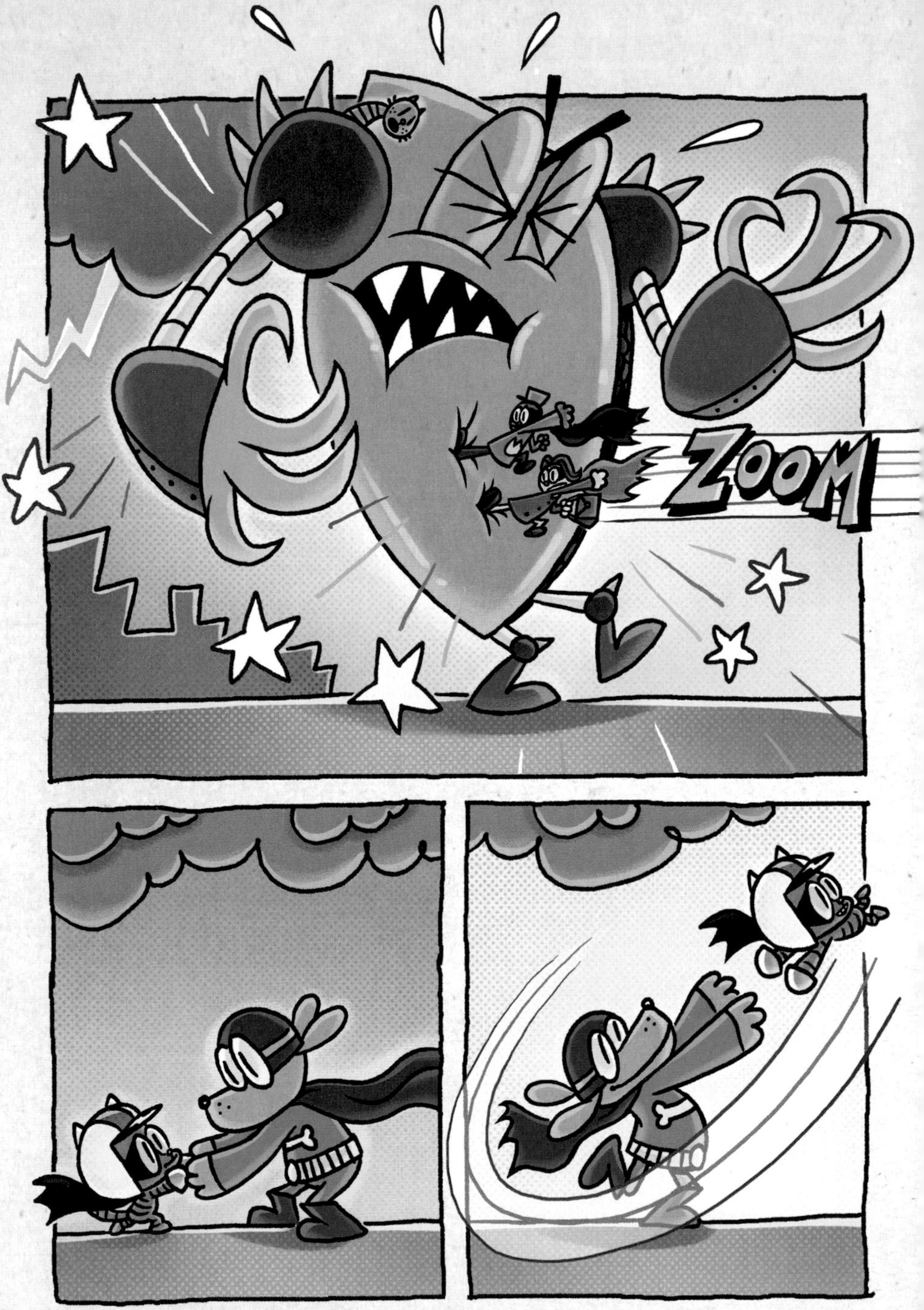
ZOOM

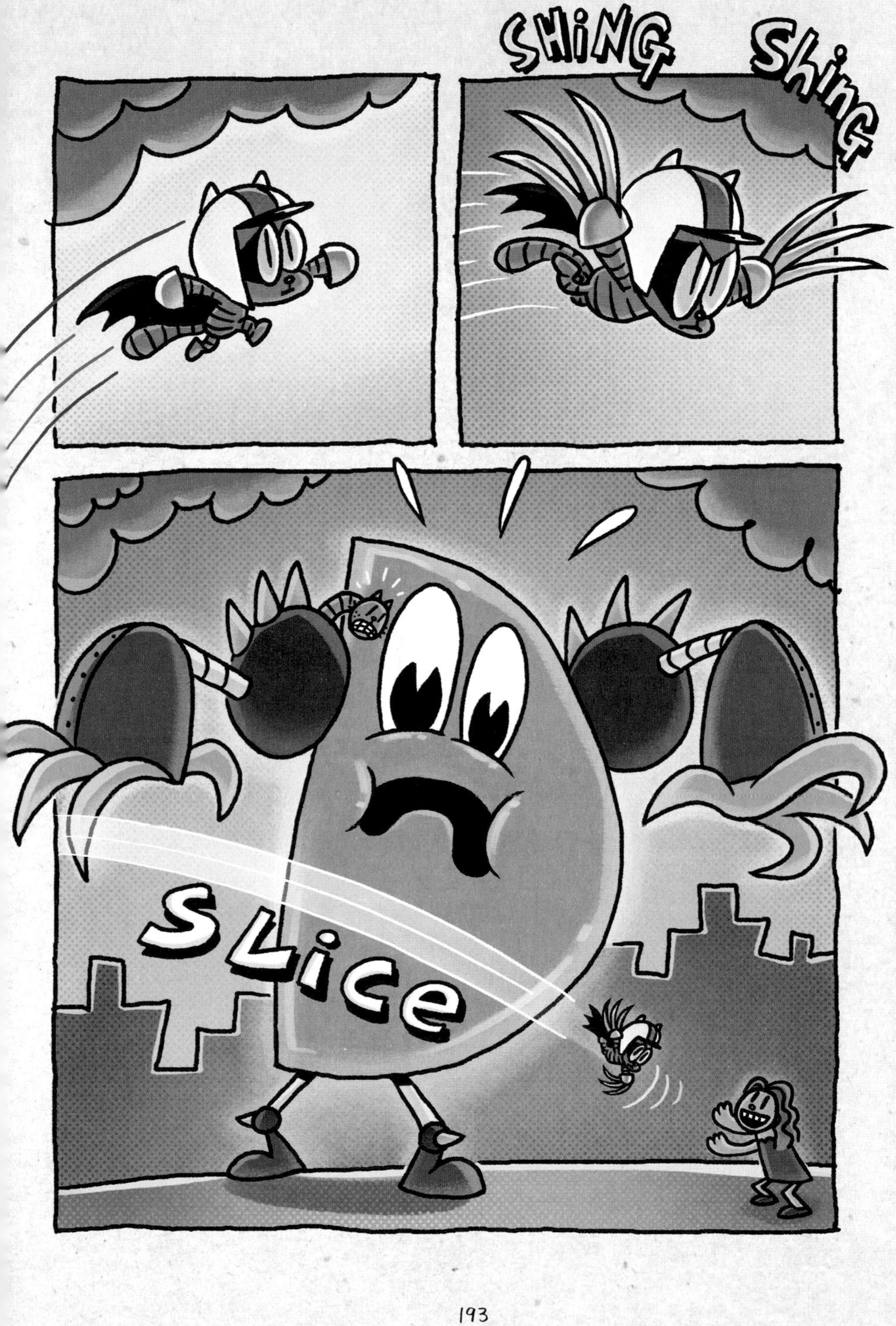
SHiNG
Shing
SLice

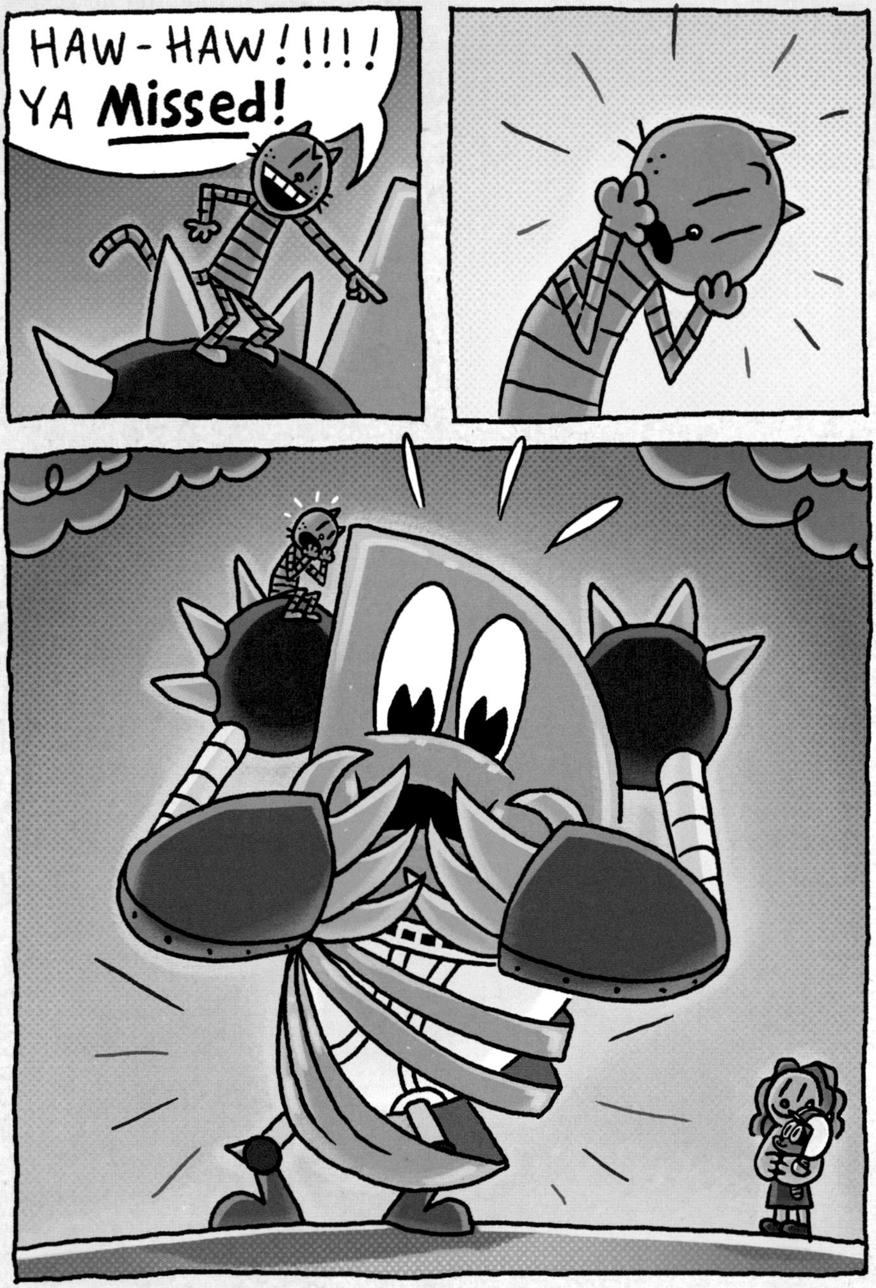
HAW-HAW!!!!!
YA Missed!

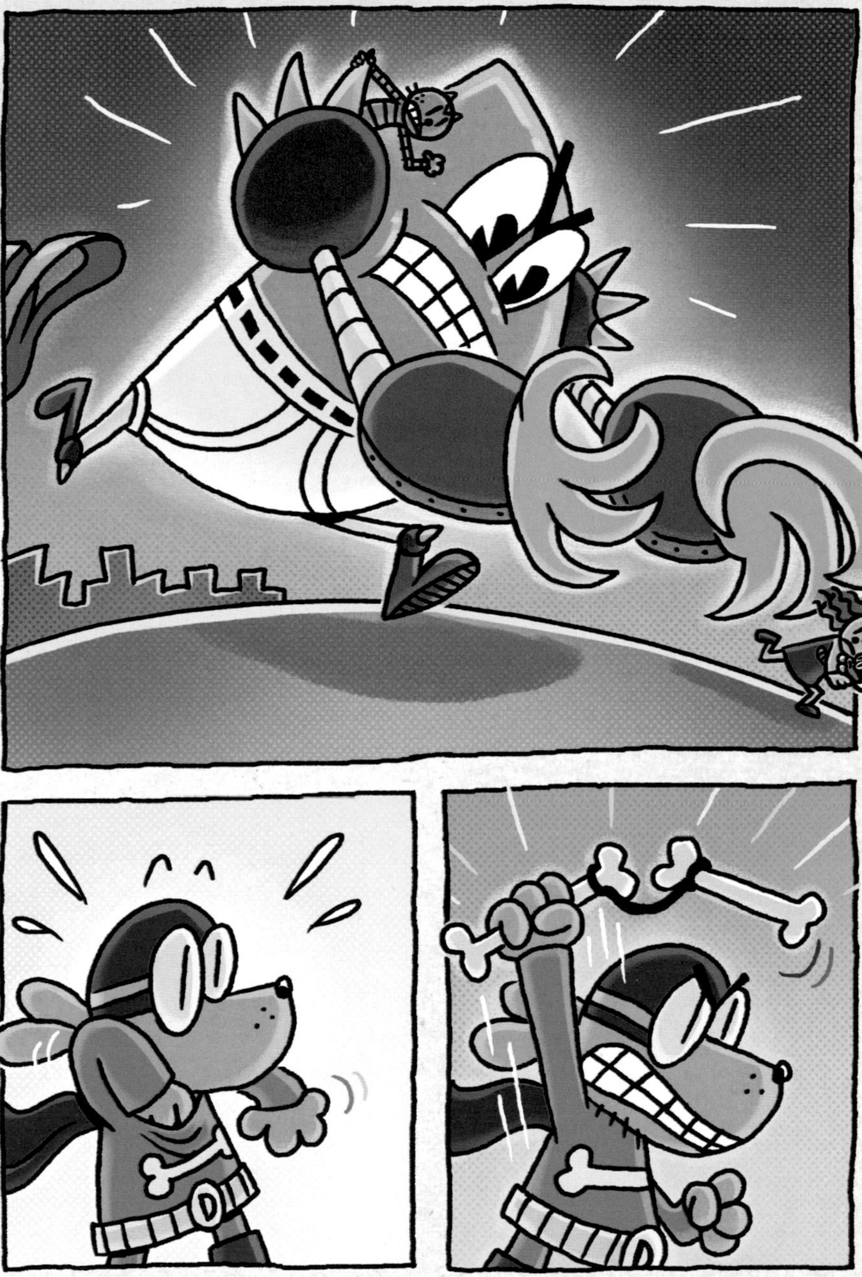

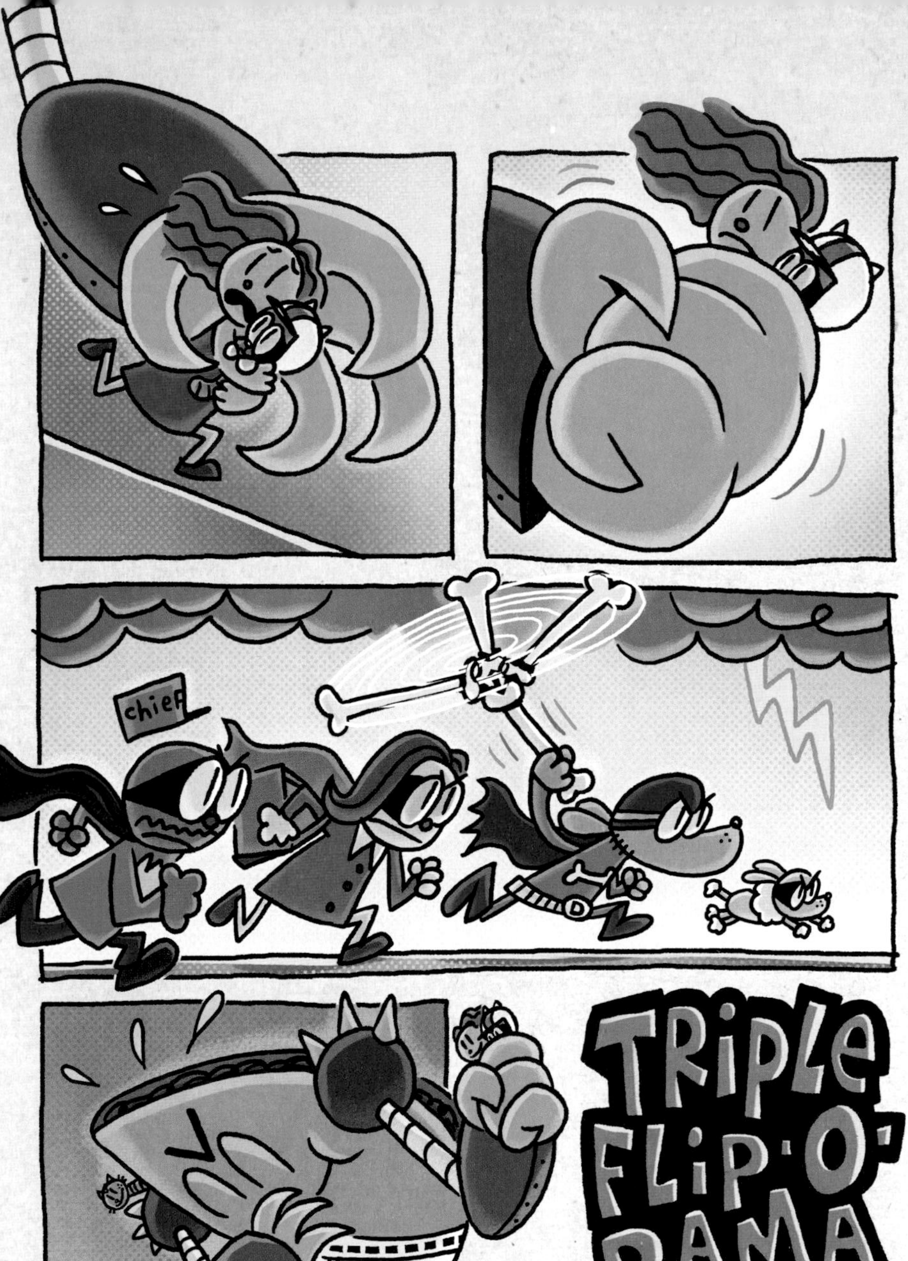
chief

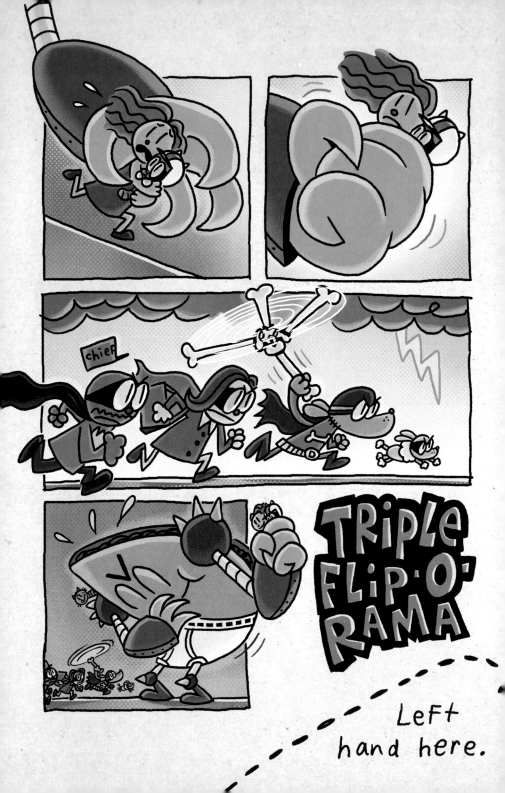

TRIPLE FLIP-O-RAMA

Left hand here.

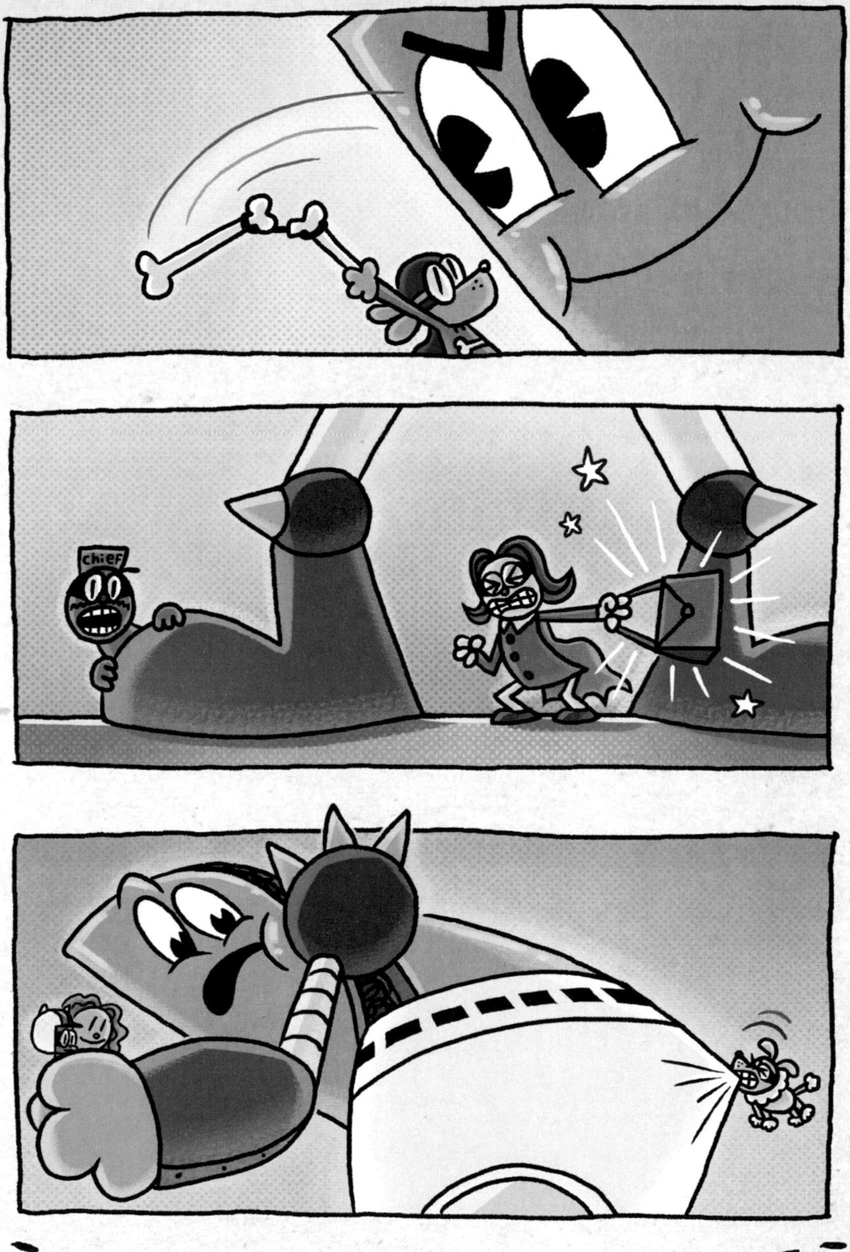
chief

Right Thumb here.

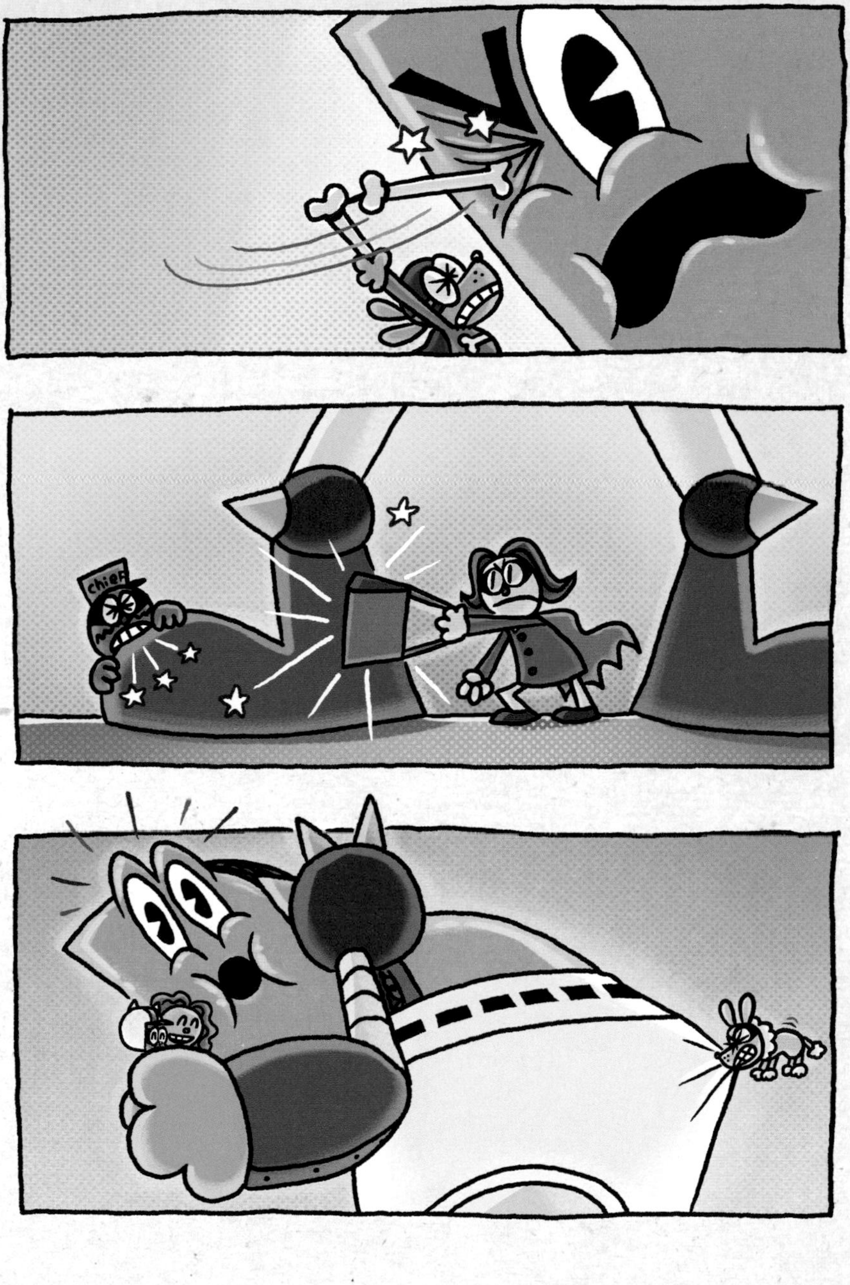
Chief

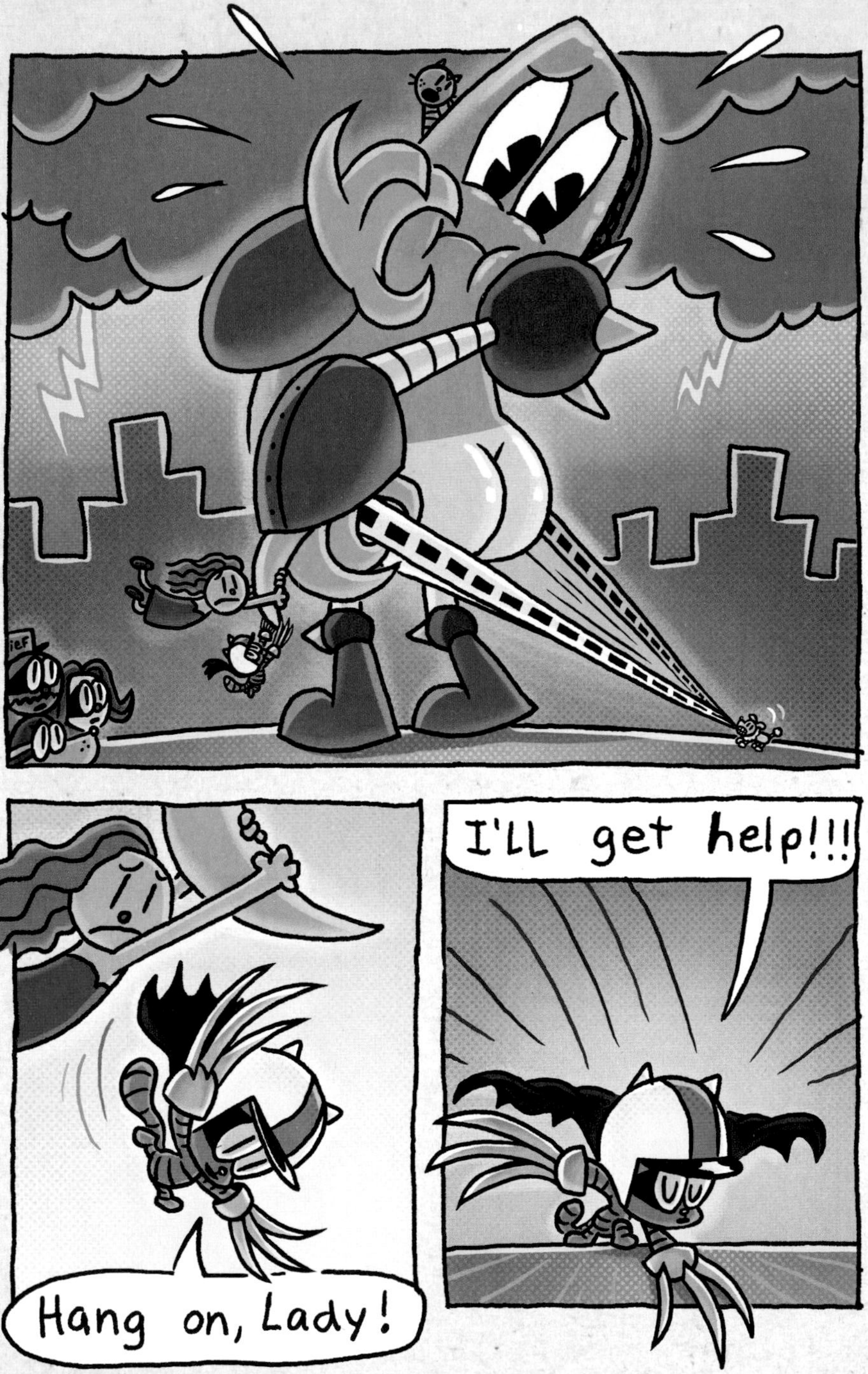
Hang on, Lady!
I'LL get help!!!

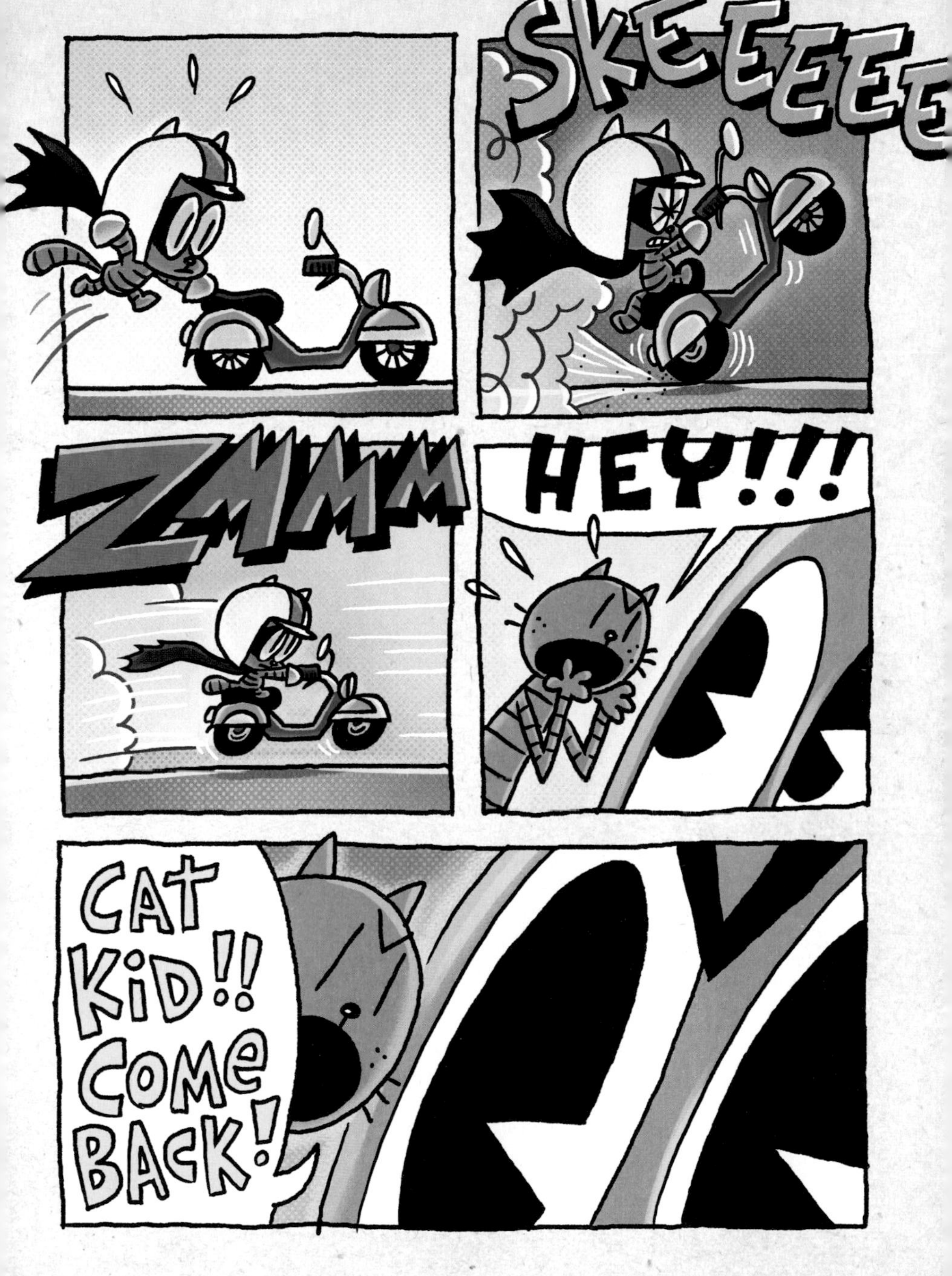
SKEEEEEE
ZMMMM
HEY!!!
CAT KID!! COME BACK!

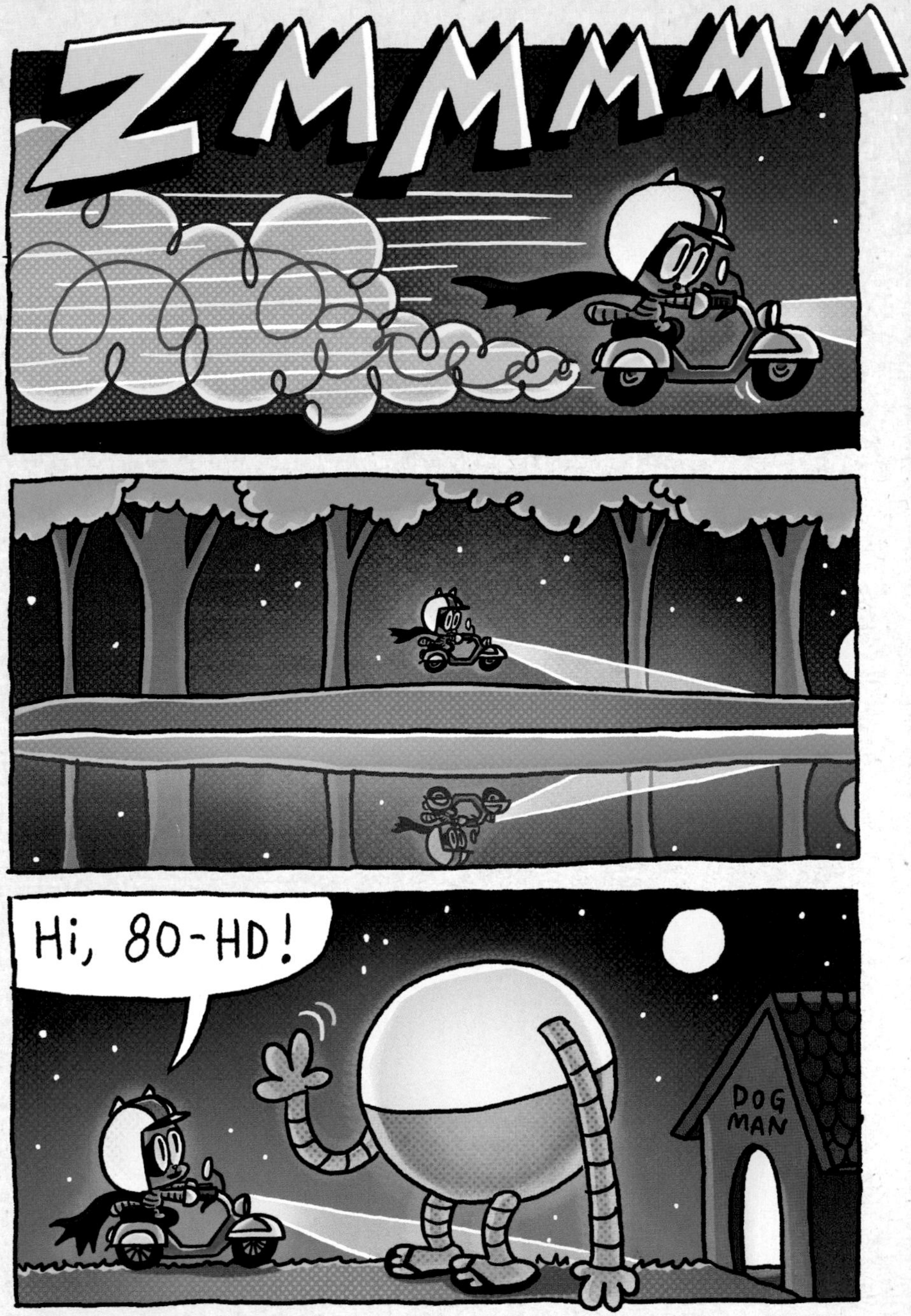
ZMMMMMM
Hi, 80-HD!
DOG MAN

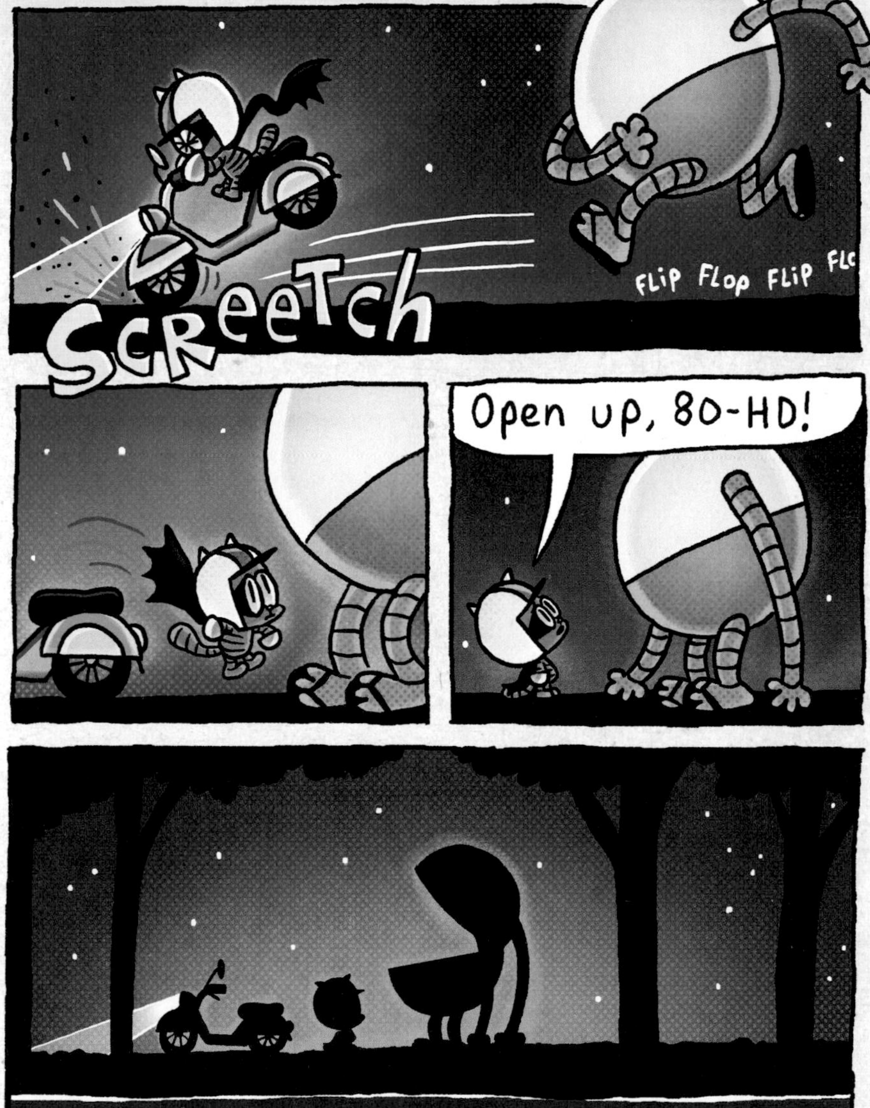
FLIP FLOP FLIP FLO
SCREETCH
Open up, 80-HD!

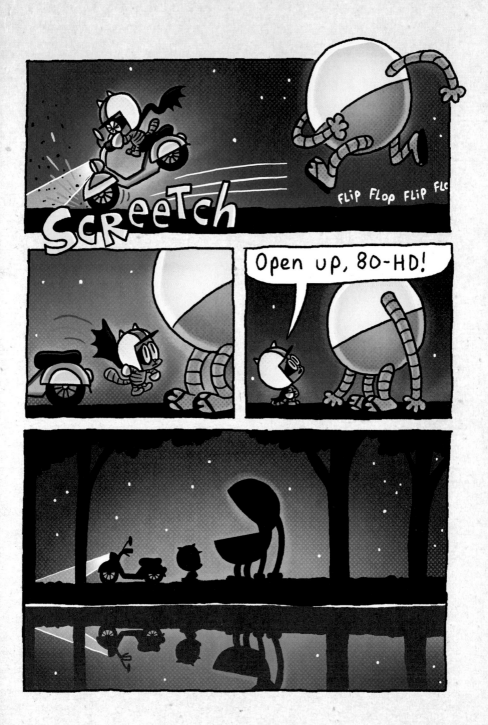

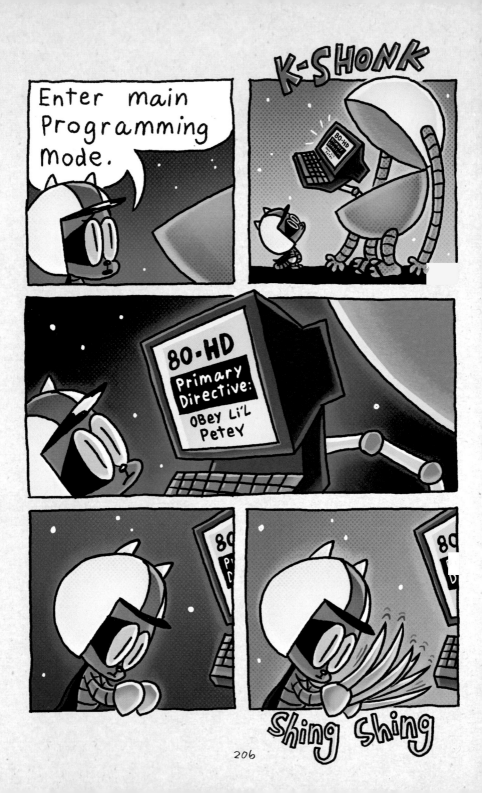

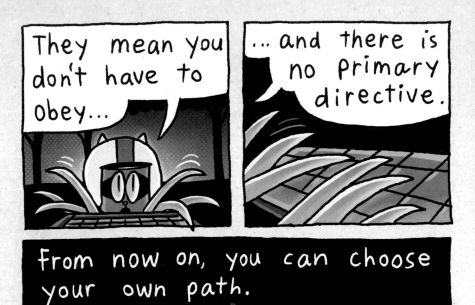

They mean you don't have to obey...

...and there is no primary directive.

From now on, you can choose your own path.

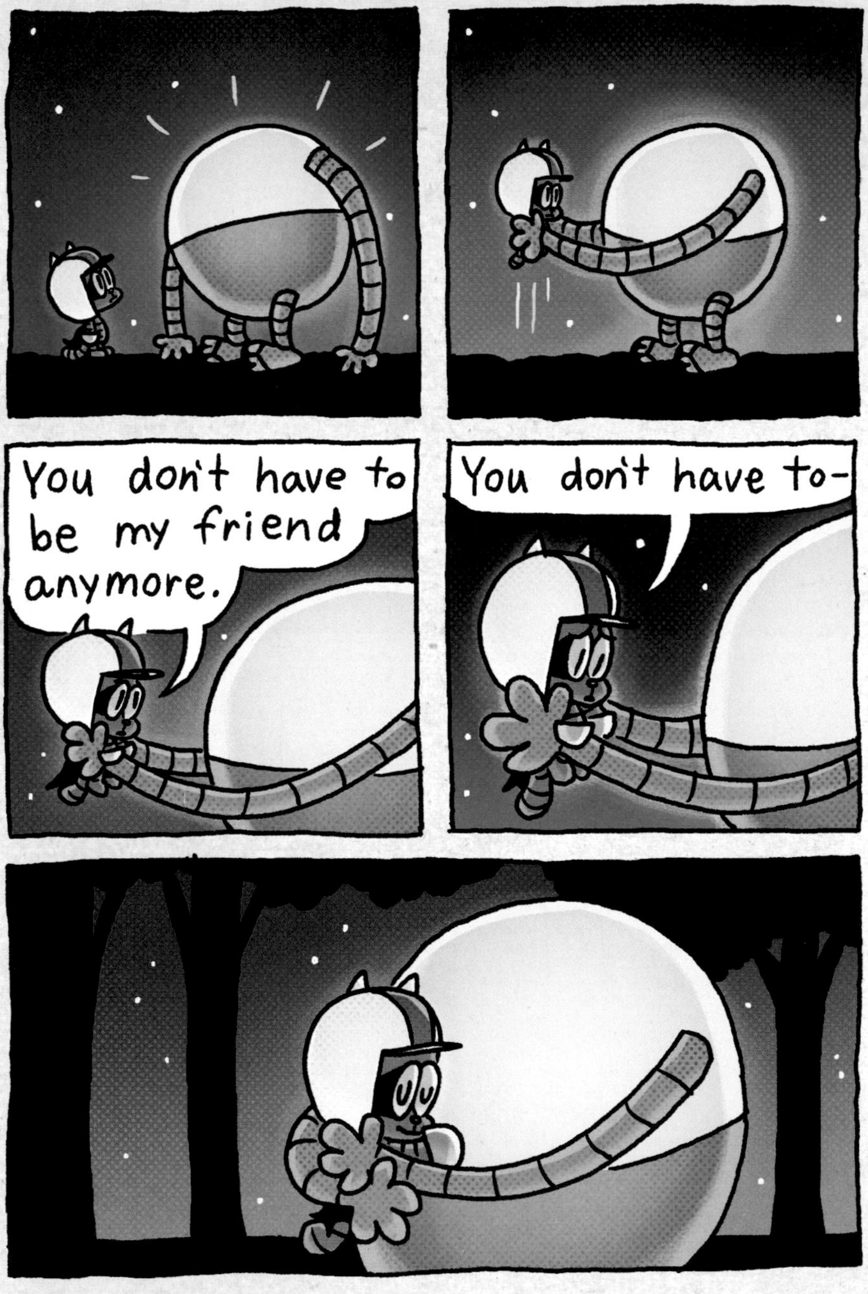
You don't have to be my friend anymore.
You don't have to-

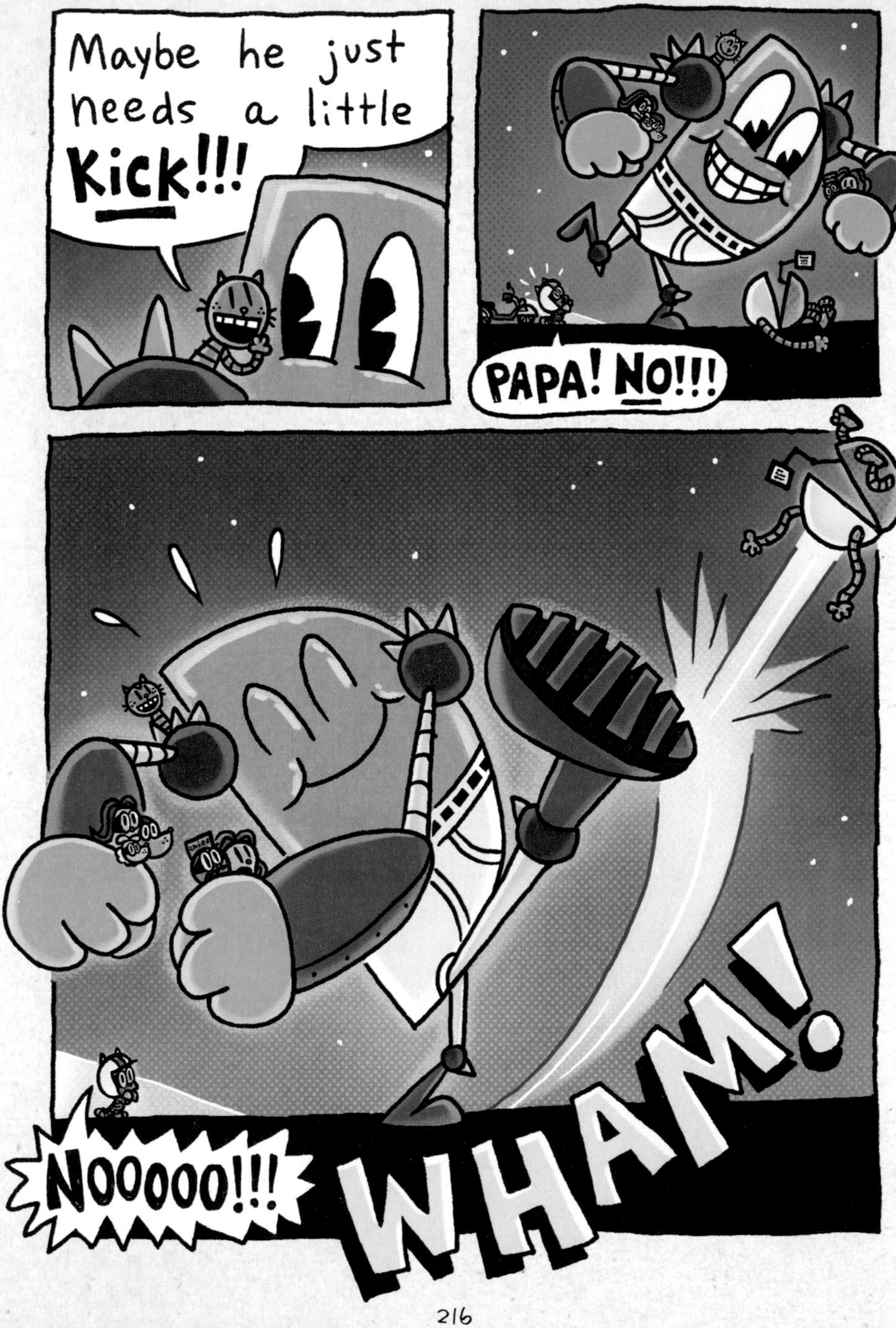
Maybe he just needs a little KICK!!!
PAPA! NO!!!
NOOOOO!!!
WHAM!

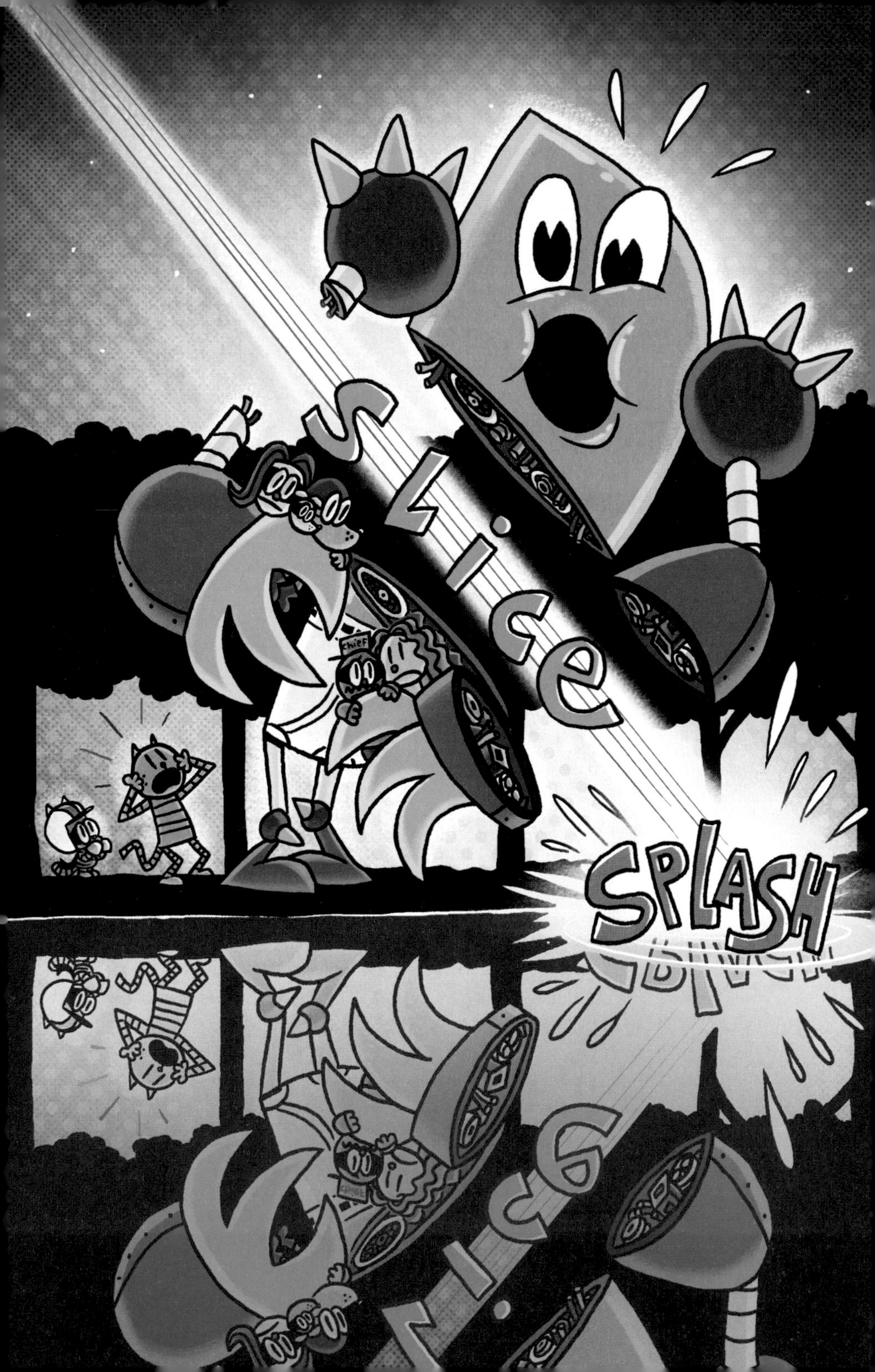
SLICE
SPLASH
CHIEF

221

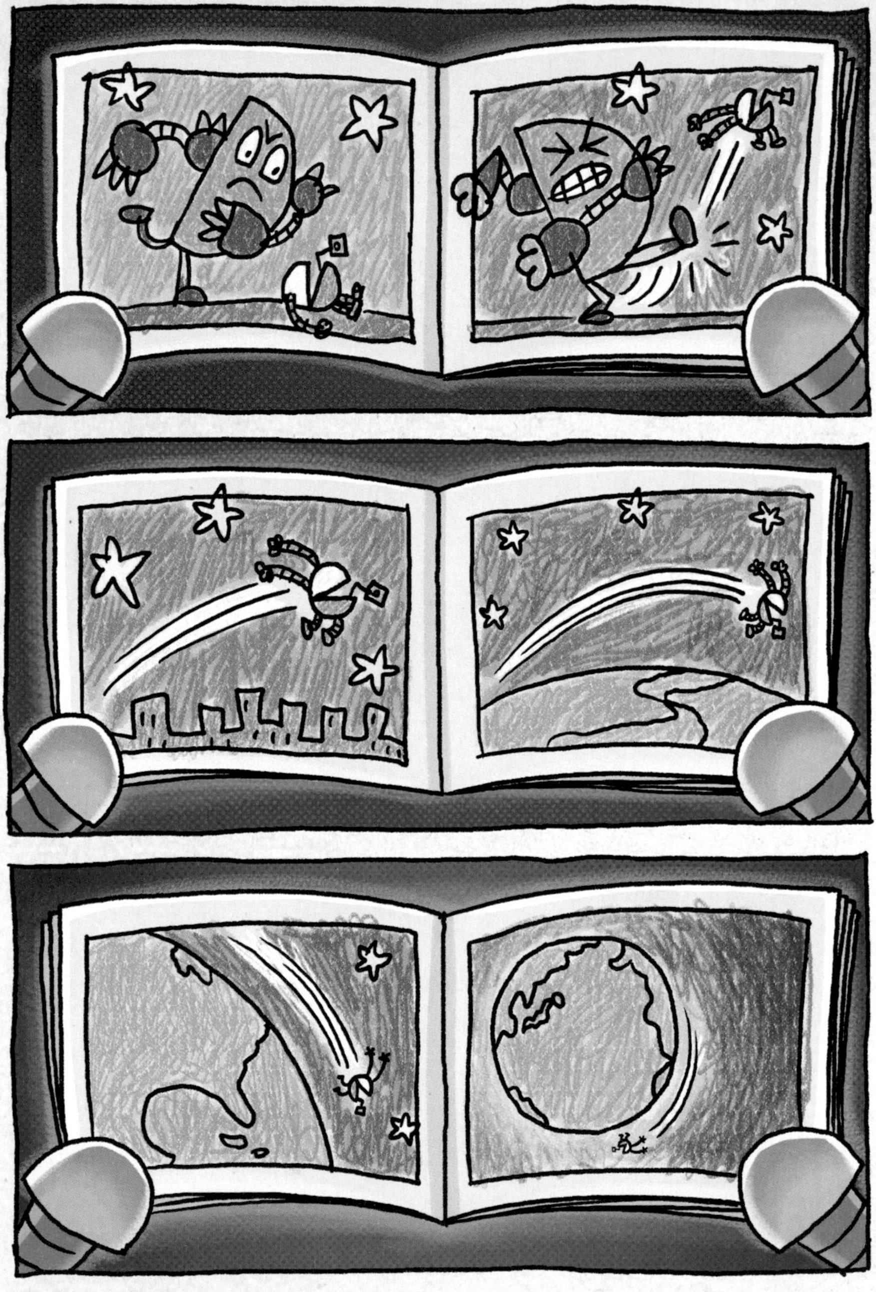

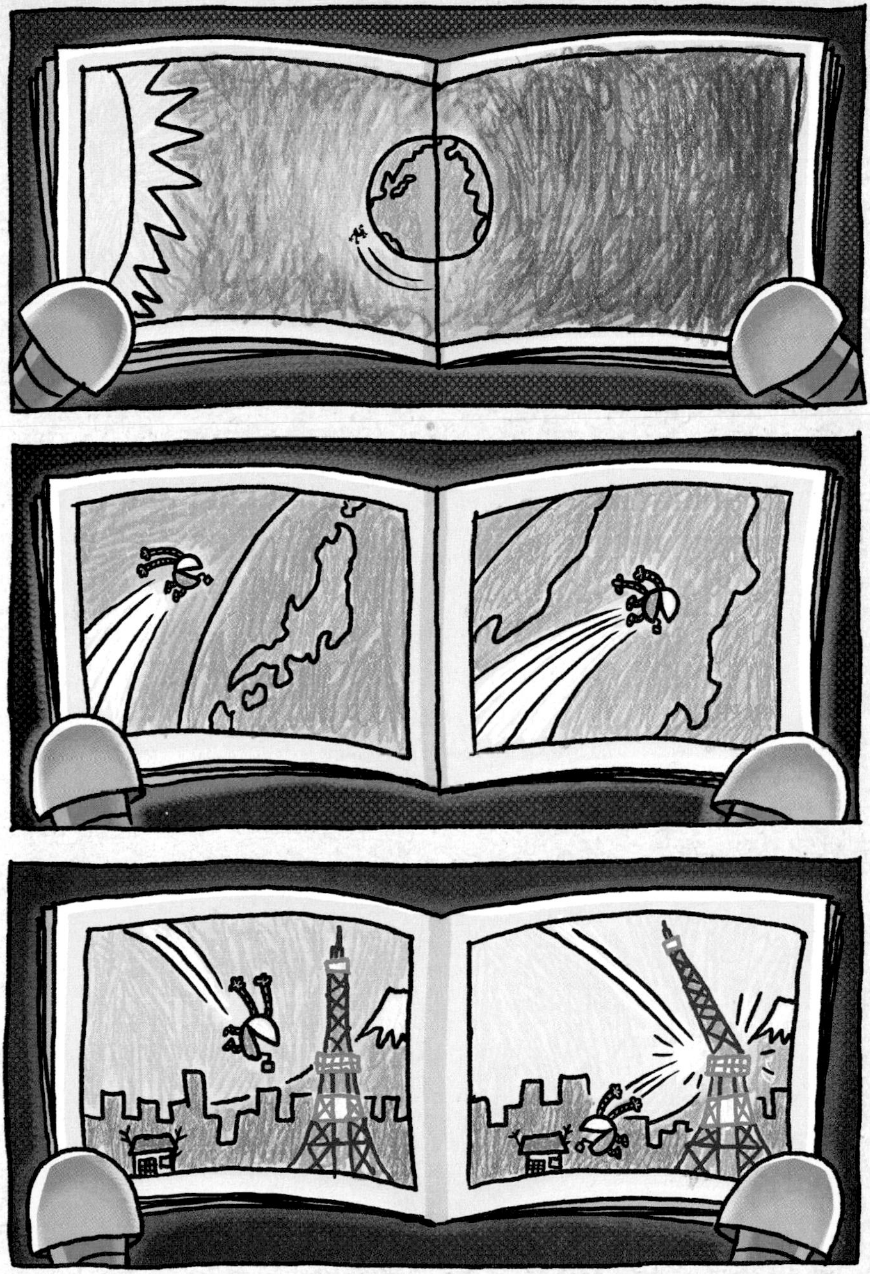

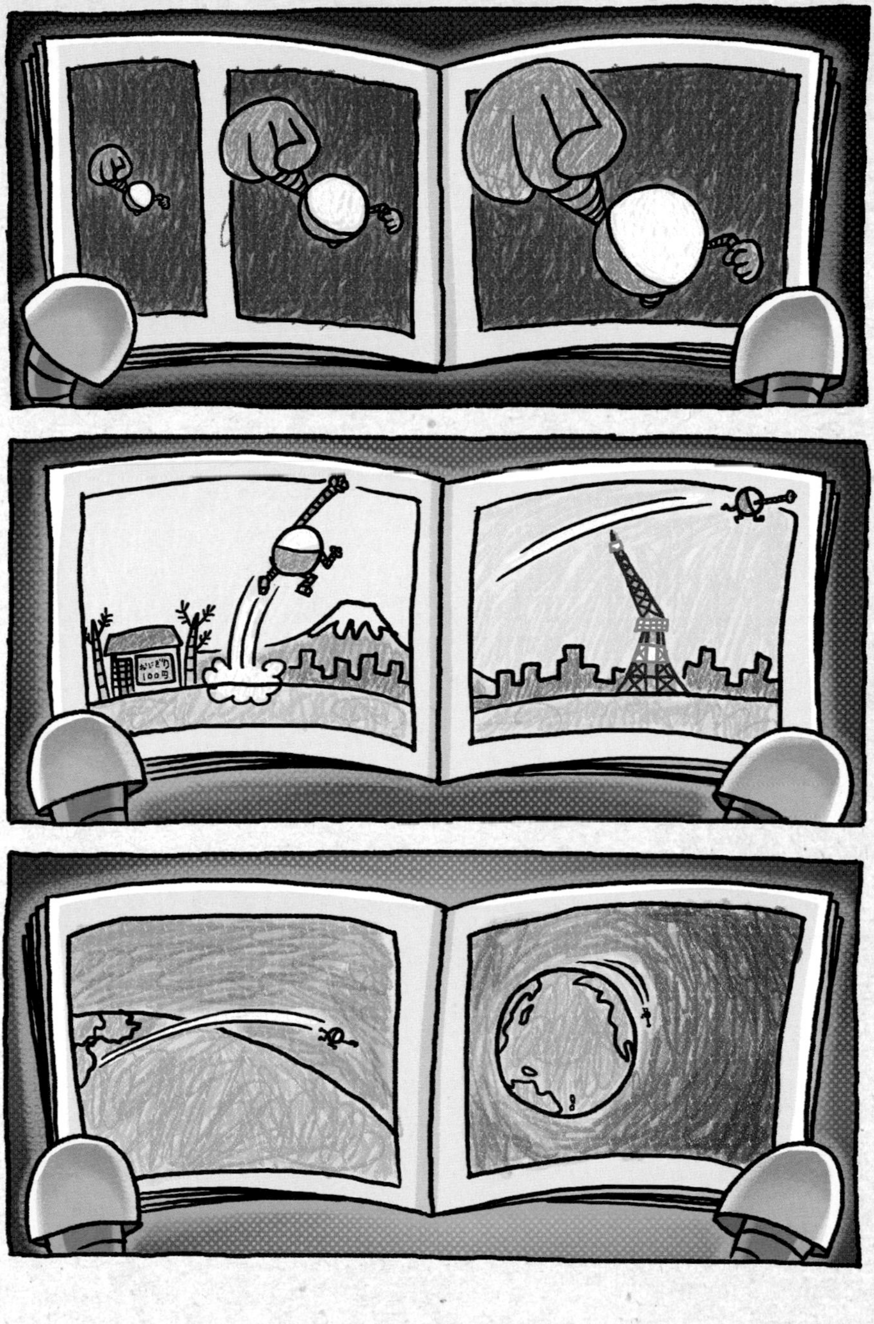
おにぎり
100円

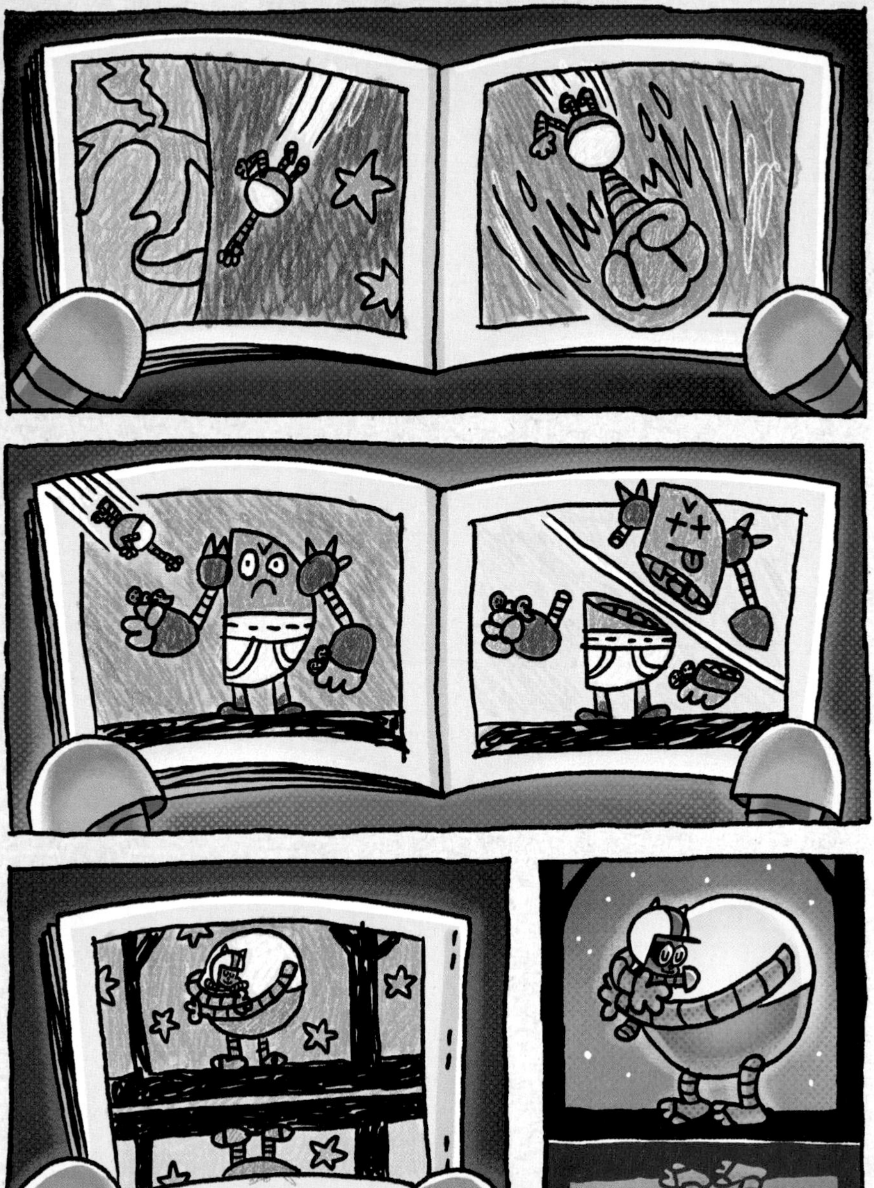

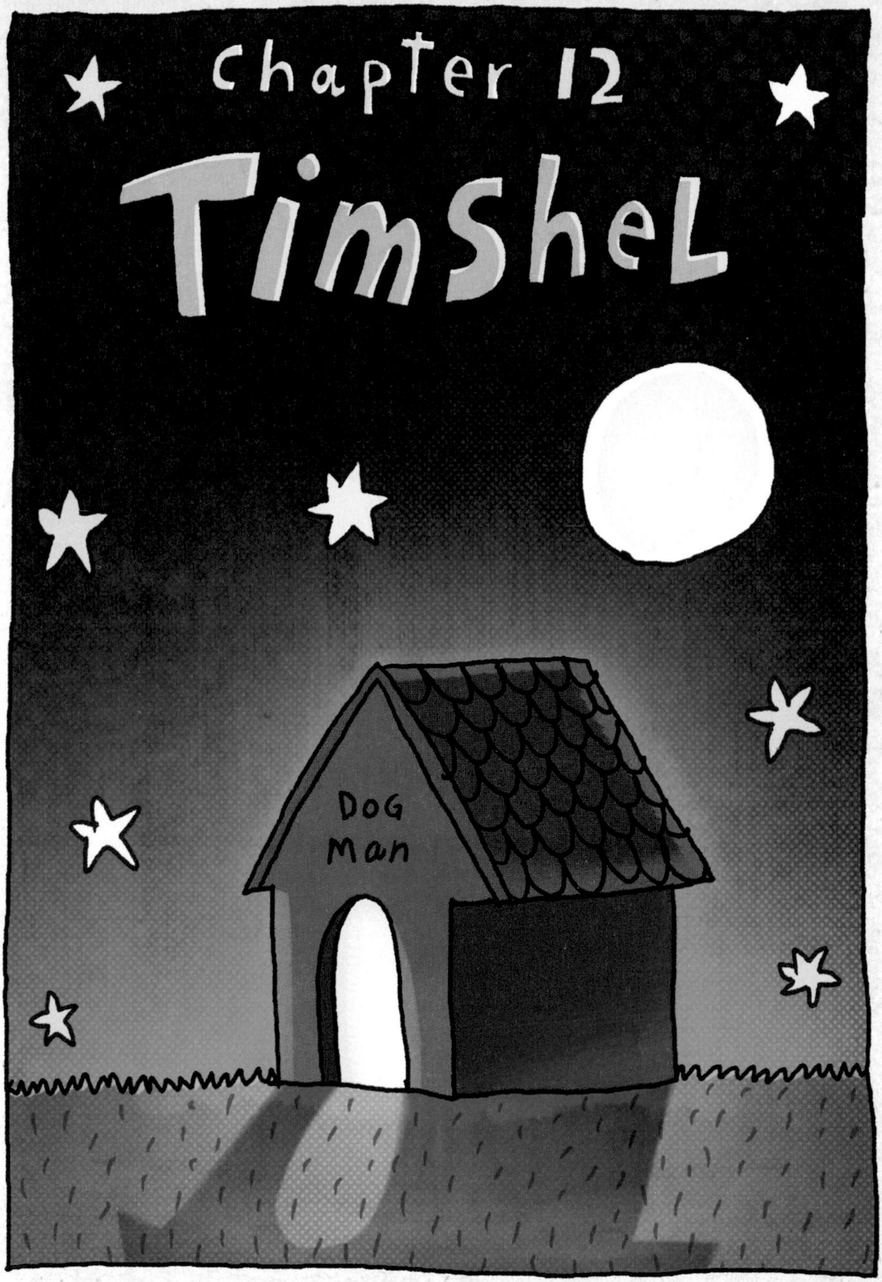
Chapter 12
Timshel
DOG
Man

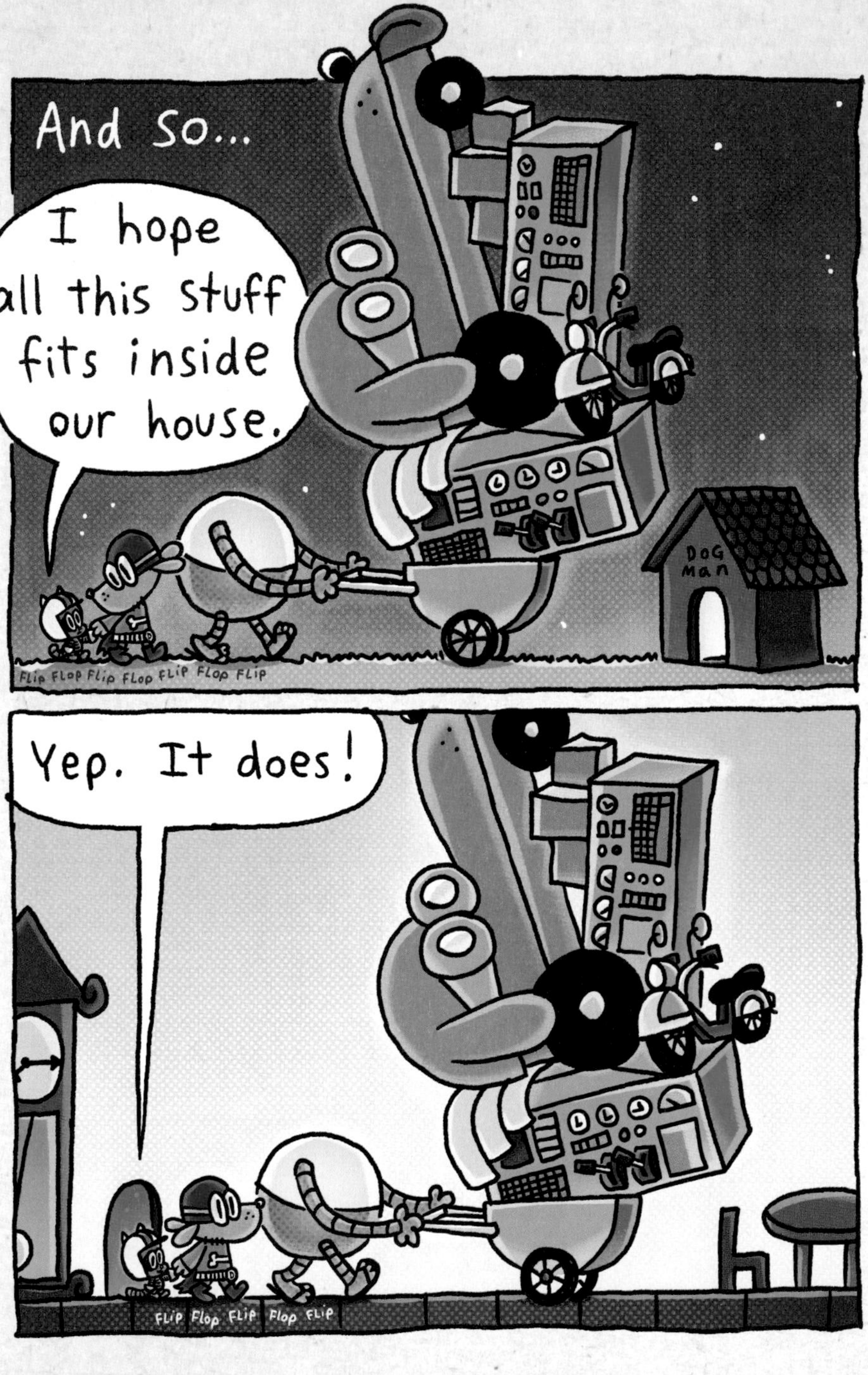
And so...
I hope all this stuff fits inside our house.
FLip FLop FLip FLop FLiP FLop FLiP
DOG Man
Yep. It does!
FLiP Flop FLiP Flop FLiP

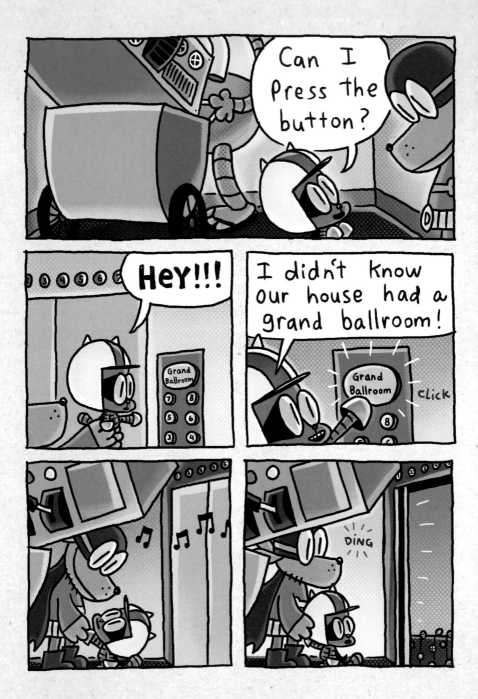

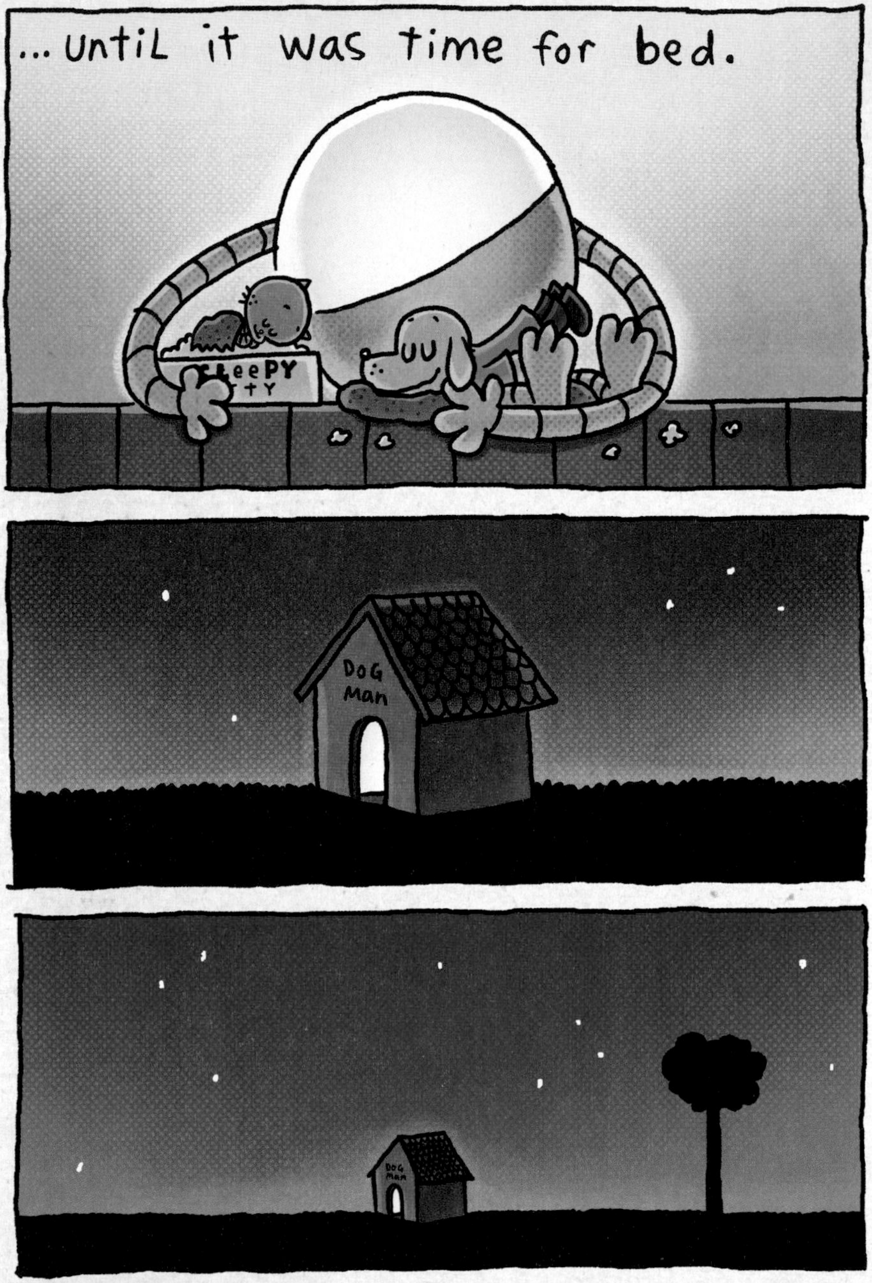
...until it was time for bed.
DOG Man

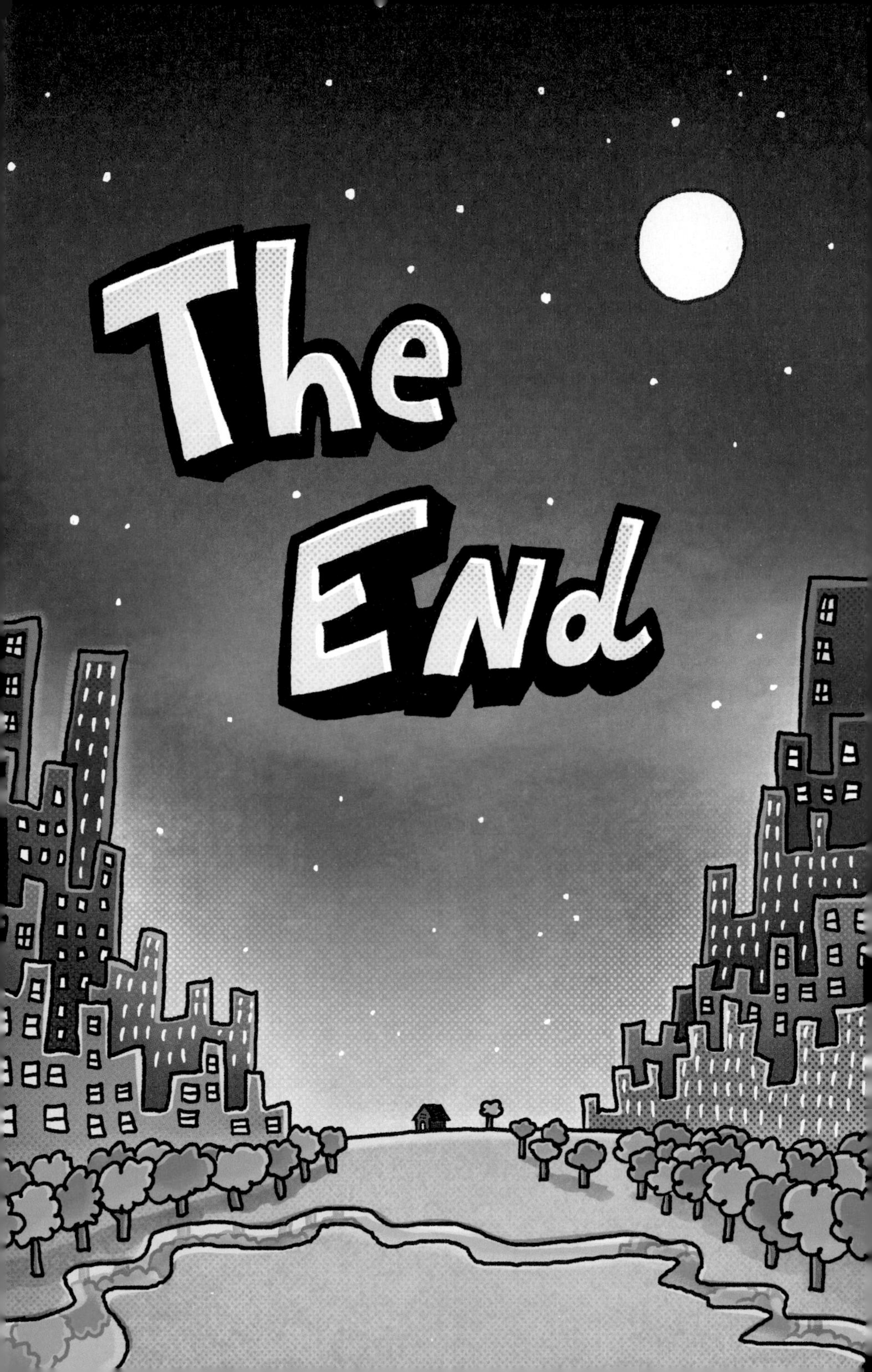
The End

HOW 2 DRAW THE BARK KNIGHT

in 46 Ridiculously easy Steps!

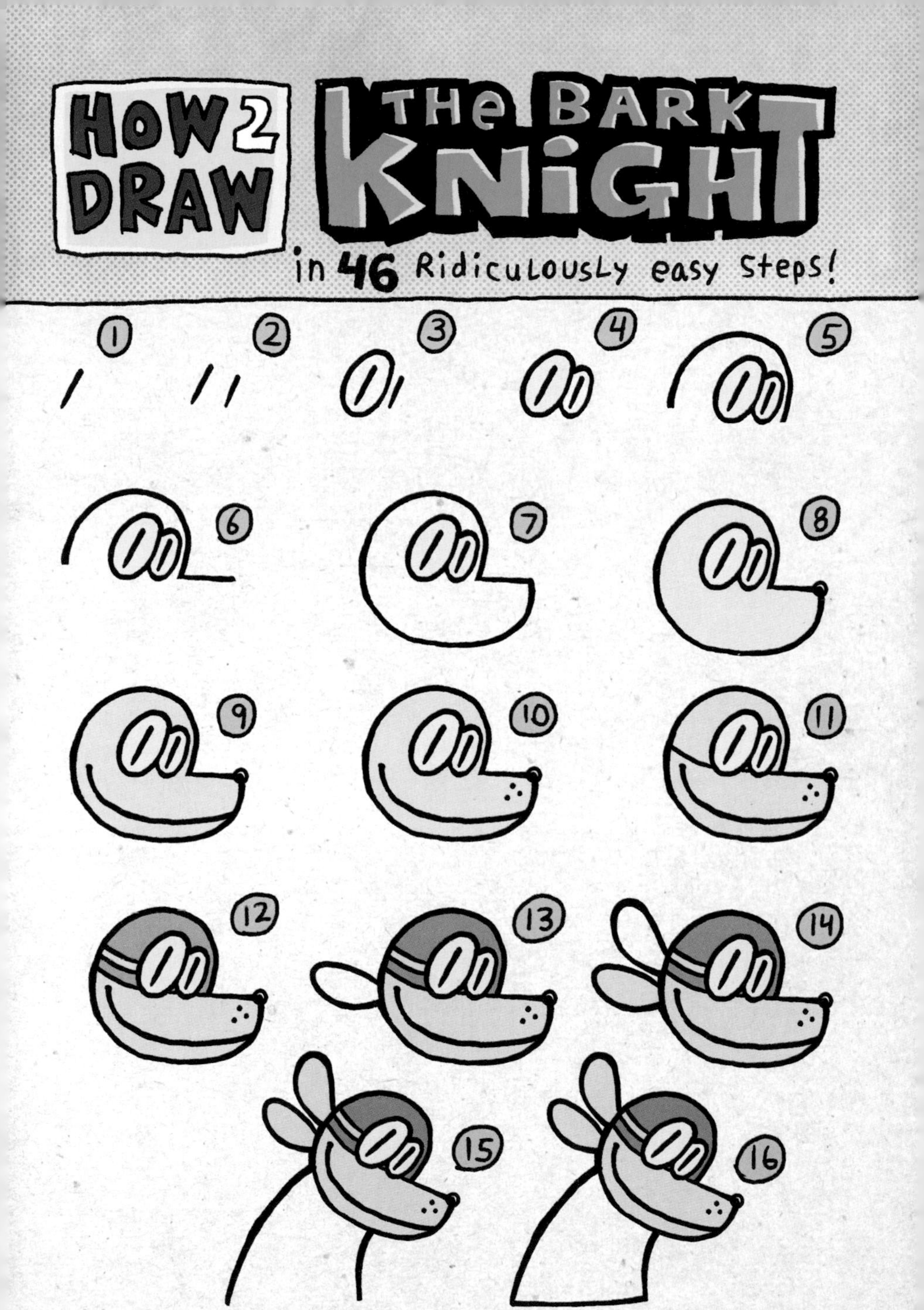
1
2
3
4
5
6
7
8
9
10
11
12
13
14
15
16

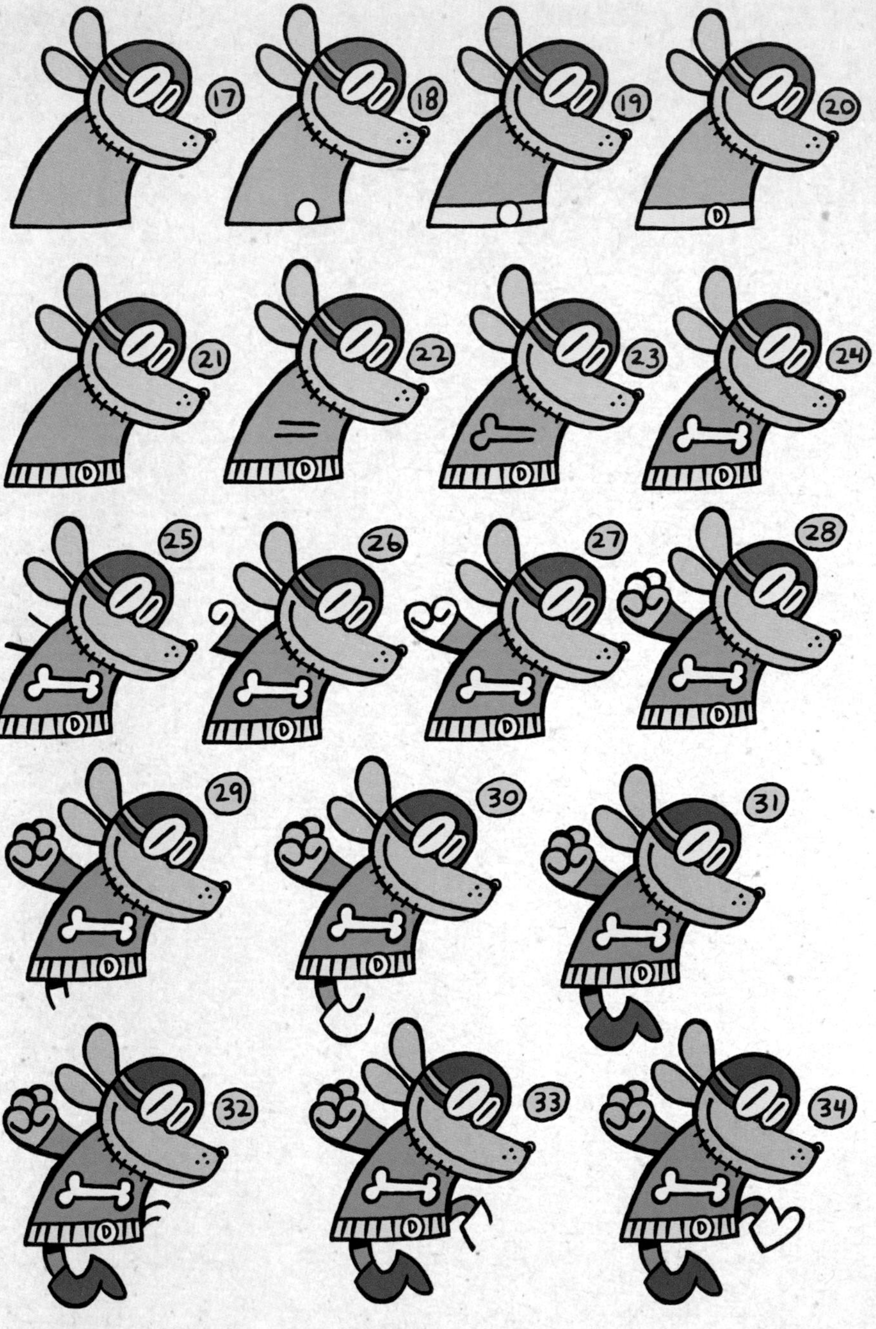
17
18
19
20
21
22
23
24
25
26
27
28
29
30
31
32
33
34

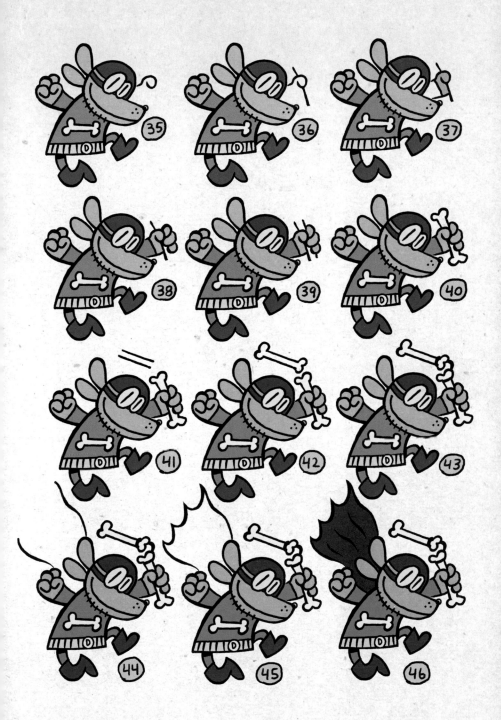

HOW 2 DRAW SUPA-MECHA PHILLY

in 37 Ridiculously easy steps!

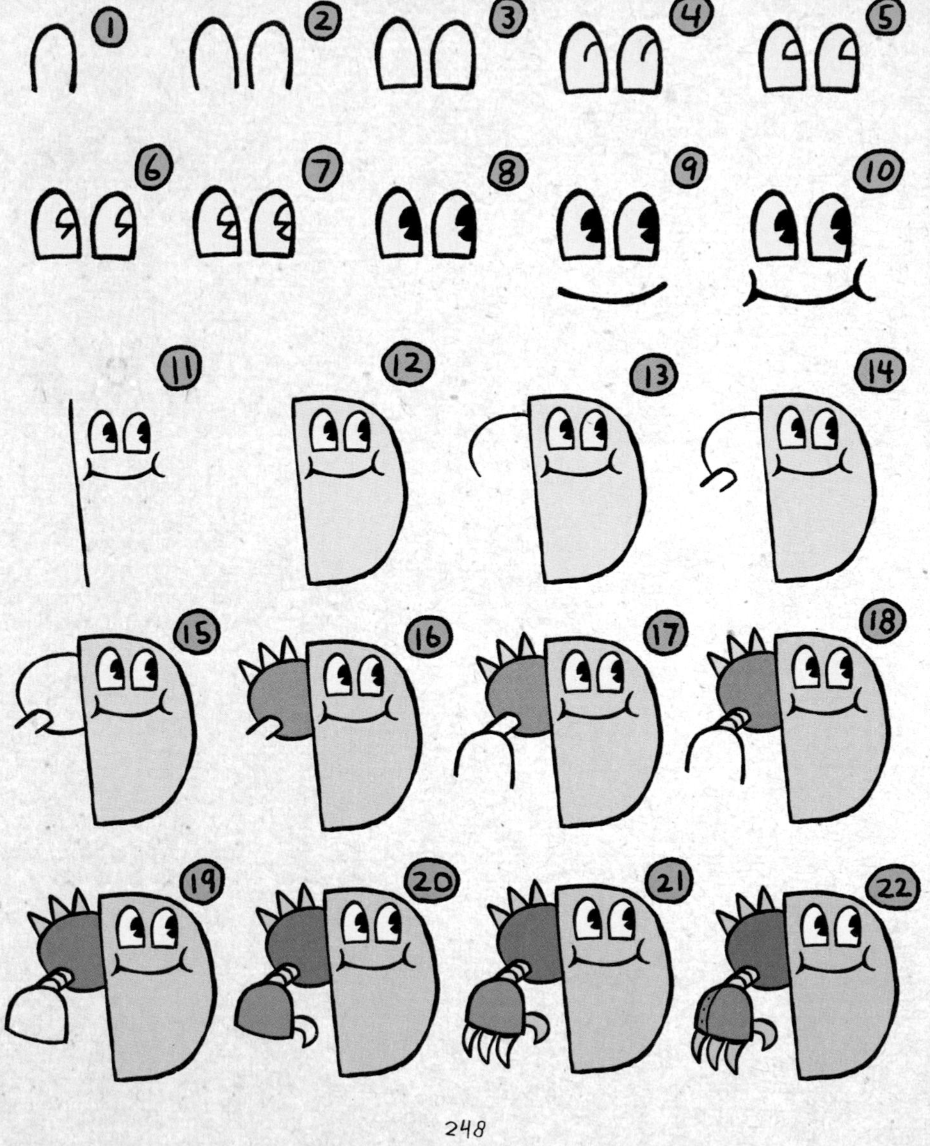
1
2
3
4
5
6
7
8
9
10
11
12
13
14
15
16
17
18
19
20
21
22

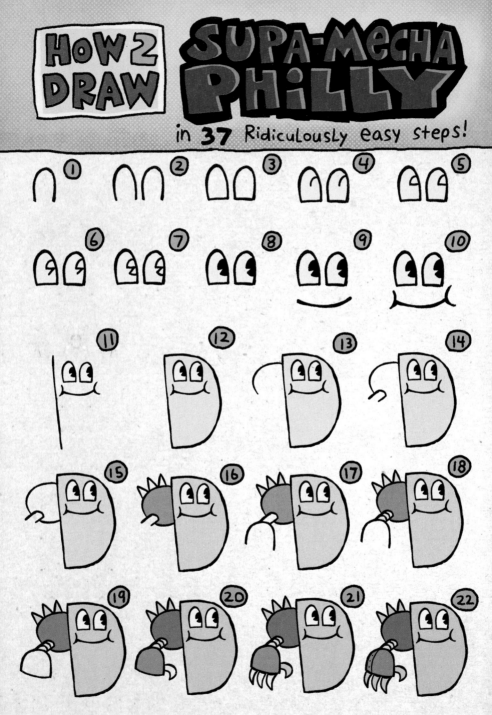

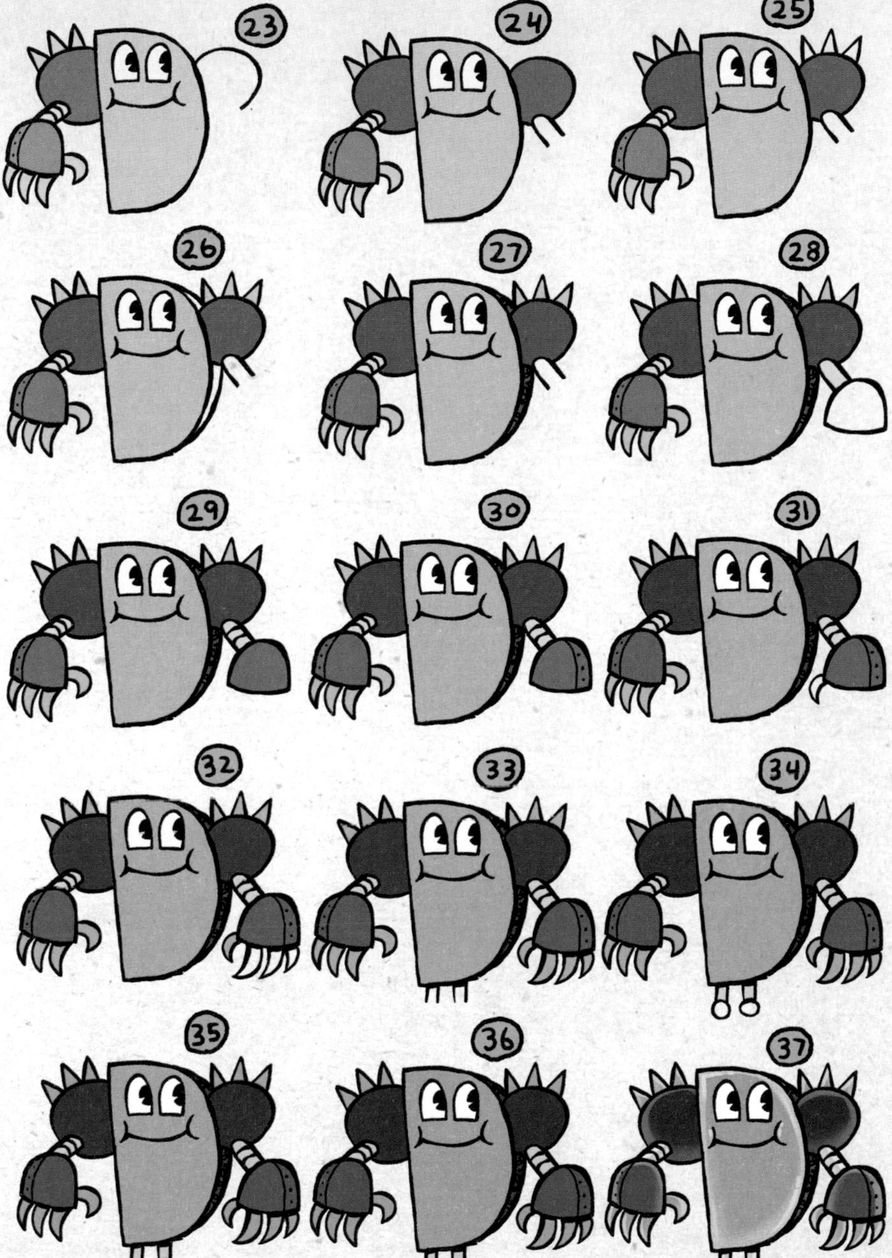
23
24
25
26
27
28
29
30
31
32
33
34
35
36
37

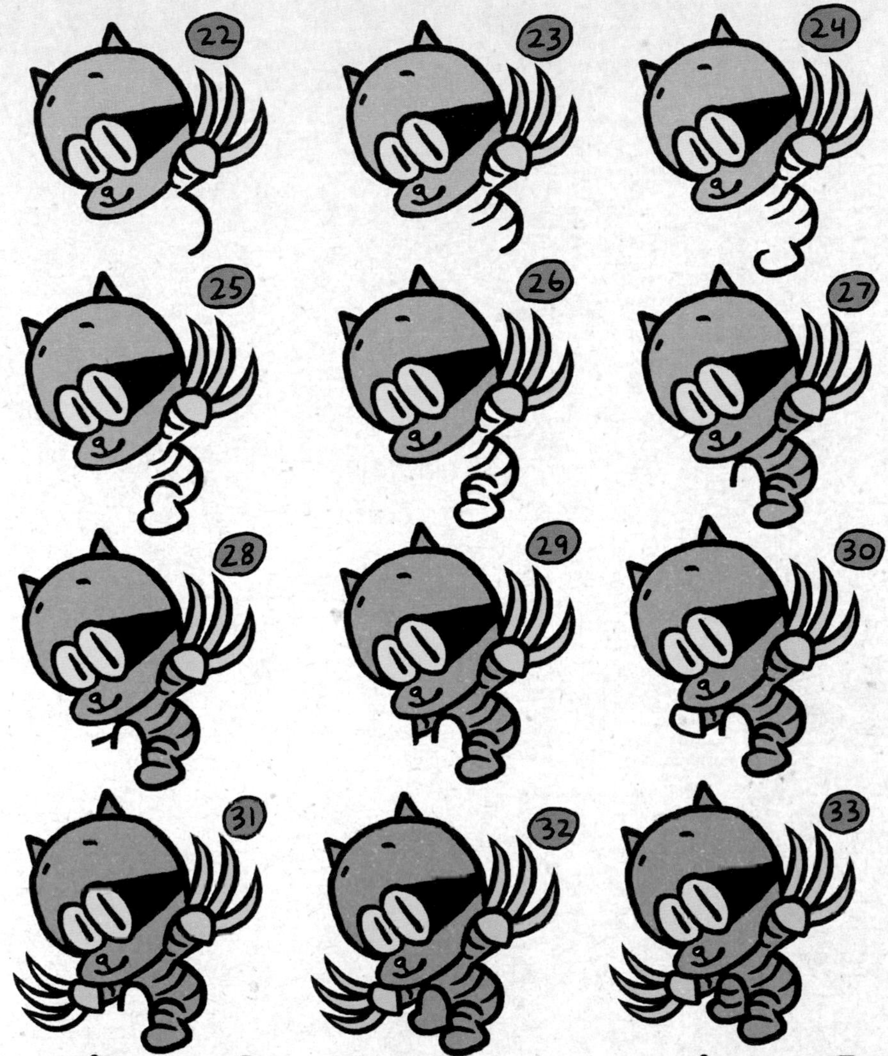
22
23
24
25
26
27
28
29
30
31
32
33
34
35
36

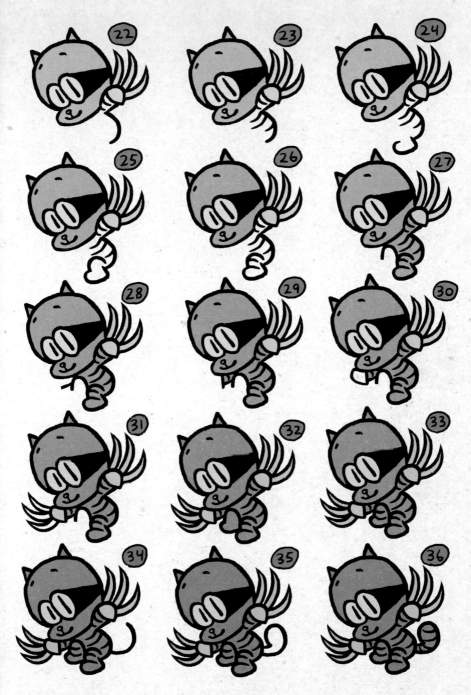

NOTES

by George and Harold

★ The titles of chapters 9, 10, and 11 are parodies of the titles of <u>Other</u> books by John Steinbeck.

★ The words on pages 57 and 233 are direct quotes from <u>East of Eden</u> by Steinbeck.

★ The Japanese words in chapter 11 mean: Onigiri (rice balls), 100 yen (about a dollar).

★ "Timshel" is the Hebrew word for "Thou mayest."

GET READING W

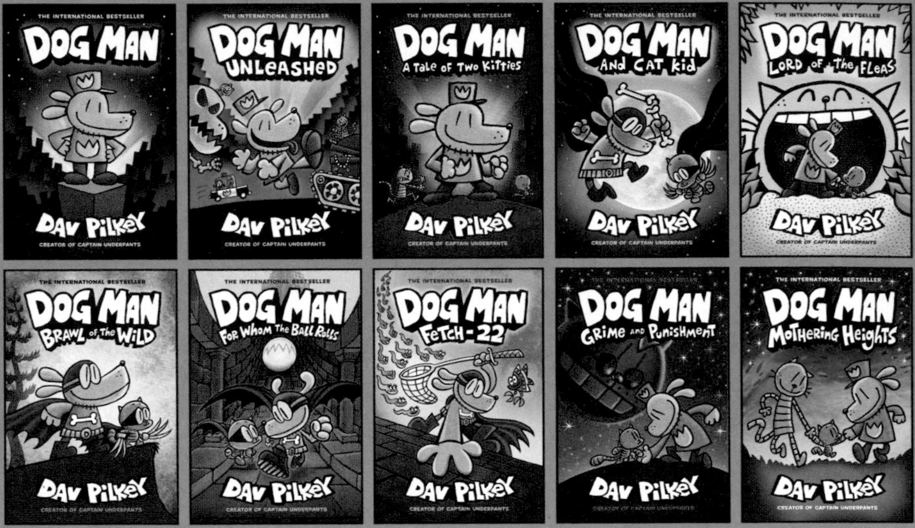
THE INTERNATIONAL BESTSELLER
DOG MAN
DAV PILKEY
CREATOR OF CAPTAIN UNDERPANTS
THE INTERNATIONAL BESTSELLER
DOG MAN UNLEASHED
DAV PILKEY
CREATOR OF CAPTAIN UNDERPANTS
THE INTERNATIONAL BESTSELLER
DOG MAN A TALE OF TWO KITTIES
DAV PILKEY
CREATOR OF CAPTAIN UNDERPANTS
THE INTERNATIONAL BESTSELLER
DOG MAN AND CAT KID
DAV PILKEY
CREATOR OF CAPTAIN UNDERPANTS
THE INTERNATIONAL BESTSELLER
DOG MAN LORD OF THE FLEAS
DAV PILKEY
CREATOR OF CAPTAIN UNDERPANTS
THE INTERNATIONAL BESTSELLER
DOG MAN BRAWL OF THE WILD
DAV PILKEY
CREATOR OF CAPTAIN UNDERPANTS
THE INTERNATIONAL BESTSELLER
DOG MAN FOR WHOM THE BALL ROLLS
DAV PILKEY
CREATOR OF CAPTAIN UNDERPANTS
THE INTERNATIONAL BESTSELLER
DOG MAN FETCH-22
DAV PILKEY
CREATOR OF CAPTAIN UNDERPANTS
THE INTERNATIONAL BESTSELLER
DOG MAN GRIME AND PUNISHMENT
DAV PILKEY
CREATOR OF CAPTAIN UNDERPANTS
THE INTERNATIONAL BESTSELLER
DOG MAN MOTHERING HEIGHTS
DAV PILKEY
CREATOR OF CAPTAIN UNDERPANTS

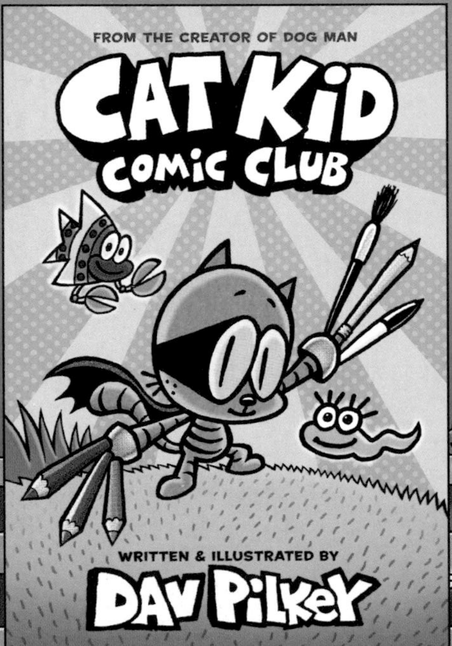
FROM THE CREATOR OF DOG MAN
CAT KID COMIC CLUB
WRITTEN & ILLUSTRATED BY
DAV PILKEY

★ "Irreverent, laugh-out-loud funny, and . . . downright moving."
— Publishers Weekly, starred review

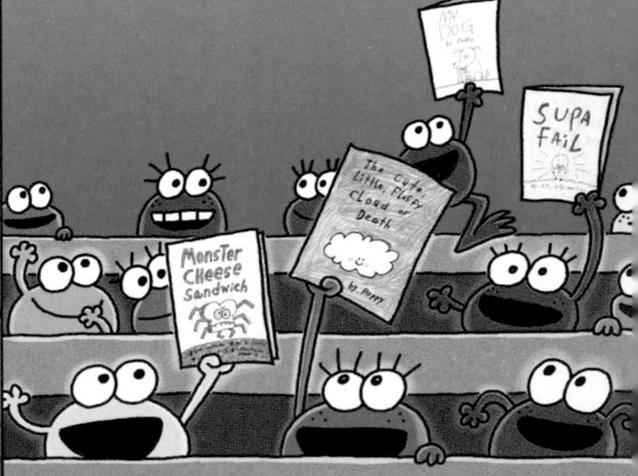
MY DOG
SUPA FAIL
The Cute Little, Fluffy Cloud of Death
Monster Cheese Sandwich